The Carnal Prayer Mat, first published around 1634, recounts the adventures of a brilliant young student who, endowed with exceptional beauty and grace, devotes himself to a life of pure eroticism. Like other classics of Chinese erotic literature, this story of one man and six women mixes the erotic and the moral to tell a tale designed to both amuse and reform the reader. Despite its age and country of origin, *The Carnal Prayer Mat* displays many of the characteristics of modern Western novels. A carefully plotted comedy of manners with abundant psychological detail—as well as dialogues on religion, sex, and morals—*The Carnal Prayer Mat* engages the reader from its first page to its last.

LI YU was born in 1610 in Kiangsu province, China, and was a dramatist, producer, and director who traveled widely with his own troupe. He also owned a bookshop and authored a collection of short stories, *Twelve Towers (Shih-erh-lou)*. Li Yu died in 1680.

The Carnal Prayer Mat

The Carnal Prayer Mat

Li Yu

Translated by Richard Martin

BOOK-OF-THE-MONTH CLUB
NEW YORK

CHAPTER I

To attract disciples, the aged hermit hangs up an
empty leather sack outside his hut. The youthful
scholar scorns the hard bast prayer mat and prefers
a soft one made of flesh.

Our story took place at the time of the Mongol dynasty
(1280–1368), in the reign-period Chih-ho ("harmony attained"—1328). In those days there lived on Kua-ts'ang-
shan, the "Mountain cloaked in azure blue," a *dhûta*, a
Buddhist hermit, whose temple name was Ku-feng, "Lonely
Summit." He came from the county of Chuchow in the
province of Chekiang and in his earlier years he had been
a talented student of Confucian political theory, expected
to attain high government office. But his natural bent was
far less toward the practical activity of a government official than toward meditation and philosophical reflection
on the root and primal ground of things.

While still a babe in swaddling clothes, he had a way
of mumbling incomprehensible sounds very much in the
manner of a student mumbling classical texts in order to
learn them by heart. His parents were puzzled.

One day a mendicant monk knocked on the door. He
was collecting subscriptions for a pious cause. The maid
had the baby in her arms as she opened. When the monk
heard the little boy babbling in a tone halfway between
whimpering and laughter, he was filled with awe and
cried out: "Why, those are maxims from the celebrated
Leng-yen-ching, Sutra of Angular Severity (translated into

Chinese in 1312), that the little one is babbling. It's plain that a former saint has been reborn in him, and is speaking out of his mouth." And he turned to the child's parents, asking them to entrust their son to him; he would train him for the religious calling and make him his helper. The parents, who were enlightened, realistic Confucians, took his words for superstitious nonsense and indignantly rebuffed him.

The child's father began to instruct him at an early age in the writing and reading of the classical books. The little boy showed a wonderfully quick understanding: he had only to read a text once over and it remained graven in his memory; he could recite it by heart. But strange to say, he was drawn from the very start to the writings of the Buddhists. Time and again his father caught him interrupting his study of the Confucian classics to plunge secretly into the Buddhist sutras. Both his father and his mother were obliged to reprove him severely and even to chastise him with the rod, before he would give up this secret occupation.

The critical moment arrived when the erect pigtails, emblem of childhood, are undone and the hair is combed down in smooth strands. He had grown to be a youth. Soon it was time for him to take his first examination, and his father sent him to the provincial academy to prepare for it. Here he so distinguished himself that the head of the school made him his assistant and monitor over the other pupils. Yet he was not so very eager to succeed in his examination; he was not drawn to the traditional government career or the worldly success that his parents had planned for him. Then, soon after he had passed his first state examination, his parents died and he was able to follow his own bent. Of course he observed the prescribed three years of mourning, as befits a dutiful son, but then he carried out his long nurtured plan of renouncing the world.

Without a moment's hesitation, he distributed his inheritance, his house and his land and his ten thousand pieces

孤峯長老

Lonely Summit.

of silver, among the members of his family. He packed a leather sack, which he himself had made, full of the few articles required by a hermit, a wooden fish, a prayer mat, some prayer scrolls and sutras, had his head shorn bare, and went off into the mountains to become a hermit.

From that time on the people who knew him personally spoke of him respectfully as Ku-feng chang-lao, "Priest Lonely Summit," while those who did not know him personally referred to him in jest as P'i-pu-tai ho-shang, "Little Monk Leathersack."

Unlike other monks Lonely Summit did not content himself with strict observance of the traditional rules and ordinances of the monasteries—such as abstinence from meat and carnal pleasures, from wine and brandy, onions, garlic and other spices; in addition, he voluntarily imposed upon himself three strange restrictions: not to beg for alms; not to engage in exegesis of the sutras; and not to make his home in a famous pilgrimage site.

When asked why he scorned to beg for alms like others of his calling, he replied:

"One who wishes to follow Buddha must take upon himself certain of the hardships of existence. Beyond a doubt the way to Buddha is paved with bitterness. Unless you harden your nerves and sinews unsparingly, you will never attain to him. A seeker after Buddha must serenely bear his share of hunger and cold. If his stomach grumbles day after day, if he has to put up, day after day, with heat and cold, sensual desires will not even put in an appearance. The less sensual desire he has, the less he will be plagued by impure thoughts and the better able he will be to make daily progress toward purity and peace of soul. In this way he will gradually attain perfection by his own efforts and will become like Buddha. To feed yourself without tilling the fields, to clothe yourself without setting hand to the loom, to rely on alms and benevolent patrons, and to fill your belly without effort—this can lead only to idleness. Warmth and comfort make a man drowsy. Idleness gives

4

rise to lascivious desires, drowsiness lulls the mind in sensual dreams. That is the exact opposite of what the imitation of Buddha should mean to us, and leads inevitably, step by step and willy-nilly, to ruin. That is why I decline to take alms and rely on the strength of my own hands."

When asked why he declined to interpret the sutras, he replied:

"What is written in the sutras comes from the divine mouth of Buddha. Only Buddha himself can explain his words. Who else can pretend to do so? No attempt to interpret Buddha's words through a profane human mouth can produce anything but foolish babble. Tao Yüan-ming* went so far as to forbid all exegesis and commentary even in the study of Confucius and his classical books—although he himself was a Chinese and these were Chinese doctrines couched in his own language. How much more futile and presumptuous would it be for a Chinese to attempt exegesis in his study of the Indian sutras, foreign books which he is obliged to read in Chinese translation. I have no ambition to become a minister in Buddha's cabinet, all I wish is to avoid betraying him through misinterpretation. And so, fully aware of my simplicity and ignorance, I refuse to have anything to do with exegesis of the holy sutras."

And when, finally, he was asked why he declined to set up his hermit's cell on mountains that are famous as places of pilgrimage, he replied:

"One who dedicates himself to the imitation of Buddha must take care not to let his senses be distracted by outward pleasures. But the outward pleasures of existence include not only good living, the lusts of the flesh, and music, but also such things as bracing mountain air, entrancing moonlight, the sweet singing of birds, graceful mountain ferns and lovely flowers; these, too, are of a nature to delight the senses and distract one from meditation. A life in the midst of a particularly beautiful countryside, sur-

* Famous poet and chrysanthemum grower, 365–427.

rounded by fantastic precipices, raging torrents, and resounding waterfalls makes for idle nature worship, lyrical
transports, poetic preoccupation with "moon sisters" and
"wind brides," and interferes with inner concentration and
clarity. Even a scholar, a conscientious disciple of Confucius, who set up his cell on a famous mountain, would be
deterred from serious study by the natural beauties around
him, and for the same reason a student of the Tao will
never in such surroundings achieve the composure he needs
if he is to reflect upon the origin of things.

"How much truer this is of one desirous of following
Buddha. To what distractions is he exposed in a famous
pilgrimage site!—There are the pretty young women and
girls, all finery and coquettish smiles, who come tripping up
to the shrines to burn incense and perform their devotions.
There are the rich and noble, borne in litters, accompanied
by a great retinue, who eat lavishly and drink uproar-
iously, and turn the pilgrimage into a merry excursion.
How, with worldly impressions such as these crowding in
on him from all sides, can a seeker after Buddha expect to
achieve abstraction and concentrate on holy doctrine?—
That is why I decline to set up my cell on a mountain that
is the site of a famous pilgrimage."

His answers made a deep impression and won him the
greatest respect. Even the ancient patriarchs, thought those
who had questioned him, had not been so earnest or so
principled in the performance of their holy task. His three
unyielding answers were bruited about and brought him
undesired fame. From far and near admirers came to pay
him their respects. Nor was there any lack of candidates
who would have taken it as the greatest honor to be accepted as his pupil or helper. But on this point he was
extremely critical and particular.

He would subject the young applicants to the most
exacting tests, by way of determining whether their nature
was good to begin with and whether they meant seriously
to shake off the dust of earthly striving. Thus far none had

withstood his rigorous examination; he had found not a single one worthy to be his helper. And so it happened that he was still living alone in the hermit's cell he had built himself not far from a mountain stream. Beside it there was a small field, on which he himself raised all he needed for food. As for drink, he contented himself with clear spring water.

It was an autumn day, in the season of the cool golden wind, when the trees cast off their raiment of leaves, when the bees leave off from their humming and the crickets give over their chirping. As usual, Lonely Summit had arisen early in the morning; he had cleared his doorway of the leaves that had fallen during the night, changed the water in the basin before the likeness of Buddha, and lighted fresh incense candles on the altar. Then he had spread out his bast prayer mat on the ground and settled down on it to meditate. As he sat thus in silent meditation, a visitor suddenly appeared. It was a handsome young man in the dress of an academician, a traveling scholar. He was obviously of noble family, for he was attended by two servants.

His appearance—it was as though a luminous springtime cloud had come floating in to brighten the gloom of the musty cell. The young visitor's person gave off the freshness of the glittering autumn wave. The light of his eyes was truly extraordinary, literally flashing with fire. But in those eyes there was a revealing glitter. A knower of men could easily discern a nature avid for sensual pleasure of every kind. The owner of those eyes was not one to content himself with a serious and regular life.

And indeed our young man's chief occupation was scouting for pretty women and young girls. He had little interest in anything else. He had become so expert in his specialty that a fleeting glance from far off, from a distance of as much as twenty yards, sufficed to tell him whether a woman was pretty or not. He had no need of closer inspection. If in his travels he found a woman worthy of his attention, he looked her full in the face. If she was modest by nature, she lowered her eyes and passed him by, without responding to his glance. But if she was afflicted with the same weakness as himself, she answered his gaze, and between the two of them there arose that silent understanding, that "exchange of love letters from the corner of the eye," which, alas, is fraught with such infinite perils for both parties. For a He as well as a She, such a pair of eyes is indeed a disastrous gift of nature. Only too frequently the loss of honor and reputation can be traced back to the possession of such eyes. This by way of warning. May you take it to heart, esteemed reader, should my remarks apply to you.

The visitor graciously signed his forehead four times, first to the statue of Buddha, then to the old hermit, then, silent and waiting, he took up his stance to one side of the prayer mat. Deep in his meditation, Lonely Summit left him waiting for a time. Only after his holy morning devotions were concluded and he had risen from the mat, did he turn to the visitor, answer his greeting with four deep bows, and invite him to sit down beside him on the k'ang. He opened the conversation with the traditional question concerning his name and lineage.

"I am from a distant region and am now engaged in travels through the province of Chekiang. My surname is Wei-yang sheng, 'Before Midnight Scholar.' In the course of my travels I heard of the exalted fame of the venerable master, whom all praise as the true living Buddha of our day. Thereupon I fasted, cleansed myself in body and soul as fitting, and set out to pay my respects to the master in the hope that he would honor me with his wisdom and counsel."

"Stop there, friend storyteller," my esteemed readers will cry. "The hermit questioned his visitor as to *hsing* and *ming*, last name and first name. Why do you have the visitor reply with a mere nickname?" Honored readers, you must know that in those days, toward the end of the Mongol dynasty, it was the strange custom in academic circles to take a pseudonym and travel incognito. More-over, three different titles were in use, depending on the man's age. Young academicians called themselves *sheng*, "scholar." Those of middle age termed themselves *tzu*, "master," and those advanced in years *tao-yen* "follower of the Tao." But the name chosen was always connected with some very personal propensity or trait. Its hidden meaning, of course, was beyond the reach of outsiders and was understood only by academicians who had known one another in their student days. As for our young man, his surname referred to a natural propensity, to wit, that he prized female company and the pleasures of love more by night than by day, and at night only until midnight, no later. Drawing on a passage from the *Shih-ching*, the holy book of songs (third millennium B.C.), in which the turn *wei-yang yeh* ("before midnight") occurs, he had taken the surname Wei-yang sheng, "Before Midnight Scholar." The hidden meaning of his surname was known only to himself and to a few of his fellow students.

"*Pu kan tang!* Too much honor! Your exaggerated praises put me to shame," the hermit protested modestly and invited the visitor to partake of his humble breakfast. It consisted of a soup of rice and vegetables, which stood steaming and bubbling in an earthenware pot on the stove. As they savored their morning repast, the hermit astutely drew his guest into a religious dispute, meaning to test his intelligence. To his surprise he discovered that the young man was extremely well informed on the most intricate matters, such as *ch'an*, or *dhyana*, exercise, immersion, ab-straction, and was well able to hold up his end of the discussion. The more he tested him, the clearer it became that he had to do with an unusually gifted and well-educated young man, who had not only read the literature of the three sublime doctrines and the nine philosophical schools, but also mastered it with ease. Even in the difficult field of Ch'an Buddhism, he proved amazingly well versed. Ordinarily, thousands of words and hundreds of explanations were needed to awaken understanding in so young an interlocutor, but with this extraordinary young man a single sentence, the barest suggestion, sufficed; he would deftly take up the master's train of thought and explore it in all its breadth and depth.

"Truly, a remarkable young man," thought Lonely Summit to himself. "So much intelligence and knowledge in one. What a pity the Creator made the mistake of endowing one whose spiritual gifts surely predestine him to be a servant of Buddha, with so sinfully seductive an exterior! To look at him, his face, his figure, his expression, his bearing, his movements—why, he is fashioned like a very demon of lust. Unless he is put in a leather sack from the very first and cut off from the outside world, the havoc he will wreak among humankind is beyond imagining. To satisfy his lusts a man of his stamp will stop at nothing: he will scale walls and wade through moats; he will devise the most intricate stratagems and hatch the wildest plans to violate virgin bedchambers. Who knows what unhappiness he will create among women, how many lives he will sully and poison! Concern for the public welfare bids me take measures to stop this wild man who is clearly a menace to all civil order and morality, and were I not to do so, I should be no true servant of Buddha, for has not Buddha commanded me to be merciful?"

To the young man he spoke as follows: "Since I have been living the life of a hermit, I have been overrun by all sorts of visitors, who have implored me to receive them as my helpers. I shall not speak of the uneducated boors who were not even worth considering, but there have also been estimable persons, men of rank and education; doctors, scholars, men of learning, even officials who sought temporary refuge in my cell, perhaps as a means of evading embarrassing proceedings over some little irregularity in their conduct of affairs. And yet, though some of these applicants had seriously concerned themselves with the study of the

Buddhist doctrine, I found no sign of maturity, of enlightenment, in any of them.

"And then—who would have thought it?—you, my esteemed young lay brother, came along, displaying so much illumination and understanding. All you need is a few years' immersion in the teachings of Buddha, and you will have risen to samadhi, to the sublime state of perfection, the earthly Nirvana. High spiritual gifts such as these weigh more heavily in the balance than outward physical perfections. It is better to surmount catastrophes than to savor brief glory. Since my esteemed young lay brother clearly has the makings of a Buddha, let him not start out upon the common earthly path, beset as it is by devils and demons; let him employ the present early hour, before the morning mists have dispersed, to cast off all earthly lusts and desires with one energetic stroke, and so enter into the gate of emptiness. Although I, paltry hermit, am only a man of common clay, I am confident that by the force of my will, in league with Providence, I can help you to live in such a way that when your hundred years of earthly life have run out, you will enjoy beatitude in the community of the saints instead of being a slave to loathsome devils and *rakshas* in hell below. Well, what do you say to my proposal?"

The young man replied: "I too have long harbored the intention of taking refuge in Buddha, and it is my firm design to return here some day in the hope of serving you as your pupil and helper. But today it is too soon. I am young in years and there are two worldly matters I should like to attend to first. Leave me time to fulfil these two tasks and to enjoy worldly happiness for a few years more; then I shall come again, and you will find me prepared to follow in the footsteps of the Patriarch Matanga.* It will not be too late."

"May one ask what these two matters are? Surely you

---

* Introduced Buddhism to China in 64 A.D.

Lonely Summit in conversation with the Before Midnight Scholar.

wish to pass an honorable palace examination, and show your gratitude to the throne by successful and glorious official activity in remote provinces. Is that not your intention?" The young man shook his head.

"Those are not the affairs I had in mind."

"What then may they be? Speak."

"Know then that vain striving for offices and dignities, for which I should have the throne to thank, is far from my intentions. What I accomplish, I wish to accomplish entirely by my own resources. I have no wish to boast, but I feel justified in saying that my learning, my memory, my gift of comprehension, and my literary style are of the first order. The literary lights of our day are all mediocrities. They wear themselves out learning texts by heart; they rack their brains, they wriggle east and wriggle west, to squeeze out a bit of literature no better than an exercise that schoolboys put together in a classroom. If they succeed in publishing the most commonplace book of poems, they plant flags of joy and gratitude on the altar of the god of literature and carry on like the most unconscionable geniuses, basking in their imagined glory. True literary glory calls for a thorough knowledge of men and great experience of the world.

"In order to become a really important writer, it is not enough, in my opinion, to be familiar with all the best literature of one's country; it is also necessary to maintain personal relations and intellectual communication with the leading literary figures of the day, to have personally visited all the famous mountains and pilgrimage sites of one's country; only then is it time to withdraw to the seclusion of a cell, where there is leisure to write a book worth handing on to posterity. If one should have the good fortune to succeed in the state examinations, to see one's name on the lists of victors, then if you will, let one perform some meritorious service for the throne. But if fortune should not favor one in the examinations, then let one confidently remain at one's desk, beneath the window of one's cell, and go on writing until old age. That is what our ancestors did a thousand years ago.

"Understand me, then. I cherish the ambition to write an important work and to go down in the literary history of my country as the 'tenth master of prose writing.' "

"That is the one affair. And the second?" asked Lonely Summit. The young man opened his mouth, but not a sound came out. Apparently he was afraid to speak.

"I see that you hesitate to confess your second intention. Would you like me to name it for you?"

"Ah, you think you can read my mind? Well, all success to you."

"Yes, I think I can, and if I miss the mark, I shall be glad to make amends. But if I am right, you must not deny it."

"How should I! If you really guess, you will be not only a Bodhisattva in my eyes, but a master of magic, a demigod."

"Very well, then, you wish to win the fairest in the land."

The hermit spoke with perfect certainty and composure. The young man gaped with amazement and for a time remained speechless. Finally he owned with admiration:

"Master, I believe you are indeed a higher being, to have read my innermost thoughts!"

"Do you not know the saying:

What men plot together in secret
Heaven hears it loud as thunder."

"Seriously, I should have thought it unseemly to strike up the worldly theme of love and sensual pleasure in your holy presence. Now that you yourself have touched upon it, I can speak openly. Know then that in me the longing for worldly pleasure sometimes outweighs even my desire to withdraw from the world. From time immemorial the notions of spirit and beauty have been inseparably linked. A young man of spirit requires a beautiful companion, and conversely; and so it has always been. I need waste no more words on my intellectual advantages, but when it comes to externals I am also well endowed. Sometimes, when I look at myself in the mirror, it seems to me that I should have no need to hide my face in the presence of a P'an An,* should there be one alive today. If heaven has made me so, am I not entitled to something very special? If there were no beauties in the world, then very well, the matter would be closed for me. But since there are beauties, why not for me too? I am barely twenty, and still unengaged. Would it not be downright ingratitude to heaven which has favored me with such spiritual and physical advantages, were I not to seek after a woman capable of satisfying my justified demands?

"Therefore, venerable master, let me go into the world and seek out the one who is destined to be mine. Have patience until I have found her and married her and begotten by her a son who will carry on my devotions at the shrines of my ancestors. When that is accomplished, no further desires will bind me to the world of dust. You may be certain that I will not only come back to you, but that I shall also convert my wife to the sublime doctrine, and with her climb the bank of redemption. What do you say to that, master?"

The master showed a frosty smile.

"Very convincing! If such is your intention, the hand of the Creator and Prince of Heaven must have slipped when he made you. If instead of an attractive exterior he had given you a repulsive one, your lucid intelligence would no doubt guide you straight to your true destination. That is why from olden time men with physical disabilities, lepers, epileptics, cripples, aware that Heaven has imposed penance on them for some offense in a former life, have so often renounced the world and chosen the holy life of a hermit in Buddha or Lao-tse. With you, esteemed young lay brother, it is just the opposite. In creating you, the Prince of Heaven, through oversight no doubt, endowed you only

---

* Chinese ideal of masculine beauty.

too well. It is as when parents spoil and coddle their children from excessive love. For fear of hurting the child, they hesitate to scold, let alone strike him when he is naughty. Therein lies a serious danger for the child. When he grows up, he says to himself defiantly, Heaven and Earth created me as I am, so my parents raised me; can I help it? With such thoughts he lulls his conscience and exculpates himself in his own mind. Without restraint he follows his bent for evil; it begins with foolish tricks and peccadilloes; it ends with crime. He is haled into court and punished severely, sentenced, perhaps to imprisonment or execution. Then he realizes—too late, alas—that he has come to this sorry end because he was spoiled and coddled by his parents in his childhood. All of which goes to show that beauty, talent, and arrogance are not enough to guarantee happiness in life.

"You harp too much on your looks and your intellectual gifts, as though they made you the most remarkable man in all China. And now this most remarkable of men wants to go out looking for the most beautiful of women. Let us assume for the moment that you find the woman you are looking for and make her yours, who can guarantee that she is really the foremost beauty in the land? Somewhere, perhaps, there is one still more beautiful. Do you expect the words 'most beautiful' to be stamped on her forehead? What if one day you find a woman still more beautiful than the first; will you not turn away from the first and pursue the one who is more beautiful? And that is not all. What if your paragon of beauty has a nature akin to yours? Then she too will be ever so exacting in her choice of a husband. Who can be sure that you will come up to her demands? How do you mean to prevent our exigent beauty from taking a lover behind your back? It all goes to show that if you persist in employing a hundred stratagems and a thousand ruses to win the fairest of women, you will ineluctably, step by step and stage by stage, make your way into the pit of damnation. Would you rather go to Hell than to Heaven? If you have no objection to ending up in Hell, very well then, go out into the world and search for your fairest of the fair. But if you would prefer the Palace of Heaven, give over your earthly designs, erase them from your mind, renounce the world, and stay with me."

Now it was the young man's turn to smile indulgently.

"It seems to me that to season your arguments with commonplaces and catchwords like Heaven and Hell is not exactly worthy of a holy servant of Buddha; childish beliefs of that sort are more what one would expect of an unreflecting layman. If I understand the Buddhist doctrine correctly, it tells us to achieve wisdom and enlightenment through the powers that are within us and so attain to a state beyond life and death. Accordingly, 'Hell,' 'Palace of Heaven' are empty catchwords, book covers without a book, for there is no such thing in reality. If sheer love of life should lead a fellow like me to overstep the bounds a little, you may say in a pinch that he is offending against Confucius' ethical principles, but isn't it going rather too far to damn him out of hand and relegate him to a non-existent Hell?"

"Granted, the terms 'Hell' and 'Palace of Heaven' are empty catchwords, book covers without a book; granted that it is childish, naive if you will, to say: 'The doer of good goes to Heaven, the doer of evil goes to Hell.' But we need such sayings. We need the notion of a blissful life in Heaven to encourage mankind to do good, and we need the notion of tortures in Hell to frighten man away from doing evil. Yes, you young people, who swear by Confucius and his doctrine of reason, you may do your best to cast off childish beliefs, but you cannot dispense with some sort of moral code. Very well, since you reject empty catchwords, I shall speak to you no more of retribution in the hereafter. What of retribution here on earth? There is a maxim that runs:

Court not your neighbor's wife,
And your neighbor will not court yours.

Of course that too is a commonplace, a catchword, but it
has been borne out time and time again in actual practice.
A man who seduces another's wife or daughter is usually
deceived in his turn; his wife or daughter is usually seduced
by another. Only those who go the way of virtue can
expect the virtue of their own wives and daughters to
remain unsullied.

"Yes, my esteemed young lay brother, you must make
up your mind: do you wish to suffer such deception in
your own skin, or would you prefer to guard against it? In
the first case, go and search for your fairest of the fair. In
the second case, abandon your mad scheme, renounce the
world, and remain with me."

The young man replied:

"The logic of your argument is compelling; an ignorant
beginner would be enormously impressed, his hair would
stand on end and his teeth would chatter. But unfortunately I am not an ignorant beginner. To intimidate me,
you'll need better arguments than that. Permit me to raise
an objection: the commandments of the Prince of Heaven
may be very strict in theory, but in practice he turns out to
be a very indulgent and merciful judge. It may be true
that most seducers meet with the punishment and retribution which you speak of, but cases of seducers getting off
scot free are by no means infrequent. I believe that if one
went from house to house, listing all the instances in which
the seducers of other peoples' wives and daughters have
been punished by the seduction of their own wives or
daughters, and those in which they have not been punished
at all, we should have to conclude that the Prince of Heaven
is a very partial and arbitrary judge. By and large of course
—far be it from me to deny it—the idea of the wheel of
destiny, of a higher retribution, is perfectly sound. What
would become of us without ethical discipline? It is one

of the pillars of all civil order, and it goes without saying that nothing must be done to shake it."

Lonely Summit said:

"It is your opinion then that in some cases seducers go free, without punishment and retribution? I very much doubt it. I fear on the contrary that the Prince of Heaven permits no evildoer to slip through the meshes. It is conceivable that *you* would be broad-minded enough to let evildoers slip through the meshes of His law, but the Prince of Heaven will certainly do nothing of the sort. That is my opinion, and it has been confirmed time and time again by the experience of ancient and modern times. It has been demonstrated a thousand times over by our official history, our literature, and our oral tradition.

"Furthermore, if you please, bear this in mind: Though men commonly boast of their amorous exploits to friends and strangers alike, the woman's way is to keep her secret dealings very much to herself. Modesty, concern for her reputation, prevent a victim of seduction from breathing a word to her own husband, not to mention friends and relatives. Her secret will go down into the grave with her. The list you were speaking of would surely be incomplete, because it is very hard to find out when a seducer is punished by the seduction of his own wife or daughter. Consider, too, that a woman can commit adultery in her heart. At the first suspicion that her husband is unfaithful to her, she may conceive the desire to pay him back in kind, and she does so with the help of her imagination. At night, during his embrace, which perhaps does not fully satisfy her or perhaps even repels her should he chance to be ugly and unprepossessing, she imagines to her great satisfaction that she is embracing some handsome young fellow at whom she has been gaping during the day; and the reverse is conceivable, it may be the man who does the imagining. What I am saying is not empty theory; these things happen in real life. In this case there is no physical assault upon a wife's honor, but she is guilty of infidelity just the same, and that, too, must be counted as retribution for her husband's infidelity and debauchery."

Again the young man smiled condescendingly.

"All quite logical and reasonable—up to a certain point, but permit me to raise one little objection: the retribution you speak of strikes the seducer through his own wife or daughter. But what if he has no wife or daughter; then what becomes of your retribution? The Prince of Heaven himself will be unable to carry out your promise. And one more thing: There is a limit to the number of wives and daughters that one man can afford. Now let us suppose that a man has two wives and two daughters; what if he seduces several times that number of other men's wives and daughters—for the wives and daughters of the land are as numberless as the sands of the sea—how is the Prince of Heaven to find a fair way of apportioning his punishment and retribution? Even if the seducer, in such a case, is punished by having his two wives and two daughters seduced, he will be coming off rather well. Wouldn't you say so?"

"What a sophist you are! This poor little monk is no match for your glittering foolishness. I give up. You refuse to believe me because I cannot support my words with proof. Very well, let us wait. Do what you think best, but one day you will come back and admit I was right. Go searching for the fairest of the fair. Your eyes will open in time. You will find your way to enlightenment on the Jou-p'u-t'uan, the 'prayer mat of flesh.' I'm sure of it, for I see you have capacities that raise you far above the profane crowd. You have the makings of a saint, you are predestined to climb the steep bank of redemption when the time comes. That is why it is so hard for me to let you go. But today's leave-taking will not be a separation for ever. When the great illumination comes to you, return to me. I shall be waiting for you. Beginning tomorrow, I shall think of you tearfully in my morning devotions and wait for you."

After these words of leave-taking, Lonely Summit took out a sheet of paper, mixed some ink, picked up his brush, and wrote an epigram:

So be it, cast away the leather sack of withdrawal from the world. Take flesh for your prayer mat and the place of your devotions. Patience, the hour of late repentance will come. Do not lament if by then your coffin has closed over you.

Lonely Summit held out the paper to the young man. "Take it, and forgive the poor *dhûta*, if in his epigram he has touched on a point that most men shun to speak of. We *dhûtas* have left all such taboos behind us. Don't take my primitive scribble as an expression of displeasure, consider it rather a token of my affection and solicitude, keep it, and some day you will see that my warning was not unfounded." He arose, giving it to be understood that the interview was at an end. Well bred enough to realize that he must not leave so venerable a hermit and master in anger, the young man bowed his head humbly and stammered a few gracious words of apology:

"Put it down, if you please, to my youthful simplicity and obstinacy, if I cannot incline at once to your wise counsel. But I fervently hope that if I return some day, you will open your heart wide and receive me in grace." Each bowed four times, the hermit accompanied his visitor to the door, and the young man went his way.

Exit the aged hermit. He will not appear again for some time, and from now on the Before Midnight Scholar will occupy the center of the stage. We shall see how he went astray and lost himself to woman and worldly pleasure. If you wish to learn how the hermit's prophecy was fulfilled word for word until the end returned to the beginning, you must read the next chapter.

CHAPTER II

O folly! The stern guardian of virtue takes the dissolute young man into his house as his son-in-law. O blindness! The honorable maiden loses her heart to a heartless rake.

After leaving the hermit, the young man went his way mumbling and grumbling:

"A fine saint indeed! Here I am, just twenty, barely at the threshold of manhood, and he expects me to take the tonsure, to renounce the world, and to suffer the bitterness of a monkish existence. Has such heartlessness its like in all the world? I only went to pay him my respects because formerly, before becoming a hermit, he was regarded as one of the leading lights of Confucian scholarship. I fancied he would dig up heaven knows what magic spells and bits of occult wisdom to help me on my way. But instead, he has the gall to treat me as a stupid child, and his only gift to me is this absurd and utterly uninspired epigram, which is like thunder without lightning. The whole thing is preposterous. As a future official and dignitary, I shall some day govern a whole district with a population numbering tens of thousands, and he fancies that I won't be able to govern my own wife. Is it unreasonable of me to desire a little practice in the wind-and-moon game, a little experience before marrying? That's what he was trying to forbid. But otherwise I should be going into marriage with my eyes closed and might even choose the wrong woman. And to top it all, he tells me that someone might requite me for past transgressions by violating the securely

guarded honor of my house. As though the woman who gets a paragon of manly qualities like me for a husband had any need to be seduced by another man! My own wife unfaithful!—Why, it's out of the question.

"I should really tear up this incompetent epigram and stamp on it. But no, I'd better not. I can use it as evidence later on, to stuff down his venomous throat. If I ever meet him again, I'll show him his epigram and put him to the test, to see whether he admits his mistake."

After thus deliberating, he folded the epigram and put it into his belt pocket.

Returning home, he bade his servants seek out all the marriage brokers they could find and commission them to search the city and countryside for the most beautiful of marriageable girls. She must be of respectable and distinguished family; and he insisted that she must be not only beautiful, but intelligent and well educated as well. There was no lack of offers. What paterfamilias would not have been glad to have him for a son-in-law, what daughter would not have taken him for a husband? Each day a number of marriage brokers came to him with their suggestions. Where the candidate was not too high in the social scale, the matchmaker would bring her along to be introduced and inspected at first hand. But in the case of a distinguished family which insisted on its forms and observances, she arranged to have the young man, as though by chance, cross the young lady's path in the courtyard of one of the temples, or while she was taking the air outside the city walls.

All these meetings and tours of inspection proved to be quite useless. A certain number of worthy young persons were unnecessarily jolted out of their peaceful routines and sent home again with vain pangs in their tender little hearts. For of all the candidates who were brought forward, not a one met with the exacting suitor's approval.

But one of the marriage brokers said to the young man: "Now it is clear to me that among all the young candidates there is only one who is worth considering: Miss Noble Scent; her father is a private scholar, known throughout the city by the surname T'ieh-fei tao-jen, Iron Door Follower of the Tao. She alone can meet your stringent requirements. But in her case there is a difficulty: her father is an old crank who adheres rigidly to the ancient customs. He would certainly not permit you to inspect his daughter before marriage. Consequently I fear that even this last hope must be abandoned."

"Iron Door Follower of the Tao? How did he come by such a strange surname? Why does he not wish his daughter to be seen? And if he keeps her hidden from all eyes, how do you know she is beautiful?"

"As I have told you, the old gentleman is rather crochety; he cares only for his books and avoids all society. He doesn't see a living soul. He lives in a splendid country house outside the city, with fields and meadows round it, and it makes no difference who knocks on his door, he refuses to open. One day an unknown admirer came to see him, a respected gentleman from another part of the country, who wished to pay his respects. He knocked at the door for some time and when no one answered, he cried out, but in vain. Before going away he wrote an epigram on the door:

> For a wise man ivy and vines
> Are protection enough, he needs no door.
> Yet this noble lord—who would have thought it—
> Hides behind an iron door.

When the master of the house found the epigram, he decided that the two ideograms, *t'ieh*, iron and *fei*, door, summed up his character perfectly, and he chose them as a surname. From then on he called himself T'ieh-fei tao-jen: Iron Door Follower of the Tao. He is a wealthy widower and his daughter is his only child. As for her beauty, it is no exaggeration to liken her to a lovely flower, a precious jewel. In addition, her father has given her an excellent education and her little head is full of learning. Poems, essays in poetic prose, songs, stanzas—she is familiar with them all and can compose in any form. Her upbringing, as you may easily surmise, has been extremely strict, and she has hardly ever set foot outside her maidenly quarters. She never goes out, not even to the traditional services on temple holidays, and there is simply no question of visits to relatives and friends. She is sixteen years old and has never been seen in public. Even we three go-betweens and six marriage brokers have no wings, we can't fly into her living quarters. It was only by the purest accident that I myself caught a glimpse of her not long ago.

"Yesterday I chanced to pass the house while the old gentleman was standing outside the door. He stopped me and asked if I were not Mother Liu, whose trade it was to arrange marriages. When I answered in the affirmative, he invited me in and presented his daughter. 'This is the young lady, my only child,' he said, and continued: 'Now I should like you to look around and bring me a suitable son-in-law who is worthy of her and has the qualities he would need to be a son to me and the prop of my old age.' At once I suggested that the young gentleman would be an appropriate match. He said: 'I have already heard of him, he is said to possess high intellectual gifts as well as external advantages. But what of his character and his virtue?' To this I replied: 'The young gentleman is distinguished by a spiritual and ethical maturity far in advance of his years. His character is without the slightest blemish or weak point. There is only one thing: he absolutely insists on seeing his future bride with his own eyes before the betrothal.' At once the benevolent look vanished from the old gentleman's face, and he became very angry: 'Nonsense. He wants to see her first—that may be permissible in the case of a venal powder-puff, a rutting mare from Yangchow. But since when is it the custom to expose the honorable daughter of a good family to the eyes of a strange man? A fine thing that would be. An impudent demand, which makes it clear to me that the young man is not the right husband for my daughter. Not another word!' With this he broke off the interview and sent me on my way. So you see, young man, there is nothing more to be done."

The young man thought the matter over carefully.

"If I were to marry this beautiful young girl and take her into my own house, there would be no one but me— for I am without parents or brothers—to keep an eye on her. I should have to stay home all day guarding her, there would be no chance whatever to go out. But if I went to live in her house, there would be no such difficulty, for this ancient guardian of virtue, my father-in-law, would keep a good watch over her in my absence. I should be able to go out with an easy heart. The only point that bothers me is not to see her first. What confidence can I have in a matchmaker's prattle? Why, there's no limit to what her kind will say in praise of a possible match." Such were his thoughts. To Mama Liu he said:

"If I am to believe you, she would be an excellent wife, yes, just the right wife for me. I should just like to ask you this one thing: to find some way of my getting the merest glimpse of her and hearing the sound of her voice. Then if the general impression is favorable, the match is made."

"See her first? It's out of the question. But if you don't trust me, why not go to a soothsayer and consult the little straws of fate?"

"There you have given me a very good idea. I have a friend who is an expert at conjuring spirits and telling fortunes, and his predictions have always been confirmed. I shall ask his advice. Let us wait to see what fate decides. Then I shall send for you and tell you what has happened."

So it was agreed and Mama Liu departed.

Next day the young man fasted and bathed and asked his friend the diviner to his house for a consultation. In the house-temple lit by candles and filled with incense, he solemnly explained the business in hand, humbly bowing his head and speaking in a muffled voice as though praying to a higher being:

"The younger brother has heard of the unsurpassed beauty of Miss Noble Scent, daughter of Iron Door Follower of the Tao, and would like to take her for his wife. But only his ears have heard of her charms, his eyes have not seen them. Therefore he begs leave to ask the exalted spirit whether she is indeed so beautiful and whether the exalted spirit recommends a marriage with her. If there should be even the slightest blemish in her, he would prefer to abandon the idea of marrying her. He fervently implores the exalted spirit to give him some gracious hint, for he does not wish to forfeit all happiness by trusting in idle prattle."

After stating his request, he made the fourfold sign on his forehead in reverence to the unknown spirit. Rising once more to his feet, he took from his friend's hand a piece of wood from the magic *luan* tree, symbolizing the spirit, held it chest high, and waited with bated breath to see what would happen next. Then he heard a sound, as of a brush passing softly over paper. A pluck at his sleeve awakened him from his trance. His friend was holding out a sheet of paper. On it was written a quatrain:

Number 1:

No need to doubt this message of the spirits:
She is first in the grove of red flowers.
Yet there is cause for alarm. So much beauty attracts suitors.
Whether the marriage is happy or not—is a question of morality.

The young man reflected: "It is clear then that she is a first class beauty. That is the main thing. As for the second part of the communication, it does not mince words about the danger such beauty involves. Can it be that the melon has already been cut open?—No that is very unlikely. Let us wait and see what the second communication says. There must be another since the first one is headed Number 1."

Again he held out the magic wood, then again he heard rustling and received the second communication, which ran:

It would be presumptuous to bank on your wife's fidelity;
Accordingly, if the husband values domestic harmony,
He will lock the gates and not admit a fly.
The tiniest fly-dropping will spoil a jewel.

Written by Hui-tao-jen
the returned follower of the Tao.

The three ideograms Hui-tao-jen were familiar to our young man; as he knew, they spelled the surname behind which the Taoist patriarch Lü Shun-yang (Lü Yen, also known as Lü Tung-pin, b. 750 A.D.) had hidden; he was also acquainted with the patriarch's life and personality; in his time, the young man recalled to his satisfaction, he had been a great devotee and connoisseur of wine and women. So, it was *his* spirit that had entered into his friend during the séance and guided the brush. Well, yes, he had thrown a little cold water on his projects by warning him of women's infidelity and bidding him to be on his guard. But there was no need to worry on that score. He would have his father-in-law, that old-fashioned guardian of morality, in the house to watch over his wife's virtue. What else was Iron Door good for? Moreover, lines three and four of the second communication were a clear allusion to him. There could be no doubt that the spirit approved of his choice.

He made a bow of thanks toward the empty air, intended for the spirit of the patriarch Lü Shun-yang. Then he sent for Mama Liu, the marriage broker.

"The spirit has spoken in favor of my marriage with Miss Noble Scent. A personal inspection is not necessary. Go quickly and settle the details." Thus dismissed, Mama Liu made all haste to the house of Dr. Iron Door, and informed him that her client no longer insisted on previous inspection of his bride-to-be.

"But he did at first," Dr. Iron Door grumbled, "and by so doing showed himself to be deplorably superficial, the kind of man who attaches more importance to externals than to superior character. He is not the son-in-law for me. I must have a man of the utmost moral rigor, who takes a thoroughly serious view of life."

Intent on her fee, Mama Liu summoned up all her ingenuity to overcome his resistance:

"If he wished at first to see the young lady, his only motive was one of kindness and tact. He was afraid that she might be too frail and delicate for married life. Once I was able to set his mind at rest on that score, he was overjoyed to hear how strictly and carefully she had been raised, and how, thanks to your guidance, she had become a veritable epitome of maidenly virtue. That decided him, and he bade me intercede with you to honor him by taking him into your worthy house."

Flattered at these remarks, Dr. Iron Door nodded his approval. Then it was a sense of delicacy that made him wish to see her first? And it was her sound upbringing that decided him? That sounded sensible and argued very much in the young man's favor. And he gave his paternal consent.

And so on a lucky calendar day the young man was received in Dr. Iron Door's home, and with Noble Scent on the carpet beside him, made the traditional bows to heaven and earth, ancestors and father-in-law. At nightfall when he was at last alone with her in the bridal chamber and she lifted her veil, he fixed his eyes upon his bride in feverish expectation. For to the last moment a doubt had lurked in a corner of his heart; to the last moment he had thought that Mama Liu's assurance must be slightly exaggerated, a product as it were of poetic license. But now that he was able to view her close at hand, in the full light of the lamps and candles, his heart leapt with delight. Her beauty exceeded his wildest expectations. Perhaps the best way to give an idea of her charms will be to quote a passage from a recent essay "in memory of the glorious lady of Tsin":

"Over her person hovers a cloud of dark mystery, a veil of unyielding reticence. Her face and every part of her body are bathed in purest beauty. When she smiles, one would like to take her charming face in both hands. But her charm becomes truly irresistible only when she pouts and knits her brows.

"To be sure, her tender waist and the nine sensitive zones of her body seem almost unequal to the battle of wedlock. Her body seems as soft as if it were devoid of bone structure; even a soft chair offends it."

How shall we describe the joy of union between bridegroom and bride? Once again we leave the task to a recent essay, this one entitled "Springtime in the Tower of Jasper":

"From beneath half-closed lids the stars that are her eyes flash an angry message: no! Awakened from deep slumber, the peach blossom declines to open its slender calyx. But eager for the fray, the tongue forces a narrow passage between the lips of the fragrant mouth. A blissful moan—and long pent-up feelings pour forth unrestrained. The dew of desire forms into tiny beads on the silken skin of her breasts. Two pairs of eyes open slowly and gaze plunges deep into gaze. Two hearts flare up into red fire."

Unquestionably Noble Scent was a peerless beauty, but to her partner's grief she was an utter failure at the "wind-and-moon game" and the hopes with which he had looked forward to his wedding night remained at least seven-tenths unfulfilled. Small wonder. Thanks to the traditional upbringing she had received from her strict, ultra-conservative parents, she wore an armor of virginal modesty and reserve, against which his tender assaults bounded off without the slightest effect. He was quite dismayed at her lack of response to his advances. If he allowed his language

On a lucky calendar day, the young man was received in Dr. Iron Door's home.

to become even mildly daring or frivolous, she blushed and took flight. He liked to play the "wind-and-moon game" not only at night but also in broad daylight, for it seemed to him that his pleasure was very much increased by the possibility of looking at certain secret parts of the body. On several occasions he attempted, in the morning or afternoon, to insert a bold hand beneath her clothing and to strip off her undermost coverings. The reception was not what he had bargained for. She resisted vigorously and screamed as though threatened with rape. At night, to be sure, she permitted his embraces, but quite apathetically as though merely doing her duty. He had to stick to the stodgy ancestral method, and any attempt at more modern, more refined variations met with fierce opposition. When he attempted the "fetching fire behind the hill" position, she said it was perfectly disgusting and contrary to all the rules of husbandly behavior. When he tried the "making candles by dipping the wick in tallow" position, she protested that such goings-on were utterly nasty and vulgar. It took all his powers of persuasion even to make her prop up her thighs on his shoulders. When their pleasure approached a climax, not the tiniest little cry, not the slightest moan of happiness was to be heard from her. Even when he smothered her in tender little cries of "My heart, my liver," or "My life, my everything," she took no more interest than if she had been deaf and dumb. It was enough to drive him to despair. He began to make fun of her and to call her his "little saint."

"Things can't go on like this. I must find some way of educating her and ridding her of those awful moral inhibitions—the best idea would be some stimulating reading matter." So saying, he repaired to the booksellers' quarter. There after a long search he procured a marvelously illustrated volume entitled *Ch'un-t'ang,* "The Vernal Palace." It was a celebrated book on the art of love, written by no less a man than the Grand Secretary, Chao Tzu-ang. It included thirty-six pictures, clearly and artfully illustrating the thirty-six different "positions" of vernal dalliance, of which the poets of the T'ang period had sung. He brought the book home with him and handed it to the "little saint." As they leafed through page after page, he whispered to her:

"You see that I haven't been asking you to join in any monkey business of my own invention. These are all accepted forms of married love, practiced by our venerable ancestors. The text and pictures prove it."

Unsuspectingly, Noble Scent took the volume and opened it. When she turned to the second page and read the big bold heading: *Han-kung yi-chao*, "traditional portraits from the imperial palace of the Han dynasty" (second century B.C. to second century A.D.), she thought to herself:

"There were many noble and virtuous beauties at the court of the ancient Han rulers—the book must contain portraits of them. Very well, let us see what the venerable ladies looked like." And eagerly she turned another page. But now came a picture that made her start back in consternation: in the midst of an artificial rock garden a man and woman in rosy nakedness, most intimately intertwined. Blushing crimson for shame and indignation, she cried out:

"Foo! How disgusting! Where did you ever get such a thing? Why, it sullies and befouls the atmosphere of my chaste bedchamber."

Whereupon she called her maid and ordered her to burn the horrid thing on the spot. But he restrained her.

"You can't do that. The book is an ancient treasure, worth at least a hundred silver pieces. I borrowed it from a friend. If you wish to pay him a hundred silver pieces in damages, very well, burn it. If not, do me the favor of letting me keep it for two days until I have finished reading it; then I'll return it to my friend."

"But why do you have to read such a thing, that offends against all human morality and order?"

"I beg your pardon, if it were as offensive and immoral

as all that, a famous painter would hardly have lent himself to illustrating it, and a publisher would hardly have been willing to defray the production costs and distribute the book. You are quite mistaken. Since the world was created, there has been nothing more natural and reasonable than the activities described in this book. That is why a master of the word joined forces with a master of color to fashion the material into a true work of art; that is why the publisher spared no costs and as you see brought the book out in a de luxe edition on expensive silk, and that is why the plates are preserved along with other literary treasures in the archives of the Han-lin Academy, in the Forest of Brush and Ink, so that future generations may draw knowledge and profit from it. Without such books love between the sexes would gradually lose all charm and ardor; husband and wife would bore one another to tears. Gone would be the pleasure of begetting children, dull indifference would take root. It is not only for my own edification that I borrowed the book, but wittingly and I think wisely for yours as well, in the hope that it would prepare you for motherhood, that your womb would be blessed and you would soon present me with a little boy or a little girl. Or do you really think that a young couple like us should espouse the ascetic ways of your *ling-tsun,* your 'venerable lord,' and condemn our youthful marriage to barrenness? Are you aware of my good intentions now? Was there anything to be indignant about?"

Noble Scent was not entirely convinced.

"I cannot quite believe that what the book represents is really compatible with morality and reason. If that were so, why did our forebears who created our social order not teach us to carry on openly, in broad daylight, before the eyes of strangers? Why do people do it like thieves in the night, shut away in their bedchambers? Doesn't that prove that the whole thing must be wrong and forbidden?"

The Before Midnight Scholar replied with a hearty laugh.

"What a comical way of looking at things! But far be it from me to find fault with my *niang-tzu*, my dear little woman, on that account. It's all the fault of the preposterous way your honorable father raised you, shutting you up in the house and cutting you off from the outside world, forbidding you to associate with young girls like yourself who could have enlightened you. Why, you've grown up like a hermit without the slightest knowledge of the world. Of course married couples conduct their business by day as well as night; everyone does. Just think for a moment; if it had never been done in the daylight with others looking on, how would an artist have found out about all the different positions shown in this book? How could he have depicted all these forms and variations of loving union so vividly that one look at his pictures is enough to put us into a fine state of excitement?"

"Yes, but what about my parents? Why didn't they do it in the daytime?"

"I beg your pardon. How do you know they didn't?"

"Why, I would surely have caught them at it. I am sixteen, after all, and all these years I never noticed a thing. Why, I never even heard a sound to suggest that. . . ."

Again the Before Midnight Scholar had to laugh aloud:

"Ah, what a dear little silly you are! Such parental occupations are not intended for the eyes and ears of a child! But one of the maids is sure to have heard or seen a little something from time to time. Of course your parents would never have done anything within your sight or hearing; very wisely they did it behind closed doors, for fear that if a little girl like you were to notice anything, her mental health might be upset by all sorts of premature thoughts and daydreams."

After a moment of silent reflection, Noble Scent said as though to herself:

"That's true. I remember that they occasionally withdrew to their bedchamber in the daytime and bolted the door after them—can that be what they were doing? It's possible. But in broad daylight! To see each other stark naked! How can it be? They must have felt so ashamed."

"I beg your pardon. For lovers to see each other naked in broad daylight, why, that's the whole charm of it; it gives ten times more pleasure than doing it in the dark. And that is true of all lovers—with two exceptions."

"What are the two exceptions?"

"Either he is ugly and she is beautiful, or she is ugly and he is handsome: in those two cases dealings by daylight are not advisable."

"Why?"

"Dealings between the sexes give full enjoyment only when both parties feel drawn to one another body and soul, as though by a primordial force, and long for physical union with every fiber of their being. Let us suppose that she is beautiful, that with her full, soft forms and her delicate, luminous, smooth skin she resembles a well-polished jewel. Drawing her close to him, her lover will strip off layer after layer of her garments, and the more he sees of her, the more his desire will increase; his member will stiffen of its own free will and stand up big and hard and strong. But then suppose that she looks toward her partner and discovers ugly features, misshapen limbs, coarse, hairy skin, in short a veritable goblin. He may have been almost acceptable as long as he had clothes on, but now he lies there before her in all his ugliness. And the greater the contrast between his fiendish aspect and the soft radiant beauty of her own body, the more horrified and repelled will she be. Even if she was fully prepared for physical union, must her desire not turn instantly to nothing?. And he in turn, must not his javelin, which only a moment before was standing up so proud and big and strong, shrink to the most dwarfish size at the sight of her obvious revulsion and distaste? In short, there can be no joyous battle of love between a pair so unequally matched.

If they should attempt it just the same, the end is sure to be a lamentable fiasco. Better let them do battle at night when they cannot see each other plainly. That is the one exception.

"The other is the reverse: he is handsome, she is ugly. The situation is exactly the same, no reason to waste words on it.

"And now we come to our own case: here it is equal to equal, radiant skin to radiant skin, well-formed youth to well-formed youth. And now I ask you: Have we any need to take refuge in night and darkness, to crawl under the covers and hide from one another? Should we not do better to show ourselves to one another in broad daylight and delight in the sight of our bodies in all their natural beauty? If you don't believe me, let us make a try. Let us just try it once in the daytime."

By now Noble Scent was half convinced. Despite the modest "no" of her lips, she was almost willing. A slight flush came to her cheeks, revealing her mounting excitement and anticipation of things to come. This did not escape him, and in secret he thought: "She is gradually becoming interested. No doubt about it, she would like to play. But her senses have barely begun to awaken. Her hunger and thirst for love are very new to her. If I start in too brusquely, she is very likely to suffer the fate of the glutton who gobbles up everything in sight without taking time to bite or chew. She would get little enjoyment from such indigestible fare. I'd better bide my time and let her dangle a while."

He moved up a comfortable armchair and sat down. Drawing her to him by the sleeve, he made her sit on his lap. Then he took the picture book and leafed through it page by page and picture by picture.

Unlike other books of a similar kind, the book was so arranged that the front of each leaf bore a picture and the back the text that went with it. The text was in two sections. The first briefly explained the position represented;

the second gave a critical estimate of the picture from the standpoint of its artistic value.

Before starting, the Before Midnight Scholar advised his pupil to examine each picture carefully for its spirit and meaning, for then it would provide an excellent model and example for future use. Then he read to her, sentence for sentence.

"Picture No. 1. The butterfly flutters about, searching for flowery scents."

Accompanying text: "She sits waiting with parted legs on a rock by the shore of a garden pond. He, first carefully feeling out the terrain, takes pains to insert his nephrite proboscis into the depths of her calyx. Because the battle has only begun and the region of bliss is still far off, both still show a relatively normal expression, their eyes are wide open."

"Picture No. 2 shows the queen bee making honey."

Accompanying text: "She lies on her back, cushioned in pillows, her parted legs raised as though hanging in mid-air, her hands pressed against 'the fruit,' guiding his nephrite proboscis to the entrance of her calyx, helping it to find the right path and not to stray. At this moment her face shows an expression of hunger and thirst, while his features reveal the most intense excitement, with which the viewer becomes infected. All this is brought out by the artist with remarkable subtlety."

"Picture No. 3. The little bird that had gone astray finds its way back to its nest in the thicket."

Accompanying text: "She lies slightly to one side, dug into the thicket of cushions, one leg stretched high, and clutches his thigh with both hands as though his obedient vassal had finally found its way to the right place, to her most sensitive spot, and she feared it might go off and get lost again. This accounts for the shadow of anxiety on her otherwise happy face. Both parties are in full swing, quite preoccupied by the spasmodic thrill of the 'flying brush' and the 'dancing ink.' "

"Picture No. 4. The hungry steed gallops to the feed crib."

Accompanying text: "She, flat on her back, presses his body to her breast with both hands. Her feet propped up on his shoulders, he has sunk his yak whisk into her calyx to the shaft. Both of them are approaching ecstasy. The way in which the artist pictures their physical and mental state at this moment, their eyes veiled beneath half-closed lids, their tongues enlaced, reveals the master of the brush."

"Picture No. 5. The dragons are weary of battle."

Accompanying text: "Her head rests sideways on the pillow; she has let her arms droop; her limbs feel numb as though stuffed with cotton. Resting his head sideways against her cheek he presses his body to hers. He too feels as numb as cotton. The ecstasy is gone. The 'aromatic soul' has fled, the beautiful dream has passed the peak and evaporated into nothingness. The barest thread of life is discernible. Without it one might think the two of them were dead, two lovers in one coffin and one grave. The picture brings home to us the sublimity of bliss savored to the very end."

Up to this point Noble Scent had obediently studied the pictures and patiently listened to the commentary. But as he turned another page and began to show her Picture No. 6, she pushed the book away in visible agitation and stood up.

"Enough!" she cried. "What's the good of all these pictures? They are just upsetting. You look at them by yourself. I'm going to bed."

"Just a little patience, we'll run through the rest quickly. The best is still to come. Then we'll both go to bed."

"As if there weren't time enough tomorrow for looking at books. For my part, I've had quite enough."

He embraced her and closed her mouth with a kiss. And as he kissed her, he noticed something new. They had been married for a whole month. In all that time, she had held the gates of her teeth closed tight when he kissed her. His

"Come, let us play at being gods."

tongue had never succeeded in forcing or wriggling its way through the solid fence. Until today he had never made contact with her tongue; he hadn't so much as an idea what it was like. But now when he pressed his lips to hers—what a wonderful surprise!—the tip of his tongue encountered the tip of her tongue. For the first time she had opened up the gate.

"My heart, my liver!" he sighed with delight. "At last! And now—why bother moving to the bed? This chair will do the trick, it will take the place of the rock by the pond, and we shall imitate the lovers in Picture No. 1. What do you say?"

Noble Scent with affected indignation:

"Impossible. It's not a fit occupation for human beings. . . ."

"There you are perfectly right. It is an occupation and pastime more fit for the gods. Come, let us play at being gods." So saying, he stretched out his hand and began to fiddle with the knot of her sash. And despite her grimace of disapproval, she cooperated, letting him draw her close and permitting him to strip off her undermost covering. As he did so, he made a discovery that fanned his excitement into a bright flame. Aha, he thought, just looking at those pictures has sprinkled her little meadow with the dew of desire. He undid himself and set her down in the chair in such a way that her legs hung over his shoulders. Cautiously he guided his bellwether through the gates of her pleasure house, and then began to remove the rest of her clothes.

Why only now?, you will ask. Why did he begin at the bottom? Let me explain: This Before Midnight Scholar was an experienced old hand. He said to himself that if he tried to remove her upper garments first, she would feel ashamed and intimidated, her resistance would make things unnecessarily difficult. That is why he daringly aimed his first offensive at her most sensitive spot, figuring that once she surrendered there she would easily surrender on all

other fronts. Herein his strategy was that of the commander
who defeats an enemy army by taking its general prisoner.
And the truth is that she now quite willingly let him undress her from head to foot—no, not quite—with the
exception of a single article of apparel which he himself
tactfully spared: her little silk stockings.

After their three-inch long (or short) "golden lilies"
have been bound up, our women customarily draw stockings over the bandages. Only then do their toes and ankles
feel at ease. Otherwise their feet, like flowers without
leaves, are unlovely to behold.

Now he too cast off his last coverings and flung himself
into the fray with uplifted spear. Already his bellwether
was in her pleasure house. Groping its way to left and right,
slipping and sliding, it sought a passage to the secret
chamber where the "flower heart," the privy seal, lies hidden. She helped him in his search by propping up her hands
on the arms of the chair and, in tune with his movements,
lithely twisting and bending her middle parts toward him.
Thus they carried on for a time, exactly in accordance
with Figure 2 of their textbook

Suddenly, way down deep, she had a strange feeling of
a kind that was utterly new to her; it did not hurt, no, it
was more like a sensation of itching or tickling, almost
unendurable and yet very very pleasant.

"Stop," she cried, bewildered by the strangeness of the
thing. "That's enough for today. You are hurting me."
And she tried to wrest herself free.

Thoroughly experienced in these matters, he realized
that he had touched her most intimate spot, her flower-
heart. Considerately acceding to her wishes, he moved
away from the ticklish spot and contented himself with
moving his bellwether slowly back and forth several dozen
times through her pleasure house with its narrow passages
and spacious halls. The intruder made himself thoroughly
at home on her property, and she was overcome by an

irresistible desire to punish him for his insolence. Choking would be a fair punishment she thought.

Removing her hands from the arms of the chair, she let his back slip down and dug her hands into his buttocks. This enabled her to press closer to him, an operation in which he helped by clasping her slender waist in his hands and holding her as tightly as he could. Thanks to the intimate conjunction thus achieved—they were now exactly in the position illustrated in Figure 3—she held his stiff thick bellwether firmly enough to start slowly strangling it. While sparing no effort and answering pressure with pressure, he saw that her eyes were clouding over and the stately edifice of her hair was becoming undone.

"*Hsin-kan*, my heart, my liver," he panted. "You seem to be on the verge—but it is very uncomfortable in this chair; shall we not continue on the bed?"

This suggestion did not appeal to her. She had the rascally intruder just where she wanted him; just a little longer, and she would choke the life out of him. At this late stage, she was quite unwilling to be cheated of her pleasure. If they were to move to the bed now, he would slip away from her. No, this was no time for interruptions! She shook her head resolutely. Then closing her eyes as though she were already half asleep, she said—this was her pretext—that she was much too tired to move.

He decided on a compromise: leaving her position unchanged, he placed his hands beneath her seat in such a way that she could not slip down, bade her throw her arms round his neck. Pressing his mouth to hers, he lifted her up carefully and thus enlaced carried her into the bedroom where they went on with the game.

Suddenly she let out a scream: "Dearest, ah! ah! . . ."

She pressed closer and closer to him and the sounds that issued from her mouth were like the moans and groans of one dying. It was clear to him that she was on the threshold. And he too at the same time! With his last strength he pressed his nephrite proboscis into the sanctum of her flower-temple. Then for a time they lay enlaced as though in a deathlike sleep. She was first to stir; she heaved a deep sigh and said:

"Did you notice? I was dead just now."

"Of course I noticed. But we don't call it 'death.' We call it 'giving off an extract.' "

"What do you mean by 'giving off an extract'?"

"Both in man and woman a subtle essence of all the bodily humors is at all times secreted. At the peak of amorous pleasure one of the body's vessels overflows and gives off some of this extract. Just before the flow, the whole body, skin and flesh and bones, falls into a deep, unconscious sleep. Our physical state before, during, and after the flow is called *tiu* 'a giving off of extract.' It is depicted in Figure 5."

"Then I was not dead?"

"Of course not. You gave off an extract."

"If that is so, I hope I may do it day after day and night after night."

He burst into a resounding laugh.

"Well, was I not right to recommend the picture book as an adviser? Is it not priceless?"

"Yes, indeed. A priceless treasure. We must consult it over and over again. A pity that the friend you borrowed it from will want it back again."

"Don't you worry about that. It was I myself who bought it. The whole story about the friend was just made up."

"Oh, that is good news."

From then on the two of them were one heart and one soul. Noble Scent became an assiduous reader of *The Vernal Palace* and from that day on she could not praise it too highly. Like a diligent pupil, she made every effort to put her learning into practice, and never grew weary of experimenting with the new forms and variations of the wind-and-moon game. The prim "little saint" grew to be a past mistress at the arts of love. Determined to keep her vernal fires supplied with fuel, the Before Midnight Scholar ran untiringly from bookshop to bookshop, buying more books of the same kind, such as the *Hsiu-t'a yeh-shih*, "The Fantastic Tale of the Silk-Embroidered Pillows," or the *Ju-yi-ch'ün chuan*, "The Tale of the Perfect Gallant," or the *Ch'i p'o-tzu chuan*, "The Tale of the Love-Maddened Women," and so on. In all he bought some twenty such books and piled them up on his desk.

Together they devoured each of the new acquisitions and then put it away in the bookcase to make place for new reading matter. Both of them were so insatiable in their thirst for discovery that three hundred and sixty pictures of vernal positions could not have stilled their appetite. They were like the lovers we encounter in novels: an orchestra of lutes and guitars, a whole concert of bells and drums would not have sufficed to express the harmony and happiness of their hearts.

So far all was for the best between them. And yet something was amiss; something that injected a discordant note into the harmony of their young marriage.

The relations between father-in-law and son-in-law left much to be desired. As the reader already knows, Dr. Iron Door was a crotchety, old-fashioned gentleman, an eccentric if ever there was one. He looked back fondly on the good old times, cherished the honesty and simplicity of our forebears, and abhorred the empty affectations of the profane crowd. Licentious talk was strictly taboo in his presence. What he liked best was earnest discussion on themes drawn from the teachings of Confucius.

The very first evening after the Before Midnight Scholar came to live under his roof, Dr. Iron Door looked askance at his fashionable clothing and his smooth, ingratiating ways which the old man judged to be quite superficial. From the very first moment, he took a dislike to this smooth, excessively handsome young man.

"Plenty of fine leaves," he grumbled in secret, "but no

fruit, no solid kernel; from his kind my daughter will get little support in her old age and affliction. However," he continued with a sigh of resignation, "the forms of this marriage have been observed; he has punctiliously provided his betrothal and wedding presents, and we have draped our house in the traditional red; the mistake has been made and cannot be unmade. Let us wait until the wedding is over; then I will take him under my strict paternal discipline and teach him to be an honest and in every respect scrupulous man." Such was his plan.

And he put it into execution. From morning to night he brooked no misconduct. The least mistake, whether of commission or omission, brought the young man a sound paternal scolding. Even the slightest incorrectness in walking, standing, sitting, or reclining called forth severe criticism and long-drawn-out commentaries.

But as the only son and heir of parents who had died while he was still a boy, our Before Midnight Scholar had long been accustomed to a good deal of independence. He could hardly have put up for long with all this tedious discipline and pedantic backbiting.

Several times he was on the point of giving his father-in-law a piece of his mind, of telling him in no uncertain terms that he had had enough of his schoolmasterly ways. But then he thought of Noble Scent. A serious dispute with the old gentleman might upset her and introduce an unwelcome dissonance into the hitherto so admirable harmony of their conjugal lyres. Accordingly he controlled himself and swallowed his indignation. But when there seemed to be no end to his swallowing, the effort became too much for him and one day, after long deliberation, his mind was made up.

"From the very first," he said to himself, "it was his daughter I was interested in. But because he was so attached to her and the thought of her leaving home was so distasteful to him, I did him a favor and moved in with him. His only thanks was to subject me to the crushing weight of his *T'ai-shan* authority, to tyrannize me in every way he could. By what right? What entitles a worm-eaten old pedant and doctrinaire like him to lord it over me? Do I have to stand for it? He should be grateful to me for putting up with his nonsense and not telling him what I think of his antiquated ways. But instead of that, he goes on scolding and bickering and trying to make me over in his image. Let him practice his pedagogic arts on some-one else, not on a dashing young genius like me. And besides, who says that his daughter is the only pebble on the beach? I was planning all along to go out into the world sooner or later, to "steal perfumes" and "fish for pearls" and do some writing on the side. Who says that I have to be chained to a single woman all my life?

"I'm good and sick of being nagged at all day, of being taken to task every time I say a word. Well, it's a good thing I haven't stirred up any scandals outside the house; why, the old tyrant would be quite capable of condemning me to death. What is to be done in such a situation? Would an open quarrel help? Nonsense, it wouldn't change him a bit. Should I be patient and keep swallowing my griev-ances? No, enough is enough. There is only one pos-sibility: to go away and leave Noble Scent to his care. I shall simply tell him that I must withdraw somewhere to continue my studies undisturbed and prepare for the next examination. That sounds innocent enough, the idea will surely appeal to him. If in the course of my travels chance should favor me and cause another beauty, a love pre-destined me from another existence, to cross my path, so much the better. Of course I shall not be able to marry her, but to pass a few pleasant hours with a 'cloud sprite on the magic mountain' will be very nice too."

His decision was made.

His original idea was to speak first with Noble Scent and then to take leave of her father. But then he told him-self that she would no doubt be dismayed at the thought of foregoing her accustomed bedtime pleasures, that she would stir up a tearful scene and possibly talk him out of his plan. To forestall this eventuality, he modified his tactics and unbeknownst to her spoke first to his father-in-law:

"Your submissive son-in-law is beginning to feel rather lonely and cut off from the world in this remote mountain town. He feels the need of the inspiration that comes of association with eminent professors and with students of his own age. He is wasting his time and making no real progress in his studies. In view of all this he begs leave of his revered father-in-law to set out on a journey; he wishes to visit the big cities in the plains, to look around him and extend his horizons. His aim is to seek out a worthy citadel of cultural life, where he will meet inspired teachers and form valuable friendships among fellow students. There he will pitch his tent. Then when it comes time for the great autumn examinations, he aspires to betake himself to the provincial capital and show his mettle on the intellectual battlefield. He will do his best to carry off first or at least second place, so proving that he was worthy to be received into so honored a family.

"What is your treasured opinion? Are you inclined to grant your permission?"

The stern father-in-law was obviously surprised and pleased.

"At last a sensible word. In the six months since my esteemed son-in-law came to dwell beneath my roof, these are the first words worthy to strike my eardrums. I can only commend your wish to depart with a view to continuing your studies. Excellent, excellent! What possible objection could I have to your plan?"

The Before Midnight Scholar continued:

"You have given me your paternal consent, but there is still a difficulty: I am very much afraid that your *ling-ai*, your 'commanding darling,' will accuse me of heartlessness if I leave her now, so soon after our marriage. In my modest

After taking leave of his father-in-law and wife, the Before Midnight Scholar set out on his journey.

opinion, it might be best to put it to her as though the decision had originated with you, my estimable father-in-law, and not with me, your insignificant son-in-law. Then she is unlikely to create difficulties, and I shall be able to go my way with a clear conscience."

"Very true! I am entirely of your opinion," said Dr. Iron Door. Soon afterward, within hearing of his daughter, he suggested to his son-in-law that it was high time for him to bestir himself into the world and prepare to win a meritorious place in the second state examination. At first the Before Midnight Scholar showed little enthusiasm for the idea; now the old man adopted a tone of severity and repeated his suggestion in the form of a command, to which his son-in-law could only incline.

Poor Noble Scent was at the very height of her newly discovered conjugal transports. When she heard of the impending departure and separation, she felt like a baby torn suddenly from its mother's breast. At first she was quite inconsolable. But at length, since it was her father's will, she inclined like a good, obedient daughter. As compensation, to be sure, she demanded, during the last days and nights, as much advance payment as was humanly possible, on the love debts that would accrue during his absence. He for his part was well aware of the lonely nights ahead of him on his long journey, and did his very best to fortify himself against the impending period of continence. Thus the couple's last nights built up to a veritable orgy; the young people clung together like glue and lacquer, drinking their fill of the delights which are ordinarily kept secret and of which lovers are reluctant to speak in the presence of outsiders. Then at last the time had come. After taking leave of his father-in-law and wife, the Before Midnight Scholar set out, accompanied by his two personal servants.

My esteemed readers will learn in the next chapter of the extraordinary adventures he was to meet with on his way.

CHAPTER III

*In the dismal suburban inn a stranger takes the
lonely traveler under his wing. To shorten the long
night, the noble bandit enlightens him on new aspects
of the wind-and-moon game.*

The Before Midnight Scholar had set out on his travels
without any set goal. Somewhere to find an unusual beauty,
that was the only thought that guided him. Where he
found her, there he would settle. And so he journeyed
from province to province, from district to district.

Wherever he went, his reputation went before him: a
coming talent, a highly gifted *hsiu-ts'ai*, who had gained
first place at his first state examination, a brilliant conversationalist, poet and writer. Wherever he halted, the news of
his presence spread at once to all the academicians within
a radius of hundreds of miles and he was literally overwhelmed by young people of his calling who vied for the
honor of his friendship and showered him with invitations
to attend their social and literary clubs. Nothing could have
interested him less. He set no store whatever by all this
literary bustle. As far as he was concerned, there was but
one urgent task: to keep looking for an extraordinary
beauty.

Day after day he arose at an early hour and strolled
through wide and narrow streets, always on the alert—in
vain. Never did any of the women who met his eyes day
after day rise above the average. He found none who
seemed worthy of the predicate *t'ien-tzu*, "image of heaven"

or *kuo-se*, "fairest of the land." Deeply disillusioned, he journeyed from town to town, from city to city.

One day he was sitting alone in a gloomy suburban inn. Both his servants were sick in bed. Concern for his prestige forbade him to go out unaccompanied. What would the ladies of the city think if they were to see him wandering about without an escort? One thing was sure, they would not take him for a distinguished young gentleman. Thus he sat disconsolate and alone in the lower common-room of his inn, sipping tea in utter boredom.

Suddenly he was awakened from his thoughts. A stranger was speaking to him. It was another guest, who had been sitting for some time over a jug of wine in the adjoining room and had now stepped up to his table.

"The esteemed gentleman is all alone and seems to be bored. My insignificance is sitting over there with a jug of tolerable wine. If you should not despise my company, perhaps you will let me invite you to join me at my table and accept a cup of my wine?"

"We have met one another quite by chance, after the manner of leaves floating on the surface of the water," said the Before Midnight Scholar with the traditional affectation of reticence. "What claim have I to your hospitality?"

"I have always heard say that you scholars are fond of a little chat. Why button up so tight? Perhaps you are offended because I am not a member of your privileged class but a plain man of the people. I know that you may expect to rise rapidly in the world, that a brilliant future awaits you, while I am only a little man. But you need not fear that I am trying to attach myself to you in the hope that you will raise me out of my lowly state and take me along with you in your high career. That is far from my intention. I am simply a lover of sociability. Since chance has brought us together in this inn, why should you not condescend to join me at my table for a little while?"

"Why not, indeed?" the young man finally consented. "I have been frightfully bored, literally pining for a taste of conversation." And only too gladly he followed the stranger to his table. After a little argument about the seating order—the young man firmly declined the proffered place of honor at the end of the table and insisted that they sit across from one another as equal to equal—they introduced themselves. As usual the young man gave his pseudonym, Wei-yang sheng, the Before Midnight Scholar.

"And your respected name?"

"As a son of the common people, I have no family name, but only a popular street-and-market name. Sai K'un-lun, 'K'un-lun's Rival,' that is what they call me."

"What an unusual name! What does it mean?"

"I am afraid you will be frightened if I tell you. You will not wish to drink with me any more."

"Have no fear. I am no coward. I am afraid neither of devils nor of ghosts—in case any of them should wish to honor me with their company. Nor am I pedantic in my judgment of my fellow men; I do not inquire after a man's class or education. All I ask of a companion is that he be congenial."

"Very well then. I am by trade a burglar, a robber, a bandit. I can scale walls and climb over roofs. Thick walls and high towers are no obstacle for me; it costs me little exertion to capture them. I am able to penetrate people's innermost rooms, their very bedchambers, and, without attracting the slightest attention, to make off with everything that catches my fancy, wrapped up in cloths and blankets. Often my victims notice nothing until days later.

"Our historical tradition speaks of a certain Moorish slave named K'un-lun, who lived in the days of the T'ang dynasty (618–907) and is said to have committed a truly heroic burglary: from the thick-walled and closely guarded border fortress of a certain Prince Kuo, he is said one night to have carried away a beautiful slave girl by the name of Hung-hsiao, 'Red Radiance.' But this one heroic deed is all our intrepid Moorish slave ever accomplished. I have performed such feats by the hundred. That is why I am commonly known as Sai K'un-lun, K'un-lun's Rival."

And now the young man looked rather frightened after all.

"You have been practicing your trade for a long time. Apparently you are well known among the population and even enjoy a kind of celebrity. Under the circumstances," the young man inquired with visible anxiety, "must you not come into conflict with the law?"

"If I had ever allowed myself to be caught and dragged into court, I should be a nobody. There is a saying that goes:

To convict a thief, you must find the goods.

There are never any goods to be found on me. Now and then, to be sure, I am questioned, but I always manage to talk myself out of it; they can never prove a thing. On the contrary, I am held in high esteem by the population far and near; and people are very careful not to bring down my vengeance on their heads by doing me an injustice. For everyone knows that I commit no injustice. I am no common bandit, I have my professional honor. There are five exceptional cases in which I make it a point of honor never to commit a theft: I spare people in times of domestic misfortune and of domestic rejoicing as well; I never touch the belongings of good friends; I never rob those who have already been robbed; and lastly, I spare unsuspecting souls who take no precautions against theft."

"That is very illuminating. But would you explain to me at greater length why you make these five exceptions?"

"With pleasure. Let us consider the first case. Suppose a man is going through a period of domestic misfortune, sickness, death in the family, or a 'flying calamity' such as fire or sudden business reverses or imperial disfavor. Would it not be unspeakable to rob a house that has been thus sorely tried, to pour oil on the fire and add misfortune to misfortune? Second exception: A family is celebrating a joyful occasion, a wedding or the birth of a son, a recovery from severe illness, a birthday, or the completion of a new house; would it not be a wretched thing to spoil the festive mood with a theft, to dishearten the family at such a moment and destroy its hopes in the future? Third exception: I have no scruples about robbing strangers; I see no injustice in it. But when it comes to good friends, people I meet every day in the street, with whom I exchange warm greetings, fellow men who bear me no ill will whatever—rob such people, no, the very idea would cover me with shame.

"Exception number four: in the exercise of my trade it seems to me the most natural thing in the world to give top priority to wealthy persons with an excess of gold and silver. I am merely levying a little tax, a tribute as it were, on their excess. But I content myself with taxing them once. To come back for more—why, that would be sordid greed. Such vulgarity would not be at all to my taste.

"Exception five: There are close-hearted, anxious, and overcareful people who try night after night to guard against theft with all manner of security devices. The words thief and burglar are forever on their lips. This I regard as an unfriendly attitude which I requite with an equally unfriendly attitude: when I wish to commit a burglary, it is to their houses that I give top priority, thus proving that their beastly security devices mean nothing to one of my talents. It is a matter of professional pride with me.

"On the other hand, there are great-hearted, generous souls who are well aware that money alone cannot confer happiness and has no bearing on a man's intrinsic worth. They think so little of their money that they sometimes forget to close the main gate at night or to bolt their bedroom door. Were I to rob such people, I should feel guilty of persecuting the weak and of fearing the strong. Here again I should be covered with shame.

"These then are the five principles that I conscientiously observe in the practice of my trade. And that is why I am respected far and wide. I am known to be a thief and burglar, but I am not treated as such. On the contrary, it is considered an honor to share my company. In short, if you do not consider it beneath you, let us swear an oath of brotherhood on the spot. One day, perhaps, you may need my services. Then you may be sure that I shall help you with all my strength, even if it means laying down my life."

The young man heaved a deep sigh of admiration, and thought to himself: "Who would have thought that the brotherhood of thieves could boast so noble, so high-minded, so heroic a member!" And pursuing his thoughts: "He has offered me his services—what if I should make use of them for my purposes? Perhaps, indeed, he will play the part of K'un-lun, the Moorish slave, and help me to win a beauty, a second Red Radiance, who is hidden away from the world behind high palace walls. What if I should bid him steal a hidden beauty for me? What a daring, intoxicating thought!"

Quite beside himself at the thought, he waved his arms and stamped his feet in excitement. But then, recovering his outward composure, he said as calmly as he could:

"*Chi hao*, very good. Your idea of drinking brotherhood meets with my approval."

However, he was not quite easy in his mind, and the other sensed as much.

"Do you really mean it? It seems to me that you have secret misgivings. But you may set your mind at rest. It is true that my undertakings are rather daring and that a certain amount of violence is involved; but there is little danger of trouble with the authorities, and at the worst, should the improbable come to pass, it is I alone who would be condemned to death, certainly not an innocent by-stander like yourself. On that score you really have nothing to worry about."

"What psychological insight! He has guessed my secret fears!" thought the young man in silent amazement. Relieved of his doubts, he gave his joyful, wholehearted consent.

They set to work at once. Having agreed to share the costs, they sent for the usual sacrificial offerings, a carp, a rooster, and a duck, and arranged to have them slaughtered and prepared in the kitchen of the inn. Then they exchanged the eight ideograms of the hour, the day, the month and year of their birth, smeared each other's mouths with the blood of the three victims, and solemnly swore fraternal loyalty to one another until death. It turned out K'un-lun's Rival was ten years older than the Before Midnight Scholar. From that moment on, accordingly, they employed the terms of address *hsiung*, "elder brother," and *ti*, "younger brother." To conclude the ritual, they partook of the succulently roasted offerings and drank quantities of the best wine and punch to their brotherhood. Their banquet continued until midnight. Then the elder brother wished to retire, but the younger brother was not of that mind.

"To go to bed separately now would be a dreary end to our festivities for both of us. My suggestion is that you come to my room and share my couch. We shall shorten the long night with intimate conversation."

The elder brother agreed at once and followed the younger to his room.

When they had undressed and lain down side by side, our scholar struck up his favorite theme:

"Is it not strange," he began, "that in this otherwise attractive region, one never catches so much as a glimpse of an attractive woman?"

"What have you in mind? Are you still a bachelor, on the lookout for a suitable companion?"

"Not at all, I am already married. However, I have been away from home for a long time, and who says that a man should content himself with one woman? After all, there are other women in the world. I should be so pleased to find a little female company in the course of my travels.

Frankly, I am a great friend of the wind-and-moon game. I cannot help it, that is how nature made me. Yes, the ostensible purpose of my journey was to study and prepare for the next state examination, but that was merely a pretext for the benefit of my wife and father-in-law. My real motive for leaving home was something very different: I desired new experience, amorous adventures. That is why I started out on this wearisome, uncomfortable journey. I have explored cities and countrysides, whole provinces, and thus far, I must admit, I have been unsuccessful. The women who crossed my path have been common, average at best, hardly worth mentioning. One kind plaster their faces with rouge and powder to hide their horrid swarthy complexions; the other kind hide their ghastly yellowish hair beneath pounds of beads and blue enameled arrows. I have not met a single one whose natural beauty had no need of such artifice. In short, I have looked about for a long while and I am beginning to be sick of the whole business."

"It is no wonder. Your whole method has been wrong. As a rule, the wives and daughters of good families do not show themselves in public. Those who do exhibit themselves are simply not of good family. Generally speaking, even public harlots and sing-song girls do not appear in public. It is only the ugly, faded ones, who can no longer awaken love, who stand in the doorway, offering their smiles for sale. All the rest, all who possess the least bit of reputation and worth, stay in their rooms waiting for the right man to come and find them, and draw them out of their obscurity. If that is true even of public women, I leave you to judge how it is with the daughters of private families. Surely you cannot expect them to stand in the doorway, showing themselves to strange men. You will look a long while. If you wish to find beauties hereabouts, the best thing you can do is to consult me."

The younger brother raised his head in surprise.

"But how so? You are not an actor on the stage of the wind-and-moon game. What can you know?"

"True, I am not an actor, but no one is in a position to observe so closely what takes place on the stage. There is no better eye-and-ear witness than I. Let me ask you a question: Where do you think more beauties are to be found, in the houses of the rich and distinguished or among poor, simple folk?"

"In the houses of the rich and distinguished, of course."

"Correct. And that fits in with my trade. Poor, simple folk are of no interest to me in my activities; they are not worth robbing.

"And now bear this in mind. When it comes to the wives and daughters of wealthy, distinguished families, appearances are often deceptive, for ladies of their class make free with silks and jewelry and all sorts of artifice. But how much natural beauty is concealed beneath their elaborate exterior? Only my colleagues and I are in a position to judge. It is in the dark, silent night that I creep into the houses of my wealthy and distinguished clientele. Consider the scene: one of our beauties is undressing—perhaps she is sitting in the moonlight, by the open window or on the balcony; or she may be lounging in bed, reading by lamplight with the curtains still open; or strumming on the lute or embroidering. She may not go to sleep for hours, she has not yet pulled up the covers. There she lies stark naked, giving me an opportunity to watch her at leisure. I am only a few steps away, somewhere in the dark, my ears on the alert, my eyes glued to her, and I don't stir. Not a sound, not a movement that she makes escapes me. Who else has occasion to observe a beautiful woman so carefully and thoroughly? Her hair, her face, the color of her skin, the forms of her body. Is she slender or skinny, well rounded or frankly stout? Is her hill-of-delight flat or arched, covered with sparse grass or dense brush? Nothing, not the slightest detail escapes me. In this way, I have been able to build up a solid stock of information about all the ladies of distinguished houses, beautiful and otherwise, within a radius of a hundred miles and a clear, unfalsified picture of each one is graven in my memory. If it's a real beauty that interests you, you can confidently apply to me."

At first the younger brother had lain beneath the covers, listening eagerly. But what he now heard so stirred him that he leapt to a sitting position and cried:

"How wonderful! Why, of course, who else has so privileged a view of our fashionable ladies in the secrecy of their boudoirs! To the rest of us they remain hidden: we can gain only a partial picture and even that is bound to be false. Now another question: When a beautiful woman lies naked before you and you are free to feast your eyes on her most intimate parts, it seems to me that you must get rather wrought up. Now what is the truth of the matter?"

"At first, I cannot deny, when I was still a young fellow and a beginner, that kind of thing did indeed put my senses in quite a turmoil, and often as I stood there in the dark, looking and listening, I could not resist the temptation and was compelled to do a little 'sleight-of-hand,' imagining the while that I was actually playing the game with the lady in question. Later, after I had enjoyed such sights many dozens of times, my senses grew dulled and indifferent. I began to look upon the secret part quite matter-of-factly as a common appurtenance of the female body, an article of daily use. After that, the sight left me cold, except when I chanced to see the lady in violent embrace with a man of her acquaintance and to hear certain cooing sounds issue from her mouth. That continued to upset me a little.—But so much for theory. Would you like me to season it with some of my actual experiences? Or perhaps I am being too garrulous; perhaps my chatter is getting on your nerves."

"Quite on the contrary; I should be simply delighted to discuss such matters with you all night; it is far more instructive and stimulating than ten years of book learning. Go right ahead. I am all ears."

"Ah yes, but where shall I begin? I have seen so much in my time. Here is what I suggest. You bring up a topic, and I will find an experience of mine to throw light on it."

"Excellent. This is what I would like to know: do women enjoy the game as much as we do?"

"Why, of course! As a general rule, that is. Among a hundred women, there may be one who takes no pleasure in it. As for the others, they are not all the same. There are two exceptional types. One of these makes a great show of passion, but her flame is a mere flash in the pan; when put to the test, she gives up very quickly and wants no more. The other acts coy and unwilling, but beneath her apparent crust of ice, she is actually burning with insatiable desire. It cost me no great pains to observe the first case. The lady in question made a great display of desire, and employed every artifice to arouse her partner. Aha, I thought, there's a wild one, brimful of passion; she will keep her man busy all night. To my surprise, things turned out very differently: her partner had barely got started, when suddenly she wilted; after that she just wanted to sleep. Her little bit of vitality had run out long before he had attained his goal.

"As to the second case, I have observed that too, but it cost me dearly. Well, there I was again in my hiding place, all ready to plunder a wealthy house. But I had quite a wait in store for me. First the man tried, very affectionately, to embrace the lady, to draw her close, but she resisted and squirmed away. He tried to straddle her, but she shook him off. At this point, he gave up, stretched out full length and fell asleep; I could hear his snores distinctly, note for note. I rubbed my hands; soon she too would fall asleep, I thought, then I would leap into action. How mistaken I was! She began to toss and turn, making as much noise as possible, obviously in the intention of waking him. He went right on snoring. She shook him, still to no avail. He just snored. Then she tried a third method; all at once she let out a piercing scream: 'Thieves! Burglars!' Any other thief in my place would have taken fright and run away. Not I. I said to myself that she was simply trying to wake up the lazybones beside her. Quite right. He actually did wake up and wanted to jump out of bed, but she held him back with all sorts of explanations: she must have mistaken the creeping of a mouse and the tread of a cat stalking the mouse for the soft steps of a burglar. Then she clasped him and embraced him and twined herself round him so skillfully that her hill-of-delight came into contact with his vassal, whose crest swelled up luxuriantly. The inevitable consequence was a resumption of the battle that had been broken off by her resistance. At first he was not very enthusiastic, for he had been wrenched out of a deep sleep; the proceedings were slow and sluggish, and it was midnight before she showed, by moving her lips in a way that might suggest a nibbling fish, and by moaning and groaning as though preparing to give up the ghost, that she had enough. But not for long. For her it was a mere intermission, a kind of truce, for her exhausted partner a brief breathing spell. He had barely begun to wheeze and snore again when she revived completely; she began to moan louder than ever and to toss restlessly about, complaining that she had an ache, first here and then there. She made him thump and rub her chest, then massage her whole body, in short she molested him until he resumed operations. So they carried on all night until cock crow; only then did she have enough and finally let him sleep. For me, of course, such goings-on meant a very unwelcome loss of business. It was already light outside. How, under the circumstances, was I to carry out my plans? There was nothing for me to do but slip away as quickly as possible. I had been cheated out of a whole night's profits. I can fairly say that for me the study of this type of woman was an expensive entertainment."

"Most illuminating! Now another question: are women just as unrestrained as men at the decisive moment, or do they maintain a certain reserve?"

"With very few exceptions they are just as unrestrained as we are. They make three different sounds, and it is only my colleagues and I who can distinguish all the subtle shadings between them."

"What are the three sounds?"

"At the beginning of the battle, before passion has really taken hold of them, they utter certain superficial cries of affection, such as 'my coco,' 'my heart,' 'my liver,' whose purpose is to stir up their partner and to arouse his desire. When these sounds issue from their mouths, it is still possible to understand each word plainly.

"The second variety of sound is made when, as the battle of love proceeds, passion reaches deep inside her, tingling and throbbing through all five entrails and all four limbs, to the tips of her toes and fingers. Her breathing quickens and becomes irregular, her upper breath misses contact with her lower breath; consequently, these sounds are confused and indistinct. Finally, in the third and last phase of ecstasy, at the peak of passion, she is so utterly exhausted that her brain as well as her limbs refuse to function; in this state, the sounds stick in her throat and become quite inarticulate, without recognizable meaning.

"On one occasion I was able to hear all three types of sound quite distinctly at close quarters, and to distinguish between them. As long as the couple was actively battling, the sounds—some of which one would have called screams —came to me perfectly plainly and distinctly, but toward the end, the woman fell silent and moved no more. From my hiding place it looked as though the man had killed her. I crept closer and strained my ears. Now I was able to make out feeble sounds, though they seemed more like sighing and moaning, and it was no longer possible to tell whether she was uttering words. That gave me an idea of how insensible, how numb, a woman can become immediately after the onset of ecstasy. There, now I have described the three varieties of feminine love sounds."

As he listened, the young man himself felt seized with a kind of numbness and sat for a time with mouth agape. By now it was broad daylight outside. He reserved his main question, or rather, his main business, until breakfast.

"Oh, what luck to have met you and drunk brotherhood with you!—I just can't get over it. I think it is the greatest blessing fate has sent me in all my three existences. You know what women mean to me. They are my whole life. And you, for the first time, have opened my eyes. If not for you—why, it is scarcely imaginable what mistakes I should have made in my judgment and treatment of them. And now I have a great favor to ask of you: you have had occasion to observe so many beautiful ladies in the silence of their boudoirs and to form an expert opinion of them— could you not help me to catch a glimpse of the most beautiful of them all? And if she should conform to my tastes and needs—well, I have no need to hide it from you, a kindly fate has so made me that I have only to lay eyes on a woman, but no need to run after her, for on the contrary it is she who runs after me. So you could leave the rest to me. I need your brotherly help and magical power only for the first meeting, that is all. Can you grant me that?"

The elder brother shook his head.

"That is impossible. To rob a house that I have already robbed, and still worse, to rob it of a highly honorable wife or virtuous daughter—no, that would be incompatible with my principles and my professional honor. That I cannot do.

"But beginning today, I shall gladly look round for you elsewhere and keep my eyes open. If I discover a remarkable beauty, I shall spare her house for the present and notify you. Then we shall take counsel, and I shall gladly help you to make her acquaintance, if you should so desire."

"You are perfectly right. Why, of course. How could I! I have eyes in my head, and yet I failed to see the nobleman in you. Yesterday you set forth your high-minded principles quite clearly. Then I may count on your friendly assistance? That is splendid. But don't forget your promise not to rob the house of our beauty. If you can really help me to the goal of my desires, I shall naturally reward you for your services."

"Reward? Despite the eyes in your head, you continue to overlook the nobleman in me. If I were out for thanks and rewards, I should lay hands on your purse right now. Such a thing would never occur to me. I shall be quite satisfied if some day in the future, when you have risen to high office, you close both eyes and permit me now and then to levy my tax on the excess treasure of the rich. That will be reward enough for me. For the rest, you may trust me: Once I promise to make you acquainted with a beauty, you may be sure that I shall keep my word. The sooner the better as far as I am concerned. For the present you need go no further in your travels. Stay here. Rent a nice little house in the vicinity and pursue your studies on the side. But don't rely entirely on me, keep your eyes open, and proceed independently if you make a discovery. Meanwhile, I shall be active in your interests and let you know as soon as I have found something. If we both do our best, each in his own way, we are sure to succeed."

The younger brother was overjoyed at these words and at once commissioned house agents to rent him a suitable dwelling. When it was time for them to part, he insisted on expressing his thanks and respect by kneeling and making the fourfold sign on his forehead.

You will learn in the next chapter what adventures awaited him.

CHAPTER IV

Applying the strictest standards, he draws up a list of the fairest flowers. He meets with inviting looks and enamored glances and decides in favor of the lady with the curly forelocks.

After taking leave of his new friend and adoptive brother the Before Midnight Scholar had gone house hunting. Strange to say, his choice fell on a temple. The temple was dedicated to the love god Chang Hsien, the "Bowstringer God," patron of love-sick maidens and of young expectant mothers, who were confident that he would help them to find a husband and make them fertile. This temple included a small number of guest rooms that were available to travelers, and the priest was always glad to turn an honest penny. The price was rather steep, coming to two silver pieces a month. Our young man might easily have rented a nice little three-room apartment elsewhere for half that much. Why did he put himself to unnecessary expense? Why, indeed, did he positively insist on lodging so expensively at the temple?

Well, what decided him was that this temple was visited by flocks of women from far and near. It was not for nothing that the patron saint of the place was reputed to be a wonder-worker who actually showed his gratitude for offerings and gave ear to the pious prayers of his female devotees. The daily procession of women to the temple offered our young man (and this was what he counted on) a priceless opportunity to observe the daughters of the region and subject them, without the slightest inconvenience to himself, to a critical examination.

What particularly favored his designs was that among the visitors to the temple the younger element was distinctly predominant. In this respect the present temple differed strikingly from other places of pilgrimage. Ordinarily most of the visitors to such places are middle-aged or elderly women who come to make burnt offerings and say their prayers, worthy matrons who are past child bearing, or soon will be.

The present temple, however, whose god was expected to confer happy marriage and male offspring, was visited chiefly by young women; though from time to time a lady of riper years might come along as a chaperon. And even when a young lady between fourteen and twenty is not beautiful, her youthful bloom gives her a certain attractiveness, the kind of charm that delights us in peach blossoms. Our young man definitely received his money's worth; even applying his severe standards, he could be confident that among ten young women who came to the temple at least one or two would deserve his attention.

He proceeded quite methodically. He arose early in the morning, had his breakfast, and dressed carefully. Then he took up his observation post beside the statue of the love god. Here he strolled up and down, always keeping an eye on the entrance to the temple. As soon as he saw anyone in petticoats approaching in the distance, he hid behind the god's broad back. Himself unseen, he was able to look through a little gap that the carver had left between the god's sleeve and his gown and tranquilly observe the worshippers as they knelt before the statue, offered up their prayers, and burned incense. He inspected them very thoroughly, noting each one's figure, headdress, attire, the play of her features, her bearing and movements. Not a single detail escaped his critical eye.

In the midst of their devotions, while they were still kneeling and the priest was solemnly reading the prayers they had brought with them, he would suddenly emerge from his hiding place, to swagger slowly past them and saunter through the vestibule to the entrance of the temple.

Naturally his sudden apparition created a considerable stir and confusion among the suppliants. In their pious simplicity quite a few of them wondered whether this exceptionally handsome youth might not be the love god himself, whom their fervent prayers had moved to come forth from the clay statute. Perhaps, they thought, he would approach them in grace and personally fulfil their desire for offspring, and they continued in their delusion until they saw him nonchalantly descending the temple steps and strolling up and down outside the entrance quite in the manner of a mortal. At last it became clear to the poor things that this was no god but a young man of common earthly origin.

But until this knowledge came to them, they felt their bosoms swell and already, in spirit, they had given themselves to the supposed god of love. Stirred to her innermost soul, one or another of them would start for home in innocent confusion, not without granting the strange youth an enamored sidelong glance. One or another would intentionally let her handkerchief fall to the ground in the hope that he would pick it up and keep it as a memento.

So much success went mightily to his head, inordinately inflating his already ample opinion of himself. He was now quite convinced that he was irresistible and took it for granted that at a sign from him the proudest and most virtuous of the lot would simply lie down at his feet.

In order to make his search still more methodical, he drew up a careful and meticulously detailed list. He always had it by him in the form of a memorandum book which he carried in his sleeve. In this little book he entered the name, address, and exact description of every young lady, seen at her devotions, who seemed worthy of his attention. "Vernal apparitions from far and wide"—this was the lovely title that he inscribed in large letters at the head of his list. The details concerning their persons—name, age, whether still single or married and if so to whom—he took from the mouth of the priest who, as we said, read the written text of the ladies' prayers in a loud voice. All this was carefully noted and entered in the list. In addition he would mark the names with little cinnabar red circles just as a high examiner marks the examination papers of the candidates, and group them according to quality. One red circle next to a name meant "good," two red circles meant "very good," and three "outstanding." After name and description there would be a brief description of the candidate's advantages.

In the course of time the list grew to considerable proportions. But despite the large number of names, they were all marked with the red circle meaning "good," or at most with two red circles, signifying "very good." The exacting young examiner had not yet seen fit to favor a single name with the three red circles signifying "outstanding." Rather disillusioned, he thought to himself: "I have always dreamed of a really outstanding beauty who would not quickly find her equal. I thought I had found one in Noble Scent. But now it turns out that there are many more like her. I am forced to admit that she is not so remarkable, one could not call her a peerless beauty. But somewhere under heaven there must be one!

"In the state examinations there is not only a *t'an-hua*, the 'third victor,' and a *pang-yen*, the 'second victor,' but also a *chuang-yüan*, the 'strongest of all,' the 'first victor.' Similarly among beautiful women there must also be a *chuang-yüan*. It is only logical.

"But where may she be hiding, this fairest of them all? Why can I not find her? But I will and must find her. These women and young girls I have seen here in the temple and entered on my list would be quite satisfactory as a reserve to fall back on if I should not succeed in finding the one, the most glorious of all. Very well, if the worst comes to the worst, I will content myself with the best among them. But for another few days I shall bide my time and keep searching, and during that time I will judge more severely than ever."

One morning he slept through his usual early rising time. He felt weary and discouraged and stayed in bed far into the morning. Suddenly one of his servants came running into the room and gave him a good shaking.

"*Hsiang-kung*, young sir, you must get up quickly. The most beautiful of women, the one you are looking for, has come. As a matter of fact," he reported breathlessly, "there are two of them."

With one leap our young man was out of bed, beginning to dress. Vain as he was, he wasted a good deal of time making himself pretty, arranging his hair, picking out a fashionable new hat, and studying himself from all directions in the mirror.

It was already too late to take up his usual observation post behind the temple god. The beauties, his servant informed him, had already completed their devotions and were about to leave. Well, he decided, in that case he would cut off their retreat. He slipped out through a side door, ran around the temple as fast as his legs would carry him and then, moderating his gait and assuming a dignified bearing, climbed the steps to the entrance. He arrived just in time to head the ladies off. There were two youthful beauties, one in a gown with a silver and red pattern, the other clad in the delicate light green tint of the lotus shoot. They were accompanied by a beauty of riper years. All three had just tossed the stumps of their incense candles in the copper ash receiver and were preparing to depart.

Our young man raised his eyes, and it seemed to him that after a long and arduous journey he had finally attained the desired goal, after the manner of the late Prince Hsiang who was wafted in a dream to the summit of the Magic Mountain, where a miraculously lovely fairy held out her arms to him. The other women he had seen, those he had entered on his list, could not hold a candle to these magnificent creatures. For a time he stood there bewildered and almost lifeless, as though he had suffered a stroke.

Then the spell was broken and consciousness returned, bringing with it an idea. They were about to go away. He simply had to prevent them from leaving or at least delay their departure. With remarkable presence of mind he sank down on his knees and deftly kowtowed—not just once, oh no, time after time he tapped his forehead on the ground. Not only his two servants but the temple priest as well gaped and stared with horror at his clownish behavior. Convinced that he had gone quite out of mind, they were in a cold sweat for fear the ladies would be displeased and create an embarrassing scene.

It never occurred to them that there might be method in his madness, and a very sly method at that. Our young man's calculation was as follows: "Either the young ladies are amenable to tender feelings—then they will interpret my kneeling and kowtowing as a homage to themselves, an expression of my admiration and adoration, and forgive the unusual mode of expression; they will not make a scene; or else, they are so rigorously respectable that no homage can touch them. Then of course, they will be furious and start to make a fuss. But I shall have my story ready. I shall say that I have come from far off to sacrifice in the temple of the bowstringer god and pray that he may bless me with children. Finding three ladies in the temple, I had thought it would be unseemly of me to enter and had remained on the threshold, offering up my prayers to the god from a respectful distance. The ladies are not likely to know that I have actually been living in the temple for some time. They will not see through the deception."

Such was the tactical calculation that had guided his strange, apparently insane behavior. He had not been mistaken. Far from seeing through his maneuver, the ladies really believed that he was paying his devotions to the god from afar. Far from creating a disturbance, they stepped considerately aside and waited for him to complete his

*With remarkable presence of mind he sank down on his knees
and deftly kowtowed.*

supposed devotions. During this time they did not all behave alike. The two younger ladies cast a little squint in
his direction from time to time but with so much maidenly
modesty and reserve that it was hard to tell whether they
were indifferent to him or not; the oldest of the beauties, on
the other hand, showed unmistakable interest. Covering
her mouth with one hand, she bestowed upon him a linger-
ing and unquestionably benevolent smile. When at length
the three of them moved on, they were obliged to pass
quite close to him, and now the glances she shot at him were
something more than benevolent.

Transfigured with rapture, he stood staring after them
as they entered their litters that were waiting outside, and
he looked after the litters for several minutes until they
vanished round a bend in the road. It was only then that
he awoke from his trance.

"Who were the three ladies who just left the temple?"
he asked the priest. But the priest sternly refused to answer.
He was quite scandalized at his tenant's insane behavior and
it cost him considerable self-control not to give him a
sound tongue lashing.

It was a sorry situation. Having slept through the reading of the prayers, the Before Midnight Scholar had missed
his opportunity to learn the ladies' names and addresses. He
could get nothing out of the priest. What was he to do?
What a fool he had been! Why had he not followed the
litters and at least found out where they lived? Why had
he not sent his servants? What were servants for? In his
bewilderment he had neglected to take the most obvious
measures. Now it was too late. The litters were far off, he
would never overtake them. Disgruntled and utterly furious
with himself, he withdrew to his chamber.

"Very annoying!" he thought. "The rest don't begin to
meet my standards, and here I have their names and addresses and a complete file of information on them. And
nothing whatever about the ones I am interested in, who
exceed my wildest hopes. It's really too absurd. There they

were, hardly two steps away, the loveliest, most splendid creatures in the world, and all I can do is mourn for them as if they were phantoms that had vanished into thin air."

Mechanically, he took out his diary. Despite the sorry circumstances, he decided, he had his duties as a chronicler. But what was he to write? He had nothing to go by. Racking his brains, he began to write and as he wrote the dry notations of the chronicler were transformed into the lyrical outpourings of an enraptured poet:

"On such and such a day of such and such a month: meeting with two great beauties. Name, origin, address unknown. Instead, a detailed description of their appearance and dress:

"The first, apparently between seventeen and eighteen years of age, wore a gown of red and silver. Seems very emotional, but undecided in what direction to guide her feelings. The floodgates of erotic desire are still unopened.

"Gloss: Oh, how shall I frame her beauty in words? She is a fragrant jewel, an eloquent flower; her mouth is a cherry burst open. The way in which she sets down her feet in walking suggests the graceful gliding flight of a swallow and recalls a historical beauty of olden time, Hsi Shih, who at a royal banquet utterly bewitched her noble lord with her dancing. She danced amid the golden plates and platters and transformed him into a puppet. (Prince Fu Chai of the State of Wu, fifth century B.C.). Her brows —in this too she resembles Hsi Shih—are always slightly drawn together, not only as with Hsi Shih when she is in a bad humor, but also when she is gay. Like a second Yang Kuei-fei (celebrated favorite of Emperor Ming Huang, T'ang dynasty, eighth century A.D.), her gaze is veiled, not only, as in the case of Yang Kuei-fei, when she is drowsy, but also when she feels fresh and alert. When she turns to go, the last impression she leaves behind is not so much the gentle tinkling of the jade ornaments on her sash, which echoes in the ears, as a strange yearning which lingers long in the heart, especially if in departing she bestows a glance, be it ever so slight, for her eyes are as moist as the radiant autumn wave. Who would not, in his heart of hearts, grant her the crown over all lovely creatures who have grown to womanhood in the seclusion of their virginal chambers?

"The second is also a great beauty; about twenty years of age; her dress is the delicate light green of the lotus shoot. One would say that she had been the object of men's ardent glances for some time, but the bud of her womanhood would seem to be still closed and intact.

"Gloss: Her forms are full and exuberant, but she is supple and lively in her movements. Her brows are finely arched, no court painter could have traced them with greater elegance. The natural rosy freshness of her complexion requires no help from powder or rouge. Her build represents the golden mean between fat and thin; she is neither slender to the point of skinniness nor so plump that one would wish some of her flesh away. Indeed, she is one who may well make demands, who has no need to content herself with the first comer. Similarly in dress and adornment, she maintains the golden mean between obtrusive elegance and exaggerated modesty. She dresses simply but with taste and distinction. Poor girl! Her innermost feelings still seem confused, as though caught in a dense thicket. A lotus bud that hesitates to blossom, she restrains her secret impulses, she has not yet found her way. She glows and sends forth fragrance like fine incense, but she has not yet begun to worry as to whether her feelings are reciprocated. Like the first, she must unquestionably be praised as a great beauty; the rare fragrance of her charms is far beyond the average. She would assuredly carry off first prize in a beauty contest."

Having written thus far, he laid down his brush and reflected: "There is still the third, the lady of riper years. She would seem to be scarcely inferior to the two younger girls. To say nothing for the present of her other charms, the ardent bewitching look of her eyes is in itself worthy of the highest praise. And she lavished more than one such glance on me! Unfortunately, my attention was so distracted by the two younger girls that it never occurred to me to respond. Come to think of it, she merits no less attention than the others, if only because she is their companion. Possibly she is their sister-in-law, in any case a close relation. If I wish to approach the two younger ones, perhaps it would be a good idea to pay her some attention. Perhaps she will be willing to help me; perhaps she will move her companions to look upon me with benevolence— who knows? I am a stranger to this place. If I can only find her, why should I not succeed in luring her within arrow's shot and engaging her in an amorous adventure? Very well, I will include her in my list and favor her with an eloquent gloss, partly out of gratitude for her ardent glances, and partly as a precaution. Once I make her acquaintance, I shall read to her from my diary and she will be flattered by my gloss. Then perhaps she will smile upon me and grant my wishes."

No sooner said than done. He took up his list again and changed the heading of the day's entry from "Two Great Beauties" to "Three Great Beauties."

"The third, the lady of riper years, is clad in the saturated colors of the evening sky in summer. She is approximately in her mid-thirties but both in mien and in bearing seems at least ten years younger. Her features, marked by noble passion, promise the expert who knows how to awaken her a lavish range of amorous pleasures. She is high-spirited. When she is in a lively humor, her mind takes wings. Although her body and limbs are fuller than those of young girls, her fine features are as fresh and charming as those of any youthful bride, her rosy cheeks need not fear comparison with a peach; her skin has the smoothness and subdued radiance of jasper, but what is most bewitching, most menacing to the beholder's reason is her eyes: even when the eyeballs are motionless, the pupils emit sparks and lightnings. And one thing more. Without so much as stirring her feet, she is able to lend her body a sudden movement, a graceful twist, so that her radiant face shines forth quite unexpectedly against the interior of the temple. It is as though a little white cloud, driven by a sudden gust of wind, should suddenly come to rest upon a dark mountain peak. All in all, she is quite the equal of the other two. Absolutely first class. Why argue about first place?"

He had finished writing. All that remained for him to do was to fill in the gaps he had left in his list, in which he would ordinarily have entered the names of the three unknown beauties, with three little cinnabar red circles. Then he folded up his diary and as usual concealed it in his sleeve pocket.

The temple of the bowstringer god had now lost all interest for him. Though from time to time he still occupied his observation post behind the temple god, his mind was no longer on his work, and he scarcely had eyes for the new arrivals who knelt down to perform their devotions. His mind was quite taken up by the three unknown beauties who had made such an impression on him. With his diary in his pocket he wandered through the streets of the city, always in the vague hope of coming across them, but in vain; he could not discover so much as a trace of them. Then he thought of his friend, K'un-lun's Rival.

"He knows every nook and cranny in these parts. Why should I not confide in him and ask him to help me?—Yet there is an objection: he offered to find me a beauty; perhaps he has succeeded in the meantime. If I tell him about my discovery, he may think I have no further need of his services. What if he has already unearthed a priceless jewel? He might decide there is no further need of it and let it slip through his fingers. And moreover, since I can provide him with no precise information about the three unknown beauties, how can he be expected to find them?

"I shall do best to conceal my secret for the present and wait to see what he has to report. For several days he has given no sign of life; he is sure to call on me soon."

He began to spend his days in his room, burying himself in his classics, tormenting himself with literary essays, and waiting impatiently for his friend to appear. But soon his nerves were frayed with waiting, and one day he ventured out again. As chance would have it, he met his friend.

"How does it stand with our business? Where have you been keeping yourself for so long? Have you forgotten your promise?"

"Never fear. I have given the matter plenty of thought. The difficulty was simply that I met with no really exceptional beauties. It was only yesterday that I found one who might meet your requirements. I was just on my way to see you. What luck that we have met!"

"Splendid. Then come with me to my humble cell. There we shall be undisturbed."

Sleeve to sleeve, they repaired to the temple. The young man sent away his servants and barred the door. Then the two conspirators put their heads together and discussed the situation.

My esteemed reader will surely wish to know the lineage and place of residence of the three beauties whom a capricious fate destined to cross the path of our enterprising young man; and perhaps he would like to know whether some poor cuckolded husband or outraged father will appear to wreak bitter vengeance upon our frivolous seducer.

Very well. There is no need for you to guess at riddles; you will be enlightened in the next chapter.

CHAPTER V

The braggart grossly exaggerates the size and en-durance of his "talent." The great expert laughs with glee at the evidence.

"Well then, has anything of interest happened to my esteemed young brother in the meanwhile?" With these words K'un-lun's Rival, squatting on a mat, opened the conversation.

"Not that I know of," the Before Midnight Scholar lied, fearing that if he revealed his own experience, the other would keep his news for himself. "But what of the dis-covery you were hinting at?" he asked. "What is her name? Where does she live? How old is she? What does she look like? Out with it! The suspense is killing me."

"My discovery is not just one. There are three of them. But I have promised you only one. You mustn't be greedy and expect to have all of them. You must choose and con-tent yourself with one."

Our scholar was taken aback. Three of them? Had not he himself been smitten by three at once, the three beauties he had met recently at the temple? Could it be the same three? That would be wonderful. Then he would start with .the older one and approach the two others through her; there would be no problem. Already he rejoiced, though he carefully concealed his feelings.

"You are perfectly right. Of course I only need one. It would indeed be greedy to want all three."

"Very well, on that score we are agreed. Now the ques-tion is which one do you want? All three are beautiful, but each has her qualities—and I don't know whether the two of us have the same taste. It is quite possible that what appeals to me would not be to your liking. Let me ask you a question: do you prefer them buxom or slender?"

"It all depends. Buxom and slender, both can have their charms. But by buxom I do not mean so fat that her dress bursts at the seams; nor by slender do I mean so skinny that her bones pierce holes in her gown. It is all a matter of degree."

"Good. In that case all three would meet your wishes. One more question: do you prefer them passionate or prudish?"

"Passionate, of course. As far as I am concerned, prudes are simply insipid. They lie there apathetically and they don't do anything to help. How, under the circumstances, can you get into the right frame of mind? It's better to sleep by yourself; then at least you can rest undisturbed. No, no prudes; I've always had a horror of them."

The other shook his head thoughtfully. "In that case all three are probably out of the question."

"Really, how do you come to be so well informed?"

"No need to go into that. Just let me assure you that for beauty all three are more than equal to your demands. But when it comes to temperament, I fear that they fall short of specifications."

"No matter. I am willing to put up with that. Provided they are beautiful. Passion can be developed by training. I speak from experience. In the early days of our marriage, my little wife at home was revoltingly modest and prudish. She hadn't the faintest notion of how to make love. But it only took a few days of pedagogic effort. After that she was a different woman. Her passion became almost uncontrollable and there was no end to her eagerness for new variants of the vernal act.

"In short, any of the three would suit me; best of all, I should like to have all three. Even if they are somewhat lacking in temperament, it doesn't matter—I know how to drive the modesty out of them."

"Very well. But there is still a question. Would you like to possess the one in question right away, immediately after the first meeting? Or would you be willing to wait a few months?"

"Frankly, I am very much in a hurry. Even under ordinary circumstances my desire for women burns with a bright flame. If I am compelled to go without for three or four days, I have lascivious dreams and give off my surplus energy in my sleep. And now, just imagine. I have been away from home for heaven knows how long, and on my travels I have scrupulously abstained from whoring. You can see what a state I am in. As long as nothing worthwhile crosses my path, I can control myself. But if the proper party comes along and shows the slightest response to my affections, I fear there will be no holding me. The sooner the better."

"Then you will have to forget about two of the three right off. They are daughters of a wealthy and distinguished house. They would be hard to approach and you would have a long time to wait. If you are in a hurry, only the third remains to be considered. With her there should be no difficulty in attaining the goal. She is a member of the lower middle class, the wife of a silk merchant. As I have already told you, I am inclined in my undertakings to spare the little people and the middle class. Only for your sake, because I have promised you and my promise is with me day and night, I have deviated from my principles just this once. Otherwise I should not be willing to set my snares for this honorable wife of a simple, honest silk merchant. How I discovered her? By accident. Not long ago, as I was strolling through the streets, I saw her sitting in a shop behind a bamboo door curtain. Although the curtain obscured the view, I could see one thing clearly; that was the rosy freshness of her face. Like a diamond or a pearl, her features gave forth a radiance that burst through the cracks in the curtain. My eyes passed over the curves and lines of her body and found perfection. As she sat there almost motionless, I had the impression of gazing upon a beautiful portrait hanging on the other side of the curtain and stirring from time to time, ever so slightly, in an air current. For some minutes I stood spellbound. Then I crossed to the other side of the street and continued to observe her. It was not long before I saw a man push the curtain aside and come out—a hulking, uncouth sort of fellow. He had on a shabby smock and was carrying a bundle of silk on his back. Obviously he was on his way to market to sell his wares. I waited until he was out of sight, then I went about the neighborhood, hearing what I could hear. So I learned that the house and shop belonged to a silk merchant named Ch'üan. Because he was a quiet, accommodating man, who would never have hurt a fly, he was generally known as Ch'üan Lao-shih, 'Ch'üan the Honest.' The beauty whom I had seen sitting in the shop turned out to be his wife. So you see, my observation had not been entirely without results. But I was not yet satisfied. That bothersome curtain had impeded my view. I was determined to make absolutely sure.

"I let a few days go by. Then I revisited the house in question. Again I saw her sitting behind the curtain in the shop. I hit upon a daring plan: I pushed aside the curtain and entered. Saying that I wished to buy some silk, I asked after the owner of the shop. Without rising, she told me that her husband had gone out, that if I wished to make a purchase, she would be glad to serve me, there was an ample selection of goods right here in the shop. Wishing to judge her as a whole, I was determined to see her in motion. So far I had only been able to examine her hands, which protruded from the sleeves of her gown. What well-formed little paws she had! Ah, the fine, delicate fingers—like lotus shoots! I was also able to catch a fleeting glance of her dainty little feet which looked out from time to time from under the hem of her skirt. She had on simple flat silk slippers without the thick felt soles that most of our women wear in the hope of acquiring the swaying gait that suggests a flowering branch stirred by the breeze. In other respects as well, I found her to be without artifice; everything about her was quite natural, especially the rosy freshness of her cheeks that had so struck me at my first glimpse of her.

"But I had not yet found out what the skin was like on the rest of her body, whether it was light or dark, and whether she was well upholstered. To find out, I had recourse to a new stratagem. I pointed to a bolt of goods on the uppermost shelf, saying that the other samples had not appealed to me; would she be so kind as to bring it down for me to examine more closely? She was now compelled to stand up and to raise her arms. I must tell you that it was a very hot day and that she was dressed accordingly; all she had on was a simple dress of thin raw silk. In short, as she stretched out her arms toward the uppermost shelf, her wide sleeves fell down as far as her shoulders, exposing her firm and shapely arms in all their snowy nakedness. But that was not all. Through her light dress I was able to make out the gentle contours of her twin hills and to see them bobbing up and down. Take it from me, you have never seen such perfect curves. And what radiant smoothness, what glittering snow-white skin! In the end I bought a piece of silk for the sake of appearances. I had kept her pretty busy with all my picking and choosing and wished to leave a favorable impression behind me. Well, what do you think of my choice? Would this woman suit you? Would you like to have her?"

"Of course, why not? She seems to be quite my type. But what makes you think that it would be possible to possess her after only a brief acquaintance?"

"I am sure it would not be difficult. At the worst there would be certain expenses. But that is usually the case when one is out for amorous adventures. I have hidden a few silver nuggets in my belt pocket as a precaution. If you wish, we can proceed at once. We shall simply wait outside the shop until her husband goes out. Then we shall follow the exact same tactics as before. We shall go into the shop and pretend to be innocent purchasers. This will give you a chance to see her and to make up your mind. If you like her, you can pay her a few little compliments right away. Why should she not be attracted to you? Chained to that uncouth husband of hers, she must be frightfully bored. If a handsome cavalier like you suddenly comes along and courts her, why should she not accept it as a welcome change, as a relief from the usual monotony of her existence? If she does not take offense at your little compliments and liberties, you may be sure that the game is half won. Then I should merely have to run an errand or two as the messenger of love, and I'll wager you will be in her bed within three days. Well, what do you say to that?"

"If you are willing to do that for me, I shall be infinitely grateful. But there is still one point that is not clear to me. You who have so many well-nigh miraculous ruses and stratagems at your command, not to mention the astonishing acrobatic gift of jumping over roofs and scaling high walls; you who seem to be in league with higher spirits, to whom nothing seems impossible: why has your obliging assistance been limited to one of the three? Why have you so carefully avoided saying the least word about the other two, the two daughters of illustrious family? Am I to suppose that you feel capable of dealing only with little people and carefully keep your hands off the high and mighty?"

"The very idea is ludicrous. We are dealing with an exception to the rule. The general rule is that it is more risky and more dangerous to provoke the rich and powerful than the little people—but there is one exception: it is less risky to seduce the women of high families than the wives of little people."

"How so?"

"Because your moneybags does not usually content himself with one wife; as a rule he has three wives and four concubines. But the master of the house cannot divide himself into parts. While he is sleeping with one, the other six feel humiliated and neglected; they are desolate on their lonely beds. There is an old maxim that says:

A full stomach and a soft bed arouse lascivious desires.

And so it is clear that your unsatisfied women of the upper classes, living as they do in idle comfort, have nothing in their heads but vernal thoughts and are positively languishing for an adventure. If the right young blade sidles up to them, he has no need to beg for favor, it is granted in advance. The idea of rebuffing him never even enters their heads. Supposing the master of the house catches them in the act, he will think twice before haling the lover before the judge, for that would create a public scandal injurious to the honor and prestige of his house. Similarly he will hesitate to kill the couple on the spot. For he will not willingly deprive himself of a pretty and valuable concubine who has cost him good money. But if he spares her, why kill her lover, who is no more to blame than she? He will let them both go.

"Not so the little man. He can afford only a single wife; he guards her like the apple of his eye and watches over her day and night. Thanks to simple fare and cold uncomfortable living conditions, a woman of that class is not as a rule inclined to sensual thoughts. But if a strange man should succeed in arousing her sensual desires and (as happens very rarely, perhaps in one case out of ten thousand) in seducing her, then the little man, should he catch them, is not likely to hesitate: he will either kill the two of them on the spot or drag the seducer to the judge. Little people care nothing for scandal or the reputation of the house. So you see, it is riskier to offend against the domestic honor of the little man than of the moneybags."

"That is very illuminating. But permit me just one objection. In practice you have advised me to court the wife of the little silk dealer but to keep away from the two ladies of illustrious family. Isn't that contrary to the theory you have just developed?"

"No. Here we have an exception to the exception. It so happens that the circumstances favor you in the case of the silk merchant's wife, but not in that of the two ladies of illustrious family. You would have a hard time approaching them and would have long to wait."

"Will you be so kind as to explain that a little more clearly. Of course I am perfectly agreed about the silk merchant's wife, but I should like to know how the chances are with the other two. If you will only consent to speak a little more plainly on that score, I shall be still more convinced of your zeal in my behalf."

"Very well. I will explain. The two of them—the one is about twenty, the other sixteen—are full sisters, daughters of the legitimate principal wife of their late father, a high dignitary of great wealth and standing. They are married to two full brothers; the elder has been married to the elder for four years, and the younger to the younger for just three months. So you see, the sisters are also sisters-in-law. The two brothers are also descended from a patrician family which for centuries has supplied the throne with meritorious officials. They themselves to be sure are degenerate types, without higher ambition. They just barely managed to carry off the *hsiu-ts'ai,* the doctorate of the first degree, and show no inclination whatever to climb higher on the academic ladder or to qualify by serious study for the two remaining state examinations. They are extremely cultivated young fellows, but as I have said, degenerate, idle fops. That is quite plain from the pretentious pseudonyms they have taken: the elder calls himself Wo-yun sheng, 'Scholar of the Resting Cloud,' while the younger calls himself Yi-yun sheng, 'Scholar of the Reposing Cloud.' Sounds mighty conceited. Clearly they regard themselves as far superior to their fellow men, riding in the clouds so to speak. In form and beauty the two young ladies are the equal of the third, the silk merchant's

wife. All three are unusual beauties, but cold. All three
lack that certain something that you call passion or temperament. When they go to bed with their husbands, they
take no interest whatever in the proceedings. They lie
there apathetically and no sound of passion issues from
their mouths. In itself, this circumstance would favor you.
But unfortunately the two dandies, unlike most other
wealthy young men, do not keep three wives and four
concubines, but content themselves with these two. Day
and night they never leave them. You would have to think
up a hundred ruses and a thousand stratagems even to get
near such closely guarded young women. To wait until
you found them alone and unguarded would cost you a
fortune in money and patience. Whole months might pass.
As I have said, the circumstances are far more favorable
with the third, the silk merchant's wife."

Our young man had listened intently. How well all that
applied to the three beauties he had seen in the temple.
Surely they must be the same. He was still interested
chiefly in the two younger girls. He simply could not tear
his thoughts away from them.

"Is it not possible," he remarked thoughtfully, "that the
two younger women are cold because their husbands are
not up to the mark in bed? Who knows! Perhaps their
equipment is inadequate, perhaps their performance leaves
something to be desired. In that case would the coldness
and indifference of the two beauties not be perfectly
natural?—Well, wait till they fall in with me. I'll liven
them up. I'll teach them a thing or two."

"Your guess is wrong. On the basis of personal observation I can assure you that while their equipment is not
of unusual size it is quite adequate, and that their performance is perfectly normal. Which reminds me of something I have been meaning to ask you for some time. What
about your own equipment and performance? With your
rakish airs I can only hope that you have what it takes.
Will you please be kind enough to let me have a look at

your instrument—just to set my mind at rest. I shall be able to take your part with a clearer conscience once I've seen for myself that everything is satisfactory."

"Oho! No need to worry about that," said the young man with a complacent smirk. "I can assure you without boasting that my equipment is up to all possible requirements and that my performance is absolutely reliable. Regardless of the lady's caliber and demands, take it from me, she will be sated and tipsy when she rises from the table I have to offer her. She won't find a miser who sends his guests away hungrier and more sober than when they came and furious with themselves for having accepted so empty an invitation."

"That sounds perfectly marvelous. But would you mind being a little more precise? How many thrusts can you manage in the course of a bed battle?"

"Well, I have never counted them. Moreover, I do not adhere to fixed rules, I lean to free style. But I can think of a lady or two or three who has had to withstand innumerable thrusts before I gave her and myself time to breathe."

"Then you cannot supply an exact figure? Can you at least be precise about the time? How long, in terms of hours, can you hold out in a contest of this sort?"

The truth of the matter was that the outside limit of our young man's endurance was one hour; after that he was exhausted. But wishing at all costs to impress the other and so insure his zeal, he thought it best to exaggerate a little:

"Oh, as a rule I can keep up for a good two hours, and if that is not sufficient, if the lady in question still wants more, I am always good for another quarter of an hour or so."

"Ah! That is the normal time for home consumption. You'll have to do better than that if you want to go about town courting this one and that one, not to mention venturing into walled castles to abduct and seduce strictly guarded young chatelaines."

"Have no fear. In addition, I possess a powerful vernal ointment. I bought it only recently and it is in my trunk, just waiting to be used. Unhappily there has been no opportunity. But if thanks to your friendly assistance the need should arise, I have only to rub in my ointment and you may be sure that my javelin will do its duty without flinching."

"Hm. There is a limit to what those ointments can do for you. At the most they can stretch your endurance a bit, but they cannot be expected to stretch or stiffen your implement. If you apply a vernal ointment to a naturally powerful instrument, it is exactly as though a gifted and well-prepared candidate should take a ginseng stimulant just before his examination. He will feel doubly fresh and alert, and his dissertation will pour out of its own accord. But his kind would have passed his examination even without the help of a drug. On the other hand a lover whose implement is feeble by nature will no more be fortified by ointments than an ignorant and untalented candidate would be helped by drugs—even if he consumes whole pounds of them before his examination. All the ginseng in the world will not produce an acceptable dissertation, even if he should sit in his numbered cell for three whole days and nights, sweating over his subject. Besides, you can't put too much reliance on vernal drugs, there are all sorts of frauds on the market. Who can guarantee that your ointment is really effective? But enough of that for the moment. What I want to know first of all, what I am determined to see with my own eyes is this: how big is your implement in reality, or to be precise, how many inches long is it?"

"Well, it's not exactly little. That should satisfy you."

"But it doesn't. Come, show it," the other insisted and reached unceremoniously for the young man's trousers in the intention of pulling them down. The young man resisted and struggled loose twice or three times. He was quite unwilling to lay himself bare.

"Very well then. I won't insist. But I am forced to as-

sume that you are afraid to show your implement because
it is just too insignificant. In that case, I regret to say that
I can no longer act in your behalf. Just imagine, if you
please, the embarrassing consequences if you should approach an exacting young lady with your inadequate
article. She will not feel the slightest tickle of pleasure. In
her rage and disappointment, she will make a terrible fuss!
She will scream like a madwoman and accuse you of trying
to rape her. The scandal you would provoke with such
folly is beyond imagining. And you expect me to get mixed
up in such a mess, to shoulder the responsibility for such a
fiasco? No indeed, you can count me out."

Under the pressure of these convincing arguments, the
young man finally gave in.

"It's not at all as you suspect," he stammered with a
sheepish smile. "My implement can bear inspection. I was
only embarrassed to display it in broad daylight, even to a
friend. But since you insist, I shall comply, if only to
dispel your unwarranted suspicions. Here you are."

He opened his fly and brought out the witness to his
manhood, a device compounded of the tenderest flesh and
the finest membranes. He laid it in the palm of his right
hand and, as though to gauge its weight, flipped it up and
down a few times before the other's eyes.

"Permit me to introduce my humble equipment, my
modest implement."

The other took a step closer to examine it in detail. What
did he see?

A pale, white stalk
A pointed bright-red blossom
Beneath a copse of sparse hair,
Veins and sinews barely discernible,
Length barely two inches
Weight three ounces at most—
A frail tube—
One might mistake it for the thin tube

In which a Mongol collects camel hairs.
The head with the fine slit
Might be taken for the bowl of a tobacco pipe
Such as those smoked by the women of the northern
steppes.
An article suited at most
To a maiden of thirteen.
A pleasure boy of fourteen
Might take some joy in it.
Before the battle it burgeons into a hard stylus,
And then it resembles a parched razor clam.
Afterward it bends like a bow
And shrivels till it looks like a dried crab.

After a thorough inspection the elder brother raised his eyes and stared at the young man in silence. "He is speechless with amazement over my impressive equipment," thought the younger brother and remarked complacently: "You have seen nothing. That is how it looks afterward when it is weary of battle. But before the battle starts— then it is something to see. Then you would have something to stare about."

"Quite unnecessary. I am perfectly satisfied with what I have already seen. Now I know what is what. Put it away," the elder brother motioned and burst into an uproarious laugh.

"My good friend. How can anyone be so completely bereft of eyesight and judgment? Your equipment is not even a third as large as that of the average man. And with that you planned to invade strange houses and seduce other people's wives. Ha ha! Does it seem likely that a woman whose gate is as wide as a shoe and who is dissatisfied with her husband's last would attempt to fill out the gap with your pitiful stylus? The way you boast, the way you chase after women wherever you go, I really expected to see something impressive, a bludgeon to strike awe in any woman's heart. I hesitated at first to ask for evidence. How could I suspect that you had nothing more than that deplorable scratch-pen, fit perhaps to fumble round a while in your companion's moss and bushes, but quite incapable of penetrating the innermost passages of her pleasure house."

"Come, come. My utensil can't be as bad as all that. It has always stood up in practice. I have no way of knowing whether your own article is so gigantic. But I can tell you one thing: this pitiful utensil of mine has called forth a *ho-ts'ai*, a cry of approval and admiration, from more than one beauty."

"Don't make me laugh. A *ho-ts'ai?* Maybe from an innocent young thing whose melon had not yet burst, an inexperienced maiden who had never seen that kind of thing before—yes, such a one may have looked upon it with desire. But I very much fear that a woman who has once encountered a utensil of my caliber would have mighty little praise left over for yours."

"Do you mean to say that my utensil is not even up to the average in length and thickness?"

"Precisely. And I may say that I am an expert in these matters, that my judgment is based on ample observation: In the practice of my trade I have seen not hundreds but thousands of these articles; and never have I seen one—to put it politely—so diminutive as yours."

"Let us forget about other men for now and speak only of those three, the husbands of the two distinguished beauties and the silk merchant. How are their members built in comparison to mine?"

"Oh not so much bigger. Perhaps twice as long and thick."

It was the younger brother's turn to laugh.

"Now I see. You are pulling my leg. You are telling me pure nonsense with a straight face as an excuse for dropping the difficult task you had undertaken to perform. Allow me one question. I realize that you may have observed the two young husbands in the course of one of your burgla-

After a thorough inspection the elder brother raised his eyes and
stared at the young man in silence.

ries, but how can you claim that the silk merchant's implement is twice as big as mine? You've only seen him from a distance, on the street and in broad daylight. What do you say to that?"

"Easy does it! It is true that I had occasion to observe the two young husbands at night. As to the third, the silk merchant, I know about him from hearsay. The day I first saw his wife, I reconnoitered in the neighborhood and learned the man's name and profession. Then I asked why so beautiful a woman should have chained herself to such a lout of a husband, and how so unequal a pair could possibly live together. The answer was that though her husband was indeed crude and ungainly in appearance, his weapon was so imposing and so bold in battle that his wife gladly forgave his other failings for the sake of this one physical advantage. She had grown used to him, by and large their married life was happy and harmonious, they seldom quarreled. When I inquired as to the exact size of this remarkable peacemaker, a neighbor replied that he had not measured it but had seen it one hot summer day when the silk merchant had thrown off his clothes, and that what he had beheld dangling below the man's belly had the length and general appearance of a club, a flail, or perhaps a pestle. His metaphors made a deep impression on me, that is why I recall his exact words. You see now that I have not deceived you and understand no doubt why I insisted on examining you at first hand. I just had to make sure that your implement would not be at too great a disadvantage beside the silk merchant's mighty armament. That was the reason for my unusual and somewhat rude behavior."

The young man sat silent for a time, beset by gloomy thoughts. Then he said:

"Is it only the sensual urge that brings the sexes together? That is an idea I find hard to accept. Might a woman not be attracted to a man by his wit, his intelligence, his good looks? Of course if these are lacking, she will be concerned only with his equipment. But I am favored by both intelligence and good looks. For their sake a woman might be inclined to overlook the deficiency of my equipment. Who knows! In any event I beseech you in the name of our friendship to carry out your promise and not to leave me in the lurch because of this one failing."

The other shook his head gravely.

"Granted that wit and good looks perform useful services in leading up to a love affair; they are agreeable seasonings, as it were, which lend a bitter medicine the taste of ginger or dates and make it easier to swallow. But once the medicine has been downed, the patient expects but one thing, that it cure him of his sickness. He is no longer the least bit interested in ginger or dates. It is exactly the same with a love affair. Of course intelligence and good looks make it a good deal easier for a young blade to approach the lady of his heart; thanks to them, he obtains admittance. But once he is admitted to her intimacy, what matters is the hard reality of his manhood. Do you suppose that when a woman has her lover between sheets she expects him to hatch out witty essays and graceful, well-constructed verses? If you can't hold up your end of the bed battle, your lady won't care a fig for your wit or your handsome face, she will give you your walking papers.

"And there is another bit of advice I should like to give you: if ever at the risk of your life you win the lady of your heart's desire and make her your own, content yourself with this one love; try to build up a relationship based on harmony and mutual affection; in short, make her your life companion. If all you care about is a brief passion, a few hours of bliss, why so much plotting and conniving? With your niggardly natural endowment you simply can't afford such extravagance. Take an example from me. Before I run the risk of breaking into a wealthy house, I must be sure that the venture will net me at least two thousand silver pieces. That much I owe to my honor and reputation as a thief. I don't bother with chicken feed. It is beneath my dignity.

"Now put yourself in the position of your lady love. Imagine all the difficulties and obstacles she must overcome, all the fear and agitation it will cost her to arrange a meeting with you behind her husband's back. It goes without saying that she expects to be repaid for her sacrifice; she expects you to show your gratitude by satisfying her, by acquitting your debt not ten but a hundred fold. If you should disappoint her and prove to be a lamentable failure, the whole romance will amount to no more than the brief amours of a rooster and a hen. The soul will go out of it. Should she be expected to risk her honor and reputation, perhaps even to ruin her whole future, for the sake of a brief and unsatisfactory adventure? I feel sure that in your heart of hearts you yourself would say no.

"My dear friend, don't take it amiss when I tell you quite frankly: your wee bit of equipment is just barely enough for domestic use; save it up for your little wife. Abandon all thoughts of byways and detours. Don't be a fool, stop making yourself ridiculous with your unwarranted ambitions. Give up your ideas of dishonoring other people's wives and daughters. You would only bring curses and righteous retribution down on your head. In any case, you will have to count me out.

"Once again, don't take offense at my plain talk. I am a plain-spoken man, I say what I think frankly and without embellishment. You would be wrong to suppose that I wish to shirk my obligations as a friend, to make things easy for myself by diverting your attentions to damsels of light life. I know they do not interest you and that is far from my intention. I wish you well and I am at your disposal for any other service. In case you require money or clothing, you may count on me for all you need. But in this other matter, I must say regretfully that there is nothing I can do for you."

The young man reflected. The brush-off was unmistakable. The elder brother would do nothing to help him fulfil his heartfelt desire. Gifts of money or clothing? What did he care about money and clothing. Besides, such gifts would be stolen goods. To accept them might involve him in the most disagreeable complications.

He cleared his throat and replied rather coldly:

"Thank you, but you must not go to any expense on my account. My treasury is not exactly overflowing but neither is it exhausted. My clothing is simple but I am plentifully supplied."

The elder brother arose, uttered a few appeasing formulas, and took his leave. The young man made no attempt to keep him. He was in no mood to play the host. His good humor was thoroughly demolished. The esteemed reader will wish to know whether he took his friend's grave words to heart and changed his way of life. Patience, you will find out in the next chapter.

CHAPTER VI

Sorely grieved over his physical failing, he bitterly accuses the Prince of Heaven. On his knees he begs the itinerant physician to operate.

The grave words of his experienced friend had depressed our young man from top to toe. To say that he was dejected would be a gross understatement. He felt as though his life were at an end, as though he were dead. He had lost all desire to speak with anyone or even to eat. In utter apathy he huddled in his solitary cell, a prey to dark thoughts. "I am twenty years of age," he said to himself, "that means I have stopped growing. Why has the growth of this one organ lagged behind? I am otherwise well developed. I have been blind up to now. It took my experienced friend to open my eyes. I never gave the matter a thought. I studied everything else under the sun, but it never entered my head to carry on the most elementary investigation in comparative anatomy. Oh, yes, I have amused myself now and then with a pleasure boy; of course we looked at each other's frontispieces, but such boys are usually very young, their frontispieces are correspondingly small. Consequently I thought mine was large. As a school-boy, I sported with a friend of my own age, his frontispiece was the same size as mine. I have regarded my own as normal ever since. And now my experienced friend comes along, shatters my illusions, and informs me that in all his long career he has never seen so puny an article as mine. That is the bitter, crushing truth! What use is my whistle to me now? It is nothing but a worthless appendage. And yet my little wife at home was satisfied with it; and when, occasionally, I ventured into a palace of joy or tried my hand with a lady's maid, they showed no sign of disappointment or dissatisfaction; on the contrary, they seemed delighted. It seems hardly likely that their pleasure came more from themselves than from me. If my weapon showed its mettle on these occasions, it cannot be as useless as my experienced friend wishes me to believe. Perhaps he was not being sincere after all and was just trying to get out of his promise?" Such were his thoughts. With all the doubts and ifs and buts that raced through his mind, he could not decide where the truth lay.

"I have it. Did my experienced friend not teach me that women are deceitful creatures, quite capable of simulating pleasure? Perhaps these women, whom I thought I had satisfied so completely, were only being polite. Maybe they just made a display of admiration to show their gratitude for all the money I had given them? Who knows what to make of a woman? Perhaps my friend's words were true after all. Very well, I shall make up for my past neglect of comparative anatomy. From now on I shall take advantage of every opportunity to see how other young men are built, and draw the proper inferences. We shall see whether or not my friend's disheartening diagnosis is correct."

He now adopted a strange habit. Whenever, as he sat with fellow students, studying or writing essays, one of his friends had to withdraw, whether for big or little purposes, the young man would accompany him and take advantage of the opportunity to scrutinize his implement and compare it with his own. He did the same whenever he saw a stranger relieving himself in the open country or in a public sanitary ditch. On the strength of comprehensive observations he was compelled to admit, much to his dismay, that his friend had not exaggerated. Neither among acquaintances nor strangers was he able to find a frontispiece as small and insignificant as his own. Everyone he was able to investigate proved to be better endowed than himself in this respect. There was no longer room for doubt: his friend was right and had not been deceiving him.

Unfit! The word resounded in his ears like a brass gong and passed into his brain which received it as an ineluctable death sentence. His exalted opinion of himself toppled like a melting iceberg.

Sorely dismayed but resigned and again relatively master of himself, he spun out his reflections to the end:

"It is a bitter pill that my experienced friend has given me. Word by word, a bitter but salutary pill. But it could have been worse. Instead of learning the truth from a man's lips, I might have learned it from a woman. It was bad enough to have him laugh at me; I wanted to sink into the earth. What if it had been a woman! The disgrace of it! Supposing I had gone to bed with an exacting young lady and my pitiful equipment had reached only half way. Supposing she had made disparaging remarks, what would I have done? Would I have broken off the futile battle of my own accord or struggled on until she spat at me and repulsed me? Horrible thought. I shall take good care that no such thing happens to me in the future. From now on it's all up with wild adventures. From now on I shall be meek and well behaved. I shall devote all my thoughts, all my strength to study, to preparation for a successful career. Once I have come by a profitable position, I shall fill up the extra rooms with a few cute young things, but I shall seek out very young ones, inexperienced in love, who will not despise me but honor and respect me. Why waste my money and vitality on difficult, jaded women? Why squander precious incense and expensive statues of Buddha on vain courtships? Enough!"

These resolutions were the beginning of a new way of life. A great transformation took place in him. From that moment on, he felt delivered from the lecherous preoccupations which had sat on him like a heavy burden, lashing him like a whip, and depriving him of all stability. A great peace descended on him. The impetuous voluptuary was suddenly transformed into a retiring, well-behaved young man.

He kept his room at the temple, but now it was devoted to its proper purpose: study. He no longer concerned himself with the women who came to the temple day in, day out to sacrifice to the love god. From time to time the need for air and exercise led him to take a stroll in the temple grounds. But if a woman crossed his path, he would turn aside and hasten back to his cell for fear she might look through his light summer clothing, made transparent by the sunlight, and laugh inwardly at his physical defect. The diary he had carried about in his sleeve was buried deep down in his trunk and forgotten. When he saw a girl or woman in the street, he lowered his gaze and passed quickly by.

He endured this way of life for two whole weeks. But

after all he was a normal young man. After the lapse of a fortnight his little fellow began to take on so restlessly at the approach of womankind that despite the searing heat he was obliged to pack it up in a girdle to remove it from their inquisitive glances. One day as he was sauntering through the streets, he happened to catch sight of a young woman in the distance. She lifted her door curtain, leaned out a little way, and began chatting with a neighbor across the way. Involuntarily he quickened his pace, in the hope of viewing her more closely and hearing what she was saying. There were two things about her which suddenly shook him out of his lethargy and attracted him with the force of magic: her face and her voice. Ah that voice! It was as melodious as the sweetest flute music—now soft and lilting, now louder and more emphatic, but always wonderfully clear and pure. The words bubbled from her lips with so charming a tone that her sweet voice seemed to linger on in his ears after she had finished speaking. And then the face! As he came close, he could see it clearly. What could account for its very individual quality? Other beauties had full, finely cut oval faces, others had expressive features. This face owed its particular enchantment to the unusual radiance of the strikingly light skin. Radiance—had his friend, ordinarily so down to earth, not recently employed the same word in describing a certain beauty? Had he not gone into ecstasies and employed the poetic turn: "Like a diamond or a pearl, her features gave forth a radiance that burst through the cracks in the curtain." This was just what captured his attention now. And with his own eyes he was able to confirm the soundness of another of his friend's observations: "I had the impression of gazing upon a beautiful portrait hanging on the other side of the curtain and stirring from time to time ever so slightly in an air current." The young man had exactly the same impression. Could this be the very person of whom his friend had spoken? It certainly seemed so.

Wishing to make sure, he sauntered on a little way and questioned a neighbor.

"I am looking for a certain silk merchant by the name of Ch'üan. He is said to live somewhere in the neighborhood. Can you tell me where?"

"You have just passed his house," was the reply. "Where the young woman is chatting with her neighbor from behind the door curtain, that is where he lives, and the young woman is his wife."

"Then it is really she!" thought the young man. He turned about and once again strolled slowly past the house. Then after taking a good look at her, he returned to his cell.

He had to admire his friend's gift of observation. "At the time I did not quite believe him. His description struck me as exaggerated. I did not give him credit for so thorough a knowledge of feminine beauty. Now I must admit that his eye is unerringly keen. His description is exact to the last detail. Beyond any doubt she is a woman who might make a throne totter. I have always been looking for one like her. I even have the bold helper who might have conquered her for me—that is, I had him until recently. But now, on account of my inadequate armament, he has refused to be of any assistance. How stupid it all is! To miss three magnificent opportunities at once. I could die of rage." Such were his bitter thoughts.

He shut himself up in his room, opened his fly, and took out his misfortune. He examined it from the right and from the left, and the more he examined it, the more he succumbed to an impotent rage. He would have liked to take out a knife and cut off the useless appendage.

He addressed a bitter prayer to heaven: "You are to blame for it all, O Prince of Heaven. If in your magnanimity you wished to favor me over other men, you should have finished the job. Why did you curse me with so momentous a failing? Intelligence and good looks may be all very well, but they are outward advantages without intrinsic worth. In all other respects you made me perfect, why did you let this particular imperfection slip through, why were you so stingy and unloving in fashioning the one organ that really matters? What would it have cost you to make it a little longer and thicker? You have blessed certain other men with too much of a good thing. Why could you not have deducted a little from their excess to make good my deficiency? Or if the bodily elements you mete out to each man are measured once and for all, why could you not make my equipment satisfactory at the expense of my own body? Why could you not spare a little skin and flesh and sinew from other parts of me and add them on to my ill-favored member? Why, O Prince of Heaven, have you done me so cruel an injustice? Having seen the most magnificent of women, I am condemned to inaction and pitiful renunciation. To die of hunger and thirst while sniffing the delicious aroma of the choicest fare—that is my wretched lot."

After this fervent prayer accompanied by much weeping and wailing, he packed his little fellow up again and went out in the hope of distracting his thoughts.

As he was walking up and down outside the temple, his eyes fell by chance on something he had not noticed before: a poster. It was affixed to the temple wall near the entrance and obviously had not been there long, because the ink was still fresh and shiny. He stopped and examined it more closely. A strange poster both in form and content. Since when were posters conceived in the form of quatrains?

> Heaven has sent me in the right hour
> To teach you the art of bringing happiness to women.
> If you are distressed by the shortcomings of your armament,
> Come to me: I make little into big.

"He has certainly come at the right hour!" was the young man's first thought, and he wondered whether the

Prince of Heaven may not have heard his prayer and taken pity on him by sending a good genius to help him in his affliction.

The quatrain was followed by a few prose sentences in small letters:

> *On my way through the region I have taken up quarters at such and such a temple, in room number so and so. Those desiring further information or treatment are requested to honor me with their visit. But they are advised to make haste if they wish to catch me before my departure.*

The young man read the quatrain and the prose text several times over, and the more he read the more excited he became. "Who would believe it? Why, it is a miracle! To think that this strolling healer has turned up in the hour of my greatest despair when I did not know which way to turn. To think that he has put up his poster right here on the wall of my temple, right before my eyes! If that is not divine Providence, I should like to know what is!"

He hastened back to his cell, dressed carefully, opened his trunk, took out a few silver nuggets, stuffed them in the card case that his young servant always carried along for visits, and started for the itinerant doctor's headquarters.

Then he was face to face with him. An unusual, awe-inspiring figure! Despite his advanced years and gray hair, the freshness of his skin and the suppleness of his bearing gave him the air of a young man. That was the visitor's first impression. They saluted one another with a slight bow and the *shou-kung* gesture, which consists in clenching one hand in the other and raising them first to chest, then to forehead level.

"Does my esteemed young friend wish to be enlightened in *fang-shu*, in bedroom technique?"

"*Jan yeh*, so it is."

"Does the desired information concern a 'she' or does it concern your own person?"

"What difference does that make, if I may ask?"

"If you merely wish to please your companion and increase her pleasure but are not concerned with adding to your own enjoyment, there is a very simple recipe: you take some essence of lichee; that will retard your flow; in addition, you rub your prepuce with a vernal ointment which numbs your member, making it hard as iron and insensitive. By this method you can postpone the flow as long as you please. Obviously this treatment serves only to increase and prolong your companion's pleasure. But if on the other hand you wish to share her increased enjoyment, to feel a pleasant tickling when she feels a pleasant tickling, to swoon with bliss when she swoons with bliss, if your aim is what is known as 'mutual bed pleasure,' the ideal situation in which he fears that his ecstasy may set in too soon and she fears that her ecstasy may set in somewhat later than his; if that is what you are striving for, I must disillusion you: that kind of bedroom technique is very hard to come by and cannot be acquired from one day to the next. You must enter upon a course of spiritual purification and work very hard at it; you must be willing to renounce the world and active life for a time, to lead the life of a hermit far from humankind and practice meditation until gradually illumination and enlightenment come over you. Years can pass before you have achieved the necessary maturity. Once that stage is attained, you will be able, with the help of certain tonic aphrodisiacs, to enjoy the highest bliss that sexual relations can confer. Is that what you desire?"

"Impossible. I could not possibly endure so long a period of trial. And as for the other aspect of bedroom technique, the art of conferring enjoyment on the woman alone, no need to waste our breath on it; I already possess the ointments of which you speak and I should hardly have inconvenienced you for that. I have something else in mind.

In your esteemed poster you publicize your art of turning little into big. That is what I have come to see you about. How do you effect an anatomical change of this kind? How do you enlarge the member? That is what I should like you to tell me."

"It is a matter of surgical skill. But before treatment can be undertaken, light must be thrown on three questions: First, how is the patient's member constituted? This I must see for myself. Second, how much enlargement does the patient wish? Third, has the patient sufficient patience and endurance? Is he willing to risk his life if need be? Only when these questions are answered, can I undertake the treatment. Otherwise I cannot shoulder the responsibility."

"May I ask you to explain your three questions in greater detail?"

"If your member is not abnormally small by nature and only a slight enlargement is required, questions two and three are superfluous. In this case the member is first locally anesthetized with hashish, so that it can no longer distinguish hot and cold and becomes insensitive to all pain. Then it is smoked with an extract made of the disinfecting blossoms of the *hsün* plant, rinsed in water, then rolled for a time between the fingers, massaged, and finally stretched. The smoking lends firmness, the rinsing strengthens, the rolling and massaging make it thicker, the pulling longer. After three days and nights of this treatment, good results may be observed. The member is one-third longer and thicker than it was. This treatment is extremely popular because it involves no danger or pain whatever.

"Now to the other case. It is more difficult. Let us suppose that your member is exceptionally short and thin, and you desire a considerable enlargement. This can be accomplished only by a rather painful operation. Here the third question becomes essential: has the patient sufficient patience and endurance? Is he willing to risk his life? If the patient is timid by nature and fears bold undertakings, that settles it, the operation cannot be performed. But if he has courage and his longing for amorous pleasure is so intense that he shrinks back from no risk, even that of his life, then I too take courage and risk the operation. This is how we proceed: First a young bitch and a young male dog must be procured; for a time they are penned up separately, then they are brought together; inevitably they will mate; before the act is completed they must be separated by force. A dog's member is a very hot-blooded affair; once it has entered a bitch, it swells and stretches to several times its normal size; it is so tightly wedged in that even after the flow he cannot pull it out for some time. Just before the flow his member must be cut off with a sharp knife; then it is carefully removed from the bitch and cut into four lengthwise strips. The patient's member is now rubbed with hashish and anesthetized. Then four deep lengthwise slits are made and in each slit a strip of the still swollen dog's member is inserted. The four incisions are then rubbed with a suitable ointment which soon heals the wounds. In making the incisions and applying the grafts, care must be taken not to injure the urethra, for the slightest injury can cause an inflammation that will inhibit erection later on. As long as the urethra is unharmed, there is no ground for concern. After a month of bed rest the grafted strips of dog member will have merged and blended with the patient's member like milk and water. The result will be a new and homogeneous member whose human and animal parts are indistinguishable; but in future sexual dealings the new member will have the nature and power of a hot-blooded dog member and will swell to several times the thickness of the patient's member. What do you say to that, my young friend? Imagine the pleasure and satisfaction you will give your companion with such super-armament."

Listening to this surgical disquisition, our young man felt as though he had gradually woken from death to life.

Even before he could utter a word, his knees had sunk to the floor of their own accord.

"Master, if you could do that," he cried, "you would be giving me new life."

The master lifted him to his feet.

"Why the exaggerated homage! If you desire the operation, I shall of course be at your disposal."

"Ah, master! You must understand: women and the pleasures of love are everything to me, they are my life. That is how nature made me. But the Prince of Heaven has endowed me with a pathetic little fellow quite out of proportion to the ardent flame in my heart. And now I have had the rare, the incredible good fortune to meet you—must I not indeed bow in humility and kneel to you, turning my face to northward?"

He called his servant, took the silver nuggets out of the card case and held them out to the miracle man.

"Take these as a small advance against your fee. Once the operation is performed, you may count on me to make every effort. You will not find me stingy or ungrateful."

"Not so hasty! I cannot accept your far too generous fee so lightly. Don't cross your bridges before you come to them. It is not yet certain that I can do it."

"Why the hesitation? Even supposing you might fail, I have no misgivings. Supposing your knife should slip, that your hand should make a blunder and I should be dispatched before my time to the Land of the Nine Springs, rest assured that I should not blame you for it; I should not bear you a grudge in the other world but accept my death serenely as my predestined fate. Hesitate no more, put your trust in heaven, and go to work."

"Not so fast. It is not as though I lacked confidence in myself and my surgical skill. Were my hand not sure and practiced, how could I ever take the responsibility for such an operation? Why, that would be to gamble unscrupulously with human life. If I hesitate, it is for other reasons. I must know whether, once the operation is performed, you will be willing to put up with three grave inconveniences. From what I know of your nature and inclinations, they would cost you a heavy sacrifice. I shall describe the three inconveniences one by one. If after that you still insist on the operation, I shall comply with your wishes. But if any of the sacrifices should dismay you, if you cannot accept it gladly and willingly, I regret to inform you that the operation is out of the question and that you must press the matter no further."

"What are the three sacrifices?"

"First: for one hundred and twenty days after the operation you must abstain from sexual intercourse. During this period any sexual activity would involve grave consequences for your health: the animal and the human components of your member would separate, the grafted animal components would cease to merge and blend with the rest, and the original human components would shrivel up and die. That was the meaning of my third question: has the patient sufficient patience and endurance? I was referring to endurance not of pain but of sexual abstinence.

"Second: after the operation you must not engage in sexual intercourse with girls under twenty years of age. They must be absolutely taboo for you even if their melon is broken, and the same taboo applies to all women, regardless of their age, who have not yet borne a child or had previous sexual dealings. Your reinforced armament would give them too much pain; indeed, they would suffer sheer torture. And I hardly need tell you that you must keep away from little girls; your super-armament would simply be the death of them. This much self-control is mere decency and common sense. You do have a conscience after all and I am sure you would not wish to weigh it down with guilt. And for the same reason I, as your physician, cannot tolerate abuse of my professional skill.

"Third: this operation always results in considerable loss of seed; the patient's fertility is seriously impaired. Children begotten after such an operation usually die young. Are you willing to face the possibility of remaining without progeny? This consideration was implicit in my third question: is the patient willing to risk his life? The danger to which I referred is not so much to his own life as the possibility of living on in his children.

"The strong-willed young man I see before me has two qualities that arouse my misgivings: on the one hand, your violent sensuality—will it allow you to dispense with cohabitation for four months, or even three? On the other hand, your intense desire for women—will it permit you to abstain from young things, not to mention little girls? And I find still a third ground for concern: in view of your youth I fear that you have not yet begotten a son and will not willingly renounce the possibility of progeny. Under these circumstances, you must see that it is hard for me to consent to the operation."

"Oh, if that is all that troubles you! I shall gladly accept these inconveniences. To me they are no sacrifice at all. You may set your mind at rest, revered master, and perform the operation with an easy heart."

"How can it be that they mean nothing to you? Explain yourself."

"As to the first: I have long been practicing continence, ever since I started on my travels. I am quite hardened to lonely, womanless nights. It will mean nothing to me to go on a little longer, for four months after the operation if necessary.

"On the second point: It is only mature married women who interest me in any case. I have no desire whatever for immature young things, and the dubious pleasure of puncturing maidenheads has no appeal for me at all. The experience with my little wife at home was plenty for me. Your ingénue hasn't the vaguest notion of the art of love; it never occurs to her to answer caress with caress. Only insane ambition can make anyone want to seduce an innocent virgin and the pleasure is purely imaginary. It takes a mature woman—preferably between twenty and thirty—

to give the sexual act any real meaning and sweetness. Younger women are capable only of taking, whereas she also knows how to give, to answer feeling with feeling. The situation is exactly the same in literature. Your immature young things are like clumsy beginners: you supply them with a thesis and they can find no appropriate antithesis. On this second point you may set your mind at rest. It will cost me no sacrifice at all.

"As for the third point. Admitted; other men attach great importance to progeny. To me personally it is all one whether I have sons or not. In this respect I am different from other men. After all a father seldom derives much pleasure from his sons. They are far more likely to turn into disobedient, rebellious, good-for-nothings than into obedient, intelligent, and worthy heirs. Of course there is a certain pleasure in raising a well-bred, intelligent son and in marrying him happily and well; if one is lucky, he may even turn out to be the prop and pillar of one's old age. But it is not as wonderful as all that. And supposing one is punished with an ill-bred monster who heaps disgrace and ruin on his family and brings his parents down in sorrow to an early grave. Cursed with an unworthy scion, the father may well regret, but too late, the effort he made on his marriage bed. In any case, one may safely say that at least one out of ten members of the male population remains sonless. If that is to be my lot, I shall be sharing it with many others and so accept it with equanimity as the decree of fate. Anyway, it is up to Providence whether I have sons or not. The operation would probably have very little to do with it. In short, my mind is made up: I insist on the operation."

"Very well, since you are so firmly resolved and have dispelled all my misgivings, I shall abandon my scruples and do your bidding. The next step is to choose a favorable day of the calendar and decide where the operation is to take place. Shall we do it in your dwelling or mine? Of course there must be discretion. All gapers and idlers must be strictly excluded."

"Then I should like to suggest that we do it here. In my lodgings we should be rather cramped for space, and there are too many people coming and going."

"Very well."

Only now did the doctor agree to accept the generous advance payment. He noted the patient's date of birth and selected, in accordance with the principles of astrology, a suitable day from the calendar. Thus the pact was concluded. Beside himself with happiness, the young man made his farewells and withdrew.

CHAPTER VII

The operation, followed by four months of absti-
nence and seclusion, results in an improvement that
makes his good friend rub his eyes in amazement. A
single application of his charms suffices to topple the
fair lady's steadfast heart.

That night our young man lay tossing for hours and could find no sleep. His memorable meeting with the miraculous physician kept running through his head. Ah, he mused, with what vigor and fury he would fling himself upon womankind once his operation had healed! Small wonder that his voluptuous visions of the future made his little fellow rise up in premature eagerness.

"I have been leading this solitary life for ages," he reflected. "Masses of unsatisfied desires have accumulated; intertwined and compressed, they are like a hard ball in my entrails. It is sheer torment. And now I have this operation ahead of me, which means more waiting, more suffering. Would it not be a good idea to go to a woman first and rid myself of painful congestion. A bowl of yellow meat broth, and then a thorough house-cleaning. I shall feel better afterward."

At this point in his meditations he jumped up. He would throw on his clothes and visit a certain flower garden he knew of. But then he lay down again with a sigh. A difficulty had occurred to him: at this late hour the little ladies would already be occupied; the green and red lacquered door would not even be opened to him, and he would have gone all that way for nothing. He continued to ponder and another idea came to him:

"Why have I brought my factotums, my two young servants, with me on my travels? Why scorn the southern passage when the northern passage is blocked?"

He called in the younger servant and gave him to understand that he was to come into bed and play the role of a "she." Shu-t'ung and Chien-shao, these were the fanciful names by which our scholar called his factotums. The younger, a bright young lad of sixteen, knew something of the written language; it was he who took care of his master's books and manuscripts; our scholar regarded him as a kind of living book chest, hence the nickname Shu-t'ung, "Book Chest." The elder servant was eighteen years of age; one of his duties was to take care of an old heirloom, a double-edged cavalry sword, to protect it from rust like a scabbard, and accordingly he was nicknamed Chien-shao, "Scabbard." They were handsome, attractive lads. With their smooth fresh cheeks they might have been taken for girls if their big feet had not betrayed their sex. But the two differed in character. The elder was a simple, rather pig-headed sort, utterly incapable of posing or dissimulating. Our scholar liked to make fun of Chien-shao; he

Shu-t'ung, the servant "Book Chest," artful and sly as a fox, knew how to take his master's hints and incline to his desires.

would drop little hints and innuendos and be mightily amused at his servant's utter failure to understand them. The younger was a very different sort, artful and sly as a fox. He knew how to take his master's hints and incline to his desires. He had learned to raise his "rear audience chamber" just like a woman and to wriggle his belly muscles in such a way as to facilitate his esteemed visitor's entrance. He was also able to emit cries of pleasure and moans of bliss, which though simulated were just like those of a woman. This explains why his master was so fond of him and why the honor of this evening's invitation fell to him rather than to the older boy.

During a breathing spell, the young scamp, overcome by curiosity, could not resist a question:

"*Hsiang-kung*, young gentleman, for a long time now you have been interested only in women and neglected us entirely. May I ask why tonight you are suddenly in a mood to warm up your cooled affections?" The question was uttered in a flutelike, designedly feminine voice.

"In celebration of a leavetaking."

"Leavetaking? Are you planning to discharge me from your service and sell me to another master?"

"How ridiculous! My meaning is not that I intend to part with you, but rather that this is my ambassador's farewell visit to your *hou-t'ang*, your 'rear audience chamber.'"

"Why does he wish to say farewell?"

"As you know, I have recently decided to make him a little more stately and imposing by means of a surgical operation. The operation will make him so big and thick that in the future every female 'audience portal,' however spacious, will be too small for him. He will have to force his way in. The tiny gate of your 'rear audience chamber' will then be quite impracticable. Now do you see why I have spoken of a farewell visit?"

"Your ambassador may be a little on the small side, but

he is otherwise in good shape. Why," asked the inexperienced boy, "are you in such a hurry to operate?"

His master explained that in this point women were far from having the same tastes as men, that while men esteem dwarfs, women prefer giants.

"Then after your operation you will always be chasing after women and have nothing to do with boys like me?"

"*Pien shih,* just that."

"One day you will have so many women you won't know what to do with them. Could you, please," the lad pleaded, "pass one on to me from time to time? It could be a lady's maid—fine ladies always have maids, don't they? When you go to see the lady, could you take me along? I should be so glad to get a taste of a woman. Then it would not be for nothing that I had served so gallant a cavalier, so eminent a master at the wind-and-moon game."

"If that is all you wish! No general who is worth his salt allows his troops to go hungry while he himself is stuffing his belly full. Very well then, I shall sleep with the lady and you may take your pleasure with the maid. And not just once, you will have the pleasure dozens—what am I saying!—why, hundreds of times."

The young scamp was glad to hear this and spurred by joyful anticipation, redoubled his efforts to make the farewell reception as warm and pleasant as possible for his master's ambassador.

Next day the Before Midnight Scholar purchased the dogs required for the operation, an uncommonly vigorous young male and a sturdy young bitch. He tied them up separately in the courtyard of the temple, and during the interval preceding the operation provided them with all the tasty morsels a dog's heart can desire.

When the time had come, he set out for the doctor's establishment, accompanied by both his servants. Book Chest led the dogs on a leash, Scabbard brought up the rear with a load of boxes containing the choicest of fare and a jug of wine. It had been decided that the operation would be accompanied by a banquet. This pleasant setting would dispel the lugubrious thoughts ordinarily associated with surgery.

In view of the mysterious character of his professional activity, the miraculous physician had set up his quarters in a lonely spot, remote from all human activity. He had chosen for his dwelling place an abandoned temple in an uninhabited spot, far outside the city. The grounds were very spacious and there were neither priests nor worshipers. There he lived all alone, carrying on his obscure craft unnoticed and undisturbed, behind barred doors.

After a brief greeting, the physician went to work without further ado. First of all he effected local anesthesia by smearing a prepared ointment on the member and rubbing it in. The patient felt as though the organ in question had suddenly been doused in ice-cold water. In a little while it seemed to him as though the organ had ceased to exist. He could rub it and scratch it, squeeze it and press it as much as he pleased; he felt nothing. This half reassured him, for now he was certain that he would not feel the sharp knife. Merrily he sat down to table with the master and enjoyed the meal he had brought along.

Between sips and mouthfuls he looked on with interest as the action developed. The two dogs appeared on the scene, led in on separate leashes by the servants and then let loose. They had come willingly, without barking or tugging at the leash. Perhaps in their canine minds they reflected, not without gratitude, that their master was now, at long last, going to grant them a little fun and freedom, and that if he brought them to such a remote, deserted place it must be to let them sow a few oats, undisturbed by any other jealous males. Poor beasts. If they had only known their master's real intentions. If they had only suspected that he would cruelly interrupt their pleasure and rob the poor male of his imposing canine member, to make good his own deficiency!

Young and well fed as they were, they were at it in an instant, firmly "sewn together." The leashes had not been removed but only slackened. Once the dogs were in full swing, the doctor gave an order and the servants pulled the leashes in opposite directions, as though to part the canine lovers. Of course the dogs were quite unwilling to separate. In their desperate resistance to the taut leashes, they presented the image of a torn lotus root, its two halves still joined by a few fibers.

The male barked furiously and clung harder than ever to his companion's rump. The bitch protested no less violently, pressing her buttocks all the more firmly round her mate's envoy, determined to hold him until he had said the last word.

Taking advantage of a favorable moment when the male dog's envoy was half in and half out, the master severed it at the root, snicker-snack, with a swift movement of his knife and deftly pulled it out of the bitch's sheath. Then he cut it lengthwise into four strips.

Now it was the patient's turn. He lay down, the master made four painless lengthwise slits in his member, and into the four gaping incisions he stuffed and grafted the still warm and stiff strips of tissue which had formerly been the male dog's pride and joy. Thus fortified, the patient's member was then treated with a healing ointment and heavily bandaged. The operation was over. Doctor and patient resumed their places at table and went on wining and dining as though nothing had happened.

That night the patient stayed with the doctor who wished to keep him under observation for a time. Before turning in, they engaged in an animated bedtime chat in the course of which the experienced medical man gave his young guest a number of valuable pointers on the technique of love-battle.

Next day the young man returned to his own quarters, which he was not to leave for four whole months. Throughout this period he exerted an iron will. The strict discipline

Young and well fed as they were, they were at it in an instant.

he imposed on himself was mental as well as physical; he succeeded in banishing every thought of women and red dust from his heart, and in dismissing all lecherous fancies. Day after day he dwelt in the ethereal realms of the spirit. He did not even concern himself with the health and well-being of his member, but bravely resisted the temptation to loosen the bandage a little, to take a peek at the patient, or to feel him. With an admirable display of philosophy, he immersed himself in his books for four whole months.

At length the four months were at an end. He undid the bandage, washed the patient thoroughly and inspected him. He could not help laughing aloud.

"How the little fellow has shot up! Why, he has grown to be a real giant. That's what I call an operation! With a weapon like that I shall take every fortress by storm." Thus he rejoiced in his heart.

He waited another day, then he set out to see his friend, K'un-lun's Rival. What gaping he would cause! Our scholar did not have far to go. As chance would have it, his friend was on his way to see him. Our scholar gave him an eloquent wink and tugged him by the sleeve.

"Esteemed friend," said K'un-lun's Rival, "you haven't shown yourself for a long time. You haven't so much as stirred from your four walls. I presume that your seclusion has proved beneficial to your studies."

"My studies? Nothing to write home about. More important is the progress I have made in *fang-shu*, 'bedroom technique.' That is more impressive."

The other laughed disparagingly.

"Progress, you say. In view of the lack of raw material I have my doubts. Did I not expressly advise you to abandon the study of bedroom technique?"

"Ha ha! You think I have made no progress during these four months. You expect to laugh at me again. But now it is my turn to laugh. You'll rub your eyes with amazement when you see the progress I've made."

"Well, well. It can't amount to much. In theory perhaps,

but not in practice. You are simply wasting your time. It is perfectly conceivable that an undersized weakling should acquire theoretical knowledge of all eighteen battle techniques by assiduous training with straw puppets. But will he hold up his end in real combat?"

"You forget: little fellows grow to be men, and every part of the living body shares in their growth."

"Yes, yes; that may apply to growing boys of twelve or thirteen, but you are over twenty. You cannot grow any more at that age. In a very exceptional case, I grant you, the organ in question might grow by a hair's breadth."

"A hair's breadth? Would I bother to speak of that? Even if it had added a mere inch to its girth, I shouldn't waste my breath. If I speak now, it is because the article in question has got to be several times thicker than it was."

"Don't talk nonsense. Such sudden growth has never been seen or heard of. But if your claims are founded, why all this talk—show it here!"

"To make myself ridiculous again? No. That first time I swore a sacred oath—in fact I put it down in writing and posted it on the wall—that I would never again display my nakedness to anyone."

"Come, come. Don't be so squeamish. Show it here. If I really detect an improvement, I shall not fail to express my admiration in the most solemn terms and to apologize humbly for my previous words of disparagement."

"Fine words don't help me—unless they are accompanied by deeds. You can only convince me of the sincerity of your friendship by giving me an opportunity to exercise my new armament, to triumph amid drums of victory and dances of joy."

"Done. You may rely on me."

Only now was our scholar prepared to lay himself bare. He made the proceedings as slow and complicated as possible. In view of the cold weather—it was the beginning of winter—he was wearing his warmest winter clothing, both his jacket and his trousers were heavily quilted. For fear that the wads of quilting might bar the passage and impede the view, he first wound a silk scarf round his body. Then he raised the edge of his jacket and stuffed it under the scarf. Finally he undid his trousers, let them slip to the floor, and propped up his weapon on the palms of both hands. As he stood there displaying his new implement, he presented the aspect of a Persian peddler, exhibiting his wares on a tray held against his belly.

The other, who was at first standing on the far side of the room, thought to himself: "He has tied on a donkey's hose to deceive me—where did he ever find such a thing?" But when he approached and looked more closely, he realized to his amazement that this colossus had not been borrowed from a donkey, but was his friend's honest-to-goodness property. And indeed he could not help rubbing his eyes in amazement.

"Will you just tell me, my good friend, what magic you have employed to transform your pathetic little runt into so mighty a warrior?"

"It seems as though he just couldn't stomach your insults. You offended him in his honor. The next thing I knew— I myself had nothing to do with it—he began to rear up in anger. Obviously," our scholar went on with a perfectly straight face, "it was the rage you kindled in him that made him swell up."

"Enough of your jokes. I can see four scars that were obviously made by knife cuts. The thing has been doctored, that's plain, and it must have been a mighty skillful hand to bring about such a change. Stop telling me fish stories and tell me what really happened." After joking a little more and goading his friend's impatience, our scholar finally gave in and described the whole course of events. The other gaped so hard that his tongue hung out.

"You are indeed capable of great sacrifices to satisfy your craving for women and the pleasures of love. That is will power. My compliments. Now that I see you so excellently armed, I can no longer oppose your wishes. Very well, you may count on my support. Make yourself ready. We shall storm the fortress without delay."

This was just what our scholar wanted to hear. He quickly changed his clothes and put on his newest winter hat. The two of them sallied forth. Their goal was the house of a certain silk merchant. K'un-lun's Rival bade the scholar stand nearby and wait. He himself went reconnoitering in the neighborhood. A little while later he returned. His smirk gave promise of good news.

"*Kung-hsi!* Congratulations. You are in luck. Your wish will be fulfilled this very night."

"What? Are you so certain? I haven't even met her yet."

"I have just been making inquiries in the neighborhood: her husband just happens to be absent on a long business trip; he is not expected back for ten days. You will be able to take your pleasure with her for ten days. I'll vouch for that. Now we shall simply drop in at the shop. All you have to do is to give free play to your charm and anchor yourself in her heart. I shall attend to the rest and I'll wager she will admit you to her intimacy this very night."

"Very well. I put my trust in you." The elder pushed the curtain aside and they stepped into the shop.

"Is Mr. Ch'üan at home?" he began.

"No, he is away on a business trip," said the fair lady, who was sitting in her usual place behind the counter. She was engaged in needlework and did not even look up.

"That's a pity. Your humble servant would have liked to buy a few bolts of silk. What shall we do?"

"There are other silk shops," she said with indifference and still she did not look up from her work. Now our scholar intervened:

"Other shops indeed, but not such fine ones, we fear. Other shops do not carry such pure and flawless goods. Besides, my friend is an old customer of your esteemed house. He has confidence in it and would regret to change." At the sound of his voice the young woman had raised her eyes for the first time and secretly looked him over.

"Very well. If he is an old customer of our humble house, why should I not oblige him?" The tone was not nearly as cool and standoffish as before. Now it was K'un-lun's Rival who once again took up the thread of the conversation.

"*Ta-niang*, noble lady, the last time I came here to buy silk, last summer it was, the *ta-yeh*, the worthy lord, happened also to be absent. On that occasion you sold me some goods with your own hand and took down several bolts from the uppermost shelf—do you recall?"

"Ah yes, now I remember."

"Splendid," the scholar broke in, "then you surely remember that he did not speak empty words or attempt to bargain, but made his purchase and paid promptly. Why then do you wish to send us to your competitors?"

"It seemed to me that my mediocre wares were not worthy of so distinguished a gentleman."

"On the contrary. More likely they are too fine for a peevish scholar like me."

"Very well. Then may I ask the gentlemen to be seated while I take down the samples."

K'un-lun's Rival was tactful enough to leave his friend the comfortable upholstered chair by the counter, where he would be closer to the fair lady. He himself sat on a stool behind him.

She set a sample before the scholar. Her manner was still indifferent, correct, almost severe. She did not favor him with the slightest sidelong glance nor so much as the shadow of an encouraging smile.

"Too yellow," he remarked before even taking the sample, only to reverse his opinion the moment he had it in his hands.

"Strange," he said, turning back to his companion. "As long as the lady was holding it, the silk seemed too yellow; now that I have it in my own hand, it strikes me as perfectly white—how can that be?"

Then after stopping a moment to think he continued with animation:

"I have it. It must be because of the striking whiteness of the lady's skin. In so lovely and white a hand the material naturally seems yellow, while in my repulsive black paw it looks white."

The young lady's attention had been captured. In spite of herself she inspected her young customer's hand.

"The young gentleman's esteemed hand does not look so black to me," she remarked. She still wore the frozen mask of severity which refused to thaw into the tiniest bit of a smile.

"It is certain," K'un-lun's Rival broke in, "that compared with my paw his hand cannot be regarded as dark, but neither can it be termed light in color beside the white hand of the exalted lady."

"Since we all agree that the silk is passably light, why do the gentlemen not wish to buy it?"

"Precisely because it is not light enough for me. It seems light only in my hand, but that is not the kind of lightness I am looking for. What I am after is silk of the same, magnificently light color as the exalted lady's adorable hand. Please be so kind as to bring me a material of that kind."

"I doubt if there is any silk so beautiful and light in color in all the world," said K'un-lun's Rival, "but a silk as light in color as the countenance of my young friend here would not be so bad. In my opinion it would be perfectly acceptable."

This remark and the gesture that accompanied it produced the desired effect. For the first time the lovely lady raised her eyes and looked the young man full in the face. What she saw was a source of pleasant surprise, and suddenly her features, hitherto impassive, lit up in a friendly smile.

"Now it is my turn to fear that there may be no such silk in all the world," she let fall in a mischievous tone.

My esteemed readers may wonder why it was only now that she took note of the scholar's person and smiled. Let me explain: she was nearsighted. At first she regarded her visitors as run-of-the-mill customers and paid no attention to them. When the younger of the two, by employing the term *suan tzu*, "peevish scholar," made himself known as an academician, a *hsiu-ts'ai*, or doctor of the first degree, a spark of interest had been aroused in her, but not enough to make her strain her eyes. That is how it is with nearsighted people. To focus an object clearly they must make a considerable effort. They are reluctant to do so unless there is reason to suppose that their pains will be rewarded. Most nearsighted women are pretty and intelligent. And for women there is a certain advantage in nearsightedness: it makes them save their feelings for the serious business of marriage instead of squandering them prematurely on passing adventures. There is truth in the popular saying:

> *She may be nearsighted, but in the marriage bed she knows what she is doing.*

Women, just like men, suffer occasionally from the pressure of sultry "clouds"; they too crave the "rain" that will release the pressure. It is perfectly obvious that a woman endowed with sharp eyes can be thrown into a turmoil by the mere sight of a presentable man. Should the opportunity arise, she will easily succumb to the call of her senses, lose her accustomed self-control, and sacrifice her virtue. Thus nearsightedness may be taken as a boon on the part of Creation. For nearsighted women are largely immune to temptations of this kind. Apart from their husbands they have eyes for no man, not even for a paragon of masculine beauty, a likeness of P'an An or Sung Yü. Thus all manner of conjugal misconduct is averted. It has been recognized from time immemorial that marriage with a nearsighted woman is usually happy and free from scandal. Though a man may come within two steps of her and court her ever so persuasively, a nearsighted woman remains reserved and indifferent, as though wrapped in a cloud. Considerable diplomacy is needed to bring about the exceptional case in which she will take notice of a strange man.

By their clever teamwork, our scholar and his friend had managed to bring about an exception of this sort. A first glance at his hands and a second at his face had awakened the hitherto closed bud of her senses and made it bloom. All at once she was ready and willing. But woman's pride forbade her to open the gates of intimacy. That was up to him. Consequently she fell back for the moment into a purely businesslike tone and asked a very practical question:

"Well, then, do you seriously wish to buy something or not? If you do, I shall bring you some particularly fine goods from the storeroom."

"Of course I mean to buy something. What else have I come for?"

She disappeared into another room and soon returned bearing a bolt of goods. With her came a young maid bearing two bowls of tea on a tray. The visitors helped themselves.

Our scholar only half emptied his bowl and then, with a glance of invitation, held it out to the lady. She received his gracious but familiar gesture with a delicate smile. With this he had opened the gates and she was able to accept his courtship without sacrificing her feminine pride. He made his intentions still clearer by touching and gently pressing her hand as she was showing him the silk. Her expression remained unchanged but she indicated her secret complicity by lightly scratching the back of his hand with her fingernail.

"The silk is excellent. We shall buy it." With these words K'un-lun's Rival put an end to the elaborate inspection of the goods and the couple's secret love play. At the same time he took a silver nugget from his sleeve pocket and handed it to his friend. The scholar did not try to bargain but declared himself in agreement with the price and set the nugget on the money scale to be weighed.

"Sterling silver," he remarked with a hidden allusion to

his own person. "I beg the exalted lady to see for herself."

"Hm. Looks good from outside. The question is only whether the inside is genuine and fit," she replied, taking up his allusion.

"Oh, if the lady harbors any doubts, I suggest that we leave the goods and the nugget here for the present. We shall come back this evening with pliers and break the nugget open. Then we shall see whether the inside is genuine or not."

"That will not be necessary. If your money is good, you can make up the difference on your next purchase. If not, you will have been my customer just this once."

K'un-lun's Rival took the bundle of silk under his arm and plucked the scholar's sleeve, so giving him to understand that it was time for them to leave. Before turning to go, the young man took a last long look deep into the lady's eyes. Despite her nearsightedness she grasped the general import of his languishing farewell and answered it in her own way, narrowing her eyes to produce an expression that could equally well be interpreted as mockery or benevolent promise.

Returned to his cell at the temple, the young man remarked to his friend:

"It seems to me that the success of our undertaking is already eight or nine tenths assured. But now what? How shall I get into her house tonight?"

"Don't worry. I have learned by my inquiries that she lives all alone—except for the little maid, who doesn't count; she is a mere child of twelve; early in the evening she falls asleep from exhaustion. She will hear nothing and see nothing."

"But what about the neighbors? What if they see us breaking in? They will cry 'thieves' and 'burglars.' What then?"

"Have no fear. As long as I am with you, nothing can go wrong. I shall take you on my back and climb up the wall to the roof with you. Then we shall let ourselves quietly down into the court. Even if a shingle should come loose, it doesn't matter; the sound of falling shingles is nothing unusual, the neighbors' ears are used to it. No, what worries me is something entirely different: did you pay close attention to her words? In speaking of the silver nugget, she intimated her doubts as to your fitness. Yes, yes, your appearance is satisfactory, but what of your core, your virility? Does it come up to your appearance? If not, you will be her customer just once—that was what she meant by her figure of speech. Remember my recent warning. Will you satisfy her demands? Tonight is the night, you must show your worth. Do you feel equal to the test? Take care not to make a pitiful botch of it. Use your head. and content yourself with one round. Don't get yourself involved in a second or a third."

"Never fear. A failure is out of the question. You can rely on me. You can stay in the vicinity if you like and listen." Laughing aloud, the scholar banished his friend's misgivings and infected him with his merriment.

He could scarcely wait for evening when the Golden Bird should descend in the west and the Silver Hare arise in the east. He felt like a candidate before a great state examination. What sort of problems would the fair examiner set before him? What subject would she select for his dissertation? That is what you will learn in the next chapter.

CHAPTER VIII

*Already in possession of sensational pleasures, she
has no difficulty in maintaining a certain decorum. She
lets the other share in her enjoyment, but reserves the
preferred stock for herself.*

The wife of Ch'üan, the honest silk merchant, was named
Yen-fang, "Aroma." The clever, enlightened child of a
small town private scholar, she had learned as a child, under
her father's guidance, to master the difficulties of the
written language and was well read in every branch of
literature. In view of her intellectual and outward advantages which were far beyond the average, her parents
were unwilling to marry her to the first comer and postponed her betrothal longer than usual. She was already
sixteen when her parents thought they had at last found a
worthy son-in-law. It was a young man who had just
carried off first place at the preliminary examination in the
district capital. Convinced that a young man of his caliber
could assure his family a secure future, they quickly sent
the usual marriage broker to see him and won him as their
son-in-law.

Unfortunately they had been mistaken in their speculation. After hardly more than a year and a half of marriage,
the young man died of neurasthenia and exhaustion. Aroma
observed the prescribed year of mourning and then decided to remarry. Her choice fell on Ch'üan the silk merchant. Despite her marked sensuality, she always managed
to keep up appearances. Whenever a married woman was
caught in the act and her scandalous behavior became the

talk of the town, Aroma liked to give herself the most self-righteous airs. In the company of her friends, she would pass judgment more or less as follows:

"There are certain truths we must face: if, in punishment for some crime we have committed in an earlier life, we are born into the world as women, we must resign ourselves to the fact that we are less fortunate than the other sex. They can travel about and see the world, lead a busy social life and sow all the wild oats they please—all that is denied us poor girls. All our lives we are penned up in our women's quarters, and the only amorous pleasures we may enjoy are those of the marriage bed—insofar as our husband saves up a little of his energy for us—and our social life is limited to association with our children, provided children are granted us. Consequently, we should be reasonable and banish any thought of amorous adventures from our minds. To engage in dealings with other men behind our husbands' backs, is to offend against the ethical and civil order and surpass the limits which destiny has set our happiness. Not to speak of the risks involved—scoldings, reproaches, possibly even beatings if our husbands should catch us, gossip and disparaging remarks on the part of the neighbors, should they learn of our escapades. Thus our very honor demands that we control ourselves and hold our senses in check. If our senses cry out imperiously for activity, it is to our own husbands that we must turn. That is the only sensible thing to do. In the daytime, of course, he is likely to be busy with his affairs, but at night, if all goes well, he is ours. To go quietly into the bedroom together, to undress slowly, to slip into bed side by side, without the least worry or nervousness—believe me, my dears, that is not a bad way to live. Think of the anxiety that is invariably the companion of secret embraces, think of how our hearts pound if a man so much as touches us behind our husband's back. Is there really any sense or pleasure in that kind of thing? I can only laugh at the foolish women who stray off into the byways. Why did they not pick the right man when it was still time? Every woman has her own preferred type; why not pick a man of this type for a husband? They were free to do so. One woman attaches importance to name and social position; very well, let her take a man of promise, a gifted young academician, for her mate. Another is more interested in good looks; very well, let her pick a handsome young blade. A third cares neither for name nor for looks; what matters to her is matrimonial effectiveness; very well, let her pick a virile, robust young fellow. Each one of us has the possibility of forging her own happiness from the very start so she has no need to go out manhunting once she is married."

Her feminine audience looked upon these disquisitions as mere theory, all very sage and high sounding, but quite unrelated to practical experience. Actually personal experience was the source of all Aroma's ideas.

As a young girl Aroma, like so many young girls, had elaborated an ideal of manhood combining all three qualities: cultivation, good looks, and matrimonial effectiveness. The young academician her parents picked for her seemed indeed to be a man of promise; his looks, too, were perfectly satisfactory. Jumping at conclusions, she imagined that he would live up to her ideal in the third point as well. But there she was in for a disappointment: he proved to be singularly short on "equipment," and there was absolutely no relying on his vigor or endurance in bedtime hostilities. He had hardly mounted, she had scarcely begun to feel a pleasant warmth, before he was ready to dismount. How could a robust, normally constructed young woman have been expected to put up with a weakling who drooped in three seconds flat and crawled off to a neutral corner? Her idea of the meeting between the sexes was something very different: an ardent battle, an ecstatic temple dance accompanied by gongs and drums. Utterly unsatisfied, she did everything she could think of to arouse him. But the poor young fellow was a weakling born and the strain was too much for him. Before the year was out, the candle of his manhood was spent completely and he died of sheer exhaustion.

From this bitter experience Aroma learned her lesson: what counts in a husband is not cultivation or good looks; these are mere window dressing, nice to look at, but useless. Only one thing counts: effectiveness as a husband. If a woman does not find all three advantages together and has to choose, she will do well to forego such frills as cultivation and looks, and hitch her wagon to the one thing that really counts, efficiency in bed, the more the better.

Aroma chose her next husband on the basis of this insight; Ch'üan the silk merchant had neither name nor looks nor cultivation to his credit. But she was undismayed by his uncouth features; she did not trouble her head about money and easily accommodated herself to his modest circumstances. The main thing for her was that her candidate was healthy and strong and, as the marriage broker confided to her and the neighbors whispered, possessed a weapon that might have honored a wolf or a tiger. This was the man she took for a husband.

She had no need to regret her decision. Her expectations were far exceeded. At first she had been somewhat skeptical about Ch'üan's vigor and dimensions—surely she thought, there must be some exaggeration. She was prepared for a medium battle, fought not with heavy swords and great battle axes, but rather with light deft rapiers. Thus she was agreeably surprised when he leapt to the attack with a gigantic spear, whose thick shaft her little hand could not even encompass.

From that moment on a great peace descended upon her. She was utterly satisfied and convinced that she would be happy and content forever after with her husband, even if heaven and earth should cave in. Her heart had grown still as though dead, a stranger to all idle thoughts and desires.

The earnings from her husband's modest silk business were meager. And so she made herself useful by helping in the shop, plucking silk fibers and spinning them into fine thread from morning to night. But now fate with its incalculable whims had caused our Before Midnight Scholar to catch sight of her as she was chatting from under the door curtain with her neighbor across the street. And fate had been in a particularly gracious mood: for as the Scholar strolled back and forth, he had managed to catch two successive glimpses of her. She, for her part, had hardly taken notice of him. She had indeed observed the presence of a man, but only in blurred outlines; his features and the particulars of his appearance had escaped her nearsightedness.

But the sharp-sighted neighbor across the street had inspected him all the more closely. She had quite lost her head and had been unable to tear her eyes away from him. As far as she was concerned, he was the ideal, the handsomest, most attractive man in the world.

She was in her early thirties and a fine figure of a woman —apart from her one blemish, an exceptionally homely face. Her husband was also a small silk dealer, a close friend of Ch'üan his neighbor. Although their businesses were quite separate, they went to market together when they had wares to sell, and they took journeys together to purchase silk cocoons from the peasants.

Healthy and endowed with very normal instincts, this woman of thirty desperately craved a love affair. But the face that nature, like an unkind stepmother, had given her was poor publicity; it drove men away by the dozens. They looked at her with the white eyeballs of indifference, or rather, they looked away.

Thus shunned by men, she yearned all the more for something to happen before it was too late. How she longed for the tingling sensation of one who inspires secret, forbidden desires. And in addition she was restive under a heavy domestic yoke. Her husband was a tyrant who scolded her mercilessly when he did not actually beat her at the slightest neglect of her household duties. Fear of her

husband's rages had taught her caution and thus far kept
her on the straight and narrow. But for a long time she had
been itching to play a little trick on her domestic tyrant.

She waited until the young stranger had gone away.
Then she came running across the street.

"Do you know him?—I mean the charming young man
who was just looking you over," she blurted out, still
breathless from running.

"Not that I know of. With my nearsightedness I don't
pay much attention to passers-by. I hardly look up from
my work. Men are always stopping outside the curtain to
stare at me. Let them stare."

"Yes, yes. You are right to pay no attention to them,
that is, the common everyday variety. But the one I'm
talking about, it's not every day that you see his likes; if
he were to come courting outside my window, I should
gladly feast my eyes on him for three whole days and
nights."

"Tut-tut! A man like that would have to be twelve tenths
perfect. There is no such man."

"Aha! If I tell you that he is not twelve but a hundred
and twenty tenths a perfect young cavalier, I shall not be
exaggerating. What else do I do all day long but stand outside the door, watching the men who pass by? And never
among hundreds have I seen such a one as this. Such fine
distinguished features, a complexion so light and fresh! Incomparable! And those vaulted eyebrows! And the finely
arched nose! And the shapely little ears! And the gleaming
eyes! Why, every single part of him is worthy to fall in
love with. He is like a silk doll or a jade figurine, in fact
he is as beautiful to look upon as a masterwork of painting,
though I doubt whether the greatest of painters could ever
capture the supple grace of his bearing and his movements.
Ah, a man like that could make a body die of longing."

"Don't be ridiculous. You are raving. There are no such
men as that. And even if there were, what is it to me? Why
should I be interested in any old Mr. Li or Mr. Chang?"

"But he is all the more interested in you. The way he looked after you! He just couldn't tear his eyes away. He would have stood there forever, but obviously thinking he was making himself unduly conspicuous, he continued reluctantly on his way. But he did not go far. A moment later he turned back and once again paced slowly past your door. What a pity we have no idea where he went! Oh, I know, you took no notice of him, he means nothing to you. But he means all the more to me. I am positively lovesick in your place. Is it not strange?"

"My guess is that not I, but you yourself, must have been the object of his attentions, and that it's just your bashfulness that makes you drag me into it."

"With my face? Don't make me laugh! Who would ever stop to look at me? No, no, it's you he was looking at. And if you don't believe me, you will soon have occasion to convince yourself. He is sure to come again. I shall be on the lookout, and when I see him in the distance, I'll run over and let you know in plenty of time. Then you can step outside to observe him close at hand and let him gaze his fill of you."

"Very well," said Aroma indifferently, "let us wait until he comes back." Despite her show of indifference, she spent the next three days in a flurry of expectation. But her unknown admirer showed himself neither on the next day nor those that followed. She had banished him from her thoughts and began to forget him. And then one fine day, her waning memory of him was rekindled.

This was some four months later. Her two customers had just left the shop when she remembered her neighbor's fulsome description. "The handsome young man!" she thought. "That must have been the one." And she went on musing:

"Yes, indeed, his looks are certainly appealing. In that respect I doubt whether he has his match anywhere—but the question remains: is the inside, the heart and core, equal to the outside? If I am to risk my honor and reputation, the undertaking must be worth my while, and that depends on the inner man. If despite his appealing husk, the kernel is no better than middling, it would hardly pay to take him into my intimacy. Then a different policy would be in order. I should merely lure him to the shop day after day, encourage him to make purchases, and benefit by the opportunity to feast my eyes on his handsome exterior—but wait a minute! That reminds me of a turn of phrase he used before: did he not speak of 'pliers' with which to break the nugget open and make sure of its genuineness? Such expressions have a double meaning, they can be taken in two ways. What then? If he should really come tonight, what ought I do? Should I dismiss him or welcome him and keep him overnight? Should I risk my good reputation or not? That is the question . . ." As she thus weighed and pondered the situation, her neighbor came rushing in, breathless with excitement.

"That was he. That was he."

"Who?"

"Why, the young cavalier I was raving about. Don't you remember? He was just here buying silk with an older gentleman."

"Oh, you don't say so."

"Well, what do you think of him? Isn't he just wonderful?"

"Well, yes, in appearance at least—but otherwise he strikes me as pretty much of a fly-by-night. Doesn't seem to be anything serious and solid about him."

"What nonsense you talk! Since when do serious gentlemen go chasing after women? Why do you always insist on judging people—especially men—by their moral worth? Can't you just accept him as a man and a very attractive one at that?"

"If you insist. But even so, he might have controlled himself a little; he might have shown a little more discretion in the presence of third parties. You can't imagine the liberties he took with me. It's lucky my husband wasn't there, or ..."

"Ah, liberties? What sort of liberties?"

"I see no need to describe them. Suffice it to say that he was not exactly well behaved."

But vague hints were not nearly enough for the sex-crazed neighbor. Her overheated imagination demanded lurid realities. Had he caressed her? Had he drawn her to him and taken her in his arms? Had he kissed her? Had he gone still further? She wanted all the details. Oh, it was all so exciting! She begged like a little dog and put an arm round Aroma's shoulder and patted her cheek, and did not desist until Aroma consented to give her a detailed report—which she found very disappointing:

"Of course he took no such liberties as you have been imagining. However, the way he kept looking at me, the piercing glances he sent my way, it was as though he were trying to hook himself fast in my heart. In addition he used certain ambiguous and pointed turns of phrase, on purpose I am sure. And that isn't all. Just imagine, while supposedly feeling and examining the materials I was setting before him, the impudent fellow had the audacity to touch my hand and even to press it a little. Well, that was plenty for me. I call such conduct provocative. Remember, we were not alone."

"Oh, if that's all! And how did you respond? Graciously, I hope."

"Graciously! He can call himself fortunate that I didn't give him a good tongue lashing right in front of his companion!"

"How unfeeling you are! Don't take it amiss if I tell you frankly that the two of you, you, so rare a beauty, and he so handsome a young cavalier, were destined for one another by heaven and earth, if not as husband and wife, then as lovers. When I think of you with your old man—you mustn't get angry; it is God's truth, I can't think of a better comparison—it is as though a freshly blossoming, deliciously fragrant rose were to be thrown on a dungheap by mistake. It's pitiful. I feel so sorry for you. With all my heart I shall be glad to help you as a go-between should he turn up again. And now stop behaving like such an old-fashioned prude. What does all your virtue get you? Stone monuments are erected only for virtuous widows who remain faithful to their one and only beyond the grave and refuse to marry again. When did anyone ever make a fuss about a woman just because she controlled herself during her husband's lifetime and refrained from taking lovers? Am I right?"

Her arguments were quite unnecessary. Even as she was speaking, Aroma—who had long since made up her mind—had forged her plan. She was well aware that she needed her neighbor's discretion and that the best way of buying it would be to give her a bite—and indeed, the first bite—of the tasty morsel. For by letting her neighbor go first and administer a preliminary examination so to speak, Aroma would be enabled, without committing herself, to test her handsome admirer's heart and core, his bedtime efficiency. Taught by sad experience, she did not wish to be misled by mere appearances. If the candidate should fail in his preliminary examination, she would stir up a scene and chase him out of the house in disgrace. Then everything would be as before, with no harm to her honor or reputation. But if the preliminary examination turned out satisfactorily, she herself would administer the main examination immediately afterwards. A clever, well-thought-out plan if ever there was one.

Aroma shook her head emphatically.

"No, no. I myself wish to keep out of it and leave the pleasure to you. You will not play the go-between for me; on the contrary, I shall play the ax-handle for you. I shall be content to eavesdrop while you are enjoying yourselves."

"What? Me? You can't be serious. You expect him to put up with this repulsive face of mine? Why, he will

simply send me packing. Oh, if you wish to be generous
and give me a bite of your pasty, that might be possible.
But you would have to go first; then, after you have had
your fill of pleasure, I could come bursting in. You would
run off in a fright after I had taken your place in bed.
That way you would carry off first honors and I should
content myself with a modest consolation prize. That might
work out all right."

"No, no. I meant my proposition seriously and I stick to
it. Don't misunderstand me. I have no intention of satisfying the frivolous pretensions behind his little hints and
allusions; however, he has cast a mesh or two around my
heart—oh those looks, that face of his! You see what I
mean, he has aroused a certain curiosity in me. So pay close
attention, this is my plan. It so happens that our husbands
will be out of town tonight. They have gone off again to
buy new silk cocoons in the villages. I shall be all alone in
the house, my little helper doesn't count. She will be fast
asleep and snoring. Should he really come tonight, the
circumstances will be favorable. As a precaution I shall put
out all the lamps and candles. It will be pitch dark; you need
have no fear that your face will put him to flight. He will
mistake you for me; you will do nothing to disabuse him,
and you will take your pleasure with him in my stead.
Meanwhile, I shall be sitting nearby in the darkness, eaves-
dropping and taking my share of the pleasure. Thus my
honor will remain intact, no one will be able to accuse me
of a thing. Well, what do you say to my idea? Isn't it
ingenious?"

"I should say so. Oh, I am so excited already. I can
hardly wait. But there is still something I don't understand. Why do you absolutely insist on foregoing the main
pleasure? You are really carrying your moral principles
too far."

"Oh, it has nothing to do with moral principles. I shall
simply be imitating the proverbial thief who stops up his
ears while stealing the bell. With this little self-deception

he appeases his conscience; he just doesn't know what is going on. To be perfectly frank, I am rather spoiled when it comes to bedtime pleasures. Confidentially, another man is not very likely to equal the caliber of my husband's last. Too small a last would scarcely touch the walls of my shoe, even if it should toil and sweat for a year and a day. Now do you see what I am driving at? You will explore the terrain for me; you will be my spy and my scout in one."

"Ah, now I understand. You mean to keep your share in the profits after all. But there is one favor I should like to ask of you: in case you should wish to take a hand in the battle, please don't interrupt me at the height of my transports. Remember the old monk's saying:

Prevent a man from eating his fill after a long fast?
Oh no! Rather bury him alive.

That would be cruel."

"Have no fear. I shall not be so unkind."

With this their arrangements for the evening were concluded.

Thanks to the delightful commission with which she had been entrusted, an exceptionally ugly woman was to enjoy an hour—alas, only a brief hour—of happiness beyond all her hopes and dreams. Would the freshly repaired and renovated last fit the shoe? That is what you will find out in the next chapter.

CHAPTER IX

*From the embattled din of the preliminary skirmish
she draws inferences concerning the strength of the
adversary. But it is only in the main encounter that
he shows his true mettle.*

In the twilight hour when lamps were being kindled in the
houses round about, the neighbor woman softly closed her
house door and darted across the street under cover of
darkness.

Aroma was in a waggish mood. "What a pity," she said,
putting on the longest face she could manage.

"Nothing is going to happen after all. He has just sent a
letter saying he could not come—an urgent appointment,
a banquet he is absolutely obliged to attend. You may as
well turn around and go home again."

The neighbor woman listened with disappointment
bordering on rage. Sparks flew from her eyes and steam
spurted from her nose. She boiled inwardly. Why had
Aroma not told her sooner? She would not have put herself to so much pains. Suspicion was born in her heart: no
doubt Aroma had regretted her promise. She had decided
that her friend would only be in the way, that she preferred to keep the night's pleasures all to herself. The
neighbor woman was working herself up into a resounding
tantrum when Aroma's merry laughter dispelled the clouds.

"Fooled you! How can you be so gullible! I just wanted
to tease you a little. Set your mind at rest. He will come.
Quickly now, we must get ready."

She led her friend into the kitchen. There they set a

kettle full of fresh water over the hearth fire and prepared a warm hip bath in a large tub. Returning to the bedroom, they moved an upholstered love seat close to the foot end of the bed. Here Aroma planned to make herself comfortable and play the eavesdropper during the first part of the night. Then she sent her friend out to listen behind the outer gate of the house.

"Bolt the door and wait until he comes. He is sure to make his presence known by knocking softly. At the very first knock pull the bolt and let him in. Don't give him time to repeat his knocking or knock more loudly; the sound might be heard in the neighborhood and arouse suspicion. As soon as you have let him in, bolt the door again. And one thing more: when you return to the room and get into bed with him, speak as little as possible. If he asks you questions and you can't help answering, do it in a whisper. Don't give yourself away by your voice, or our whole stratagem will be ruined."

The neighbor woman promised to follow her instructions to the letter and repaired to her listening post behind the outer door, while Aroma put out all the lights in the house and settled down on the love seat.

A whole hour passed. The neighbor woman came in again, footsore from standing there and unnerved from listening: no one had knocked. She was just opening her mouth to report to Aroma when suddenly someone embraced her and kissed her in the darkness. First she thought it was Aroma. Another of her jokes, no doubt. To make sure, she let her hand slip down along the someone's body. Lo and behold, she encountered something long and hard —a he!

"Dearest!" she whispered, fighting back her impulse to cry aloud. "Oh, oh, however did you get in?"

"Over the rooftops."

"Oh, what a wonderful man! Come, let's go to bed."

They undressed. But though far from reluctant, he could not keep pace with her. She was lying stark naked on her back while he was still removing his clothes. At last he had finished. He climbed in, lay down on top of her, and groped for her legs, meaning to toss them over his shoulders as usual. But his hands met with the void. She had already raised her legs and spread them wide. She had prepared an eager welcome for him.

"She certainly comes straight to the point," he said to himself. "Well, so much the better. There will be no need to waste my time beating around the bush. I too shall come straight to the point." And he poised his battle-ax for a frontal attack. But she had not been prepared for so violent an onslaught. What a vigorous warrior was storming at her gate and demanding admittance! And she began to squeak and struggle.

"*Hach . . . bh . . . !* Take it easy. You are hurting me," she pleaded, gasping for air.

Gentleman as he was, he granted her a respite which he utilized to finger her portal, gently parting the wings of her gateway and rubbing persistently this way and that. Then he attacked again. But again he failed to breach the fortress. The head of his "tortoise" squeezed in an inch or so, while the van of his army was repulsed.

"There is nothing to be gained by pussyfooting," he explained to her. "The best strategy is an all-out offensive. It may hurt you at first, but if you can stand it, your pleasure will be all the greater afterward."

And he attacked vigorously. But again she struggled and resisted.

"*Shih pu-te!* It won't work that way. Please, a little saliva would help."

"Certainly not. That is contrary to all the rules of the game. That may be permissible when there's a maidenhead to be pierced, but not otherwise." He attempted another assault, but her resistance was undiminished.

"*Shih pu-te!* It can't be done. If you are too proud to break the rules, I'll attend to it."

She struggled loose, spat in the hollow of her hand, and

used one half the saliva to lubricate her gate, the other half to anoint the head and neck of his tortoise.

"It will be better now. But gently please."

He disregarded her plea. On the contrary, he wished to show her what he could do. Clutching her hind cheeks firmly and pulling her to him so brusquely that flesh met flesh with a loud report, he attacked with all his might. This time he broke through, successfully introducing his entire armament into the fortress.

She uttered a soft scream, this time less from pain than from admiration.

"Goodness! Who would have expected a young scholar like you, a stay-at-home bookworm, to be so mighty a warrior! He doesn't even care whether his victim lives or dies. He just pushes his way in and that's that. You've reached rock bottom, you can't get any further. So out with you, and make it quick!"

"Oho! We're just beginning. A fine how-do-you-do if I were to retire from business now," he replied with a merry laugh and began to heave and thrash with all his might and main. At first each of his thrusts brought forth a moan; "*hach . . . hh.*" After fifty odd strokes she fell silent. After he had passed the hundred mark, she began to moan again, the same sounds of "*hach . . . hh . . .*" issued from her lips. At first her moaning had been from pain, but now it signified rapture. It is indeed a strange fact about women that they can express very different feelings with the same sound; first it is a sound of suffering and then it becomes a sound of pleasure. With her pleasure moan a woman makes it known that her ecstasy is approaching the peak, that the cloud over the magic mountain is close to bursting.

Now Aroma's neighbor exerted all her guile and cunning. Her cloud had already burst twice, but when our young man asked her if she had come to the point, she said no no and insisted that he persevere in his efforts. Why did she lie? Because she knew that she was only Aroma's substitute and that Aroma was listening. If she admitted that her joys

She knew that she was only Aroma's substitute and that Aroma was listening.

had come to a head, Aroma would step in and take her place. She wished to enjoy the rare pleasures of this night to the full, to prolong them as much as possible. She observed the well-known practice of the substitute officials described in the popular saying:

These worthy gentlemen are substitutes in office:
Slowly does it, take your time.
The public may be good and sick of waiting their turn.
What matter! Meanwhile we draw our wages.

In this love battle there was a certain amount of cheating on both sides. She cheated in defense of her interests. He for his part cheated in defense of his prestige. When in answer to his question she kept saying no, she had not yet come to the point, he felt himself in honor bound to give the same untruthful answer to the same question, and to continue bravely in his efforts. He didn't want her to be disappointed in him, though by now he was hard pressed and would have welcomed a breathing spell. In this phase of the battle, he was very much like a drunken man riding a donkey, his head tottering alarmingly at every step.

She must have noticed the difference between the easy spontaneous vigor with which he had started out and his present convulsive effort. Taking pity on him, she asked:

"Dearest, have you come to the point?"

And still his pride would not let him give in. Her question produced the same effect as the scolding with which a master shakes up a sleepy pupil and spurs him to new wakefulness. He redoubled his exertions and struggled bravely on. But when he began to sweat and pant, she relented.

"*Wo tiu la!* I've done it. Stop. I can't go on. I am dying. Put your arms around me and let us go to sleep side by side."

With these words she offered him the armistice for which he had been secretly longing. He was only too glad to accept.

Meanwhile Aroma had played the eavesdropper. The whole time she had lain motionless on the love seat at the foot end of the bed, listening intently.

In the beginning, when the neighbor woman had squeaked and struggled and his attack seemed to be making no progress, she had said to herself, well, his utensil can hardly be so insignificant; it must indeed be quite imposing and serviceable. Already half her doubts were dispelled. And as the battle progressed, when she saw, or rather heard, how perseveringly he held up his end and how, after a brief moment of weariness, he rallied his flagging troops and led them back into the fray with redoubled vigor, she was wholly reassured. "He is a born conqueror of ladies' chambers, my chosen hero," she said to herself. "I shall belong to him with joy and without regrets."

Taking advantage of the deep sleep into which the couple had fallen, she slipped quietly off the love seat. For a time she stood in the dark and pondered. She might slip unnoticed under the covers and simply join in when the couple woke up. But in the darkness, she told herself, he would be unable to distinguish her from her neighbor; what was to prevent him from devoting his attentions to the neighbor woman? That simply wouldn't do. Or even if he should turn to Aroma, he would not perceive her beauty in the darkness. That would be depriving him of just what he needed to rekindle his passion and fire him on to new deeds. He had every right to be tired, and without the proper inspiration he would provide her with nothing but cold and savorless leftovers. No, that was not at all what she wanted. She would proceed in a very different way.

She slipped secretly into the kitchen, where she poured several ladles full of water into a kettle which she set on the hearth fire. Then she kindled a straw in the fire and lit a lamp. Lamp in hand, she returned to the bedroom, approached the bed and lifted the curtain. She removed the silk coverlet from the sleeping pair, shone the lamp in their face, and burst out in simulated rage:

"Heigh, what kind of behavior is this! Breaking into strange houses in the middle of the night and lying around in other people's beds! Up with you! Give an account of yourself!"

Our scholar gave a violent start. Drowsy and befuddled as he was, he mistook the intruder for the irate husband: no doubt he had been hiding in the house the whole while, waiting to catch his wife's lover in the act with a view to blackmail. For a moment our scholar was scared to death and a cold sweat poured down his back, but soon he gathered his wits, and when he looked up he saw none other than the object of his adoration standing before him in the lamplight. He rubbed his eyes. How was it possible? Why, he had just been sleeping with her—or did she have a double? He turned his head and looked at the woman by his side. Now, in the glow of the lamp, he distinguished her features for the first time and started back in horror. That blackened skin riddled with pockmarks! That flat nose, that broad mouth! That strawlike, lusterless hair! His eyes moved downward along her body. It was shapely enough, but here too her skin was covered with spots.

"Who are you anyway?" he asked.

"I am the neighbor from across the street. At Madame Aroma's express request I took her place just this once. She wanted me to test you. It all began that first day when you were walking up and down in front of the shop . . ." With disarming simplicity she revealed the whole truth from A to Z.

She climbed out of the bed and quickly slipped into her things, though in her haste she put on only what was strictly necessary: her lined trousers, her padded cotton jacket, her felt slippers. All the rest—stockings, underwear, tunic, sweat cloth—she gathered into a bundle which she tossed over her arm. At the door she turned back:

"Plain as I am," she said, "I shall forever be your humble

servant. It was as a favor to my friend that I shared your couch tonight, but perhaps we were predestined from an earlier existence to lie together. Who knows? If ever you should come again and have a few minutes to spare for me, your devoted handmaiden will always be at your disposal. Do not treat her too unkindly."

She bowed to him and then to Aroma, muttered a few words of thanks for the friendly reception, and departed. Aroma accompanied her to the house door, let her out and barred the door behind her.

When she returned, our young man was still quite bewildered. He felt as though he had just awakened from a deep dream or a drunken stupor.

"Well," said Aroma with an affectation of coldness, "why are you still lying here? The other has settled accounts for me. We are quits. You have had your pleasure. Why don't you go home?"

He protested vigorously. "Oho, we are far from being quits. Quite on the contrary. You owe me reparation for the injustice you have done me by defrauding me with so inferior a substitute. It is midnight already, soon it will be dawn. We have no time to lose. Quickly. Crawl in here beside me, and not another word!"

"Do you really mean it?"

"I certainly do."

"Very well. In that case, will you kindly get up and dress? Before we go to bed, there is something important to be done."

"What can be so important? As far as I can see, the one important thing is that we go to bed together."

"Stop asking questions and come along."

He jumped up and flung on his clothes. Taking him by the hand, she led him through several rooms and inner courtyards to the kitchen. There she pointed to the bath-tub and the kettle full of boiling hot water on the hearth fire. Now he understood. He was to take a bath, and since it was far to the kitchen and the way led through open courtyards, she had bidden him dress, fearing that he might catch cold if exposed to the cool night air. How considerate of her! In his thoughts he performed a kowtow of thanks.

Meanwhile she plied the ladle and filled the tub half with cold, half with hot water. The result was a fine warm bath, not too hot and not too cold.

"There. Now you can get in. You will find soap and washcloths over there. Help yourself."

And she continued:

"An unsavory smell of strange woman still clings to you. I should not like you to pass it on to my sensitive body."

"You are perfectly right," he agreed. "It is indeed of the utmost importance. I shall also wash my mouth out to obliterate every trace of kisses."

And he reached for the water bowl and the toothbrush which had been placed in a rack affixed to the outside of the bathtub. He was very much impressed to note that despite the late romantic hour she was still the perfect housewife, attentive to every imaginable domestic detail. How carefully she had prepared his bath, complete with soap, washcloths and steaming warm towels! When he had finished drying himself, she had wiped off the wet bath mat with a rag, and later on in the bed chamber she had prepared a sweat cloth and placed it in readiness beside the pillow.

"What an excellent housekeeper!" he thought in silent admiration. "She thinks of everything."

She put out the lamp and sat down on the edge of the bed. Slowly she undressed, carefully smoothing out each garment and folding it over a chair.

Graciously she let her lover finish undressing her, loosen her silk brassière and remove her thin batiste panties. He embraced her and kissed her and sent out a hand to explore. He found her twin hills, so full and elastic that they slipped out of his hands when he tried to pull and pluck at them. Everywhere her flesh was firm, but at the same time it was soft and tender; nowhere did he find a hard place. Further down, on the vault of her fortress wall, he met with the same soft firmness, but here the skin seemed to be even smoother and more supple than elsewhere.

He moved her carefully into place, raised her legs over his shoulders, and opened the battle, employing the same tactics as with her ugly precursor; a frontal attack without introductory love play. His calculation was that though this approach might hurt her at first, her pleasure would be all the greater afterward. The offensive ran off without a hitch. But contrary to his expectations, she remained utterly apathetic as though she felt nothing at all, giving no sign either of pleasure or of pain. Then he remembered what his experienced friend, K'un-lun's Rival, had told him about the mighty caliber of her husband's last. No wonder his forces had been able to slip into the enemy fortress so easily, without encountering the least resistance. He had not been prepared for a shoe of such dimensions. In a shoe so deep and wide his last, though by no means unimpressive, seemed to shrivel into nothingness, to lose itself like a needle in a haystack.

Aware that he would get nowhere by the old methods, he decided on a change of tactics. Removing the pillow from under Aroma's head, he pushed it beneath her loins. In so doing, he intentionally neglected to provide her head with another support. This impressed her and inspired her with a secret admiration. Thus far she had experienced no pleasure at all, but she saw by his preparations that he knew a thing or two about bedchamber technique and was confident that everything would come out all right in the end.

Esteemed reader, the battle of the sexes is in many respects not unlike the art of warfare: before the opening of hostilities, the two contestants spy upon each other, feeling out one another's strengths and weaknesses. He tries to find out whether she is deep or not so deep, in order to plan his offensive and retreat accordingly. She tries to obtain accurate information about his armament, whether short or long, thick or thin, in order to meet it with suitable movements and adapt herself to it. Success in battle depends on knowledge of the enemy's strength or weakness. The length and thickness of men's utensils vary exceedingly, and the same applies to the depth and width of women's pleasure houses. If she is not particularly deep, an over-long utensil is out of place; there will not be room for it, at least not for all of it. If he should nevertheless attempt to force the whole of it in, he will give her not pleasure but pain. Ought he to get all the pleasure? That would be unfair. But if she possesses an extraordinarily deep pleasure grotto, she needs a mate with unusually long and powerful armament; otherwise she will get no satisfaction. But the length of the male organ is fixed by nature once and for all; it does not go on growing and there is no way of lengthening it artificially. Consequently a knowing lover resorts to a stratagem: he removes the pillow from beneath his lady's head and wedges it under her waist. Thus raised, her pelvis lies flatter and the lover's utensil is so enabled to reach the bottom. This should not be taken to mean that the pillow beneath the waist is indispensable or should be employed in every case. It is indicated only in cases when the lady's pleasure grotto is too deep for her lover's armament. We see then that this shortcoming can be remedied. But there is another discrepancy that cannot be made good: when the lady's shoe is too wide for her lover's last.

The itinerant surgeon's operation had considerably increased the thickness and stamina of our young man's equipment, but had not lengthened it. On his first attempt to penetrate Aroma's pleasure grotto, his utensil had proved too short and had failed to plumb the depths. By hitting on the above-mentioned stratagem of wedging the pillow under her waist, he had impressed her with his competence; she said nothing but secretly she was very pleased.

This use of a pillow is a simple and widely known trick,

but few men are considerate enough to bother and still fewer know how to do the thing properly. In addition to supporting the waist, most men leave the pillow under their lady's head. This is a big mistake. For her body is then raised at both ends, with the result that she is bent in the middle. If, to make matters worse, her lover rests his whole weight upon her, it is easy to imagine how uncomfortable she must feel. In this unnatural position, a kiss requires the most painful contortions on both sides: *he* must hump his back in order to reach her mouth; *she* must stretch her neck and twist her head backward before her lips and tongue can meet his lips and tongue. All this because of the troublesome and superfluous pillow under her head. And so I say, away with it! Let the lady's cloud-coiffure lie directly on the sheet. Then the heads and limbs of both parties will fit harmoniously together; his noble yak whisk will penetrate her pleasure grotto without difficulty, her purple little tongue will find its way easily into his mouth, no inequalities of position will prevent them from merging and blending inwardly, no discomfort will mar their pleasure.

After this brief digression, let us get on with our story. Raising her nephrite thighs over his shoulders, planting both hands on the bed sheet, our scholar resumed the interrupted battle—this time with success. His valiant henchman did not bely his partly canine origins and nature. The longer the battle raged, the more imposing became his stature and with it his courage; no longer was her pleasure grotto a bottomless pit; both on the sides and in the depths the desired contact was established. Aroma's attitude changed accordingly. The first assault had left her totally apathetic and inert, no sound of pleasure or pain had escaped her; but now her body began to quiver and writhe voluptuously, and moans of "*hach . . . hh . . .*" issued from her lips.

"*Hsin-kan*, dearest. It's coming! I feel a pleasant sensation."

"So soon? Why, I've hardly begun," he whispered back. "Just wait until I get going, then you will really feel some-

thing, *wo-ti kuai jou,* my perverse little lump of flesh."
And he proceeded to heave and thrash until heaven and
earth were stricken with terror and threatened to lose their
balance. Her stifled cries of "Dearest" and "Oh, I'm dying"
became more and more frequent and the grass and bushes
round her gate grew moist with the dew of pleasure. He
reached for the sweat cloth to wipe away the dew, but she
restrained him. How so? It has already been stated that
she was very passionate by nature. A battle of the sexes,
she felt, should be a wild frenzy, an ecstatic temple dance
with a rousing accompaniment of gongs and drums. Interrupt the temple dance with a prosaic sweat cloth? Out of
the question. Even in her everyday dealings with her
husband she had taken the same attitude. Let the dew of
pleasure sprinkle her as it might, there would be no wiping
until afterward, after the cloud had burst. This was a very
personal eccentricity of hers. I mention it only in passing
and—it goes without saying—only for the benefit of
gourmets and connoisseurs!

Our young man was still going strong when she flung
her arms round his neck, pressed him close, and groaned:

"*Wo yao tiu la!* My cloud is bursting. Let us die of joy
together."

Actually it was too soon for him. He would have been
glad to go on a little longer and impress her with his vigor
and endurance. But she would not allow it.

"Stop. I am fully convinced of your strength and endurance. You've been battling all through the night, you've
taken on two women and laid them low. Grant yourself a
little rest, save your strength for tomorrow night; I
shouldn't like you to get sick from overexertion; I want
you to stay well for my sake."

Ah, she was concerned for his health. How considerate!
How touching! Deeply moved, he folded her in his arms,
pressed her tight, and body to body, they shared the
ineffable bliss of the bursting cloud.

For a long while they lay still, in close embrace, until at last she broke the silence:

"Dawn is coming—get up, get up! Put your clothes on. You must go before it is light, the neighbors mustn't see you."

They threw on their clothes. She took him to the house door, let him out, and quietly barred the door behind him.

From then on they continued in the same vein night after night. He crept in secretly under cover of darkness, but no longer like a *liang-shang chün-tzu*, a "knight of the roof tops." Now he entered normally through the gate and stole away in the gray dawn. Sometimes, when the parting was too much for them to bear, he spent the day with her. Then they took their pleasure in broad daylight and ran about the house without a stitch of clothing, delighting in the rosy nakedness of each other's well-shaped bodies. On such occasions she pretended to be sick and left the gate bolted all day long.

On the second evening after the first night of love, the neighbor woman came and begged—she just couldn't help herself—our young man for a crumb or two. He could not just send her packing; she knew too much. And so he skirmished with her a little. Though her hunger was far from appeased, he thereby kept her in a good humor and prevented her from becoming resentful.

Despite infinite precautions it was inevitable that the neighbors should get wind of what was going on at Honest Ch'üan's house during his absence. They were curious folk, and certain suspicious sounds had reached their ears. But one and all they identified the interloper as K'un-lun's Rival, because of all the questions he had asked about the Ch'üan household. Who else could it be? No one suspected that our young man was behind him. Well, thought the neighbors, if that's who it is, we had better not incur his displeasure by spying on him or meddling in his activities. He is a dangerous man and we shall do well not to court his vengeance. Accordingly, they played blind and deaf, closing their doors and shutters early in the evening and staying carefully off the streets once night had fallen.

Ten nights on end our lovers carried on undisturbed, then the husband's return put an end to their secret pleasures. They were both heartsick at the thought that they could no longer see one another. If our scholar had been free to choose, he would at least have walked up and down in the daytime outside his lady's window. But his experienced friend refused to let him do so for fear that such youthful folly might stir up a deplorable scandal. However, he agreed to play the messenger of love. Pretending to be an innocent customer desirous of buying some silk, he would enter the shop to bring Aroma some message from her lover and on the same occasion take a message from her to him. When present at these visits, husband Ch'üan suspected nothing. As far as he was concerned, K'un-lun's Rival was merely a regular customer who paid promptly, and he saw no reason why Aroma should not wait on him. On the contrary Ch'üan would retire to the background whenever the bandit came in and let his wife handle the negotiations. He was a candid soul, incapable of imputing evil designs to his fellow men, least of all to his esteemed regular customer. He was indeed fully deserving of his nickname Lao-shih, "the guileless." Until one fine day the neighbors opened his eyes. You will hear about that in the next chapter.

CHAPTER X

The magnanimous friend bores a passage through a wall of obstacles and makes free with his money. Those who had mated in the grass and dew become a regularly married pair.

Aroma had no intention of passively bowing to her fate. She simply could not accept the idea that her precious romance of the last ten nights was all over just because her husband had come home. She sat and pondered: "I used to think it was impossible that one man should combine all three advantages: cultivation, good looks, and worthy armament. When it came to remarrying, I resolved to forego the first two advantages and chose a husband who possessed only the third, the one that struck me as essential. I picked an uncouth individual without looks or cultivation and thought it my duty to esteem him. For the sake of the one advantage, I put up with a narrow life. I did all I could to help in the shop and wore my fingers to the bone for my husband from early morning till late at night. And now—who would have thought it!—I have met a man who actually combines all three advantages. What would have become of me if I had not met him? My life would have been utterly ruined! I should have been reduced to a life without content or fulfillment. Of what use would all my beauty have been to me? None at all. I would have been no better off than my ugly neighbor from across the way. I have ten days of the most wonderful experience behind me—I regret nothing—but what is to happen now? Am I to go on vegetating as before, dragging on a shallow, empty existence? Or shall I make some bold move? Is there not, in our old chronicles, some similar case, that might give me an idea?"

Aroma closed her eyes. Her thoughts wandered into the night of the remote past. A shade, a feminine shade, stepped forth from the chorus of historical ghosts and took on shape before her eyes: Hung-fu, the lovely "Red Whisk," who had lived in the days when the star of the Sui dynasty (581–618 A.D.) was beginning to decline and that of the T'ang dynasty (618–905 A.D.) was rising above the horizon.

In those days the beautiful Hung-fu, youthful dweller in the "side chambers" of the mighty prime minister Yang Su (d. 606), achieved fame by a deed of extraordinary boldness. With the other ladies of the harem, she was permitted to attend a banquet given by Yang Su, the aging duke and illustrious general, in honor of Li Ching, a beautiful and distinguished youth from the mighty Li family which then had its eyes on the throne. Between her and the youthful guest, it was love at first sight. Despite the vigilance of the grim harem guards, she managed to slip out of the palace that same night and flee with her beloved.

Delving still further into the past, Aroma's thoughts went back to the era of the former Han dynasty (225 B.C.– 6 A.D.). Again a single shade stepped forth from the whirling sea of ghosts and took the form of a beautiful young woman. A scene from olden days came alive before Aroma's inner eye: a great banquet in the house of Cho Wang-sun, the wealthy patron of the arts. A talented young poet by the name of Szu ma Hsiang-ju (d. 117 B.C.), dazzlingly beautiful, a brilliant conversationalist, delighted all present with his singing and playing on the lute, and won the heart of Wen-chün, the beautiful daughter of the house. Again it was love at first sight. That same night she slipped away, disguised as a young man, left her father's palace with the help of a trusted chambermaid, sought out the young man at his inn, and went away with him as his wedded wife.

Aroma reopened her eyes.

"These two heroines of antiquity," so she spun out the thread of her meditation, "did not shrink from a daring venture; they shattered all the barriers of convention and took their fate in their own hands. They eloped! They allowed themselves to be abducted! And society didn't even find fault with their boldness; on the contrary, they shared in the glory which their husbands later acquired—the one, Li Ching (571–649), attained the highest offices and even the rank of duke; the other, Szu ma Hsiang-ju, basked in the imperial favor and became a respected court poet. And both these ladies were later distinguished by the throne with titles of honor! Why should she, Aroma, not do likewise? Why should she not do something drastic to end the present intolerable situation? What was she in her present state? A woman divided against herself, outwardly a Mrs. Chang, inwardly a Mrs. Li; outwardly the conventional wife of Honest Ch'üan the silk dealer, but inwardly and with every fiber of her being the mistress of her beloved young scholar. What was the saying of the wise Confucius, which my father used to insist on so strongly and recommend as a motto to take with me on life's way? 'A man of clear understanding will do nothing that cannot bear the light of day.' I have always favored clarity in human relationships. If I have gone and got myself a lover, let me be consistent about it and not do things by halves; let me belong to him entirely and him to me. I was not cut out for the role of those pitiful creatures who consume themselves in vain yearning for love, who slavishly forego their happiness and accept the idea that they will never again in this world see the object of their desire, not even from afar, who sicken and languish from disappointed love. No, that is not for me."

Her mind was made up. She took brush and paper and wrote her beloved a letter.

Aroma's learned father had given her a sound education; she had received the best of instruction in literature and the art of writing and had mastered the poised, elegant style, well larded with quotations, that is customary in the communications of the intellectual élite—that is, she had been well versed in it up to the time of her second marriage. But in the course of her life with Honest Ch'üan, a small businessman without culture or education, she had grown very rusty. Consequently she wrote her present letter in a simple style close to the language of everyday life. This unadorned style had the advantage of being intelligible; it distinguished her letter, to its advantage, from the usual bluestocking product which reads more like an essay than a letter and is so involved that the receiver cannot make head or tail of it. Aroma's letter ran:

To her beloved, known as Wei-yang sheng, the "Before Midnight Scholar," with a request for favorable attention:

Since you have stopped coming to see me, I have lost all desire to eat or drink, I can hardly choke down the slightest mouthful and when from time to time I do force myself to take some food, it is never more than a third of the usual portion. I feel that my entrails have shrunk to less than half their normal size and my face has become so dreadfully emaciated that I scarcely look like a human being. You can hardly imagine the state I am in. Now I have made a decision. I am prepared to belong to you for life. Now you too must think up a plan and do something that will bring us together as quickly as possible. It makes little difference whether you enlist the services of your friend, K'un-lun's Rival, and let him abduct me or whether I, following the example of a Hung-fu or a Wen-chün, run off on my own hook. But first we must decide at what time the abduction or flight is to take place and in the latter case, where I should wait for you. For I should not like us to miss one another. Please, please, bear all this in mind.

If you should hesitate for any reason at all or if you

cannot summon up the courage for such an undertaking —I admit that it involves danger—please write me to that effect. Then in my opinion you will be a heartless, ungrateful wretch, and I won't have anything more to do with you. If I should happen to meet you anywhere —you may as well be prepared for it—my sharp teeth will sink themselves into your faithless flesh as if it were pork.

I shall dispense with the usual oaths of fidelity unto death. Such protestations are usually mere phrases employed by faithless females to pull the wool over their men's eyes. That is all I have to say to you.

Saluting you with arms joined and upraised,
Your dishonored mistress,
Yen-fang.

She folded the letter, sealed it with strips of red sticking paper, and hid it in her sleeve. Then she took up her position in the covered gateway and waited until she saw K'un-lun's Rival passing by. She beckoned him to come close and secretly slipped him the letter.

And that is not all she did. She resolved to win her own freedom in case her lover should take fright and fail her. The tactic she hit on was to make life utterly miserable for her husband. All day long she plagued him with reproaches and complaints about one thing and another; on the slightest pretext she would make an intolerable display of righteous indignation. Or she would pretend to be sick and spend the whole day in bed, saddling him with all the cooking and cleaning. Even when he brought her her meals in bed, she found fault with everything; the rice was underdone, the meat was tough. She stopped helping in the shop, she didn't touch a single cocoon or spin a single thread. The sulking and scolding went on from morning till night. When it was finally time to go to bed, she went right on with her program of wearing him down—though in a different way. She multiplied her wifely demands ten-fold; mercilessly she let him thrash and heave until he gave up the struggle in utter exhaustion. But no sooner had he fallen into a well-deserved sleep than she ruthlessly woke him up again and sent him to the kitchen to make tea or brew some medicinal potion. With such tactics she thought she would send him to the Land of the Yellow Springs before his time, just as she had done with her first husband, the shortlived academic weakling.

Let the old fellow die—who cared!—then she would be free to marry again, and next time she would find a husband who lived up to her ideal.

These coldly calculated tactics were not long in bearing fruit. Intimidated by the peevishness and ill humor to which she subjected him all day long, the simple soul had felt at first that he must be to blame. He resolved to compensate for his imaginary offenses by worthy accomplishment in bed at night. But contrary to his hopes, his most frantic exertions failed to improve her disposition. The moment she stepped out of bed in the morning, she displayed so peevish and sullen a countenance that he was terror-stricken before she had even opened her mouth. Small wonder that after barely two months of such treatment, this man formerly so robust, a match for any she-wolf or tiger cat, was transformed into a withered, emaciated picture of misery whose last hour could hardly be far off.

His neighbors, as we may well imagine, were alarmed at the change in his appearance. But for fear of the dreaded K'un-lun's Rival, no one dared open his mouth even to express friendly sympathy. Until one day he confided in them of his own accord. A light had glimmered in his straw-stuffed skull: there must be some special reason, unrelated to his person, for the strange change in the disposition of this woman who had formerly been gentleness personified.

"Have the esteemed gentlemen observed anything suspicious in my house during my absence?" he inquired. "Has a strange man been seen going in and out?"

At first they were unwilling to speak and pretended to know nothing. But then they took pity on him; it was just too heartbreaking to see this decent, good-natured fellow wasting away under his wife's ferocious, seemingly insatiable appetite. There was no doubt that he would soon breathe his last unless something were done. At last they resolved to speak:

"Actually we have noticed something. During your absence a certain someone did go in and out of your house with suspicious frequency, a certain customer of yours— a very particular customer, yes, a dangerous customer, not the kind of man it's wholesome to meddle with. You know the old saying:

It is not hard to take cover against spears
In open combat,
But to guard against arrows shot secretly in the dark,
That is a different matter.

In short: to cross such a man would accomplish nothing and would involve incalculable dangers."

"Speak up, man, who is this mysterious bugbear?"

"Well, if you must know, it is none other than the notorious bandit, the terror of all honest citizens, the man whose felonious deeds, bordering on the miraculous, are the talk of the town and of other towns as well—it is K'un-lun's Rival.

"One day, some months ago, he came strolling past your house and chanced to catch sight of your esteemed spouse. Apparently she found favor in his eyes, for afterward he sought us out and asked us all manner of questions, among others whether and to whom she was married. We replied truthfully that she was your *ling-chung*, your 'commanding legitimate wife,' whereupon he remarked that such a one as she was not suited to such a one as you, that it would not surprise him to hear that you quarreled from morning to night and then some, whereupon we informed him that the exact opposite was true, that your married life was perfectly peaceful and harmonious. When you left for your recent business trip, he came again and inquired how long you were expected to stay away. We told him you would not be back for ten days. After that we heard suspicious sounds in your house every single night, doors creaking and closing, steps and voices; one of the voices was definitely that of a man; it sounded as though your wife were entertaining a visitor. If the visitor had been someone else, we should certainly have gone to the bottom of the matter. We should have listened and spied. But as it is—well, you know that it is not wholesome to court trouble with the mighty T'ai-sui, Star of the 'Great Year,'* to break ground and build a house when he is overhead, that is, to annoy him. Moreover, our laws do not say that citizens are supposed to investigate cases of adultery in the neighborhood. Accordingly, we did not greatly trouble our heads over what was going on in your house. We let him go about his business, and that is just what he did every single night until your return. But we are telling you all this in confidence, mind you. Lock our words carefully in your heart. We should not like you to take any action, now or later, against this certain someone; you would get us all into a peck of trouble. And don't let your wife know that you suspect anything; just play the fool. Otherwise she might write the certain someone a letter and warn him. He would avenge himself on us, and we should tremble not only for our possessions but for our very lives."

"So that is how the land lies," said Honest Ch'üan. "K'un-lun's Rival! I thought he was just a good customer. So that is why he honored my shop so frequently. Very well, I thank you for your kindness in setting me straight; without it I should never have caught on. Of course I shall hold my tongue and not tell anyone where my information comes from. But one day I shall call that certain someone to account and he will pay with his head. When

---

* The planet Jupiter, period twelve years.

that happens, may I count on the esteemed gentlemen to lend me their wholehearted support?"

"No, that would be a big mistake," the neighbors protested vehemently. "You have no proofs. Think of the old saying:

> *If you wish to convict a thief,*
> *You must catch him with the goods.*
> *If you wish to charge a cockscomb with adultery,*
> *You must catch the two of them in bed.*

Heaven knows how long K'un-lun's Rival has been carrying on the burglar's trade, and no one has ever caught him with the goods. Do you think a man of his talents will let himself be caught climbing into other men's beds? Don't take it amiss if we speak frankly: your legitimate spouse is simply not suited to you, one day she is sure to run off with him. Since you are bound to lose her in any case, you must try at least to defray the expense of her trousseau."

"What do you mean by that?"

"Don't be so thickheaded. You have certainly heard what fiendish tricks the certain someone is capable of. For him no wall is too high or thick. To sneak into your humble dwelling is no problem for him at all. He will come again, you can count on that. And what guarantee have you that he will content himself with your wife and not take along a part of your possessions for the trousseau? He will steal them both: your wife and your money. And it's a sure thing that you will not be able to stop him."

At last the honest silk dealer saw what was what. He was scared almost out of his wits. Utterly bewildered, he fell down on his knees and begged the neighbors for advice. Sincerely sorry for him, they were eager to help. After puffing at their pipes and racking their brains for a time, they circumspectly stated their opinions, which were divided. Some advised divorce: that would be to pluck out the evil at the root. Others advised him to move to some remote region, where his wife would be safe from the certain someone's pursuits. While Honest Ch'üan was still hesitating, the oldest among those present, a gray-haired man of mature experience, spoke up:

"These are idle counsels. Divorce? On what grounds? There is no proof of adultery. Move away? Do you suppose that the certain someone, who knows every highway and byway in the land, would not find you out wherever you went? In my humble opinion there is only one thing for you to do: hush the whole matter up. Play the fool. That is the only way of averting a catastrophe. Furthermore: since your legitimate spouse is estranged from you, you will gain nothing by keeping her in your house. The best thing you can do is to sell her. In that way you will make a bit of money and extricate yourself from the affair without loss. There would be no point in selling her just to anyone at all. The certain someone would soon get wind of it and be very angry with you for disturbing him in his pleasures and cutting him off from his paramour. No, the only solution is to sell her to the certain someone himself. A successful bandit like him always has plenty of money. To him it will mean nothing to cough up a hundred or even two hundred silver pieces for a woman he loves. Then you will easily be able to get a new wife, better suited to you than the present one. In this way you will avoid all unpleasantness and acquire a new wife free of charge. Well, what do you think of my idea?"

"Marvelous. That is just what I will do. But there is still another point: I myself cannot carry on the negotiations with the certain someone. I need a middleman. Which of the esteemed gentlemen would be willing to intercede for me?"

"Oh, if that is all that's worrying you! We are all willing. True, we must be assured that afterward, when the affair is all settled, you will not regret it and accuse us unjustly of conspiring with the certain someone, of helping him to filch your present wife."

"Far be it from me to do anything of the kind," Honest Ch'üan protested. "That would be rank ingratitude when I have only the esteemed gentlemen to thank if I get off safely with my life and money."

"Very well, we trust you," the grayhead replied. "We know your honesty. Now let us decide who is to be the middleman."

The matter was discussed for a while and at length a man known for his ready tongue was chosen. It was decided that he should go to see K'un-lun's Rival the very next day and open negotiations.

Meanwhile our young man was consumed with yearning for his beloved Aroma. His state of mind was exactly the same as hers. He had lost his appetite and sleep had forsaken him. He felt empty, as though hollowed out and dead. I cannot go on like this, he said to himself, something must be done. Was it for nothing that he had a friend who was in league with all the spirits, both good and bad?

He was just dressing to go to see him when K'un-lun's Rival turned up as though summoned, bringing Aroma's letter. The young man read, and his flagging energy revived.

"You've got to do something," he pleaded. "You must help me to see her again. Otherwise I am done for." And he read the letter aloud.

"Hm. In that case," said K'un-lun's Rival after brief reflection, "there is only one solution: abduction. That would be child's play for me, but then what? That is the question. You would not be able to stay in this town, you would have trouble with the husband. No, you would have to move far away, to some place where he would be unable to find you, and set up a secret love nest. An attractive idea, not bad as a long-term plan. But do you really wish to carry it out? That calls for reflection. You must make up your mind."

The young man had to think a while. Actually several of his heartstrings were still fastened to this place. There was unfinished business to be attended to, three pieces of it to be exact, namely the three beauties he had met at the temple of the love god and put down in his diary as "outstanding." He could not forget them. The parcel of earth where they lived was dear to him; to tear himself away from it so suddenly would be very hard for him. On the other hand, his dear Aroma's letter had stirred him deeply. Could he leave her urgent cry unanswered? Impossible. His decision was made.

"Very well, I am prepared to go off somewhere where our traces will be lost, where the husband will be unable to pursue us."

"Good. But there is something else to be considered. The abduction of a legitimate wife is a wrong and weighs more heavily in the balance than the theft of money and property. For money and property can be replaced; if you lose them today, you can win them back tomorrow. A wife is not so easily replaced. Imagine how a husband must feel when one fine day his dear little wife is stolen away from him. Besides, Honest Ch'üan is not exactly wealthy. Where will he find the money to buy another? It is a universal human truth that your little man, under extreme provocation, will not shrink from murder. For the sake of your own safety, you must find a way of making the affair acceptable—or reasonably so—to Honest Ch'üan. The only way to do that is for me to leave a small indemnity, a hundred and twenty silver pieces let us say, in his house for him when I abduct his wife. Then the abduction will lose its sting and seem more like a friendly business deal. Of course you will still have a wrong on your conscience, but otherwise you will have nothing to fear. As for me, my bandit's honor will remain unsullied."

"The plan has much, in fact everything, to be said for it. Unfortunately it is impracticable because . . . well, you must realize that my treasury is just about exhausted. How am I to raise the money so quickly? And as for taking advantage of my good friend, no. I should not be able to sleep at night."

"If that is all that's worrying you! Money comes to me as easily as it slips away. That is the nature of my trade. Don't trouble your head about the money, I will supply it. As for you, just sit down and write your Aroma an answer. Tell her to state a day, any day will do, when her husband will be away from home. That day I will abduct her."

With a sigh of relief the young man set to work. He crushed an ink stick and mixed it with water on the ink stone, dipped his brush, and set it racing impetuously over the paper. His letter ran:

To Yen-fang, beloved mistress of my heart, begging a favorable reception:

Two months have passed since our separation and they seem like ten long years. I too feel as though my throat were laced tight. I can hardly get down a swallow of food or drink and at night my perpetual thoughts of you keep me awake. Day after day I have pleaded with my friend to do something for us. He hesitated up to now, for he did not know what your feelings were and did not wish to take any unconsidered action.

I have just received your letter. Now I know how faithfully you love me, I know that your determination to follow me is as hard as iron and as firm as rock. Rest assured that I am of like mind. From now on, nothing will part us.

Leave everything to me. The entire responsibility is mine. You intimate in your letter that you are thinking of emulating those two heroines of ancient times, Hung-fu and Wen-chün, of running away on your own. Please drop that project, it would be dangerous. Instead, we shall take another model from antiquity. You surely know the story of the beautiful Hung-shao, "Red Sheath," which took place during the reign-period Ta-li (766–780), under the T'ang dynasty.

She was languishing like a prisoner behind high walls in the castle of an aged potentate. One night her lover had her abducted, despite all obstacles, by a devoted henchman, a Moorish slave (K'un-lun-nu). That is exactly what we shall do: one night my friend will abduct you. It is not for nothing that he was named after the famous Moor of the T'ang period. Have no fear, he will carry it off. In regard to the happy moment when your abduction will take place, I can make no prediction. That depends on when your grim guardian is away from home. That is something you must let me know at once. We shall take action that very same night.

You threaten, in case I should be faithless and cowardly, to sink your sharp teeth into my flesh as though it were juicy roast pork. Oh, you will have no need to exert your precious little mouth—if such were the case, I myself should see to it that my faithless carcass were devoured by dogs and ravens.

I have nothing more to add.

This is my answer, anonymous for reasons of caution.

In the very same hour K'un-lun's Rival brought Aroma the letter. And then he waited. He prepared a little package of a hundred twenty silver pieces to leave on Ch'üan's table as an indemnity when the time came. Days passed, and still he was waiting for Aroma's message saying the coast was clear. But no message came. Instead came Honest Ch'üan's neighbor, the spokesman and intermediary in matters connected with marriage.

After the usual introductory flourishes, he divulged his proposition:

"Honest Ch'üan's business is doing poorly. His income is not sufficient for the upkeep of a wife. Consequently he would like to sell his legitimate spouse and has chosen me as his middleman. My first thought was of you. Others lack the money, or if they have enough money they are too petty and niggardly to provide her sort of woman with the life to which her qualities entitle her. You, on the other hand, are a man of stature, famous for your generosity and magnanimity as a protector of the poor. That is why I have come to you in the hope of persuading you to add one more good deed to the many you have secretly performed in the past.

"In the first place you would be saving a splendid young woman from her present misery and from the dismal prospect of starving to death. For another, your purchase money would help Honest Ch'üan in his dire need and enable him to keep up his business and fill his daily rice bowl. You would be doing two good deeds in one."

The middleman's speech had aroused the bandit's suspicions. "Strange, very strange," he thought to himself. "I was just about to abduct Honest Ch'üan's wife, and he sends this man to offer her for sale. It almost looks as though he had got wind of my plan and had thought up this offer as a way out of the trap. Be that as it may, his offer is welcome. What was to be a secret deal becomes open and above board. The abduction will be unnecessary. What better can I wish for?"

He turned to the intermediary:

"What is Honest Ch'üan's real reason for wishing to sell his wife?"

"Poverty. Nothing else."

"And what about her? Does she consent to the sale?"

"I should say so. With her present husband she would be doomed to starvation."

"Very well. What is his asking price?"

"He spoke at first of two hundred silver pieces. But I talked him out of it. He was being too greedy. He will be satisfied with a little more than half of that."

"Very well. I offer one hundred and twenty."

"Done."

K'un-lun's Rival gave the middleman the package of a hundred and twenty silver pieces that he had intended to pay as an indemnity. The middleman went his way, sent

K'un-lun's Rival surprised his young friend with the finished love nest.

for Honest Ch'üan, and gave him the package with the purchase money.

With that the deal was concluded.

At first K'un-lun's Rival had toyed with the idea of naming his friend, the Before Midnight Scholar, as the real purchaser. But he decided against it, for he told himself that if he, the noble and widely feared bandit, whose name everyone respected, put himself down as the purchaser, there would be no danger of an unpleasant epilogue, Honest Ch'üan would be very careful not to stir up trouble later. Not so if the young man came out openly as the purchaser. The Moor in the woodpile would probably be discovered and the end result might well be a very disagreeable trial for adultery.

Accordingly K'un-lun's Rival represented himself as the purchaser. Made out in his name, the sale and marriage contract (for supposedly he was taking Aroma as his collateral wife) was signed by Honest Ch'üan and witnessed by several of the neighbors. With his usual generosity the noble bandit gave the neighbors an additional sum of ten silver pieces for their time and services. A week later, without the usual waste of time involved in the search for a favorable day of the calendar, he called for Aroma in a rented two-man litter. First he took her to his own home, where he lodged her for the time being. Then he found the young couple a dwelling in another neighborhood and furnished it—all at his own expense. When he escorted Aroma to her new home, she even found a charming young servant girl on hand, whom he, with touching solicitude, had engaged for her. Only then did he inform his friend of the developments and surprise him with the finished love nest.

Thus a common bandit proved to be a true friend, one of nature's noblemen, worthy of the most august models of antiquity.

If you wish to know how the story continues, you will have to read the next chapter.

CHAPTER XI

She refuses to grant him the joys of her bed until he honors her with the kowtow that she felt to be long overdue. All vinegar at first, she ends by coupling him with her bosom friends.

After two months of unclouded felicity in their new home, Aroma informed her lover that her womb had been blessed. He was overjoyed. Apparently the itinerant surgeon had been mistaken in predicting that the operation would frustrate his hope of offspring.

Some months later her body began to fill out and she felt seriously hampered during his embraces. She could no longer· take part as actively as she would have liked.

The situation was now very different from what it had been in the first ten nights of their secret dealings, when they had started with fright at the first cock crow, when, cruelly parted from his mistress, he had crept away like a thief in the early dawn, tormented in his conscience and trembling for fear of being discovered. Now a hundred cocks could crow without frightening them; they were free to savor their love at their ease whenever the desire came over them. Spoiled as he was, it came as quite a blow to him when one day she announced that she needed a respite.

"We shall have to stop for a time. My health requires it, and as for you, it can hardly hurt you to rest a while and gather new strength. Let us be patient until after the baby is born."

From that time on they slept separately. He transferred

his sleeping quarters to his study which was separated from her boudoir by two inner courts.

There he sat in frosty loneliness as formerly in his temple cell. Accustomed as he was to a woman's warmth and merry twittering, how was he to endure the crushing stillness that suddenly enveloped him? He felt as though he had been removed to the polar regions. He shivered and quaked. Small wonder that his brain began to work, that he began to consider the possibility of a substitute for the pleasures that were denied him.

At the time of his first longings for Aroma, he had supposed that if he could only win this one he would content himself with her for the rest of his days and desire no others. But no sooner had he taken possession of her than the thought began to germinate within him that it would be really wonderful to have another woman in the same class with Aroma, and that then and only then would his happiness be complete.

Moreover, he reflected, this arrangement would fall in with his future position as a high official and dignitary. An ancient model came to mind. Had not the legendary Emperor Yao married Shun, whom he had chosen as his successor, to his two daughters Nü-ying and O-huang, in order to put him to the test? For if a man can handle two wives at once and carry on a peaceful and harmonious life with them, he surely has it in him to rule a whole nation with all its many conflicts and contradictions. Such had been the wise calculation of wise Emperor Yao.

And once he, the Before Midnight Scholar, had passed his final examination, would the Throne not entrust him with some populous province to govern and rule over as representative of the Son of Heaven, as an emperor on a small scale?

Thus he had long since conceived the idea of a double marriage. Even in the period of his bedtime joys with Aroma, it had lain latent beneath the surface, though she amply met his amorous requirements. Now that her companionship was denied him and he was sorely in need of a woman, the hidden spark blazed into a wild imperious flame.

What he had hitherto kept putting off till later now became a pressing need. All at once he remembered his temple diary that lay buried, long forgotten, in his trunk, and he recalled those three most glorious creatures of all, whom he had listed as "outstanding." If only he knew where to find them! But in his confusion he had neglected to send his servants after their litters to find out where they lived.

Address unknown—what a shame! The two younger ones along with Aroma. What a wonderful trivet that would have been! In its pan the threefold flame of amorous pleasure would have crackled merrily heavenward, eternal and inextinguishable. What a pity!

In his thoughts he went through the list of the beauties he had noted as worthy of consideration, and stopped at the group classified as "very good." Why should these not help him weather the present emergency? He would track down the three most glorious of all later on. His decision was made.

Barring the doors to his cell, he dug out his diary and leafed through it secretly, behind Aroma's back. He found the name: Hsiang-yün, "Scent Cloud." And then he read the lines in which he had characterized her.

His commentary on Scent Cloud was longer and more detailed than the other commentaries devoted to those of her class, and her qualities were underscored with a heavier line.

In speaking of the others—with the exception of course of the three extraordinary beauties—he had always found certain faults. Praise had been mingled with blame. In regard to Scent Cloud he had had scarcely anything to find fault with; she came immediately after the three outstanding beauties.

The commentary ran:

"Her outward appearance shows certain unusual advantages. Her posture and movements reveal an easy grace. She walks as though gliding. So delicate is she one has the impression that one might lift her in the palm of one's hand. Her eyes, her expression are worthy to be immortalized by an artist's hand. But her most special quality is the fragrance that emanates from her person and envelops her like a cloud. Her body seems to be saturated with the scent of some rare flowers. Her speech—ah, that melodious intonation!—resembles the sweet sobbing of a nightingale or the delicate far-off notes of a reed mouth organ. In an orchestra of common brasses and woodwinds she is a hand gong of noble bronze, an ornament among ornaments, worthy of a high place in the contest for the crown of beauty."

He tried to recall her face, her appearance. He guessed her to be in her middle twenties. And yes, indeed, what had impressed him most was the special scent that had tickled his olfactory membranes as she glided past him. It was not the ordinary smell of some perfume that fashionable ladies carry in a perfume bag on their belt or in their sleeve pocket, but something very different.

Again his memory carried him back to the incident. After she had gone, he had picked up something which she —intentionally or not—had dropped. Yes, it was a fan.

He had found it to one side of the altar where she had knelt and made her burnt offering. He had picked it up and put it away among his many souvenirs and keepsakes. There was a poem by Li T'ai-po inscribed on the fan. Obviously she had written it with her own hand. Where could she live?

He looked back at his diary. Under his commentary on Scent Cloud he found the name of the street where she lived written in small letters. He smacked his thighs. Why, that was the street where he himself was now living! A short street with only a few dozen houses on it; it was safe to assume that she did not live miles away. It would not be hard to find her house.

He went out at once and made inquiries in the neighborhood. And—who would have expected heaven and earth and all the spirits good and bad to bless his sinful undertaking and make things so easy for him?—it turned out that she lived right next door and that her boudoir was separated from his study only by a partition wall.

In the course of his inquiries he learned still more; Scent Cloud's husband was a man in his fifties by the name of Hsien-hsien-tzu; recently, after the death of his first wife, he had taken her as a second string to his marriage bow. He was a well-to-do academician, a doctor of the first degree, but had never attained office, for though highly educated and greatly respected in academic circles, he was an impractical sort, averse to all official activity; his chief and preferred occupation was preparing young candidates for the state examinations. He took this activity very seriously and accordingly made his headquarters at the institute where he taught. He returned home only once a month and then never devoted more than one or two nights to his new young wife.

Could one have conceived of circumstances more favorable to our scholar's designs? He rubbed his hands.

"Providence would seem to have intended us for one another," he rejoiced inwardly. "I have no doubt been guided to this street by good spirits who wished me to console this unfortunate young woman in her loneliness."

The next problem was: how to get in touch with her? For a time he strode back and forth in his cell, deep in thought. Then he stopped still and examined the wall dividing his study from the adjoining property.

Like most partition walls, it was too high to climb and too thick to pierce. For a moment he had toyed with the idea of boring a hole through the wall but soon discarded it as absurd. He would have had to attack the brickwork with hammer and chisel, and the noise—the pounding of the hammer, the scraping of the chisel, not to mention the thud of the mortar and debris falling down on the other side—would be sure to alarm the neighbors and set them crying for help. They would suppose that a burglar was trying to break in. No, that would not do.

Once again he examined the wall, and at last found what he had been looking for—a weak spot. The top of the wall was very close to the side of the house. At this point there was a patch in the house wall, some three feet high and five feet wide, which was not made of brick like the rest of the construction, but of wooden planks—apparently the mason had run out of bricks. Our scholar decided at once to remove a few of the interlocking planks. He would be able to do so without making much noise. Then there would be little difficulty in entering the house or at least in communicating with his fair neighbor through the hole.

The first thing he did was to get a ladder and lean it against the wall. Then he went for his tool box. He had never before found any use for this tool box though he had been keeping it in his bookcase for a long time. One day while idling about the shops he had purchased the pretty cardboard box and taken it home, more as a curiosity than for any practical purpose. It contained ten different implements, including a hammer, pliers, a saw, a file, and a short crowbar. The sign over it in the shop had read: "Chest of the ten useful utensils."

Who would have supposed that these long forgotten tools would come in so handy one day! One is reminded of the wise Confucius' saying:

Nothing is useless in this world
Nothing is so trifling as to deserve your contempt.

With his tool box under his arm, he climbed the ladder and examined the planking close at hand. The planks themselves were good and solid, but he was pleasantly surprised to find that they were neither glued together nor fastened with the usual "dog tooth" brackets; they had merely been put in place horizontally, one on top of the other.

That simplified his work considerably, especially as one of the joints was not exactly tight. He inserted his file in the gap and worked at it until he had a space two inches long and wide enough for the crowbar. A bit of pressure sufficed to loosen the first plank, which he removed and laid down beside him on top of the partition wall. The second and third planks gave him no trouble at all. He was able to loosen them and lift them out with his bare hands.

That was that. He had made a hole large enough to poke his head through and look into one of the rooms.

Always methodical, he saw that his next step must be to get rid of the loose planks and the tool box. Otherwise they might topple down with a great clatter and betray his presence.

As silently as possible, he climbed down the ladder with his burden and then, no longer encumbered, sprang nimbly up again. Having sighted new land on the other side of the wall, he was in the utmost haste to begin his explorations.

He had nearly reached the top when he heard a faint sound through the opening in the wall and stopped still. Soft steps, then a rustling of silk skirts. He climbed up to the last rung and peered cautiously through the opening.

He had no sooner thrust his head through the hole than he discovered to his amazement that the room below it was a certain secret closet, no doubt adjoining his neighbor's boudoir. And there—what a delightful surprise—he saw her very own self.

She was sitting with her back turned to him on the *ma-t'ung*, the "horse bucket." He held his breath—she was doing the "lesser convenience." When she had finished, she stooped down to pick up the lid that was lying on the floor.

As she stood there thus bowed—her skirts caught up over her waist—she offered the secret observer a charming view; looking between her well-rounded moon hills, he beheld the lovely landscape of her hidden vale of pleasure. Ah, what a rare and happy moment!

But was it really she? Was it Scent Cloud? Thus far he had only seen her from the rear. He waited while she drew up her panties, tied the string, and let down her skirts. At last she turned sideways toward the window. It was she! Scent Cloud! He found her even more bewitching than when he had first seen her in the temple of the love god. He would have liked to call out some tender salutation. But two considerations deterred him from calling attention to himself now: first, the fear that other ears might overhear him; second, fear of frightening the lady herself. He was in the shadow of the overhanging roof, while she was in the bright light of a nearby window. Thus she would not be able to make out his features and recognize him, perhaps she would mistake him for a burglar and start to scream. No, he must find another, subtler way of making himself noticed. Quickly he withdrew his head and hastened down the ladder. He had an idea—the fan!

He had carefully put it away in a little trunk with many other souvenirs. The trunk bore the inscription: *Men-yen chih-yi*, "Tender mementos of lovely ladies." He had taken the four words literally from the *Shih-ching*, the "Book of Songs." The passage was in the first section entitled *Kuo-feng*, "Songs of the States." His idea was that these souvenirs would come in handy as means of pressure. For they were pledges of love, and in face of such a pledge what fair lady would be able to deny his wishes?

Quickly he fished out the fan and examined it. Three poems by Li T'ai-po (705–768), the great poet of the T'ang period, were inscribed on it in delicate little characters, assuredly by her own hand. He said to himself that if he were to recite one of these poems in a loud voice, she would be bound to hear him. Spurred by curiosity, she would show herself at the hole in the wall, and once he had lured her to the spot, once she had caught sight of him, he felt certain that everything would be all right: he would not have to fight his way up the ladder to besiege the fortress; on the contrary, she would smile down upon him. When the time came, he would not be at a loss for a few words of gallantry. His eloquence would hold her fast. This was his sly calculation.

The three poems had to do with the romantic incident with which began the disastrous political influence of the celebrated beauty T'ang Yu-huan (d. 756). Until then she had been the mere mistress of the eighteenth prince, and then one day the emperor himself (Hsüan-tsung, 713–756) presented her with an entire garden of sumptuous peonies— the peony was then looked upon as queen among the flowers. This flowery allusion was an invitation to move into his own harem. Shortly thereafter he honored her with the title Kuei-fei, "Precious Concubine," and made her his favorite.

Our young man read the three poems and a shudder of awe ran through him. Was he to declaim this sublime product of the highest poetic art, this masterpiece from the brush of the great Li T'ai-po, in his disordered every-day dress, without form or ceremony? No, that would never do. That would be sacrilege. What he had in mind was a solemn, ceremonious act requiring a worthy exterior and inner composure. Accordingly, he washed, changed his ordinary old cap and worn housecoat of cheap cotton for a handsome new cap and festive garment of sumptuous crackling silk. Then he lit a stick of fragrant aloes wood in a bronze censer and sat for a while in silent contemplation before the wisp of bluish smoke that rose from the spout.

Finally he gargled and rinsed his throat with fresh water, just as a mime or opera singer does before appearing on the stage.

After thus making himself outwardly and inwardly worthy, he turned toward the hole in the wall and began to declaim the first of the fan poems. He pronounced the words as distinctly as possible and exerted his vocal cords to the utmost.

A first breath of spring caresses
The balustrade all covered with hoarfrost . . .

And in a chanting tone he recited the whole twelve-line stanza. Then he paused for effect. Was she inclining an ear to listen? Would she show herself? But nothing stirred. He decided on a repeat performance. Louder and louder he intoned the same text, not just once or twice, no, he recited it ten times without stopping.

Then he paused again, pointed his ears and peered up. Still there was utter silence and nothing to be seen. He would have to make himself still plainer. He resorted to a trick. In the manner of an impresario or announcer who interrupts a concert right in the middle in order to introduce the diva to the esteemed public, he broke off in the middle of his recitation to weave his fair neighbor's name into the poet's text. He even went so far as to state where and on what day and hour she had dropped her fan. His trick was quite successful.

Suddenly he heard a faint sound from the cleft in the wall. A sigh, one might have thought, or a slight cough. He pretended not to hear, looked down at the fan in his hand, and addressed it in tones of anguish: "What good does it do me to possess you if your mistress is far away? Where can she be? Why doesn't she show herself? Well, I am good and sick of it—you are nothing but a useless bauble and if ever I meet her again, I'll just give you back to her . . ."

At this point in his monologue he was interrupted by a call from across the wall:

"You're quite mistaken. The mistress is right here. There is absolutely nothing to grieve about. And now will you please return my fan. Just toss it over."

Affecting surprise, he looked up from the fan toward the gap in the wall. There he beheld, like a picture in a frame, a dark cloud coiffure, a peachlike face, a gently rounded bosom—the rest of her was hidden by the wall. Well, it was high time!

"Oh what a wonderful surprise! To behold the most glorious of women so close at hand. Really," he cried out in his most pathetic tone, "I was half dead with grief." Nimbly he mounted the ladder, straddled the wall and slid along it until he reached the hole in the side of the house. Unceremoniously he thrust his head and shoulders through the narrow frame, clasped the living picture in his arms, and hugged her and kissed her impetuously. There ensued a long and passionate kiss; their tongues mingled and intertwined as though they wished never to part. Finally he bestirred himself and squeezed back through the opening. He was utterly out of breath. Small wonder, after so much emotion in so strained and uncomfortable a position. In that position a sensible conversation would hardly have been possible, and obviously a conversation was necessary at this point. She left him time to catch his breath and then it was she who opened the interview:

"You good-for-nothing, where have you been all this time? Why have you neglected me so long? And why, just today, have you suddenly remembered my fan and the poem on it?"

"I live next door. We are neighbors. Didn't you know?"

"Neighbors? Since when? Last I heard there were other people next door."

"I just moved in."

"Where did you live before? Why have you moved here?"

Wishing to flatter her, he saw fit to strain the truth a little.

"I moved on your account. I wanted to be near you. Ever since I saw your lovely face in the temple of the bow-stringer god—do you remember?—I have had thoughts only for you. Encouraged when you left the fan for me—or did you not intend it for me as a tender memento?—I racked my brains for a way of approaching you. And then at last I heard of a vacancy here next door. So I moved in."

Her whole face beaming, Scent Cloud tapped him affectionately on the shoulder.

"Then you do love me? And I thought—you know, I came very close to misunderstanding, I was almost very angry with you!—Tell me, is there anyone else living with you?"

"Oh, only a little girl friend. A friend made me a present of her. Otherwise, aside from my two servants and my girl friend's maid, there is no one but me. I didn't take the rest of the family with me on my travels. I left them home."

"Ah, I see. And why didn't you come here long ago? Why did you let me strain my eyes looking for you, for heaven knows how long?"

"I didn't know where you lived. I found out only recently. And then I moved here at once."

"Oh. I see. And how long ago was that?"

"Not long. Maybe five months. No more."

Suddenly there was a change in Scent Cloud's expression. After a pause for reflection she replied angrily:

"Five whole months! And what, may I ask, prevented you from troubling your head about me all this time? And why have you suddenly decided to strike a flame in the cold ashes of your love?"

Her tone boded no good. So she had detected something fishy about his story. Embarrassment was written all over his face. Desperately he cast about for an explanation.

"I thought . . . yes, I thought your esteemed husband was at home. I didn't wish to do anything that might attract attention to myself. But that was entirely on your account, do you see? I didn't wish any premature move of mine to put you in an embarrassing situation. The consequence is that I've been waiting patiently all these months. It has been very hard for me, you can take my word for it. It was only today that I chanced to learn that your esteemed husband was not home but at his institute. That is why I didn't dare to call myself to your attention any sooner. But you mustn't suppose for one moment that I had forgotten you, that the flame of my affections had burned down to cold ashes as you put it a moment ago—very unjustly I assure you."

Scent Cloud sat for a time in thoughtful silence. A frosty smile played round the corners of her mouth.

"I imagine you threw my fan away long ago?"

"Not at all. I've kept it like the apple of my eye. And not only that. I have carried it around with me the whole time. I've never parted with it for as much as ten minutes on end."

"You don't say so. If that is the case, bring it here to me."

Well, he thought, that would not be difficult. Already he rejoiced inwardly. The sight of the fan would dispel her last doubts and put an end to her sulking. She would open her arms to him—so he imagined. But he was imagining too fast.

He slid along the wall to the ladder, climbed swiftly down and as swiftly up again, triumphantly brandishing the fan wrapped in a green silk handkerchief.

And then something unexpected happened. Without a word, without the slightest break in the storm clouds of her countenance, she tore the fan from his hand, broke it into three pieces and flung it on the ground behind her. As for the handkerchief, she tossed it contemptuously back at him.

"Faithless scoundrel!" she fumed. "It's a good thing I haven't had any intimate dealings with you yet. All is over between us. Begone!" And she disappeared indoors.

In vain he called after her. The only answer from within was a convulsive sobbing. What could have got into her? Deep in thought, he slid along the wall to the ladder. Indeed it was high time for him to be going. From the garden which lay between him and Aroma's part of the house he could hear suspicious rustling sounds—someone moving about among the banana fronds. Could it be Aroma? What would she think if she caught him on his strange excursion to the upper regions?

He slid down the ladder and disappeared into his cell.

There he strode back and forth for a time, deep in thought. What could be the matter with her? Why was she playing the offended woman? He had said nothing to ruffle her feelings. Could it really be his neglect that had upset her so? There seemed to be no other possible explanation. Come to think of it, he had been shamefully inattentive. But that sort of offense is easily repaired. Oho, he would pay his debt with interest. What was the old saying?

> *If the heart is in the banquet,*
> *Small matter if the fare be hot or cold.*

After all, she must have felt that he was prepared to lay his whole heart at her feet. Why then all the excitement? Could there be something more behind it? It would almost seem so. Well, he would see. The first thing to do was to repent and make proper amends—she had made that clear enough.

He would best have liked to start his course of penance at once. But it seemed rather risky to go climbing around on walls in broad daylight under Aroma's very nose. Accordingly he checked his impatience and postponed his undertaking until nightfall. The few intervening hours dragged out like months. Finally the moment for action had come. First he paid Aroma the usual good-night visit and escorted her to bed. Then he barred all the doors and windows and put out all the lamps and candles. Finally he removed his cap and outer coat.

Then he climbed the ladder and slid across to the hole in the wall. First of all he would have to widen the hole if his whole body was to get through. "I may as well make a good job of it," he decided and removed all the rest of the planking. His path was clear. The space that opened before him had the dimensions of a gate. But now a new difficulty arose. How would he get down into the house? It was too far to jump. Well, he would just have to pull up his ladder behind him and set it down on the other side. Fortunately this proved unnecessary. Thrusting an exploring hand through the opening, he felt a hard object. What a pleasant surprise! She had left her own ladder in place—for his convenience. Then she must be expecting him. Despite her harsh words, he concluded, she must be in a conciliatory mood. Cautiously, but now as easy in his mind as if he were accepting an invitation to tea, he descended the ladder. This crossing of the wall, it seemed to him, was like a gentle stroll across an arched wooden bridge, up a steep hill on one side, down a steep hill on the other. His fears had left him. His adventure had ceased to be dangerous.

On tiptoes he groped his way round the boudoir, looking for his fair neighbor's couch. She lay wrapped in her blanket with her face to the wall. Apparently she was sound asleep, for there wasn't a peep to be heard from her as he approached. Boldly he reached out his hand toward the coverlet, meaning to lift it and slip in underneath. But an instant later he started back in a fright. The supposed sleeper had suddenly turned round and sat up.

She had not been asleep at all. She had heard his steps as he had crossed the wall and tiptoed about the room, but for the sake of convenience, to spare them both the need for a formal greeting, she had pretended to be asleep.

But that the impudent fellow should ignore all social forms to the point of trying to climb straight into bed with her—no, that was too much. It was like bursting into a yamen unannounced, instead of sending in the secretary with a proper petition informing the exalted mandarin of the visitor's name, lineage, profession, and so on. No, that wouldn't do. It was outrageous. Pretending that she had just awakened from a deep sleep, she snarled inhospitably:

"Heigh, who are you? How dare you come in here at this time of night?"

The intruder leaned down close to her ear:

"It is I, my darling," he whispered. "It is I, your neighbor and devoted admirer, with whom you were talking this noon. I have thought things over in the meanwhile and I see how disgracefully I have acted. How could I neglect you so! But now I have come to make amends." And again he tried to raise the coverlet and slip into the warm nest. But her reception was not what he had expected.

"Faithless scoundrel! Who told you to break in here like a thief in the night to make amends. Get out. And make it quick," she fumed, rolling herself up tight in the blanket.

"But darling! How unjust. I did everything in my power to approach you. Do I really deserve to be called faithless?"

"You fraud! You may deceive others with your fine words, but not me. You can't pull the wool over my eyes. I happen to know whom you've been chasing, and one thing is sure, it wasn't an ugly, nasty thing like me. I know all about your beauties. Of course you had no time for me. You were busy with your mistresses. And now all of a sudden you come here to me behind their backs. What for? Seems quite unnecessary to me."

"Mistresses? I don't know what you're talking about— I haven't got anybody except the insignificant little girl friend over there, whom I had to take into my house for propriety's sake, because a good friend gave her to me, as I told you quite frankly today. I can assure you that she is nothing to get vinegary-jealous and excited about."

"I'm not excited about her. And I don't find fault with you for doing your duty by your legal wife—why not, it's perfectly normal. No, it's something very different that burns me up—namely, that you've been making love all this time to certain other ladies of my own class and for-gotten me entirely. I wouldn't complain if we had lived far apart and a rendezvous had been impossible—I'd let it pass. But for the last five months you've been living right on the other side of the wall and in all that time not a single word out of you. It's unforgivable. What do you want of me? Just stick to your other mistresses, that's all I ask of you."

"But dearest, I simply don't understand you. Aside from my legitimate wife and the insignificant little girl friend over there, I have had nothing to do with any other woman.

Other mistresses! What other mistresses? Where did you ever get such an idea!"

"Very well, if you insist, I will be perfectly plain. Is it true that on such and such a day and hour you kowtowed and touched your forehead to the ground at the temple of the bowstringer god for the benefit of three fair ladies who had come to sacrifice and perform their devotions? Just tell me that. Yes or no?"

"Yes, it is true. But my homage was meant for the god, not for the three ladies. I was on my way to the temple to perform my devotions, but I didn't dare to go in because I saw that the space before the altar was occupied by the three ladies. It would have been unseemly of me to mingle with them. Consequently, I remained outside, on the temple steps, performing my devotions at a distance."

Scent Cloud laughed aloud.

"Then you admit it was you. As for the rest of your story, this homage that was supposedly meant for the god, you may be able to palm off such nonsense on other people, but not on me. Why, no intelligent three-year-old would believe it."

He realized that she had seen through him. No amount of denying could help him now. Working with the speed of lightning his mind dictated a three-point program that seemed to be the best way out of his dilemma: 1) a frank confession; 2) a contrite apology; 3) an inquiry about the three unknown beauties who had indeed been the object of all his hopes and yearnings and concerning whom Scent Cloud seemed to be well informed.

With a mischievous smile he confessed: "All right, I admit, my kowtow was addressed to the three beauties— but only half of it, the other half was for the god. But how did you find out about all this? A married woman like you is always at home. Who told you about it?"

"Oh, I don't need anyone to tell me the news—I have a magical eye and a magical ear with a range of a thousand miles."

"Hm. Well, be that as it may, would you be kind enough to tell me, since you are so well informed, the names and addresses of those lovely ladies and whether and to whom they are married."

"What? You are asking me? Here you've been carrying on with them for almost six months and you claim not to know who they are?"

"Come, come. Since I met them that day at the temple, I haven't laid eyes on them. And you say I have been carrying on with them for the last six months? I beg your pardon. I shall have to report you for malicious slander."

"There is no point in denying it. Why otherwise would you have cut me all this time? Your three beauties are at the bottom of it. They persuaded you to give me the cold shoulder. It's perfectly obvious. I know all about it."

"I really can't make you out. What makes you so suspicious? Your suspicions are absolutely groundless, I assure you."

"Really? Can you swear to it?"

"With a clear conscience."

And he lifted his voice in a solemn oath: "Bowing my head in humility and veneration before heaven and earth, I swear that I have never had dealings with those three beauties. If I have done so, let me be accursed, let the lightnings of heaven crush me, let the avenging spirits of hell pursue me and torment me, seize me and nip me and chop me to pieces and grind my bones to powder one by one. Let the same punishment be meted out to me if I so much as know the three fair ladies' names and addresses and have ever strolled up and down making sheep's eyes before the door of their house."

That sounded forthright and sincere. Scent Cloud felt relieved—not wholly perhaps but at least half—of the burden of suspicion that had been weighing so heavily upon her.

There was only one more thing that troubled her: that homage of his.

"Very well. You are forgiven—up to a certain point. But there is still one doubtful matter . . ."

"What? You are still talking of doubt? I thought I had explained everything and cleared myself completely. And now, if you please, be a good girl and let me into the warm nest," he pleaded. The night air was chilly and lightly clad as he was, his teeth were chattering. Desperately his fingers sought a breach in her blanket fortress. Vainly he sought a loose corner to pull out, so opening a passage into the bastion. But still she was adamant.

"I cannot pretend to equal the charms of your three beauties—so what do you want with me? Still your desires with them and leave me alone." Her tone was as sharp as a knife and as cold as ice.

"There you go again with those ridiculous feelings of inferiority of yours. It's maddening. Did I ever say you were less beautiful or desirable than the three others?"

"Then why did you honor them with a humble bow of homage? When you saw me all you did was to make eyes— and not for very long at that. Naturally it's because I'm not half as beautiful. I can't say I blame you. It's as good as I deserve."

"Ah, so that's it. That kowtow. That's what's been eating you. Why, it was just an impulsive notion of mine; it doesn't mean that I am any less devoted to you in my heart. Devotion is devotion, with or without kowtowing. But if that's your trouble, it's easily repaired. I'll pay my debt this minute—and with interest to cover the arrears."

And as nimbly and supplely as his frozen limbs permitted, he doubled up in a kowtow and humped his back and hammered his head not once, twice, or thrice, but twelve times in a row on the wooden floor, and with so much fervor that the ivory bedstead began to tremble and quake. Scent Cloud was filled with pride and at the same time touched.

Now she felt the last bit of doubt and suspicion slip away.

And nimbly and supplely he doubled up in a kowtow and humped his back.

She held out her hand to him beneath the coverlet and graciously drew him into the warm nest.

They were remarkably well suited to one another. His first visit to her pleasure house ran off as smoothly as the passage of a light coach along a familiar, often traveled highway.

By a tacit understanding they spared each other the usual introductory ceremonial and groping love play and took up the main theme at once. He found that the gate and passageways of her pleasure house observed the golden mean between wide and narrow. She found that he might have gone to work a little more gently. But since she was positively itching and burning with desire, she stifled her initial pain and let his doughty ambassador enter her privy cabinet without ado and spread out to his heart's desire. As the audience progressed, to be sure, it seemed to her that he was spreading out rather too much. At first he was able to move about freely in her secret cabinet, but gradually, in accordance with his canine nature, he became so swollen with the pride of victory, and grew so mightily that the room became too small for him, the walls closed in on him and cut off his retreat. Scent Cloud had never seen anything like it. This was definitely something new to her, a sensation. She could not help giving expression to her amazement:

"Strange, when my husband visits me from time to time, the going is hard at first and gets easy as time goes on. With you it's just the opposite: first easy, then hard. How can that be?"

"Let me explain. My modest jiffy may not be so imposing by nature as that of other men, but to make up for it, it has two unusual advantages: first, like a grain of rice that swells up in water, it is small at first but then in the course of its activity increases stupendously in size and vigor; second, like a flint which at first seems cold and dead but emits sparks after you have rubbed it a few times, it is cold at first, but heats up more and more in the course of its activity, and finally bursts into flame—or perhaps I should say, it is like a 'fire star' or rocket such as you see in displays of fireworks. It was only on the strength of these advantages—why should I make a secret of them?—that I dared to court you. I should be glad to hear your expert opinion."

"Why, it's just wonderful. It's a perfect treasure you've got there. Tell me—you're not fooling? But even supposing it's the truth, what good does it do us? Surely it will give us little pleasure if it keeps swelling up that way. It hurts."

"Don't worry, it just needs moistening. Just wait till the dew of pleasure spreads over it. Then things will go more smoothly."

"Very well. If that's how it is, I will bear up patiently. Do get to work and make the dew come quickly."

"Wisely spoken!" he cried, lifted her legs over his shoulders, and set furiously to work.

It was not long before the proceedings became smooth and painless. Again his jiffy heated up and the more it heated, the more pleasurable her sensations became.

"Dearest, you were telling the truth. It's a wonderful thing you've got there—oh, I am ready to faint away with delight."

This was music to his ears and sly as he was he decided to use this favorable moment of weakness to his advantage. Continuing his efforts, he spoke to her:

"See, you yourself admit that I wasn't lying, and that applies to everything else I say. You can trust me. Will you stop worrying now and please tell me what you know about those three ladies at the temple?"

"Why are you in such a hurry? No need to prod me. I'll get around to speak of them."

This too was music to his ears and in anticipated joy he kissed her and entwined his tongue in hers. And so they carried on until the third drumbeat. Then she was exhausted, fragrant beads of sweat stood out on her forehead; her hands and feet grew cold. The cloud had burst three times.

"Dearest, I can't go on. I'm done for. Come, put your arms around me and let us sleep," she pleaded in a weak voice. And obediently he lay down beside her.

As he thus lay by her side, he breathed in a strange fragrance that clung to the pillows and blankets. It seemed to him that this was the very same scent that had seemed so bewitching when she glided past him at the temple. He could not restrain himself from asking:

"Darling, what subtle essence do you use to perfume your bed and your clothing? It is perfectly exquisite."

"Perfume? I use none at all. What gives you that idea?"

"I noticed it when we first met at the temple; when you passed close to me, I sensed a rare fragrance that emanated from you, and here in bed I perceive the same rare scent. If it is not perfume, where can it come from?"

"From myself. It is the natural scent of my skin and body."

"But that seems almost incredible. Then you too can boast of a miraculous quality, a true physical treasure."

"Yes, that is perfectly true. Apart from that, I am just like all women, but in this one respect I differ from them and possess a distinct advantage. Let me explain. When my mother was in her heavy hour and about to bring me into the world, a red cloud suddenly appeared in her bed-chamber. A strange fragrance issued from it, so powerful that it seemed to buffet her in the face. And long after the cloud had gone, the fragrance lingered on. Meanwhile I came into the world and from then on this scent has clung to me. That is why my parents called me Scent Cloud.

"In daily life, when I am occupied with indifferent matters, this special quality of mine does not make itself felt. But as soon as my senses are aroused and begin to vibrate, the strange scent flows from my pores. It is not only those around me who notice it. I myself can smell it.

"Why should I make a secret of this advantage that a

kindly nature has bestowed upon me? I turned it on quite intentionally that day in the temple of the bowstringer god. I not only left my fan for you to find and keep as a token of my sympathy; the body scent released by the sight of you was also meant to serve as a messenger of love. Under its spell, I thought, you would find me worthy of favorable attention.

"You will conceive of my bitter disappointment when you so rudely disregarded my tender message and left me waiting until today for the fulfillment of my heartfelt desire."

Still rather skeptical, he wished to make sure, and so he began to sniff at her from top to toe. And indeed there was not a single spot on all her body which did not emit a thread of the subtle fragrance.

What a marvelous discovery! Why, this was a very special feminine charm that he had never even heard of until then. Carried away with delight, he embraced her and squeezed her, caressing her by turns with kisses and affectionate little names. She shook with laughter and interrupted his caresses with the roguish question:

"Have you been thorough with your sniffing? Are you sure you haven't skipped anything?"

"Not that I know of. Or should I . . ."

Scent Cloud giggled and buried her face in the pillows. "See for yourself."

He turned her over on her back and let his mouth and nose slip downwards from her twin hills.

"Eureka!" came the triumphant cry from the underworld. Rising to the upper regions he smacked his lips.

"Delicious, perfectly delicious." After a time he slipped downward again to the nether world, curving his body into an arch.

He opened the gates to her pleasure house and dispatched his tongue into her inner chambers as his vice-ambassador.

"Oh! What are you doing? Stop that. You're killing me," she screamed, shaken with laughter, and tried in vain to push him away. But the more she pushed him, the more obstinately the zealous vice-ambassador worked at his diplomatic mission, which he carried out so skillfully that the results were quite equal to those achieved by an experienced and accredited diplomat.

At length his mission was accomplished and he was graciously discharged. After a pause of silent exhaustion she stroked his hair.

"You love me that much? If that's how it is with us and if you are as serious about our love as I am, let us this very night swear a solemn oath of everlasting fidelity."

"You've taken the words out of my mouth. That is just what I was going to suggest."

They climbed out of bed, slipped into their clothes, knelt down by the window with their faces to the night sky, and swore by the moon and the stars that they would belong to each other not only in this life but in the next as well, and that nothing, not even death, would ever part them. After that they undressed again, crawled back under the bedclothes and continued their conversation until they had laid bare the innermost creases and crevices of their thoughts and feelings.

"I can't understand your husband's behavior. Thanks to heaven knows what good works in an earlier existence, he has had the fantastic good fortune to possess a dear little woman, a veritable jewel like you, and instead of profiting by his good fortune, he lives away from home, deserts his sweet little woman and spends his nights in a cold and gloomy school. It's quite beyond me."

"Oh him! He'd like to but he can't. He just hasn't the strength to make use of his domestic property as he would like to. That's why he runs off to his school. To avoid embarrassment. There he is relieved of the rigorous duties that marriage imposes."

"But I have heard that he is only in his middle years. Seems to me he ought to be able to carry out his conjugal duties at that age."

"He overdid it in his youth. He was a great skirt chaser, a notorious seducer of wives and daughters of good families. Day and night he carried on with enterprising women. And so he spent himself before his time. Today he is perfectly useless."

"Do you think he was as effective in his youth as I tonight?"

"It's possible. Not much less at any rate—except of course for the miraculous quality of your jiffy."

"Oh, I'm sure he had nothing like that. I doubt if there's another like it in all the world," he agreed, grinning from ear to ear. "And if each of us is blessed with so rare a physical quality, it means that nature meant us for one another and that we should never part. From now on I shall come over here to share your couch as often as possible, even without previous appointment."

"Tut, tut. Aren't you promising too much? You are not living alone after all. I shall be satisfied if you don't neglect me and treat me as unlovingly as in the last five months."

"Are you still accusing me of not loving you? You are being very unjust, I assure you. I'd just like to know what slanderous tongue has put such nonsense into your head. If I find out, you just wait, some chatterbox is going to get a good tongue lashing."

"If that's the case, you'll have a bone to pick with your three beauties—it is they who have slandered you—if you wish to call it slander."

"What's that? And they had no shame about revealing the tender secret of their little adventure in the temple?"

"Let me explain. They are relations of mine and good friends as well. The two younger ones are my cousins by marriage, the oldest is their aunt. The two younger ones and myself are one heart and one soul; we are like blood sisters; we share all our joys and sorrows and have no secrets from one another, not even secrets of the heart.

"When I came home from my visit to the temple that day, I told my cousins quite frankly of my meeting with you; I told them how handsome you were, how you had cast loving glances at me, and how I had fallen in love with you on the spot and left my fan on purpose in the hope that you would find it and take it as a token of my affection. Their reply was: 'It looks like love at first sight. Don't worry, he'll find you one of these days. Just wait.'

"I too was quite convinced that you would come looking for me, and to make things easier for you I began spending the whole day in the covered doorway of my house, hoping that you would chance by. But you didn't come. Ten whole days I waited for you in vain.

"Then suddenly I had a visit from my two cousins. They were on their way home from a visit to the temple of the bowstringer god.

"I could see right off that they were in a high good humor; there was a loving blush on their cheeks and their eyes sparkled with animation.

" 'Tell us,' they said, 'that young stranger you met recently at the temple and were so wild about—what did he look like? Can you describe him?'

"I described him as well as I could, your face, figure, and dress. They nodded to one another and said to me: 'That is he. We met him today at the temple—and now answer one question: did he express his love for you very plainly, let us say, by—kowtowing?'

"I replied in the negative. 'His eyes spoke clearly enough,' I replied. 'But to kowtow! To fall on his face before me in front of all those people—that would hardly have been proper.' At this they exchanged a silent glance and a deep smile expressive—or so it seemed to me at least—of secret satisfaction. That aroused my suspicions and I gave them no rest until they consented to explain.

"And what did they tell me? Visibly savoring every detail, they told me about your ridiculous kowtowing on the temple steps. And as they spoke, they kept exchanging those irritating triumphant glances of theirs.

"You can imagine how I felt. I was boiling. I was in a

wretched mood for three days. Then I began to look at things more philosophically. I said to myself: 'We were all strangers to him; that was the first time he had ever laid eyes on any of us. When he saw me, he was intimidated by all the people; he didn't dare to breathe a single word of greeting and contented himself with silent glances. But at the sight of my cousins he went literally out of his mind and threw all tact and propriety to the winds. He fell on his face in public and behaved like a perfect fool. What is the logical inference to be drawn? That my cousins made far more of an impression on him, that nature had endowed them with far greater charms, and that consequently they are luckier in love than I, that the young man in question has clearly indicated his preference for my cousins and hasn't the slightest intention of running after an insignificant creature like me any more. If that's how the land lies,' I said to myself, 'I've been languishing long enough. I am good and sick of waiting in the doorway for nothing.'

"As far as I was concerned, the matter was settled. I was only sorry that it had created bad blood between me and my cousins, with whom I was ordinarily on the best of terms. I bore them a grudge for several months, to be exact until my recent meeting with you. Your solemn oath convinced me that my suspicions of my cousins had been unjustified. That silly kowtow of yours was to blame for the whole trouble. Was it necessary?"

"Oh, I see. Now the whole thing is clear to me. I understand what a burden of disappointment must have been weighing on your tender breast and I see why you were so angry with me at first. But now everything is all right again. As for your supposed rivals, I should like to help clear up your little misunderstanding. If they are your relatives, then they are mine as well, my little cousins by marriage. It seems only fitting that I should pay them my respects—now don't get any ideas—I only wish to be polite, that's all I have in mind. I shall take advantage of my little social call to tell them how it is with us. That will cure them of their boasting and lording it over you. It will be your chance to triumph. Well, what do you think of my idea?"

"Stop right there. I see the whole thing in a rather different light. The three of us are not only cousins and friends; in addition we have taken an oath of sisterhood. We have solemnly sworn to share joy and sorrow, pleasure and pain like sisters. In taking my pleasure with you all alone, in enjoying your embraces behind their backs, I have been untrue to my oath. I have put myself in the wrong toward my sisters. My conscience demands that I make reparation.

"I shall visit them first alone and give them an honest accounting. Naturally it would be incompatible with the spirit of our oath if I should lay claim to a privilege in respect to your person. And that is just what I mean to tell them. Then we shall visit them together and they will have their part of pleasure in you. Like true sisters they will share in my joy at discovering that there is so wonderful a thing in heaven and earth as your jiffy. We shall fulfill the saying:

All wonderful things on earth
Should be the common property of all.

Of course it is up to you. But if you agree to my plan, I must set one condition. Once you have possessed them, you mustn't forsake me, you must keep on loving me as much as you do tonight. Can you promise me that? Can you swear it?"

Without the slightest difficulty! Beside himself with joy, he somersaulted out of bed like an athlete, slipped into his clothes, fell once again on his face, and swore eternal love and fidelity until death. The punishments he invited in case he should prove untrue to his oath were perhaps even more dire than on the occasion of his first oath. Then he crawled back under the bedclothes and resumed his caresses, which were in part an expression of love and in part a recompense for her volunteer matchmaking activities; in short, he served double portions of meat and wine. As you may well

imagine, the fair guest was overjoyed at his munificence
and quite tipsy with pleasure.

When the banquet was over, they fell asleep neck to
neck and cheek to cheek, and they slept until there was
light in the east and the sun arose. Then she shook him
awake and sent him back across the old wooden bridge to
his cell.

From then on they saw one another every day and loved
one another every night.

Now the esteemed reader will wish to know whether and
when he finally attained the goal of his desires, namely
possession of the three beauties from the temple. You will
have to be patient for a while. From the second chapter on
we have been concerned with our Before Midnight Scholar,
his vernal lusts and aberrations. Enough of that for the
present. The next two chapters will take up a secondary
action and constitute an intermezzo. But after the intermezzo our leading actor will return to the stage.

CHAPTER XII

*He smashes his frying pans and cookpots and leaves
home in order to vent his rage. He makes his bed on
brushwood and feeds on gall to avenge himself on the
thief of his domestic honor.*

Despite the generous indemnity Honest Ch'üan had received for Aroma, the wrong he had suffered still rankled
in his heart. To make matters worse, his cuckoldry had

made him lose face with his friends and neighbors. His fellow citizens avoided him and he no longer dared to show his face in public. He grew weary of life in general and of his business in particular. All day long he sat idle in his shop, immersed in gloomy thoughts.

He tried to obtain information about Aroma's secret doings from the little twelve-year-old housemaid: at what time of day and for how long had she entertained the imposing gentleman? Had she had dealings with other men? As long as Aroma was there, the little girl had held her tongue for fear of her mistress and pretended to know nothing. Later on, when Aroma was gone and it became certain that she would not return, she had finally opened her mouth, informing Honest Ch'üan of the exact hour when the visitor had come, how long he had stayed, and when he had gone away. Most important, she told her master that it was not the imposing gentleman of mature years who had slept with her mistress but a very different, late-born individual, a handsome, distinguished young man who had always come in the older man's company. The imposing gentleman had merely played the part of a go-between and stood guard at night.

The little girl also informed him that the ugly neighbor woman from across the way had been mixed up in the business.

At first Honest Ch'üan had his doubts. Would K'un-lun's Rival consent to play the go-between for another? He just could not believe it. Was it possible that the proud and dignified bandit would stoop to such a thing? Again Ch'üan ran to the neighbors and questioned them. They owned that they had suspected K'un-lun's Rival unjustly, that the guilty party had actually been the strikingly handsome young man whom he had once seen in the shop with K'un-lun's Rival but to whom he had paid no attention.

Did they, he inquired, know where this young man came from and where he was now? In the end, his persistent questioning brought results. The young man, he

learned, was a stranger to the town, his home was in such
and such a place, it was not K'un-lun's Rival but this young
man who had had secret dealings with Aroma. He had now
taken her as his collateral wife, for he had a young first wife
at home whom he had deserted. K'un-lun's Rival had only
married Aroma as the young man's proxy, the whole affair
had been cooked up between them.

Now Honest Ch'üan knew what was what. He turned
the situation over and over in his mind.

"If K'un-lun's Rival were the guilty party," he pondered,
"vengeance would be out of the question, I should have to
eat out my heart with bitterness to my dying day; only
after death would I be able to plead my cause before the
judge of the underworld and settle accounts with my
enemy.

"But since it is that other scoundrel who has deprived
me of my domestic honor, why should I put up with my
wrongs in silence? That is too much to expect. Why should
I not give free rein to the rage that fills my belly and rises
in my gullet and threatens to choke me? Why should I not
avenge myself? The only question is how? If I were to
make a complaint against the insolent young fop, his
friend, K'un-lun's Rival would come to his help and bribe
the judges. He has plenty of money and what judge in these
sorry times is not to be had for money? Besides the neighbors who served as witnesses at the mock marriage and
signed the papers would never dare, for fear of K'un-lun's
Rival, to testify for me and against him. No, there's no
point in making a complaint, I'll have to do something
else. Ha! I've got it. I will simply go to the young fellow's
home; with ten ruses and a hundred snares I will creep into
his house and make up to his legitimate first wife whom he
has left there—I will avenge myself through her. Then
we'll be quits. He seduced my wife, I'll seduce his wife.
Ha! Not bad! That's a pleasant kind of revenge! Much
more amusing than knocking the fellow dead—where
would that get me? A difficult project perhaps but what

counts is the determination. How does the old saying go? Ah yes:

Where there's a will there's a way.

Besides, I can't stay here any more—everybody knows that my wife has played me false; they all whisper and ridicule me behind my back. They take me for a fool and a namby-pamby; I am thoroughly sick of the whole place. So what's the good of staying on? Very well, it's time to hit the road. Perhaps merciful heaven will hearken to me and help me to obtain satisfaction, who knows?"

His mind was made up. He proceeded to sell his house and property, including the little maid and his stock of silks; in short, he "smashed frying pans and cookpots and gave away his houseboat," as they say. He broke up housekeeping, took up his walking stick and, amply provided with cash, set out for the unknown.

One fine day he reached the goal of his journey. He stopped at the nearest suburban inn and allowed himself a day's rest. Then he began to make inquiries, to find out all he could about the situation and habits of his enemy's father-in-law's household. It soon became plain to him that things would not be as easy as he had supposed. He had conceived his venture as rather like a quick snatch at somebody's pocketbook. Why, he had thought, should it be any more difficult to crawl into a bedroom here than it had been in his own house? He need only wait for the master of the house to absent himself; the gate would be unbarred as it were and easy to open. It had not occurred to him that there was quite a difference between the household of a simple merchant like himself and that of a crusty old scholar like Dr. Iron Door, a strict, not to say pedantic, observer of the old-fashioned Confucian ways. As Ch'üan's inquiries revealed, this Dr. Iron Door was so determined to shut himself off from the outside world that he did not even permit his best friends and closest relatives to cross the threshold.

Honest Ch'üan lost heart. He began to doubt and to hesitate and played with the idea of abandoning an apparently hopeless undertaking. But then he said to himself: had he taken this arduous trip, had he made his way over a thousand hills and dales in order to let himself be intimidated by an old scarecrow by the name of Iron Door? No, he was too proud a man to accept such a defeat. One way or another, he would try. If things went wrong, well, it would only mean that heaven had not favored his projects. He decided to rent lodgings in the neighborhood, somewhere near the Iron Door estate, no matter whether to the right or left of it, in front or behind. Then he would settle down to observe his neighbor until he found an opportunity to act.

With this in mind he went for a look around Dr. Iron Door's property and was in for an unpleasant surprise. The place was utterly isolated. As far as the eye could see, nothing but wild, uncultivated land. How on earth could he settle down in that wilderness?

Dejected, he was turning to go when his eyes fell on a poster. It was nailed to a board that was fastened to a tree some fifty paces from the Iron Door property. The poster said:

Untilled land to let for clearing and cultivation.
Rent free during first year.

Thoughtfully, he looked around: a wild tangle of bushes and giant weeds. His deliberate mind worked.

"If anyone is to clear this land and cultivate it, he will have to live here as well. There is plenty of room. Very well, I shall lease the land and start by building a modest little hut. I shall build it close to Dr. Iron Door's property. He can't very well forbid me to do so. That will bring me several degrees closer to my goal. Under cover of working in the fields, I shall be able to keep an eye on the house; I shall have all the time in the world to see what is going on."

No sooner said than done. He went to the nearest habitation and knocked.

"Who is the owner of the land over there?" he inquired. "I should like to rent it and clear it. Would I be able to live in the owner's house?"

"Not very likely," came the answer. "Dr. Iron Door—that is the landlord's name—lives in the solitary house you see over there in the midst of the wasteland. He never lets anyone live at his house. You would have to look around for another place to live."

"What kind of man is this Dr. Iron Door?"

The other shook his head. "A very difficult man. I doubt if you'll find another so difficult in the whole world. If he weren't such a hard customer, someone would have rented his land long ago."

"What is so difficult about him?"

"According to old law and custom, a tenant who agrees to clear and cultivate wasteland is forgiven his rent for the first three years. Dr. Iron Door will grant only one year rent free; after that he insists on payment. And in general he is an out and out miser and skinflint.

"He never has the most insignificant morsel of food to spare for his fellow men, he has never been known to give anyone any charity. For reasons of economy, he doesn't keep a single servant, not to speak of a major-domo. If he should find a tenant, he would exploit him as a servant. Whenever there is any heavy work to be done in his household, he goes chasing about the neighborhood, screaming and begging for a helping hand, and when a neighbor is friendly enough to help him out, he never gets any reward for his pains, not so much as a copper. Three years ago there was a man stupid enough to rent his wasteland. But the old skinflint found so many extra jobs for him to do that the poor fellow gave up before he had even started cultivating the fields.

"The story got around and since then there have been no more candidates. That is why the land is still unoccupied."

Honest Ch'üan was more encouraged than frightened by this report. To be called in for heavy housework? That was just what he wanted. What could be better? That would bring him a little closer to his goal. It was a way of getting into the old pedant's otherwise inaccessible house. Perhaps he would even catch an occasional glimpse of the daughter of the house.

Other men might object to performing such domestic services; he, quite the contrary, would welcome it; others might stick at working for nothing, to him it didn't matter one bit. He had plenty of money, he hadn't come here for the wages. Of course he would have to be patient, Peking wasn't built in a day. But he had time as well as money to spare. Of course he would have to give himself another name against the chance that his enemy, the old fellow's son-in-law, should turn up unexpectedly. He would naturally know the name of Aroma's former husband. But luckily they had never met face to face.

He would introduce himself as Tso Sui-hsin. This pseudonym meant "Desired Deed," a hidden allusion to the vengeance for which he yearned and for the sake of which he had come. But not wishing to confuse the reader, the author will continue to employ the name of Ch'üan.

Quite contented and pleased with himself, Honest Ch'üan returned to his inn. There he sat down and drew up a lease. He was a businessman after all, and though none too skilled at writing, well versed in the commercial forms.

With the document in his sleeve pocket, he set out for Dr. Iron Door's house. There he sat down on a stone not far from the gate and waited patiently until someone should open from within. It seemed useless to knock. The natives had told him that the old eccentric made it a principle of never opening to anyone, even if the visitor should hammer on the door for hours. He waited in vain until nightfall. Then he went back to the inn.

Early the following morning he returned to the house.

This time he was in luck. When he arrived at his post, the landlord was standing outside the door. Holding a straw basket in one hand and scales in the other, he was waiting for the cheese and vegetable vendor.

Honest Ch'üan stepped up to the man with the severe angular features, bowed respectfully, and mumbled a few words of greeting.

"Have I the honor of speaking to Dr. Iron Door?"

"I am he. What do you wish?"

"I hear you have a parcel of wasteland for rent. I am short of money at the moment and reduced to making my living by manual work. I should be willing to clear the land for the exalted gentleman. Would you be inclined to accept me as your tenant?"

"Hm. But are you up to the work? Farm work of this kind requires strength and perseverance. I am not interested in lazy bunglers who just want to fill their bellies and would only give my place a lick and a promise."

"Don't worry about that. I am very strong, accustomed to hard work and hardships. If you have any doubts, you can try me out for a few days. Then if you think that I don't work hard enough, you can look around for someone else."

"Very well. But there is still another question. What about lodgings? You can't live in my house."

"Very simple. I'll build a simple little hut out in the fields—at my own expense of course. I am all alone and my needs are modest. In this way I will save the money I should otherwise have spent in renting from strangers."

"Excellent. Go and draw up a lease."

"It's all ready. I have it here."

Honest Ch'üan drew the document from his pocket and submitted it. Dr. Iron Door read the lease and without a moment's hesitation affixed his signature. His first appraising glance had told him that this large, powerful looking applicant, the very picture of honesty, was the right man for him. He would be valuable not only for his farm work but also as a domestic servant. The deal was closed. Ch'üan engaged a few carpenters and masons in the town, bought lumber, bricks, straw and other building materials, and started to build at once. Ten days later the new house was finished and Ch'üan moved in. It was a simple hut with a thatch roof resting on wooden posts, but inside everything sparkled with cleanliness. There was a table, a tile bed that could be heated, a hearth, cooking utensils, and a storeroom already equipped with the necessary farm implements. Ch'üan had no need to stint himself on his purchases, he had plenty of money with him. His hut proved to be a perfectly satisfactory habitation.

From then on Ch'üan had no need to feel like an outsider; he was now a full-fledged resident with a roof over his head.

Dr. Iron Door soon noted with satisfaction that the new tenant took his work very seriously. The scholar lived all alone in a little cell. It was situated on a rise of ground close to the outer wall of his estate. Thus he had a good view of the adjoining land and was able to watch Ch'üan at his work.

He was delighted with what he saw. He was himself an early riser. But however early he himself arose, he saw his tenant, still unwashed and uncombed, hard at work with hoe and spade and sickle. Before he himself crawled out of bed, the man from the hut had done a good piece of work and cleared and weeded and ditched so and so much land.

This impressed Dr. Iron Door no end, and he was not chary of approving cries of *tsai*, "bravo." Ch'üan responded with redoubled zeal and gladly consented to perform all sorts of housework that was too heavy for a maid. He claimed no reward for such additional tasks and even declined with thanks the food that the master of the house occasionally had set before him.

Once, as Ch'üan was leaving, Dr. Iron Door wished to give him a jug of millet brandy as a reward for his untiring zeal. This too Honest Ch'üan declined, saying that he never touched spirits. And even if he did, he added, he could afford to buy his own and was not dependent on the generosity of others.

This proud frugality was just what was needed to reinforce and consolidate his master's good opinion of him.

Alone in his hut after the day's work, Ch'üan reflected on the goal and object of his projected vengeance, namely, the daughter of the house. Before being admitted to the house for the first time, he kept asking himself: "What can she look like? Homely, I presume; exceptionally so perhaps. Why, otherwise, would her young husband have deserted her after scarcely a year of married life; why would he have left his home to chase around after other women? But if that's the case, how shall I wreak my vengeance? If she is so ugly, how will I stir myself up? My henchman will lie down and go on strike. I have been very much spoiled by Aroma. With a beautiful woman I'm sure I could manage, but if she turns out to be ugly, I fear that I shall be a lamentable failure."

These fears and misgivings were dispelled when Dr. Iron Door asked him in to do the heavy work. On the very first day he caught a fleeting glance of an exceptionally beautiful young lady, and when he heard one of the maids address her as *hsiao-chieh*, "young elder sister"—a form of address commonly reserved for the young lady of the house—he was convinced, to his infinite delight, that she and no other was the object of his vengeance.

Back in his hut, he stretched out on his wooden bed and pondered. "Incredible, simply incredible," he said to himself. "She was made for love—why does that idiotic husband of hers desert such a jewel to go chasing around after other women? What can be the matter with him?"

The thought left him no peace. He resolved to proceed with the utmost circumspection for fear of botching so wonderful an opportunity. All his self-control was needed, for at the mere thought of this alluring fruit, his mouth watered and his henchman rose up clamoring for activity.

When Ch'üan chanced to come near the daughter of the house in the course of his housework, he took care to avert his eyes. Silent and with bowed head, he pretended to be unaware of her presence. He cut the figure of an ascetic who had turned away from the red dust of this earth.

In the course of the next few months, Dr. Iron Door conceived a boundless esteem for Honest Ch'üan. What virtues the man possessed! He was conscientious, cheerful in his work, frugal, modest, helpful, taciturn, and sober. A real treasure of a man!

Dr. Iron Door took counsel with himself. "Before his departure my son-in-law left me a few silver pieces with which to engage a manservant, for it was plain that the household was very much in need of one. But discouraged by other masters' experience of the lazy gluttons who call themselves major-domos or servants, I could not make up my mind to hire one. This tenant of mine, however, would seem to be the right man. He is alone in the world, without family ties. I wonder if he would be willing to sell himself and to become my bondsman?

"It is true that I should be taking a double risk: with all his excellent qualities it must be admitted that he is nothing but a penniless stranger from heaven knows where; if I take him into my household, what guarantee have I that he will not rob me one day and vanish into thin air? On the other hand, he is unmarried, a powerful man in the prime of life—it might be dangerous to have a bachelor like him in the house. Quite apart from the maids, I have my daughter's virtue to think of. There might be trouble. What shall I do?—Perhaps, if he is willing to become my bondsman, I should give him our little lady's maid for his wife. She would keep an eye on him and prevent him from getting any silly ideas. Moreover, that would attach him to the house. Then he would give up any idea of running away. I should have nothing more to worry about. Well, that is just what I mean to do."

His mind was made up. One day he went out into the fields, looked on for a time as Honest Ch'üan plied his spade and his hoe, and spoke to him as follows:

"I see that you are a good hard worker; sometimes I even think that you may be overdoing it. Now I wonder: a man of your abilities could easily feed a wife and children; why at your age are you alone and unmarried?"

Ch'üan stopped working, wiped the sweat from his brow and replied:

"There is an old adage:

With head and mind you can feed a thousand mouths; with brute force you are lucky to feed yourself alone.

In short, my work barely suffices to feed this one mouth of mine. Under the circumstances how can I think of founding a family?"

"But a wife and children are just what is needed to fill a man's life. If you feel unequal to making a home of your own, why not marry into someone else's household? There are plenty of marriageable young girls capable of making you happy and giving you children. Think of the future. If you remain a bachelor all your life, who is going to sacrifice and pray at your grave when the time comes? It would be a pity to slave all your life, without making any provision for the future."

Honest Ch'üan knew perfectly well what the other was driving at; Dr. Iron Door had apparently decided to take him into his own house. That, Ch'üan realized, would be a long step toward the fulfillment of his plans. But he maintained an inscrutable reserve, taking good care not to show his satisfaction.

"Yes," he said. "As the saying goes, it is a good thing to rest in the shade of a mighty tree. But there are two objections: in the first place, the master of a house is often unable to distinguish between sweet and bitter; I might work like a horse or an ox and harvest scoldings or even blows instead of thanks; in the second place, my fellow servants might well be envious or hostile; a new servant is expected to humble himself before those who are older in the service; but what if the older servant has grown accustomed to a lazy, comfortable existence and the newcomer is more zealous? The result will be quarrels and bad blood; the older servant cannot help fearing that the eager newcomer will supplant him in the master's esteem—a sorry state of affairs that can often be observed in great households, particularly among our local mandarins.

"These two considerations," Honest Ch'üan concluded, "might well deter me from selling myself into another man's household."

"Well," said Dr. Iron Door, "in regard to my household, you need have no such misgivings. There could be no quarrels with your fellow servants, for I have no male personnel. After all, I am not a mandarin. And the benevolence of my feelings toward you must be made clear by my intention of giving you a wife the moment you enter my service. What do you say to that? Would you be willing?"

"Why not? It is very kind of you."

"Splendid. In that case let us draw up a contract. Just tell me how many silver pieces you desire as a purchase price for your person. Meanwhile I shall have lodgings prepared for you in the house and choose one of my maidservants for you. You can take possession of her the very day you move in. Is that satisfactory?"

Ch'üan nodded his head. "Why yes, I seem to be settled for life. I shall bring you the contract tomorrow, but . . ."

He cleared his throat and paused as though in embarrassment. He seemed to have something on his mind.

"There is one more thing: I am a rather odd man by nature; I don't set much store by women. I can imagine having a wife, but I can equally well imagine doing without. In other words, the idea of marriage does not exactly thrill me. There's no need to give me one of your maids right away, that can wait. Let me work a few years for you first; you can marry me later on, when my strength has begun to wane and my muscles have grown slack. Now my first duty is to work for the noble lord, to clear his wasteland and till his fields; I shall need plenty of strength for that and I shouldn't like to waste it on a woman.

"As for your offer to pay a price for my person, I cannot accept it; that is quite out of the question. I am alone in the world, I have neither parents nor children nor brothers nor sisters to care for; for whom should I pile up money? I shall be perfectly content if the noble lord provides me with board, lodging, and clothing. What would I need money for? Let us leave the clause about the purchase price out of our contract. It would only be a figure on paper, for in reality I should not ask you for a copper."

The old skinflint was delighted with this proposal. His eyes twinkled with pleasure and his eyebrows hopped up and down for delight. He replied with a smirk:

"Well spoken! Every word bears witness to loyalty and a high sense of duty. As for the purchase price that you decline, I shall set the sum I had intended for you aside for the present and spend it later on clothing and similar items for you.

"In one point, however, I am not of your opinion: the question of marriage. Others in your position would be glad to achieve marital happiness in this way. But you scorn both money and wife. In view of such pride and noble selflessness, it would be hard for me to regard you as a subordinate and expect you to perform any service whatsoever; I simply shouldn't have the heart to. You might call me master as much as you pleased; I should not be able to regard you as a servant. In short, if you persevere in your refusal, I regret to say that I cannot take you into my service."

"I understand, the noble lord fears that without a wife I should not feel attached to the house and should run away sooner or later. That is why he insists on marrying me. He is mistaken. I am not the kind of man who is divided in his mind. But if it sets your mind at rest, I shall accede to your wishes and accept a wife."

With this the agreement was concluded to the satisfaction of both parties. Ch'üan did not even wait until next day but drew up the contract that very evening and brought it to his master. And Dr. Iron Door, in turn, did not wait until next day but brought Ch'üan the promised little wife that same evening. His choice fell on Ju-yi, his daughter's maid. And he gave the new member of his household the name of Lai Sui-hsin, which means "Welcome."

Now that Ch'üan had been taken into Dr. Iron Door's house, the hut out in the fields had become superfluous. At his master's behest, he tore it down again.

Ch'üan had now traveled eight tenths of the road to his goal of vengeance. How he was to negotiate the remaining two tenths you will learn in the next chapter.

CHAPTER XIII

Amorously whispering behind barred doors, they think they are unheard, but the walls have ears. Ordinarily it is forbidden to spy on ladies in their baths; the present case is an exception.

Since her husband's more or less forced departure—his father-in-law had driven him out of the house with his quarrelsome, schoolmasterly ways—Noble Scent, abandoned when she had just grown accustomed to love, found herself in the condition of a drinker who has just been obliged

*That very evening Dr. Iron Door brought Honest Ch'üan his
daughter Noble Scent's maid, Ju-yi, as his spouse.*

to give up spirits or of a gourmet whose doctor has suddenly ordered him to forego all roasts and condiments and live on insipid vegetables.

Three nights, five nights of solitary sleeping were already a torment, but now the torture had been going on for six months. She felt like a widow. Deprived of bedtime pleasures, she took refuge in fantasy and tried, with the help of the thirty-six illustrations from the *Ch'un-kung*, or "The Vernal Palace," the spicy volume the Before Midnight Scholar had purchased in the early days of their marriage, to arouse and satisfy her desires artificially. She made the same mistake as the fool who thought he could quench his thirst by looking at a still life of succulent fruit and appease his hunger by gazing at a still life of inviting pasties and incurred the same sort of disappointment; far from being appeased, her hunger and thirst for love only became more intense. She put the useless picture book back in the drawer and tried another way out; perhaps she could dispel her desperate *ennui* with light reading.

Esteemed readers, you may ask what sort of reading matter she selected to this end? In my humble opinion, she ought to have turned to the books which her father had recommended and given her as a young girl, innocent, virtuous books of an educational nature, such as the *Lieh-nü chuan*, "Biographies of Heroines," or the *Nü Hsiao-king*, "Daughters' Guide to Childlike Piety," and such like.

Reading matter of this kind might have distracted her, banished her boredom and discontent, and even made her forget her hunger and thirst. Grass widows and even real widows can derive consolation, forgetfulness, and peace of mind from the proper sort of reading matter. But what did Noble Scent do? Instead of the books recommended by her father, she selected the dissolute, salacious trash that her husband had brought home with him. Erotic novels of dubious quality, such as the *Ch'i p'o-tzu chuan*, "The Love-Crazy Women," or the *Hsiu-t'a yeh-shih*, "the Romance of the Embroidered Couch," or the *Ju-yi-chün chuan*,

"Lovers Galore," and so on. She eagerly devoured this spicy reading matter and never skipped a page.

In the course of her reading, she often ran into the most amazing passages in praise of the hero's equipment, vaunting its imposing thickness or incredible length. She encountered troubling similes such as "like a snail crawling from its shell," or "comparable in dimensions and general appearance to a skinned rabbit." As for the endurance and efficiency of these heroes, there wasn't a one of them who couldn't manage a thousand thrusts without stopping.

In reading such descriptions Noble Scent couldn't help thinking of her own connubial experience and drawing comparisons. "Is it possible?" she wondered. "Can such things be? My young husband's utensil was barely three inches long and no more than two fingers thick, and when we sported together, his outside limit was two hundred thrusts, then the cloud burst. He even used to boast of his vigor and endurance; and here I read about men capable of delivering at least ten times more than he. Seems hardly credible. Come come. You mustn't believe everything you read in books; the best thing you can do is to give up this sort of reading. Surely the miraculous items described in these pornographic books are pure invention, products of the author's imagination . . ."

She vacillated between doubt and belief, until at length belief won the upper hand. "There are millions of men in the world; that leaves room for plenty of deviations from the norm and average—why should there not be men of unusual build such as those described in these novels? Just imagine! What ineffable bliss to get one of those for your husband! A demigoddess could ask no better. Oh, why has such happiness been denied me?"

From then on the thought left her no peace. She lost all interest in her needlework. Her only distraction was the reading matter in question and the more she read the more the sultry yearning of her senses curdled into storm clouds

—oh, if only he would come home, she would . . . oh, then the clouds would burst and the saving rain would fall.

But the poor thing waited in vain. A year passed, and no sign of him, not so much as a letter.

A strange change had taken place within her; she could no longer summon up resentment at such unloving treatment. Resentment had turned to defiance. Why waste her feelings on this loveless husband of hers? There were other men. Her feelings clamored for life and experience.

"In all these novels you seldom find a heroine who hasn't carried on with several men; to judge by them there's nothing unusual about a married woman taking a lover to make up for her husband's shortcomings. Who knows? Perhaps I committed some crime in an earlier life to be punished in this one with so heartless a husband. We had been married only a few months when he left me, thrust me aside. Since then more than a year has elapsed. Am I to suppose that in all this time a skirt chaser like him has controlled himself and kept away from the bypaths? It doesn't seem likely. Very well, what's sauce for the gander is sauce for the goose! Who will deny me the right to open a secret backdoor and let a someone, a lover, in? It's just too bad that the old man runs the house so strictly. Shut off like this from the outside world, I never even get to see a strange man . . ."

Arrived at this point in her thoughts, she was seized with new resentment, directed this time not against her faithless husband but against the domestic tyrant, her own father. She could not help toying with the wicked hope—ah, where was her filial piety now!—that he might soon depart for the Land of the Yellow Springs. Then she would be free to take a lover into the house.

And now this strange tenant farmer had suddenly turned up. From the very first she looked upon him exactly as a hungry hawk looks upon a chicken that has entered its field of vision: a welcome prey. His appearance was all one to her; let it be refined or vulgar, attractive or ungainly! Only one thing mattered: he was a man. And he wasn't so bad looking at that; in any case, he was powerfully built and that seemed promising. She planned to seize this man as a hawk seizes its prey.

Her plan was conceived at once, but as long as he was living in his hut, there was no way to carry it out. He was so disgustingly modest and respectful; when he had work to do in the house, he did his best to keep away from her and when his work obliged him to approach her, he bashfully lowered his head and far from speaking to her, he never so much as looked at her. In short, he behaved as though he had taken strict vows of asceticism.

But now that he had been received into her father's house, all this would change. When she first got wind of the plan, her heart gave a jump, in fact several jumps, of joy. Originally she made plans for the very first night, but here she was in for a disappointment: it was not a lone bachelor who moved into the servants' quarters assigned him by the master, but the newly wedded husband of Ju-yi, her maid. She felt that familiar acid taste in her mouth. First she was a prey to jealousy. But then came curiosity to keep it company. What, she wondered, could his equipment be like? And what of his efficiency and endurance? She was determined to find out. It would be exciting to look on in secret as they sported together; that would offer her a certain compensation.

She kept her clothes on and stayed awake until the lamps went out in her father's study. Then she slipped out of her boudoir and crept across the court and down the passageway to the couple's bedchamber.

What a pity! The room was already darkened, she had to content herself with listening. She bent an ear toward the window, and what did she hear? Instead of the expected sounds of joyous passion, lamentable moans so pitiful to hear that her heart was like to break and she could not help sharing the pain of the poor suffering woman. She pondered. Ju-yi was in her mid-twenties. That made her quite a bit older than herself with her eighteen summers.

Thanks to the strict discipline her father maintained in the household, which excluded the slightest possibility of male acquaintance, she had thus far remained *ch'u-nü*, an "untouched virgin." It was only natural that the loss of virginity should involve a certain amount of pain. But that Ju-yi, who was a mature woman after all, should carry on so pitifully suggested that her mate's armament must be of remarkable size, so much so that it had difficulty in forcing an entrance. A promising inference, which filled the listener with anticipated pleasure. Perhaps this stranger would prove to be the equal of the heroes she had been reading about; perhaps when the time came, he would fulfill all her desires. It was just too bad that visual evidence was not to be had. But maybe she would have better luck next time.

The cries of pain within had soon given way to silence. The truth of the matter is that Honest Ch'üan, kindly man that he was, wished to make his inexperienced mate's introduction to love as easy and painless as possible. He had broken off his first lesson in the middle.

Noble Scent saw no point in continuing to strain her ears. She left her listening post and darted back to her boudoir.

The following night and the night after that, there was no change. Again Noble Scent took up her listening post; again she found the room darkened, again there was nothing to be seen, again she went away disappointed. But it seemed to her that Ju-yi's cries of pain were weakening.

Finally, on the fourth night, her patience was rewarded. This time she found the room lit by lamplight and, best of all, the window curtain had not been lowered. It seemed as though those within were about to put on a special gala performance for the eavesdropper's benefit.

The eavesdropper had arrived just on time. The show was about to begin. First the couple removed all their clothes; then she sat down on the edge of the bed and he stepped up to her, drew her head and shoulder against his chest and let her play with his armament for a while. And what armament! With a swift movement of her hand, Noble Scent covered her mouth to stifle a tell-tale cry of joyous horror. What length! That was a horse of a very different color from the modest two-three inches to which her Before Midnight Scholar had accustomed her; it was eight inches long or more, simply fantastic. And the thickness! Her tender lotus shoot fingers wouldn't even be able to encompass this mighty elephant's trunk. The couple had meanwhile completed the prologue and was putting on the main act. The assailant had breached the enemy fortress, this time without encountering much resistance; there were no cries of pain—the patient efforts of the first three nights had widened her shoe, enabling it to receive his last. And now he began to perform. And what a performance! Her amazement was aroused for the third time. What vigor, what endurance! Back and forth went the shuttle, not just a few hundred, but far more than a thousand times, and the extraordinary lover didn't show the slightest sign of exertion or fatigue. It was just like a novel. And quite otherwise than on the first few occasions, when Ju-yi had displayed no sign of pleasure and emitted the weirdest cries of pain, now she seemed to be experiencing the purest bliss and emitted the strangest cries of delight. The sounds that squeezed out of her were such as to touch the heartstrings of heaven and earth, not to mention the secret listener. While on the first occasions she had suffered along with the poor victim, now her senses were no less stirred from merely looking on than were those of Ju-yi from the reality of the thing. She had seen and heard enough. Having gained full certainty, she returned to her boudoir. Here, she said to herself, is a man who can compete with the hero of any novel. I must and will have him for myself.

As to Honest Ch'üan, his attitude toward the young lady had changed completely since he had gained a firm foothold in the household. He cast off his ascetic countenance and assumed the worldly manner of one not at all

Finally, on the fourth night the eavesdropper was in luck. The room was lit by lamplight, the window curtain not lowered, a special gala performance was about to begin.

impervious to sensuous charms. Whenever he passed her, he would give her an appealing little glance. If she favored him with a smile, he would smile straight back. If she looked grave, he too put on a similar grave look as though to show her that his soul was at one with hers.

One day while working in the garden, he chanced by her boudoir just as she sat splashing in her bath. An intentional or unintentional cough from the direction of the door—she was sitting with her back to the window—disclosed his presence. What fun it would be, she thought, to display herself in all her rosy nakedness and observe the effect on his senses.

"Who's there?" she cried. "I am in my bath. No one can come in now."

Words of dismissal, but in the alluring tone of her voice he seemed to detect the exact opposite: a friendly invitation to come closer. Still, he did not feel quite sure of himself and continued irresolutely along the house wall until he came to the window. There he stopped still, overcome by an irresistible desire to peep in. Moistening his fingertip with his tongue, he carefully dabbed at a spot in the parchment window covering, which gradually grew soft and transparent. Leaning forward and holding his breath with excitement, he peered in through his peephole. He was to be well rewarded for his pains.

As we have seen, she had at first been sitting with her back to the window. Her sensitive hearing had followed the gentle tapping of his felt soles along the boudoir wall, and when the tapping had suddenly stopped at the window, she had rightly inferred that he was trying to look in. "Let him have his money's worth!" she said to herself, laughing inwardly, and had turned half around in the tub, so that her countenance and her nephrite twin hills were facing the window. But she was not yet satisfied. Presumably he had come for the view and she wanted his view to be perfect. Thus far her most intimate parts were hidden beneath the surface of the water. She lifted herself out of the water and lay flat, with thighs widespread, across the edges of the tub. Thus she lay before him in all her glory.

For quite some time she lay there, letting him feast his eyes on her "valley of secret pleasures." Then she returned to her previous sitting position, for in the long run it proved fatiguing and uncomfortable to lie flat, supporting her head and legs on the hard edges of the tub.

Then she lowered her eyes, looked down thoughtfully at her middle parts, shrugged her shoulders, and heaved a long deep sigh. To the secret observer at the window the meaning of her sign language was perfectly clear. It was as though she had said: "Oh, misery, misery! It is unendurable! Will no one save me?"

Now Honest Ch'üan was ten tenths sure of himself. If this was no invitation, he had never seen one. A flame of irresistible desire blazed up within him. The time for hesitation was past. He turned back to the boudoir door and went in.

He knelt down courteously by the bathtub, mumbled a few words of apology for the "wretched slave's unforgivable boldness—an offense for which death would be small punishment." Then he bent forward, threw his arms around her, and embraced her without further ado.

At first she made a show of surprise and terror.

"What does this mean? What has got into you?" Words of reproach, but gently, tenderly uttered by lips obviously quite ready to be kissed.

"Ah, noble lady, do not misunderstand me: it is for your sake alone that I have sold myself into slavery. Just to be near you. I have long been awaiting the favorable moment when I might find you alone and lay bare my feelings. But how was I to do so without your permission? I simply hadn't the courage; it seemed too bold, too insolent. But today chance favored me with a glimpse of your wonderful body. I could no longer contain myself, it was stronger than I. I know it was an unforgivable crime to burst in like this, but I couldn't help it. And now here I am. Prostrate at your feet, I beseech you: have pity on me and grant me my life."

Noble Scent had no desire to waste precious time in idle discussion. If they waited too long, one of the maids might come along and frighten him away. She preferred to come straight to the point.

"What, may I ask, was your purpose in breaking in? What is your intention? Are we to take our pleasure right here in the bathtub? That is out of the question, it would be imprudent, and the fear of being disturbed would mar our enjoyment."

"I know, I know. This is not the proper place. But may I hope—would the gracious young lady grant me the favor —would she permit me to pay her my respects tonight?"

"Tonight? Why, you spend the night with my Ju-yi. I doubt very much whether she will let you out of her sight."

"Oh, don't worry about her, she sleeps like a log. Once she drops off, she sleeps soundly until morning, so soundly that I have to shake her and call her ten times before she shows any sign of life—she won't notice a thing if I steal away during the night."

"Very well, then. It's a bargain. I'll expect you tonight."

Delighted with her consent, he stroked her and caressed her and kissed her all over. Then he turned to the door. Once again she called him back:

"Are you serious? Will you really come? If so, I shall leave the door open and wait for you—otherwise, if you didn't mean it seriously, I should bolt the door as usual."

"Why, my dear, dear young lady, how can you doubt? Of course I will come—but please, please, don't be angry and impatient if it should get to be a little late."

"Very well."

With a gesture, she gave him to understand that he was dismissed in high favor.

It was already late afternoon when the two of them made their appointment. Noble Scent did not even bother to dress. Having stepped out of her bath and dried herself, she went right to bed. She was in no mood to eat supper, but she thought she would store up a little sleep in order to be well prepared for the impending hostilities. But she was so excited she could not shut an eye. Wide awake, she lay waiting. She did not have long to wait.

At the beginning of the second night watch, at the double hour of the boar, she heard the door squeak softly.

"Sui-hsin, is it you?" she asked in a muffled voice.

"Dearest young mistress, it is I," he replied in equally muffled tones. It was a moonless night, the boudoir was immersed in black darkness. For fear that he might lose his way in the dark, bump into something, and make a noise that would stir up the household, she climbed out of her warm nest, ran to the door, took him by the hand, and drew him with her to the bed.

At the thought of his mighty armament, the delicate young beauty felt just a wee bit frightened and ill at ease. Perhaps he would hurt her. Before he crawled under the covers, she pleaded with him:

"Don't be too violent. You'll be gentle with me, won't you? I know what a gigantic utensil you have. You won't hurt me, will you?"

"Why, the idea! How could I dare to injure the gracious young lady's precious body? I shall be ever so gentle and you may be sure that I won't hurt you." These were his words, but he did not take her appeal very seriously, mistaking it for a coquettish challenge to show what he could do. Forgetting his promise, he started in with a brusque frontal assault.

But he was poorly received. She pushed him away angrily.

"Don't be so rough!" she fumed at him. "You are hurting me! Is that how you keep your word?"

Contritely he broke off his attack. Apparently she had meant what she said. He would have to proceed more circumspectly.

"Forgive my enthusiasm, gracious lady. It has never be-

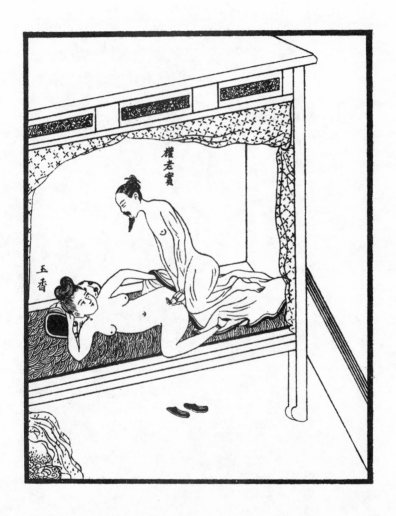

Noble Scent could not repress a giggle when she felt his am-
bassador wandering about, far from the object of his desires.

fore been my good fortune to embrace so beautiful a lady. Your bewitching presence robbed me of my reason; when I felt your silken skin, your tender flesh, I was as though drunk; I could not control my overwhelming desire—forgive me please and let me repair my wrong. I shall be doubly careful." So he pleaded with her and renewed his promise. This time he kept it.

He gave up the idea of entering her pleasure house by force; instead, he let his ambassador reconnoiter the entrance and saunter about, first through the bushes on the fortress wall to east and west of the gate, then further down, in her valley of secret pleasures. Here his ambassador sauntered gaily up and down.

This was a trick he had learned from Aroma. At the beginning of their marriage, Aroma's pleasure portal had been approximately the same size as that of Noble Scent now; it had been no easy matter for his ambassador to gain admittance to her audience chamber and privy cabinet. Aroma herself had thought up an ingenious way of remedying the difficulty: by strolling about in her valley of secret joys, by rubbing gently against the "back and shoulders" of her pleasure portal, his ambassador would call forth pleasant inner vibrations, which in turn would foster the dew of desire. Moistened by this dew, the intruder would be enabled to slip easily through the gate. Other expedients are often resorted to by youthful, inexperienced lovers, too excited to wait, but they are far from producing the same beneficial effect.

The dew of desire is very much like the spring floods in the upper Yangtse valley: a heavily laden junk has run aground on a sandbank; without the least exertion on the part of the boatmen, the flood waters lift it clear. The technical term for this stratagem which he had learned from Aroma is "to coax the source into flowing by removing the pebbles."

Noble Scent could not repress a giggle when she felt

his ambassador wandering about, far from the object of his desires.

"Why are you fumbling around like that?" she asked. "You must be lost."

"Is it possible that you are unacquainted with this little variant?"

"Never heard of it. Seems to me you are all muddled."

"Oh no, it's you who are very much mistaken. Just wait. In a minute you'll feel a pleasant sensation. Then you'll see who is muddled and who isn't."

And indeed, after he had reconnoitered her valley of secret joys for a while, the dew of desire began to make the pathway smooth and slippery. "The spring floods are coming," he said to himself happily.

The junk was floating free—almost too free, he feared. Fearing that his ambassador might skid on the slippery path and miss the entrance, he requested his companion to guide him to the right spot with her tender little hand. She complied with some difficulty—it took all ten of her lotus shoots to hold the doughty ambassador. But soon, with her willing assistance, he had the difficult passage behind him and was presenting his credentials in her audience chamber.

Noble Scent's heart overflowed with gratitude. Thanks to her companion's delicacy and circumspection, she had not felt the least twinge of pain. The man was obviously an expert. She thanked him with a tender embrace.

"It seems very strange," she said, "I am told that you have never attached much importance to women, and I shouldn't be surprised to hear that this is your first try at gallantry. And what delicacy, what virtuosity! Especially when I think of my own young husband who regarded himself as a hero of the bedchamber and couldn't think of anything else! I'd like to know when he ever treated me with so much consideration and understanding. Really, I like you. I love you madly."

Her praises increased his self-reliance and spurred him on to acquit himself of his task with redoubled zeal. And he held up his end so well that from then on she invited him into her bed night after night. She simply could not forego the unprecedented pleasures he offered her. He had become indispensable to her.

At first they carried on secretly, behind Ju-yi's back. But then they decided that since Ju-yi was bound to find out sooner or later, it would be better to tell her honestly and frankly how matters stood. To mollify her and keep her in a good humor, Noble Scent decided to stop treating her as an inferior and slave and to accord her the respectable status of a subsidiary wife; she herself, of course, would be the principal spouse.

Placated by this tactful treatment, Ju-yi put a good face on a business that was not altogether to her liking. From then on they formed a *ménage à trois*. Either the women, by turns, would share his couch all night, or else they would change places at midnight, or else all three would sleep together.

In the last case it sometimes happened that Honest Ch'üan, while only half awake, would mistake one for the other and address the lady's maid as *hsiao-chieh*, "gracious young mistress," and Noble Scent as Ju-yi. After making this blunder two or three times, he decided to use the neutral term *hsin-kan*, "dearest," for both of them.

In view of the superabundance of bedtime pleasures which Honest Ch'üan thus enjoyed night after night, the reader will not be surprised to learn that in a few months' time his powers were thoroughly spent. He was simply exhausted.

In the light of this it might be said that the sword of vengeance had cut two ways. Ch'üan had planned to attack the thief of his domestic honor through his young wife. But now the other, by the instrumentality of the very same young wife, had made a wreck of Honest Ch'üan, so avenging himself on the avenger.

Honest Ch'üan's dealings with Noble Scent had not been without consequences: three months later, she felt herself pregnant. That was the end of their pleasures. For fear of her father's wrath, she wished to do away with the undesired fruit of her womb. But try as she might, nothing helped. She was seized with despair. One night, she tearfully acquainted Honest Ch'üan with the distressing situation.

"You don't know my father and his unbending severity. He scolds me and beats me for the slightest wrong word, the slightest little falsehood. And now this scandal. If he finds out about it, he will strike me dead. I should do better to put an end to my life first—in that way, I shall at least be avoiding the loathsome family scenes."

Thereupon she prepared to hang herself in his presence. To this Honest Ch'üan was unalterably opposed and he did his best to dissuade her.

"Very well," she replied. "If you wish me to go on living, there is only one way out: flight! Let us all three slip away secretly and go to some strange place where no one knows us. Then we shall have no domestic scandal; we shall have time to set up a household and work out a plan for the future; and in this way, I shall be able to bring the child—it's yours as well as mine after all—into the world under peaceful conditions. I won't be obliged to kill it and shall be able to go on living with a clear conscience. What do you think?"

He found her plan very reasonable and gave his consent. That same night the three of them packed all their money, jewelry, and valuables, and the most indispensable clothing into bundles and, when they knew Dr. Iron Door to be sound asleep, secretly left the house.

Where they went and what became of them you will learn in a later chapter.

CHAPTER XIV

*Faithful to her oath of friendship, she tells her
friends about her night of love. Like true sisters, the
friends share their nocturnal pleasures.*

We have not yet concluded the story of Honest Ch'üan's
vengeance, but you have already heard eight or nine tenths
of it. We shall return to it after a while and tell how it
ended. Let us meanwhile go back to the Before Midnight
Scholar and see how he fulfilled his wildest desires and then,
from the summit of sensual pleasure, fell inevitably into an
abyss of suffering and woe.

In the course of the first night spent in Scent Cloud's
arms, he had learned something about those three, most
glorious of all, whom he had never ceased to desire above
all others. He had found out that they were related to
Scent Cloud, that the oldest of the three was the aunt of
the other two, who were her nieces and had sworn an oath
of sisterhood. But the shortness of the night prevented him
from learning any more.

He had already wasted a good deal of time on explanations, indispensable lies, and apologies, on two oaths and a
belated kowtow, all of which were needed to dispel her
stubborn suspicion. And after all a certain amount of the
precious night had to be spent on the appeasement of their
imperious desires. In short, any number of questions had
remained unanswered. But the second night he made up for
lost time. Willingly Scent Cloud imparted the desired information.

"The oldest of the three, whom I call 'Auntie,' was

born on the tenth day of the second month, on the day when the buds of the fruit trees burst into flower. That is why she was given at birth the name of Hua-chen, 'Happy Hour of the Fruit Blossom.' Out of respect for her age, we younger girls call her Chen-ku, 'Aunt Happy Hour.' She has been a widow for the last ten years. She would gladly have remarried, but her son by her first marriage has always been opposed to it. Like it or not, she has been obliged to remain a widow.

"The two younger, whom I call 'cousins,' are the nieces of her late husband. The elder is called Tuan-chu, 'Pearl Without Blemish,' the younger Tuan-yü, 'Jade Without Blemish.' They are blood sisters. Similarly their husbands are blood brothers. The elder husband goes by the name of Wo-yün sheng, 'Scholar of the Resting Cloud,' while the younger husband calls himself Yi-yün sheng, 'Scholar of the Reposing Cloud.'

"The houses where the three families live are close to one another. They have different street entrances, but the properties are so connected by inner gates and passages that they might be said to form a single property. The occupants can visit one another at any time without going out in the street. It is the same street where I live, only two houses away. Consequently, I haven't far to go when I wish to visit my aunt and my cousins. Now you will understand the reason for my suspicion and resentment. How could I help supposing that you moved to our street not on my account, but on theirs, when I learned that you had been living here all these months without giving me the least sign of life? But now you have set my mind at rest, my suspicions were unfounded."

The young man pondered. Her story coincided perfectly with what his friend, K'un-lun's Rival, had told him about the three distinguished ladies. And his information about the two young husbands and their strange pseudonyms also proved to be correct. He couldn't help marveling at the noble bandit's flair and gifts of observation.

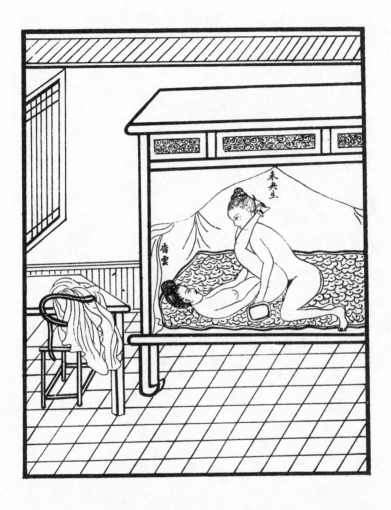

But the second night he spent with Scent Cloud he made up for time lost the first night and asked the questions that had remained unanswered.

"Yesterday," he said, unswervingly pursuing the goal of his desire, "you generously promised to make me acquainted with your two *ling-mei*, your 'noble cousins.' When may I count on that pleasure?"

"Soon, very soon. In three days, five at the very most, I shall go over to see them. Then I will tell them how it is between us and prepare them for your visit. That, to be sure, will be the end of our pleasures here in my bed. For I shall be staying with them for some time."

"What! Why, you've scarcely taken me into your good graces and already you mean to slip away from me?"

"Now, now. You mustn't worry. There's not a chance of my slipping away. You can come and see me, and that will give me an opportunity to introduce you to my cousins."

"Marvelous. But I don't quite see why you have to move over there."

"Let me explain. My husband is absolutely indispensable to my two brothers-in-law as a tutor. Their poor heads are full of great open spaces and now they've decided to take the big state examination that is soon to be given in Peking. For the last few weeks of preparation they have kept my husband with them in the house and they insist that he accompany them to Peking, for they wish to benefit by his knowledge and instruction up to the very last minute. They are counting on him to whip them into shape. They can't take a step without him. Without his help and encouragement they fear that they would lamentably fail. In short, all three of the gentlemen are setting out for Peking in the next few days. Not wishing to leave me all alone, my cousins have arranged for me to stay with them during our husbands' absence. Now you know the how and the why of it."

"That's perfectly wonderful," our young man cried in joyous surprise, inwardly thanking heaven and earth and all good spirits. How kind of them to favor his frivolous undertakings, to remove all three husbands for his sake, leaving their beautiful young wives an easy prey for the claws of his desire. He inwardly rubbed his hands. Now he would be able to vent his animal spirits to his heart's content, undeterred by anxiety or other obstacles.

And indeed, three days later, the three gentlemen set out for Peking at the crack of dawn. The same day Scent Cloud moved in with her cousins. After a brief greeting, she came straight to the point. She just couldn't wait to tell them of her triumph.

"Have you been back to the temple of the bowstringer god?" she asked. The cousins replied in the negative.

"Oh, you haven't? Perhaps another visit would have been worth your while. Maybe you would have met the handsome young stranger who courted you so impetuously. You remember, don't you? The one who kowtowed and beat his forehead on the ground."

"Oh, that fellow. Well, we didn't feel like going empty-handed, and we didn't have any fans to give away—like a certain someone."

"Oho, that sounds like a dig at me. That's true, it was extravagant of me to give my lovely fan away for nothing. He, on the other hand, kowtowed to you for nothing—he might have followed you after all. But you haven't seen hide nor hair of him since, have you? Not even his astral body?"

"That's so. You're perfectly right. And I must admit that we find his behavior astonishing, not to say inexplicable. First he acts as if he were perfectly wild about us, as though he couldn't wait one minute to get his hands on us. We felt certain that he would follow us and turn up that very evening. We spent half the night waiting for him in the bower by the garden gate. But he didn't show up. I guess he just forgot us. He could really have spared himself all that fuss in the temple."

"Oh, he hasn't forgotten you at all. As I hear from a third party, he is still sick for love of you. He just didn't know where to find you. In his confusion he neglected to send his servants after your litters to find out where you lived. He's quite inconsolable at having lost sight of you."

"Sick for love of us? Not very likely. But perhaps he has been lovesick over the owner of a certain fan that was given him as a keepsake."

"You've put your finger on it. And in this case of love-sickness, I am glad to say that the patient has been cured. The cure ran off smoothly and without complications. But he is still lovesick over someone else. And this case is much more serious. Its first symptom was that ridiculous kowtow on the temple steps. If he doesn't receive treatment soon, the worst is to be feared for him. And there's danger in it for you too. Suppose he should tell the judge of the under-world that you are to blame for his untimely death!"

The two cousins exchanged an eloquent glance. Then they tried desperately to read Scent Cloud's expression. Was she speaking seriously or merely joking? It was hard to interpret the opaque smile that played round her mouth, but they thought they detected a note of secret triumph.

"It almost looks," they exclaimed as though with one mouth, "as though you had made a conquest and been re-paid for your fan."

"In a way—and I must repentantly own that it all hap-pened behind the backs of my two adoptive sisters."

This bitter truth put the two cousins in a state of mind very similar to that of a candidate who returns home to his wife after flunking his examinations. He is dejected and crestfallen, and yet he yearns for the affectionate embrace he has been deprived of for so long.

It cost them a certain amount of self-control to put on a cheerful countenance and force a few words of sisterly pleasure at her good fortune.

"*Kung-hsi!* We wish you luck. We congratulate you on the new addition to the family—what could be sweeter!"

The note of envy, irony, and skepticism in these strained congratulations did not escape Scent Cloud's keen hearing. Someone else in her place might have felt dismayed. Scent Cloud, however, was secretly delighted at the emotional disarray into which she had thrown her cousins. She found it just too amusing to tease them with little pinpricks and shake them out of their accustomed equanimity. That was her way. She continued merrily:

"I should say that the event called for a cup of joy. You are politely invited. Actually I should invite you even if you hadn't congratulated me."

"Oh," Jade, the younger cousin broke in with animation, "then, we'll get to see our new in-law? Where does he keep himself?"

"Why do you wish to see him again? Didn't you get a good enough look at him in the temple?"

"I beg your pardon. This is something very different. Then he was a total stranger to us, and we couldn't respond to his amiable greeting; it would have been unseemly, but now that he has managed to worm his way into our clan, he belongs to us. Why on earth shouldn't we say hello to our new cousin and brother-in-law and look him over a little more closely—in your interest, of course?"

Scent Cloud knitted her brows. The vertical wrinkle that formed in the middle of her smooth forehead suggested that she was a prey to serious misgiving. Of course it was just put on. It amused her to tease her adoptive sisters and leave them dangling for a while.

"Hm, of course it would be perfectly simple to introduce him to you. That I can do for you whenever you please. But I see a possible objection. Suppose the sight of you should send him out of his wits again; suppose he should start to play the fool, kowtowing and beating his forehead on the ground the way he did at the temple. His kind doesn't care a fig for good manners once his passions are aroused. He is perfectly capable of doing something very gross and tactless. I should not like to expose my dear cousins to that."

Cousin Pearl protested: "Come, come. Your fears seem rather exaggerated. Between then and now there is an appreciable difference: then there was hardly anybody about whose presence was likely to embarrass him; but today you would be present, jealously supervising his behavior. That will make him think twice before doing anything too eccentric."

Cousin Jade was squirming impatiently in her chair. "Why waste your breath?" she broke in. "It's a pure waste of time. She simply wants to keep her darling away from us. She won't even give us a look at him. A fine sister she is! Remember how we swore to share all our joys and sorrows? Now we can see what an oath means to her. It seems to me that kowtow of his gave us certain rights over him. But we have made no claim whatever. We just wanted to take a look at him; that was all we had in mind. But it's no use insisting. Are we going to beg favors of her?"

Scent Cloud felt that she had gone too far in her teasing. She took a more conciliatory tone:

"Now, now. There's no use getting into a huff. I was just joking. And joking aside, you have no reason to be angry with me. If I had wished to monopolize him, would I have come here to see you? I should have stayed quietly at home and kept him all to myself. Isn't that right? Why then do you accuse me of sinister designs and suspect my loyalty to our oath? All we have to do now is to arrange a fair basis of division, a schedule as it were. There mustn't be any rivalry among us; we mustn't bicker or quarrel over him. Once this essential detail is settled, I shall invite him over."

The cousins' faces lit up. The younger leapt from her chair, clapping her hands with delight.

"Well said," she cried with enthusiasm. "You have proved your loyalty to your sisters in arms."

"As to the basis of division," Cousin Pearl added approvingly, "we shall be glad to follow your proposals."

"Well, then, here is what I have decided. If priority of acquaintance were the only consideration, I might point out that I was first to meet him and enter into intimate relations with him and logically infer that I am entitled to the same privilege as a legitimate principal wife. If I wished to stand on principle, I might look upon you as later, collateral wives and demand certain advantages for myself. For instance, I might demand a half share and leave the other half for the two of you. But it is not my intention to be so petty or so greedy. I prefer to bear in mind that we are not only cousins and friends, but, by virtue of our alliance, as close to one another as blood sisters. Accordingly, I think we should all have equal rights, on condition only that we adopt and observe a reasonable order in the exercise of these rights; and I can see no other basis for a reasonable order but seniority. Such an arrangement, I believe, provides the only possible guarantee against confusion. I should not like us to behave like small children in a classroom, all reciting their lesson at once. Discipline is indispensable, my dear ladies. Each one in her turn. The younger after the older. At what time you wish to exercise your rights, whether by day or night, that is up to you. But there is still another point I should like to impress on you. When it is your turn at table, give your successor a thought. Leave something for her. Don't act as though the table had been set for you alone. This applies even to the pleasures of mere conversation. None of us must be cheated out of her share, particularly not I, who hold the oldest claim. And that is my last request. Remember that I came first, and you after me. Don't press your intimacies so far that I come to feel neglected and thrust aside. That would arouse resentment and mar our friendship. Are you in agreement with these general principles?"

"Perfectly," cried the two cousins as though with one mouth. "All you have said is perfectly fitting and proper."

"Very well, then I shall compose a written invitation to him at once. Bring me writing paper." Pearl hurried off for the paper, while Jade mixed ink on the ink-stone. Scent Cloud picked up the brush and wrote briefly and succinctly on the flowery paper:

The ladies are expecting the young gentleman
On the terrace of the moon.

That was that. She folded the paper and prepared to insert it in an envelope.

Cousin Jade gave vent to her astonishment: "Why, that's nothing but an unfinished couplet. What about style and literary form? Why don't you finish it?"

"I know," Cousin Pearl blurted out. "She admires his gift of threading his way into a woman's inner life. She is leaving it to him to finish her opus, to round it out into a quatrain. Besides, that saves him the trouble of writing a long, elaborate answer. Ah, there's love for you!"

Scent Cloud's reply was an absent smile, which could reasonably be interpreted as corroboration of her cousin's theory. She gave the letter to her maid with instructions to deliver it through the hole in the wall and wait for an answer. Meanwhile the ladies passed the time over a cup of tea, chatting merrily. The subject of conversation was of course a certain He.

"How did you manage to smuggle him into your house and spend whole nights in his arms?" Cousin Pearl wished to know.

With a smirk, Scent Cloud described the course of events, how he happened to live next door to her, how he had had the brilliant idea of making a hole in the wall and attracting her attention by loudly reciting the poem by Li T'ai-po on her fan, and how he had finally passed over the "wooden bridge" in the form of two ladders.

"Wonderful! It's plain that he has his wits about him. But how is he otherwise?" Cousin Pearl inquired. "Is he a competent lover?"

"Competent is no word for it . . . he makes you want to die of bliss in his arms. The two of you know only his exterior. Yes, his very appearance is unusually attractive, one might even say incomparable. But after all an artist, a portrait painter or a sculptor, can capture outward advantages and do as well as nature. Such things can be imagined. But what you simply can't imagine is his hidden advantage—you know what I mean—his certain something, his equipment. You may take it from me that it is simply fantastic. You've never seen the like of it."

Both cousins jumped up from their seats and besieged Scent Cloud for further details. With their frantic thirst for knowledge, they were like candidates shortly before an examination, fastening on to the fellow students who have the test behind them, questioning them about everything under the sun: what was the topic? was it short or long? was it taken from the classics or elsewhere? Had any pointers been given that might serve as a candle to illumine the darkness in the candidate's brain?

"Just watch me," said Scent Cloud in response to the storm of questions. She picked up an ivory chopstick—the cup of tea had stretched out into a dinner, and the table had not yet been cleared—"I'll show you the long and the short of it. You see this chopstick? It is just about the same length as his utensil."

Then she took a tea bowl between her fingers and showed it to her cousins.

"You see this bowl? It is just about as wide as his armament."

"Oh! But what about the hardness? Does it stand up under wear and tear?"

Scent Cloud pointed to a plate of bean curd. "Just like this curd." The cousins tittered.

"What? His cudgel is like that soft, flabby stuff? If that's how it is, where's the good of all that length and thickness? What a pity!"

"I beg your pardon. You only show that you don't know much about bean curd: nothing is so hard and solid, neither gold nor silver nor copper nor iron. Metals may seem ever so hard, but in fire they soften and melt. The only thing that resists the fire and does not melt is bean curd; on the contrary, the greater the heat, the harder it becomes. That's just how it is with his utensil: the hotter the battle the harder and firmer it grows. I've tried it out. Now do you admit that my metaphor was a good one?"

"Oh, you must be exaggerating. Such things just don't exist. It would be supernatural. No, we don't believe it."

"Believe it or not, that's how it is. Far from exaggerating, I have been guilty of understatement. The little fellow in question has another miraculous quality that I haven't mentioned. But why waste my breath? You wouldn't believe me. Just wait until tonight; then you can try it out and see for yourselves."

"No, you must tell us," they insisted. "What do you care whether we take you seriously or not?" And they prodded her until she gave in. She told them how his battle-ax increased in stature as the fray proceeded and how its temperature rose from cool to red-hot.

Lovingly she brushed in the details of the picture, kindling a blaze of wild excitement in the hearts of her listeners and making them blush crimson to the tips of their ears. Ah me, they sighed inwardly, if only the possessor of such physical perfection would turn up at once; if only he would rush into bed with them without the usual detours and formalities and let them put his powers to the test.

Unhappily, they had quite a time to wait. It so happened that the Before Midnight Scholar had just gone out when Scent Cloud's maid arrived with the invitation. While she sat in her mistress's boudoir, waiting for him to come home, she was spied by Book Chest, his younger servant, who, eagerly following in his master's footsteps, rushed over through the hole in the wall to keep her company. They had time for considerable dalliance before our young man's arrival sent them scurrying in opposite directions.

At length the messenger-maid returned to her mistress. Tingling with excitement, the three young ladies put their heads together to read the letter of reply.

It was hardly a letter. Just as they had foreseen, he had

simply made Scent Cloud's couplet into a quatrain. His answer was just as succinct as the invitation:

> *Prepare a substantial meal, including a dish of leeks,*
> *To fortify me for our rendezvous.*

An acceptance if ever there was one. His literary effort could not be accused of obscurity. The message threw the two cousins into a fine frenzy. They jumped up and started for their bedrooms in their haste to make the beds, pile up the blankets, take baths, set incense burning, and make other such preparations.

But Scent Cloud called them back, insisting that the order of sequence must first be agreed upon.

Respectful of the rules of etiquette, Cousin Pearl offered the first place to Scent Cloud, who was the oldest. But Scent Cloud declared magnanimously that she would forego her priority for this night—it cost her no great sacrifice, for the pleasures of the last few nights had left her more than satisfied.

After considerable discussion it was decided that Pearl, the elder sister, should exercise her rights until midnight, while Jade, the younger, would take over after midnight.

The ladies had scarcely completed their preparations in boudoir and kitchen when the maid, whom they had posted at the entrance, appeared, lighting the way for the eagerly awaited visitor.

With a show of bashfulness, cousins Pearl and Jade withdrew to the rear of the drawing room, leaving Scent Cloud to take care of the first greetings.

He made her a deep formal bow.

"Would you kindly introduce me to your honored cousins?" he whispered to her.

Smilingly she took each of her cousins by the hand, drew them forward—they were still playing bashful—and introduced them. Pearl wished to send a maid for tea. Scent Cloud stopped her with a laugh.

"Why bother with the ceremonial tea? He has been

languishing for you enough. Forget the formalities and kiss one another. Instead of insipid tea, let him drink the noble elixir of your lips." Her sprightly words broke the ice. Our young man didn't wait to be asked twice. Deftly, he clasped both cousins in his arms, pressed them together, shoulder to shoulder and cheek to cheek, and set his lips to theirs in such a way that their three mouths formed the ideogram *p'in* 品, signifying "familiar." It was a long, penetrating kiss. At last the younger cousin tore herself free.

"I must go to the kitchen to see about supper," she said. And with a mischievous sidelong glance at him: "Especially those leeks you ordered."

"Oh, why bother! It's much too late for an elaborate meal. And as for that dish I ordered, my needs have been amply met by my sampling of your noble lips."

But Jade had already gone off into the kitchen, and a few minutes later the maids brought in the small but succulent supper. All four took their places at the table and dedicated themselves for a while in silence to the savory little cups and bowls.

Our young man, however, was not really interested in eating. His thoughts had fluttered far ahead. He poked about distraughtly in his dish of leeks and jumped up before he had finished half of it. He winked at Scent Cloud and took her aside:

"Well then," he said. "What's the order for tonight?"

"This is what we have decided: until midnight, you are to have Cousin Pearl, the elder, and after midnight Cousin Jade the younger."

"But what about you?"

"Right in the middle between the two," she said with a very straight face.

"You've managed things pretty nicely, haven't you?"

"That sounds like a reproach—I suppose you mean to say that I am behaving like the selfish host who in cutting the carp takes the meaty middle piece for himself, leaving his guests the head and tail with all their fins and bones?"

"Hm, just about. My idea was this. It seems to me that with that sort of arrangement, an awful lot of time will be lost in dressing and undressing, in running from room to room and bed to bed. Wouldn't it be more practical if we all lay down in one bed? What do you think?"

"Ah, I see what you're getting at. Mr. Greedy wants to have all three at once. You want to do the same trick downstairs as you just did upstairs with your kissing. Except that instead of the character *p'in*, that you make upstairs, your idea in your downstairs operations is to make the character *chuan* 串, "to string together." Is that it? Not a bad idea. But I wouldn't advise it the very first time. No, leave that for later. Tonight you'll have your privacy, until midnight with Pearl, after midnight with Jade, and that's that. My claim to the middle piece was only a joke. And one more thing: Take a little pains with them. Don't disappoint them."

"You don't need to tell me that. What do you take me for? But I *am* sorry you won't be with us. I was especially looking forward to your company."

Scent Cloud beckoned to the maid and instructed her to light the young gentleman to Cousin Pearl's boudoir.

She herself repaired to Cousin Jade's room. Poor little thing, having to sit up waiting her turn! Scent Cloud decided to sit with her and try, with her merry chatter, to make the time pass more quickly for her.

Meanwhile the couple had mounted the carved ivory bed. Few words were exchanged, few formalities observed; as though they had long been intimate, they helped each other undress; she undid his belt and trousers, while he stripped off her undergarments.

At first his activities gave her less pleasure than pain. She felt scarcely equal to so enterprising a foe and she was on the point of giving up. But then she remembered what Scent Cloud had told them about the sensational joys they might expect as the battle wore on. Under no circumstances

*All four took their places at the table and dedicated themselves
for a while in silence to the savory little cups and bowls.*

did she wish to forego such bliss; it would repay her for all sufferings. Bravely she gritted her teeth and submitted to the violence of his assault.

Her perseverance was to be rewarded. What she had been eagerly expecting from minute to minute actually happened; the deeper his ambassador penetrated into her pleasure house, finally forcing an entrance into her nethermost privy cabinet, the more he swelled, the higher rose his temperature. Finally he had grown into so imposing a personage that he filled her whole privy cabinet. He had cut off his own retreat with his increased girth and could no longer budge. With this the summit of bliss was attained for both of them, and Pearl experienced the wonderful sensation that Scent Cloud had so lyrically described. She had to admit that Scent Cloud's words had not been empty prattle. And passionately she embraced the bestower of such unprecedented joys.

"Dearest, your very exterior, your face, your figure, would suffice to make thousands of women die of longing for you—I just wonder why, to top it all, nature should have endowed you with so rare, so wonderful a physical treasure. It's almost too much of a good thing. You seem to have been born to drive all the women in the world mad with longing for you."

"Dearest, should I take you at your word? Would you be willing to sacrifice your life and to die of love in my arms?"

"Don't take it amiss, but having discovered that miraculous object of yours, I should like to remain alive just a little while longer—let me enjoy it a few times more, then I will gladly lay down my life. But the very first time? No, that would be too soon."

"Never fear," he said jokingly. "It won't come to that. Remember, I must devote half the night to your noble sister. The best I can possibly do is to take half your life." Whereupon he began again to thrash and to heave so tumultuously that heaven and earth were nearly thrown off their hinges.

Pearl's pleasure house was deep enough, but her "blossom heart" was not far below the entrance to her grotto. His ambassador had only an inch or two to go, and a delightful thrill came over her. She felt the pleasantest nervous tingling and it was not long before she began to moan.

"Dearest, stop. Spare my life. I fear I shall lose not just half but the whole of it."

At first he ignored her plea and went on with his thrashing until at last the increasing languor of her limbs and the cold breath that issued from her mouth made it clear to him that her delicate constitution was simply not equal to such a battle. Thereupon he forebore, threw his arms around her, and let her rest.

It was some time before she had halfway recovered her strength and was able to speak. She pointed to the water clock that was standing by the bed.

"Dearest, I should gladly expire in your arms. But it is midnight, my sister is waiting for you. You must get up and go to her."

"Right! But how am I to find my way through the pitch darkness? Would you be kind enough to show me the way?"

"I can't. You have worn me out completely. I can't even rise from the bed. But I'll send my maid to show you the way."

She clapped her hands, whereupon a young thing, holding a lantern affixed to a pole, appeared from the vestibule. She waited for our young man to dress; then she took him by the hand and drew him after her.

She was a child of barely fifteen and still an innocent virgin. She had been sitting nearby the whole time, listening with scarlet-red ears. The tumultuous sounds of the love battle had thrown her senses into a turmoil.

It was quite a long way through the dark courtyards and

*As though they had long been intimate, Pearl and the Before
Midnight Scholar helped each other undress.*

pitch-black galleries. All the while her young blood throbbed in her arteries, clamoring for appeasement. Suddenly, in a remote corner of the garden, she stopped still. At last the plea that had been gagging in her throat escaped her.

"Young Sir, please, please, won't you give me just a little taste of the sweets you have just been lavishing so extravagantly on my mistress? For the moment your way leads through me. I am the customs station. If I am to let you pass, you must pay me duty."

With these words she set the lantern on the ground, snuggled up to him, and began to poke about in her underwear.

The young man couldn't help laughing to himself. But he was gentleman enough to spare her feelings and not to offend her by a brusque rebuff. Very well, he would do her the favor. He bade her lie down on a nearby garden bench.

Somewhat distracted, his mind less on this improvised entremets than on the delicious second course listed on the menu, he set to work rather listlessly and mechanically. In any case nothing much came of his efforts, for he had poor material to work with. She was an utterly inexperienced young thing, an "unbroken melon." He encountered obstacle upon obstacle.

"Ouch, you're hurting me," she screamed. "Oh, how is it that your egg beater gave my mistress so much pleasure when all it gives me is pain. It's the same utensil, isn't it?"

Patiently and indulgently he explained that she was still an "unbroken melon," that a certain membrane had to be pierced, that this naturally involved pain and bleeding, and that she would only feel real pleasure after the ninth or tenth try.

But it seemed to him that this was hardly the time or place to instruct a beginner in the game of love, as he had once done with Noble Scent, his first wife. It was long after midnight, Cousin Jade must be waiting impatiently. Was this the moment to be teaching the elements of love on a hard garden bench in the cool night air? No, it was just too absurd.

"You see, little girl, my implement is just too big for you. Just have patience until my next visit. Then I'll bring along my nice young servant, the one who carries my books. Shu-t'ung, 'Book Chest,' is his name. He will be a much better mate for you. You can nibble all the sweets you like with him."

Quite consoled, she slipped into her panties and led him to Jade's quarters. At the door, another lady's maid was waiting who led the latecomer into the boudoir, festively illumined with candles and lamps. He found Jade lying in bed, with a book in hand.

Her expression was rather frosty as he stepped in.

"Please don't be angry, darling," he apologized hastily. "I'm sorry I'm late."

"Oh, don't mind me!" she replied testily. "Why didn't you stay there all night? Why bother to come all this long way?"

"Now, now! How can you talk like that? I am already heartbroken at having missed ten minutes of your precious company."

During this brief colloquy, he had been undressing. He crept under the covers beside her.

Jade was three years younger than her sister Pearl. She was exceptionally delicate and small boned. Her flesh, her skin were the softest and tenderest things imaginable. Her breasts felt like freshly laid hen's eggs without shells. She made the impression of a fragile figurine that the slightest pressure would break. When she strolled about the garden or floated—one can hardly speak of climbing—up the steps of the moon terrace, it seemed as though the slightest breeze would blow her away. When she sat down, it was as though someone would have to support her on the left and right to keep her from tipping over.

How could so frail a creature be expected to withstand a serious bedtime battle, let alone a contest with an adversary so impressively equipped as our young man? Her sister Pearl had already threatened to "die of love"; but she was more robust, in her mouth such words may have been a mere phrase or at least an exaggeration; in Jade's case, however, they were only too close to the truth.

Fortunately our scholar recognized the danger in time as he saw her lying there. Her eyes reduced to narrow slits by her sagging lids, her lips half parted, she struggled for breath and gasped for words she lacked the strength to utter. Perceiving to his horror that her fragrant soul was making ready to flee the fragile dwelling place of her body, he was filled with sincere compassion.

"My tender love, you can't go on? Would you like me to stop?" The question was really superfluous. Her silent nod —she was incapable of speaking—told him enough. He nimbly disentangled himself from her and climbed out of bed. For a while he sat pensively beside her, giving her time to catch her breath.

And yet how lovable she was! He felt an irresistible longing for a new intimate embrace. But this time, with tender solicitude, he chose a different position that would be sure to give her no discomfort. He lifted her over him, bedded her breast in his, set her cheek against his cheek, and threw his arms around her. Thus they fell asleep.

It was in this same, somewhat unusual position that Scent Cloud and Pearl found them in the morning when, spurred by curiosity, they appeared in the boudoir and drew aside the curtain of the bed.

"Well, well," Scent Cloud joked, poking Pearl in the ribs and pointing at the young man's portly ambassador. "There will be no need to buy a wax candle for the bed lamp tonight."

"We mustn't be unfair to our little playmate," said Pearl, laughing and falling in with the jest. "The poor candle has been burning all night and used up so much oil that I doubt whether there's very much left."

Rubbing her eyes and scurrying into her clothes, Jade participated in the general merriment.

Scent Cloud turned to the Before Midnight Scholar and addressed him in tones of the utmost gravity. "And now, listen. We have come here for serious deliberations. What is to be done? In the long run the woman in your house is bound to find out that you are having secret dealings. What is she to think when she sees you leaving the house night after night and staying out until morning? Her suspicions will be aroused and she will want to get to the bottom of the matter. And then what? What we should like best is for you to stay here the whole time and not go home at all. We should find means of passing the time—it doesn't have to be always in bed. We could play chess, compose poems together, and tell each other amusing stories and anecdotes. Wouldn't that be fun? But how are we to manage it? Have you a plan in mind?"

"Have I a plan! Have no fear, my dear ladies, I have been working on it the whole time."

"Really?" they exclaimed as though with one mouth. "Tell us. What is it?"

"Just listen. For some time now my little girl friend has been in the family way. She is *hors de combat* and needs a rest. Only recently I spoke with her on the subject. I had been traveling a long while, I said, and it seemed like a good idea to take advantage of her present condition to go back home and attend to my family.

"The trip would take approximately three months. By the time I returned, I said, the baby would no doubt be born and we should be able to resume, with renewed vigor, the pleasures of which we had been deprived for so long. She approved wholeheartedly. This very day I shall pack, take my leave of her, and taking my younger servant with me, start on my supposedly long journey. In reality, however, I shall just take the few steps from my house to yours. That will give us three full months. Not to mention the amusement we shall derive from playing chess, com-

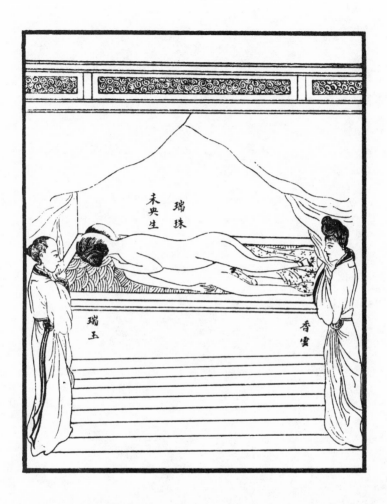

But this time, with tender solicitude, he chose a different position that would be sure to give her no discomfort. Thus they fell asleep, and they were still asleep when Scent Cloud and Pearl appeared in the morning.

posing poems, and telling stories and anecdotes, we shall also have plenty of leisure for the game of *chuan*, of 'bead stringing.' "

All three ladies jumped with delight. "Wonderful! Magnificent! Ch'en P'ing* himself could not have thought up a better plan."

"But there is still another point I should like to discuss with the honored ladies. I have two servants over there. The elder is rather stupid and obtuse, the youngest is extremely spry and clever. I am used to the lad and I should like to have him with me here, while the elder may just as well stay over there and guard the house. Would you have any objection to the younger lad living here?"

"No."

"Fine. However, there is still a small But: the boy takes after his master. He is just wild about women. Unless he finds something sweet for his palate here, he will simply run away and go back over there to live. That would attract attention and might make trouble. What should I do?"

"Oh, that is no problem," said Cousin Pearl. "We have plenty of maids in the house to satisfy his appetite if he hankers after sweets in the evening."

"Excellent."

The council of war was ended. On the same day the Before Midnight Scholar moved over to the ladies' estate with his baggage and his servant. From then on it was not only the master who enjoyed his daily fill of feminine warmth and affection, not only the master who grazed on the loveliest flowers; his servant as well was amply taken care of.

Yet alas, one day the vernal fragrance of the magic garden would pass away, and nothing would be left but sighs of grief and eternal parting.

---

* Inventor of the "six miraculous strategic plans," second century B.C.

CHAPTER XV

*Halfway to the summit of pleasure they meet with
an unwelcome difficulty. The "vernal palace" incar-
nate is carried away in a trunk.*

One day the Before Midnight Scholar made the three
beauties who had hidden him in their house a proposition
aimed at adding variety to their love game. In accordance
with the rule that had been agreed upon, one after another
of the ladies had been privileged to spend the whole night
with the young man. The order was determined by seniority. When Jade, the youngest, had had her turn, Scent
Cloud, the oldest, opened the round anew. It was after
they had completed several rounds that he suggested what
he had in mind from the very start, an arrangement which
struck him as the peak and summit of all amorous gour-
mandise.

"How would it be if after every round we were to inter-
calate a night on which all three of us should lie together?
Wouldn't that be fun?"

His proposal met with enthusiastic acceptance. The
ladies procured an exceptionally wide bed with ample room
for four persons, an enormous pillow almost seven feet
long was fashioned, and a gigantic blanket was pieced together from six ordinary blankets.

The three cousins laid down head to head, and he was
allowed, not to say encouraged, to roll and sport over them
and between them to his heart's content, taking his pleasure
with this one and that one. When he had satisfied the middle one, he honored her right-hand neighbor, and when

posing poems, and telling stories and anecdotes, we shall also have plenty of leisure for the game of *chuan*, of 'bead stringing.' "

All three ladies jumped with delight. "Wonderful! Magnificent! Ch'en P'ing* himself could not have thought up a better plan."

"But there is still another point I should like to discuss with the honored ladies. I have two servants over there. The elder is rather stupid and obtuse, the youngest is extremely spry and clever. I am used to the lad and I should like to have him with me here, while the elder may just as well stay over there and guard the house. Would you have any objection to the younger lad living here?"

"No."

"Fine. However, there is still a small But: the boy takes after his master. He is just wild about women. Unless he finds something sweet for his palate here, he will simply run away and go back over there to live. That would attract attention and might make trouble. What should I do?"

"Oh, that is no problem," said Cousin Pearl. "We have plenty of maids in the house to satisfy his appetite if he hankers after sweets in the evening."

"Excellent."

The council of war was ended. On the same day the Before Midnight Scholar moved over to the ladies' estate with his baggage and his servant. From then on it was not only the master who enjoyed his daily fill of feminine warmth and affection, not only the master who grazed on the loveliest flowers; his servant as well was amply taken care of.

Yet alas, one day the vernal fragrance of the magic garden would pass away, and nothing would be left but sighs of grief and eternal parting.

---

* Inventor of the "six miraculous strategic plans," second century B.C.

CHAPTER XV

*Halfway to the summit of pleasure they meet with
an unwelcome difficulty. The "vernal palace" incar-
nate is carried away in a trunk.*

One day the Before Midnight Scholar made the three
beauties who had hidden him in their house a proposition
aimed at adding variety to their love game. In accordance
with the rule that had been agreed upon, one after another
of the ladies had been privileged to spend the whole night
with the young man. The order was determined by seniority. When Jade, the youngest, had had her turn, Scent
Cloud, the oldest, opened the round anew. It was after
they had completed several rounds that he suggested what
he had in mind from the very start, an arrangement which
struck him as the peak and summit of all amorous gour-
mandise.

"How would it be if after every round we were to inter-
calate a night on which all three of us should lie together?
Wouldn't that be fun?"

His proposal met with enthusiastic acceptance. The
ladies procured an exceptionally wide bed with ample room
for four persons, an enormous pillow almost seven feet
long was fashioned, and a gigantic blanket was pieced together from six ordinary blankets.

The three cousins laid down head to head, and he was
allowed, not to say encouraged, to roll and sport over them
and between them to his heart's content, taking his pleasure
with this one and that one. When he had satisfied the middle one, he honored her right-hand neighbor, and when

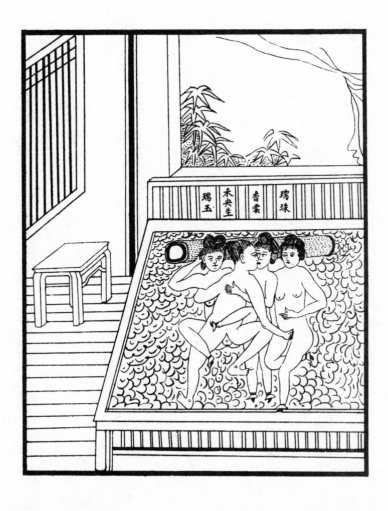

*The three cousins lay down head to head, and he was allowed,
not to say encouraged, to roll and sport over them and between
them to his heart's content.*

she had had enough—all three kept their appetites within reasonable limits—he visited the neighbor on the left.

Everyone found the game so exciting that all four of them were soon appeased: the main course was devoured in barely two hours and they spent the rest of the time caressing and fondling each other.

The Before Midnight Scholar had every reason to bless his good fortune: to lie with three beauties all at once! What young man of his age and class had ever been so smiled upon by fate? Why, it is doubtful whether even a Son of Heaven—with the possible exception of the two great imperial voluptuaries, Emperor Yang-ti (613–617) of the Sui dynasty and Emperor Ming Huang (713–756) of the T'ang dynasty—had ever indulged in such extravagances.

The three young ladies also deemed themselves fortunate. It seemed to them that they had caught the love god himself in their nets. However, there was one worry that cast a shadow on their happiness. One day when they were alone without him, they put their heads together and took counsel.

Scent Cloud began:

"So far everything has been perfectly lovely. We could wish for nothing better. Even a god could give us no greater joys. We can truly deem ourselves fortunate. But fortune is fickle. We had better take measures against possible reverses before it is too late. What if we should be surprised? What if our beautiful secret were brought to the ears of our absent husbands? That would put us in a very embarrassing situation."

Pearl broke in: "Hm. It seems to me that our estate is well hidden and excellently protected by walls and gates. Who is going to invade our ladies' chambers and poke his nose into our private lives? Certainly no man. Even our major-domo is not admitted to our living quarters; the house regulations allow him no further than the second door. Thus no danger can be expected from the male side. If there is danger, it will have to come from the distaff side, and there, I admit, I have a secret fear: there is a certain someone living in the neighborhood. If she should poke her nose in, that would be the end of our pleasures."

"What someone are you referring to?" asked Scent Cloud.

"That's an odd question. Haven't you guessed? Why, she lives right next door and bears our family name."

"Yes, of course. Aunt Chen."

"Who else? Well, you know the way she is. To the world, she displays an honorable widowhood, but in reality all her thoughts revolve around one thing: man! Do you remember when we went to the temple of the love god together? When we saw our friend kneeling before us on the temple steps and beating his forehead on the ground, she went clear out of her mind. She would best have liked to kneel right down beside him, to join him in honoring heaven, earth, and their ancestors in the hope that this would constitute a quick marriage. Don't you remember what she said when we got back home? She hadn't praise enough for his graceful figure, his beautiful face, his distinguished bearing. 'What a pity that we don't know him!' Those were her words. 'If only we knew his name and address, I'd never let him get away from me.' What do you suppose would happen if, after talking about him that way, she should find out that we had been keeping him hidden here? Imagine how jealous and envious she would be, what sinister plots she would hatch against us. I can hardly bear to think of it."

"You are right," Scent Cloud agreed. "We must be on our guard against that man-crazy female."

"What are we to do?" Jade asked.

Pearl continued: "At first I feared that our maids might talk. But fortunately we have our friend's young servant in the house. He knows how to stop their mouths. And so we have nothing to fear from that quarter, but all the more from Aunt Chen. You know her habit of coming over here unannounced, of bursting in on us and spying. Like a rat looking for bacon, she pokes into every nook and cranny, she peers to eastward and squints to westward, and always acts as if there were something to discover, some secret we were trying to keep from her.

"If we are to be armed against her eternal spying, we must take two security measures. First we must give our maids strict instructions to mount guard where our property borders on hers, to relieve one another at regular intervals, and to notify us by a secret signal, a loud cough or a sneeze, or to cry out if they see her headed this way; that will give us time to hide our friend. And that brings us to the second security measure. Where, indeed, are we going to hide him?"

"Behind the door," Scent Cloud suggested.

"Under the bed would be better," said Jade.

Pearl shook her head.

"Both would be foolish. With those lynx eyes of hers, she would be quick to find him behind the door or under the bed. No, I know of a better hiding place, where even the omniscient spirits wouldn't think of looking."

"Where?" cried Scent Cloud and Jade as though from one mouth.

Pearl pointed to a large trunk of plaited bamboo. It stood in a corner of the boudoir and served for storing old picture scrolls. It was six and one-half feet long, two and one-half feet wide, three and one-half feet high. The outside was made of plaited bamboo; the inside was lined with thin wooden slabs.

"It's just right for a hiding place," she pointed out. "Not too short and not too long, just room enough for one person. All we have to do is take out the old scrolls, then in case of emergency our friend can crawl in. There will be just room enough for him. The only problem remaining to be solved is that of air. We wouldn't want him to suffocate. But that's simple. We shall just remove a few slabs from the lining. Then he will be able to breathe through the plaiting."

"Wonderful. That's just what we will do," cried the two other cousins and went into action forthwith. The maids were summoned and instructed to stand guard without interruption on the borderline between the two properties, to relieve one another every two hours, and to give the ladies due warning should their worthy aunt seem to be heading their way. Further, they were to take the picture scrolls out of the trunk and remove a few of the wooden slabs from the lining. Finally, the Before Midnight Scholar was told what *he* must do in case of emergency: as soon as the dreaded visitor's coming was announced, he must quickly crawl into the trunk and lie there as still as a mouse.

On two occasions the security measures were actually put into practice and proved their worth. Everything went off smoothly and Aunt Chen withdrew without having unearthed any secrets.

Like many members of their sex, our three beauties loved to rummage through the belongings of their common friend. One day they made an exciting discovery. Chancing to see his card case lying about, they opened it and under the cards came across a notebook. Its contents were very startling: a long list of feminine names, arranged according to rank and class. To each name was appended a critical note—all unmistakable in his very own brush stroke.

They sent for him and stormed him with questions.

"Look what we have found. An index of your sweethearts. Where and when did you get to know them all? And when and why did you draw up this list?"

"Oh, that was when I was living in the temple of the bowstringer god. To pass the time away, I used to observe the ladies who came to perform their devotions. When one of them seemed worthy of my attention, I put her down on my list. My idea was to build up a collection of precious bamboo shoots, as it were. At some later date when I had attained office and dignity, I thought I would

花晨及子並四婢

On two occasions Aunt Chen burst into the house with her maid,
but withdrew without having unearthed any secrets.

transplant them into my yamen and sprinkle them now and then in the hope that their fresh greenery might relieve the dull grayness of my official residence—but I also intended, you may be sure, to do what I could about satisfying *their* desires."

"And have you managed to lay hands on any of your 'precious bamboo shoots'?"

The Before Midnight Scholar clenched his hands at chest level and made a solemn bow.

"You three, my treasured friends."

All three burst into gales of laughter.

"You expect us to believe that? You're just saying that to flatter us. Such insignificant little shrubs as ourselves could scarcely stand up under the severe critical standards that guided you in your work."

"I beg your pardon. If the ladies are in doubt, you have only to read what is written about you here."

He pointed to the appropriate place on his list. They were delighted with what they read. Perhaps his praises were slightly exaggerated—all three found themselves honored with the little red circles meaning extra-special—but in the main his descriptions and characterizations of them struck them as accurate.

Once they had started to read, curiosity impelled them to go on. And the very next item on the list was a note about a "dark beauty." Her qualities were very much the same as those attributed to Pearl and Jade, and his description of her was perhaps a mite more flattering than his comment on Scent Cloud. All three glowered and frowned.

"Who is this 'dark beauty'?" they asked in unison.

"Why, your companion. There were three of you at the temple. Don't you remember?"

All three laughed hilariously.

"What? That old bag," cried Pearl and Jade. "And despite her age and decrepitude you put her in the same class as ourselves. Isn't she the lucky one!"

Scent Cloud took the matter far less lightly.

"If that's the case, your comments on us are hardly flattering. Quite the opposite. With his silly standards, his opinion of us is worthless. The best we can do is to cross out all that slop he has written about us."

"Don't take on so," Jade put in. "He must have had his reasons for putting her in the same class with us. Maybe she gave him lots of love in an earlier existence, much more than we give him, and he has shown his gratitude in this existence by promoting her to the top class without even examining her qualifications. Who knows? But in that case he should have put all three of us in the lowest class right off. Be that as it may, we cannot possibly agree to so obvious a mistake. The best thing we do is strike our names off the list." Her words cut like a cold flame.

In vain he tried to explain. He couldn't even make himself heard over the cackling and gabbling of their three hostile tongues. Finally Pearl's powerful voice asserted its authority:

"Very well then, let us strike our three names and all the nonsense that goes with them off the list and leave the sole place of honor to his precious beloved from an earlier existence." So speaking, she took up a brush, crossed out the three names and commentaries and wrote in their place:

Are we, like a flock of wild geese,
To flutter about looking for triumphal wreaths?
No—let us give age its due
And modestly retire.

Thereupon she turned to the Before Midnight Scholar:

"And now we shall tell you who she is, the precious bamboo shoot you esteem so highly. You are very lucky, your 'dark beauty' lives right next door; she is our dear neighbor and beloved Aunt Chen. And now you may run along and sprinkle your beloved bamboo shoot. As for the three of us, we shall no longer trouble you to fulfill our desires."

In view of the general hostility, the Before Midnight

Scholar wisely forebore to argue. He realized that it would have been quite hopeless and he had to admit, in his heart of hearts, that he had been grossly tactless despite his honorable intentions. And so he sat for a while in silence, with bowed head, like a poor sinner aware of his wrong, patiently letting the whiplash of their anger, mockery, and scorn snap about his ears, although the more he thought about it, the less reason there seemed to be for all this excitement.

Only after the storm had died down and the waves subsided did he open his mouth and explain to the disgruntled beauties his real reason for giving the "dark beauty of mature years," the worthy Aunt Chen, so flattering a mark —he had been moved by a tactical consideration.

When she had so unmistakably given him to recognize her affection, he had thought she would be an easy mark. This had given him the idea of trying to make her acquaintance first—but only as a means to an end. The end of course was an introduction to the three nieces. It was they he had been after from the start. Should the occasion present itself, he would call her attention to the words he had devoted to her in his notebook. He had added the red circle as an afterthought to make sure that she would look upon him with benevolence and favor his desire to make the acquaintance of her nieces. Of course she didn't deserve to be put in the same special-extraordinary class as they. Would the gracious young ladies not deign to forgive his gross error in judgment in view of his good intentions? His plea was not in vain. The three beauties were instantly mollified, the last little cloud of their displeasure was wafted away, and once more there was sunshine in the boudoir.

A round had just been completed and all four agreed to spend the night together. Merrily chatting and laughing— the Before Midnight Scholar was an excellent entertainer and knew how to keep the ladies in a good humor with spicy anecdotes and jokes—they began to undress at an early hour; it was still yellow twilight. He was first to be ready and had already taken his place on their wide collective couch; the ladies were somewhat slower, they insisted on carefully folding their clothing and underclothing and piling them neatly on the pouf beside the bed. At last they had finished and were about to troop into bed when one of the maids began to cough and clear her throat in the garden. The warning signal! Aunt Chen was on her way. It was time to take cover.

With all their chatting and laughter they had failed to hear the first signal. Nimble as the waves, all four flung themselves on the pile of clothes, all reaching and grabbing at once.

Precious time was lost in the resulting confusion; the ladies had to content themselves with a meager outer covering. But the Before Midnight Scholar's clothes were on the bottom of the pile and he couldn't get to them at all. Stark naked as he was, Scent Cloud pushed him into the trunk and closed it over him.

Immediately thereafter the visitor arrived, flanked by Pearl and Jade who, as good manners demand, had taken a few steps toward the rear of the house to welcome her.

The moment she set eyes on her two nieces, Aunt Chen had smelled a rat. Fear and embarrassment were written all over their faces as they stepped up to her in the middle reception hall as though to bar her way. Suspecting that something was amiss, she refused to waste time with the usual formalities of greeting, in which her nieces wished to involve her in the hope of delaying her. Instead, she made straight for the boudoir.

"Aha! All three of my beauties together! What a charming sight! How are you? Long time since we've seen each other!"

During these brief words of greeting, she looked searchingly about the room. She ignored the polite invitation to be seated, but pursued her customary inspection of the boudoir, approached the bed, looked into it and behind it, behind the cupboards and clothes racks, and squinted into every nook and corner.

But, to her vast disappointment, she couldn't find a thing. Had all those snakes and dragons been sheer imagination? Rather taken aback, she sat down on the proffered chair and began to talk about the weather.

The three nieces heaved an inward sigh of relief. Once again, thank goodness, the danger seemed to have blown over. For a moment they thought they were safe. But then —alack, alas!—they noticed something which they had quite forgotten in the excitement, something likely to create a peck of trouble: the Before Midnight Scholar's notebook with his select list of beauties. They had left it open on the desk. How stupid of them! Now they sat there on tenterhooks, waiting for the first opportunity to make it disappear.

But Aunt Chen's eye was quicker than their hands. Before they could do a thing, she caught sight of the notebook and a moment later she had it in her grasp. As gently and inconspicuously as possible, Pearl and Jade tried to wrest it away from her. Without the slightest success. Their aunt clung to her prey for dear life. Scent Cloud quickly thought up a different and—she thought—better means of warding off the impending calamity: a little deception.

"Let Aunt Chen have it if she wants it," she said to her cousins in a tone of affected indifference. "Let her keep it if it amuses her. We picked it up on the street. It doesn't mean a thing to us."

"So kind of you," said Aunt Chen. "I'm sure it is quite without value. I simply cannot understand why you two were so dead set on taking it away from me. I think I'll have a look at it. You've made me curious." With this she stood up and took a few steps toward the window. She opened the notebook and her eyes lit at once on the promising title: "Vernal apparitions from far and wide." "Aha!" she thought, "something about love." And she decided the book must be full of pornographic pictures. With nervous eagerness she leafed through it, looking for illustrations which she thought would be more interesting than the text.

But though she leafed through the notebook from start to finish, there was not a sign of any "vernal palace" pictures; nothing but text, written in a tiny "fly-head" script.

She leafed back and began to read from the beginning. After skimming over the first few sections, she came to the conclusion that this strange list with its descriptions and critical notes must have been composed by some young academician full of wit and fine feeling. And how elegant, how poetic a style! It was a pleasure just to read it; this is much better, she thought, than some pretentious novel full of vernal episodes.

She was so entranced that she could not lay the thing down. She read and read. At last she came across a passage dealing with a certain "dark beauty." To her amazement she found that the description applied to her, stroke for stroke and line for line. Her heart began to pound. And three red circles were marked at the end of the commentary, showing that the unknown observer had put her in the highest class, that he regarded her as extra-special and outstanding. Who, she wondered, could have composed this flattering portrait of her?

She pondered. Since her visit to the temple with her nieces, she hadn't left the house; no strange man could have laid eyes on her. Visit to the temple? Why yes, that was when that handsome and charming young man had so impetuously fallen on his knees and beat his forehead on the ground in their honor—he and no other must be the author! These were the thoughts that passed through her mind.

If she had the slightest doubts, they were dispelled when, leafing back through the notebook and skipping over two sections that had been crossed out, she came across the general heading:

"On such and such an hour of such and such a day of such and such a month, meeting with three great beauties . . ."

Hadn't the three of them gone to the temple together? Next came the two crossed-out passages. Obviously they had been crossed out only recently, because the heavy brush strokes still looked suspiciously fresh. The text was all smeared over, but there were still a few signs that she could decipher without difficulty. As, for example, the words:

"Gown of red and silver . . ."
"Her dress is the delicate light green of the lotus shoot . . ."

Didn't Jade have on a gown of red and silver that day, and hadn't Pearl been dressed in light green? And now, to cap it all, the freshly written quatrain, still glistening with fresh ink:

Are we, like a flock of wild geese,
To flutter about, looking for triumphal wreaths?
No—let us give age its due
And modestly retire.

Why, that was Pearl's handwriting! She knew it well. Aunt Chen could not help laughing to herself, and in her laughter bitterness was mingled with gleeful anticipation. Just wait. She would show them a thing or two.

Nonchalantly she dropped the telltale notebook into the depths of her sleeve pocket. She suddenly put on a solemn, stern countenance as though she had a very painful announcement to make.

"Ah yes," she sighed. "Our good old Ts'ang Chieh (third millennium B.C.), the inventor of our script, was indeed a great sage."

The three young ladies exchanged looks of puzzlement. A far-fetched remark if ever there was one. What could she be getting at?

"How so?" Scent Cloud asked.

"I am thinking of the characters he invented—everyone writes them differently, in his own personal way. With their help it is possible to convict criminals—of either sex! Let me ask you a question: the three of you live here under one roof. Am I right?—Is it not remarkable that the sign which wise old Ts'ang Chieh devised for the word adultery, 姦, should just happen to consist of 'woman' written three times, as though he had foreseen thousands of years ago what is going on today here in your quarters. Am I right? Do you admit that there is something miraculous about wise old Ts'ang Chieh's script?"

Pearl tried to save the situation:

"It is true that the three of us live here together. But what grounds have you for your outrageous suspicions? We have done no wrong."

"No? And how did this compromising notebook come into your possession?"

"We found it in front of the house," Scent Cloud insisted.

"You expect me to believe that? Why, a three-year-old child wouldn't fall for such fairy tales. And now let us be serious. Where have you hidden the author of the notebook? Confess. If you confess of your own free will, I shall be merciful and spare you the scandal. Otherwise I shall write your husbands in the capital and send them this notebook as evidence. What is more, I shall advise them to come home at once and call you to account."

With courage born of despair, the three culprits persisted in their denial: "We really found it quite by accident. We know nothing about the author, whether his name is Chang or Li, or where he lives. What more can we say?" But their words sounded very feeble and made no impression at all on the prosecuting attorney. Once again she looked round the boudoir, darting her glances to eastward and to westward, until they finally came to rest on a certain object. The bamboo trunk! She had overlooked it in her previous tour of inspection.—And why was the lid closed? It had always been open before. There must be some explanation. She turned to Pearl and Jade:

"Since you refuse to confess, I shall adjourn our hearings for the moment. I really came for a very different purpose. I have always wanted to take a look at your picture scrolls but somehow I never got around to it. Won't you be so kind as to show me a few?"

Pearl and Jade exchanged looks of consternation.

"Oh," they cried both at once, "it's just too absurd! The trunk has been locked for a long while and we have mislaid the key somewhere; we have no idea where to look for it. But we shall look for it tomorrow, it must be somewhere about, and then we'll send the scrolls over to your house."

"But I happen to be just in the mood to look at them now," said Aunt Chen with an amiable smile. "It doesn't matter about the key. I have heaps of keys at home, keys to fit every conceivable lock. I'll just send one of my maids for the key basket." And that is exactly what she did. It was not long before the maid returned, struggling under the weight of a large basket. It must have contained several hundred keys.

Aunt Chen set to work at once, fitting keys in the lock.

The three young ladies stood there like statues, looking on in utter helplessness. They couldn't very well intervene, for that would only have confirmed her suspicions. Their last feeble hope was that none of the keys would fit. But it was quickly disappointed. Luck was on the side of their adversary. Their aunt had no need to try two keys or three keys, the very first one fit, the lock sprang open and she raised the lid.

And what a surprise! What did she see? No dead picture scrolls, no, an extremely living and well-shaped scroll of flesh and blood in the shape of a stark-naked, handsome youth. His skin was smooth and luminous. His truncheon —luckily for her, for otherwise the sight might have given her too great a shock—was lying in a quiet resting position across one thigh.

Even so she was so frightened that she quickly dropped the lid and closed the lock again. With a show of indignation, she turned to the three convicted culprits:

"A fine kettle of fish! So that's what you've been doing behind your husbands' backs. Since when have you had this individual in the house? And how many nights have you been carrying on with him? Confess. Where have you left your tongues?"

The three poor sinners were struck speechless. Their faces were the color of parched earth.

"Very well," said Aunt Chen sternly. "Since you are so obstinate and refuse to confess, I have no other course but to report the matter to a magistrate. There will be a public scandal. You have brought it on yourselves." She beckoned her two maids to come closer.

"I want you," she ordered, "to run and tell the whole neighborhood that triple adultery has been going on here in broad daylight. Tell them the offender has been caught in the act and that we have him safe under lock and key. Tell the people to come and look at him so they can testify when the case comes to court."

The three sinners begged for a brief adjournment of the proceedings and retired to deliberate. They quickly concluded that the threat of a public scandal was not meant seriously, that their aunt merely wished to intimidate them in order to secure a share in their treasure. Very well, that could be discussed. The most sensible policy, they decided, was to propitiate her, to make concessions, to negotiate a compromise, a *modus vivendi*.

They returned to the hall of judgment.

"We recognize the wrong we have done. We should never have done such a thing behind your back. A fault is a fault, we have no wish to deny it or embellish it. We throw ourselves on your mercy and ask your magnanimous indulgence; we further request that you open the trunk; its occupant would also like to make humble amends."

"Very well. I agree to that. But there is one thing to be settled first. What form are his amends to take?"

Scent Cloud took the floor: "We wish to inform our revered aunt that we cousins have so far enjoyed equal shares in this treasure of ours. From now on we shall be glad to offer you a one-quarter share, with the understanding that you as the oldest will take precedence over your nieces."

Aunt Chen burst out laughing.

"That is an odd, not to say ridiculous, offer. Ha, ha! As I see it, you have hidden this certain someone here for heaven knows how long and taken your pleasure with him for heaven knows how many days and nights. And now you condescend to offer me a quarter share of the future pleasures. It is as though a judge should remit a thief's punishment—no torture, no imprisonment, no restitution of the stolen goods—and merely specify that he pay the authorities a small share of the proceeds of his future larcenies. You expect me to fall for that? Don't make me laugh."

"What did you have in mind?" asked Pearl rather hesitantly.

"I am willing to let mercy prevail, to pass the matter over in silence on one condition: I will take this someone home with me and keep him for my bed companion until I have caught up on the pleasures you have swindled me out of. Once I am caught up, I shall return him to you, and you can sport with him again as you please. That is my offer. Should you decline it, I shall turn him over to the judge, and at the very best he will be thrashed until he looks like a lump of sausage with whom you will hardly wish to satisfy your appetites. Well, what have you to say?"

"In that case," Jade suggested, "we ought to specify the number of nights during which he will belong to you alone and at the end of which you must give him back. I trust that you don't mean to monopolize him for a whole month or a year."

"Let us leave that question open for the present. When I get him home, I shall question him until I find out how many nights you have been carrying on together. I claim exactly as many nights for myself alone. Then and only then will I give him back. I have nothing more to add."

The three told themselves inwardly that he would be sure to underestimate the number of nights he had spent with them in the hope of being sent back to them as quickly as possible. They said they had no objection.

"He has only been with us for two nights," they added so loudly and distinctly that the someone in the trunk would be sure to hear. "You can ask him when you get home. He will tell you the same thing."

They now wished to let him out of the trunk so that he might escort their aunt home. To this she was opposed. She feared that once free he might give her the slip.

"It is still daylight. If we should arrive together, my staff would see him and wonder what is going on. I shouldn't like that. No, we must think up a way of transferring him unnoticed."

"You go home now," the nieces suggested. "When it's dark, we shall send him over."

Aunt Chen shook her head. That too struck her as unsafe. What assurance had she that these sly young snips would keep their word and not let him escape?

"I have it. A wonderful idea. There's no need to open the trunk. We shall let my servants carry it over just as it is, contents and all. I shall tell them it contains picture scrolls which are mine but which you had borrowed for a time. It's as simple as can be."

Without even waiting for her nieces to answer, she sent one of her maids to summon her major-domo and four strong servants. They soon appeared, bringing ropes and carrying poles. At a terse command from their mistress the servants tied the ropes round the trunk and fastened them

"I have it," *Aunt Chen cried.* "We shall let my servants carry the trunk over just as it is, contents and all. I shall tell them it contains picture scrolls."

to the poles which they slung over their shoulders. A moment later the major-domo left the house followed by the servants and their burden. Aunt Chen brought up the rear with her two lady's maids.

Sad at heart, the three confederates looked after the receding procession. They felt like grieving widows looking after the coffin of a beloved husband and were very close to weeping and wailing. Away he went, their "living vernal palace"! And to make matters worse, they were worried. What would that man-crazy female do to him? It was perfectly possible that she would wear him out completely. Perhaps he would never return. That trunk was so like a coffin: an evil omen.

My esteemed readers will learn in the next chapter whether or not the Before Midnight Scholar was to find his way back to his beloved bamboo shoots.

CHAPTER XVI

Nettled by mocking verses, she demonstrates her superiority over her juniors. In possession of every possible advantage, she digs a pit for the others and falls into it herself.

On reaching home, Aunt Chen dismissed the major-domo, the porters, and even her lady's maids. She wished to be unobserved when the secret of the bamboo trunk came to light.

But first she let our young man fret for a while in his

dark cage. Meanwhile she opened a clothes chest and fished out a complete gentleman's wardrobe which had belonged to her late husband. She arranged the clothes in a neat pile on a porcelain stool beside the trunk. Only then did she insert the key in the copper lock and lift the lid. She bade the young man climb out and put some clothes on, a process in which she assisted him.

After a formal introduction and the usual ceremonies of salutation, she asked him to be seated and opened a conversation. Her manner was free and easy and she came straight to the point.

She began with the meeting in the temple and the diary and asked whether his impetuous homage and flattering commentary on her person had been meant seriously.

Our Before Midnight Scholar was no simpleton and he was not without experience in the use of soft soap. He assured her of his sincere devotion and declared that since their meeting in the temple he had thought of her day and night; consumed with longing, he had been quite inconsolable at his failure to learn either her venerated name or her honorable address. And now—he continued—he thanked heaven for having brought about so miraculous an encounter and for permitting him, after admiring her so long in secret, to enjoy her glorious presence.

Lady Chen took this bill of goods for coin of the realm and accepted it with gratitude and benevolence. She called for her maids and ordered a supper for two. After dining they went straight to bed.

Lady Fruit Blossom was a large, portly woman. While not exactly fat, she was delightfully buxom.

As he lay there, flesh to flesh, in her shapely, well-rounded arms, feeling the firm pressure of her luscious full lips, he was invaded from the very start, before even bestirring himself in any way, by a sense of blissful, almost ecstatic well-being such as he had never before experienced, though he was hardly a novice in love. My esteemed readers may well wonder how so.

Let me explain. There are two varieties of beautiful women: one is beautiful to look upon, the other is beautiful to enjoy. When a woman is beautiful to look upon, it does not necessarily mean that she is beautiful to enjoy, or vice versa. Our history records only a single case, since ancient times, of a woman, among those wielding political influence at court, who combined both these advantages: that was the beautiful Yang Kuei-fei, celebrated favorite of Emperor Ming Huang (713–756) of the T'ang dynasty.

To be beautiful to look upon, a woman must possess three qualities: she must be rather slender than stout, rather small and delicate than large and portly, rather frail and shy than robust and forward. It is thus that our painters from time immemorial have represented the ideal of feminine beauty: waists comparable to supple willow switches, limbs that do not fill out their garments but disappear far within. Our painters have not chosen large, voluptuous figures when they wished to paint women beautiful to look upon.

As to women beautiful to enjoy, it is quite a different matter. They too must have three qualities: they must be rather buxom than skinny, rather large and portly than small and frail, rather robust and self-assured than delicate and shy. Why does true enjoyment require these three qualities?

Well, I will tell you. In cohabitation a man expects three things from his companion, and it is these three things that he prizes in her: first, feminine warmth and softness; second, compatibility between her proportions and his; third, that she be able to withstand the weight of his body. To lie on a flat, skinny creature is like lying on hard paving stones. It is not very pleasant; on the contrary, it is quite uncomfortable. How different when the He has a soft, buxom She for a companion; then he basks in warmth and softness, he feels as though bedded in cushions and pillows; even before he has begun to bestir himself, a feeling of pleasure wells up in him. In addition, there is the highly estimable power of buxom, well-upholstered women to confer warmth in winter and coolness in summer. Accordingly, women of luxuriant build are preferable, for purposes of cohabitation, to skinny, cadaverous women.

Furthermore, it is a very dubious pleasure to have a little short-legged woman for a bed companion. The consequence will be a discrepancy in bodily proportions. If upstairs he holds her head to head and breast to breast, downstairs his legs will be dangling in midair; that is very unpleasant. To hold a delicate little doll of this sort in his arms may well arouse feelings of tenderness and affection in a man, but never voluptuous delight. Accordingly, big women are preferable to little ones for purposes of love.

Finally, a woman's body must withstand a considerable weight when it comes to love making. A man, after all, is likely to weigh his ninety-five to a hundred and sixty-five pounds. It takes a robust woman to endure such pressure without difficulty. It is just too much for one of your frail, willowy damsels. Her companion will be afraid of crushing her. That is bound to depress him and cramp his style. What pleasure can he have when he has to hold his passions in check and satisfy his desires in homeopathic doses? A lusty fight to the finish is out of the question. Accordingly, a robust woman is decidedly preferable, for purposes of love, to a timid, fragile, delicate young thing.

Thus we see that beautiful to look upon and beautiful to enjoy are two entirely different things. A woman who combines both qualities in her person has no need to possess all the outward charms in the world. If she is eight tenths beautiful to look upon, that will do; she will give her companion twelve tenths worth of enjoyment and satisfaction. Lady Fruit Blossom was this rare type: beautiful to look upon and beautiful to enjoy.

As our young man lay in her full bosom, upstairs enlaced by her round firm arms, and downstairs held firmly by her silken smooth thighs which were gracefully modeled for all their luscious fullness, he felt as though bedded on

How smoothly it all went off! Lady Fruit Blossom was this rare type: beautiful to look upon and beautiful to enjoy.

soft cushions, and was seized with an infinite well-being. Her bodily proportions were just right for him and his weight did not seem to trouble her in the least. Beside this sumptuous, luxuriant, mature beauty, all the others in whose arms he had lain until that hour seemed in some way deficient, either too flat and thin or too short-legged or bashful. None had ever given him such bliss.

With no other help or encouragement, his ambassador rose of his own accord to his full height and strode, proud and upright—not an ounce of humility about him—through her spacious pleasure gate—far more spacious he found it than those of her three nieces—and entered her privy cabinet to pay his due respects.

How smoothly it all went off. More quickly than usual, his ambassador had performed his diplomatic mission, and on her side as well a sigh of release indicated that the cloud of political tension had burst and the air had cleared.

After a delightful pause of relaxation, the Before Midnight Scholar, always eager for knowledge, began to ask questions:

"Dearest, how is it that you capitulate so easily? I hardly put in twenty strokes and there you are! With your three nieces I had to exert myself far more. I was never able to checkmate them in less than a couple of hundred moves. And even so, I think they were the easiest victims I had ever encountered. I should never have expected to find one who offered still less resistance."

Lady Fruit Blossom put on an expression of stern superiority.

"Pah, those young chickens! I'll pit myself against them any time! Or anyone else for that matter. You underestimate my powers. A fellow will have to shuttle back and forth somewhere between a thousand and two thousand times before I weaken."

"What's that you say? More than a thousand times! But it went off so quickly and easily just now—can it be that the noble lady was making a fool of me and only pretending to capitulate?"

"Not at all—but this time was an exception. Just remember, my boy, that I have been a widow for ten years. For ten years I hadn't lain with a man. You can imagine how things were inside me. I was literally bursting with desire, charged to the breaking point. A spark was enough to set off an explosion. Well, you happened to be the spark. But don't take me for a weakling on that account. The rapidity of the explosion was due more to my momentary physical condition than to any remarkable achievement on your part. You won't have it so easy next time."

"Hm, so that's how it is. Between a thousand and two thousand times! That takes doing. Is there not, aside from the traditional shuttling back and forth, some other, less strenuous means of satisfying so exacting a lady?"

"Unfortunately, no—though of course there are certain accessories that can help, spicy jokes, anecdotes, and so on. That kind of thing is amusing and makes for a pleasant atmosphere. Without atmosphere the game gets dull and monotonous, as though the players were deaf and dumb. Where's the charm in that?

"And while we're on the subject of deaf and dumb, that reminds me: When it really gets me, when I've really had it, I lie lifeless, as though deaf and dumb. You'd think it was *rigor mortis*. It lasts about fifteen minutes and then I come to. I'm telling you as a precaution, so you won't be worried when it happens."

"Thank you. I am forewarned. But I fear that with my modest powers I shall not be able to put the noble lady into such a state of catalepsy. Between one and two thousand times, in and out, back and forth—who can manage that? That would require extraordinary strength and endurance. I'm sure I wouldn't be up to it. My performance is second class at best. But what about your late husband? Did he meet your demands? Was he able to send you into a cataleptic trance night after night?"

"Oh him! His performance wasn't even second class; it was third or fourth. He overdid it in his youth and wore himself out before his time. He used to say that if other women's secret parts were made of flesh and blood and nerves, mine must be iron; he said they were so unfeeling that he could stand on his head without getting a rise out of me. And so he thought up certain ways and means of warming me up, and some of them actually worked. They put me in the right mood—it's the mood that counts."

"Oh, I should be glad to learn of his ways and means. In fact, I should like to try them. I might save a little strength."

"There are three of them, all very simple."

"And what may they be?"

"Vernal pictures, gallant reading matter, and suggestive sounds."

Our scholar's eagerness faded to disappointment.

"Is that all? I tried the first two in the first period of my marriage. They proved helpful, but their effect doesn't last. The first time you look at a picture or read a passage in a book, yes, it has the charm of novelty and may create a favorable mood, but the second or third time, it loses its charm and leaves you cold. I am not impressed."

"Your supply must be too small. If you keep looking at the same old pictures or reading the same books, they are bound to lose their appeal. I have several dozen albums of 'vernal palace' pictures and several hundred spicy tales. By the time I run through the lot of them, I have forgotten the first ones. I can begin all over again, and again they put me in the right mood. The main thing is to choose the right moment. Looking at vernal pictures is to be recommended before the battle begins, when both parties still have their clothes on and there is still a certain distance and coolness between them, as between host and guest. As they look at the pictures together and discuss them, a rising agitation makes itself felt in both of them. At first they should disregard it. Then, little by little, it swells into overpowering desire and all their inhibitions vanish, as though of their own accord. After that it is just a short, obvious step to undressing and hopping into bed, and it is then that the pictures will exert their full magical power.

"Gallant reading matter, on the other hand, is to be recommended when both parties have begun to undress and to exchange the first hesitant caresses. At this point they will do well to pause and read one another suitable passages from some gallant novel; then they should lie down and take their pleasure, and after they have done so for a time, let them pick up the novel again and read. When they come to an unusually gripping passage, let them lie down and resume the battle. When weariness sets in, let them resume their reading, and so on. This procedure will lend spice to their bodily entertainment, ennoble it with wit, so to speak, and there will be no room for boredom. That is the magical power of gallant reading."

"Well observed and brilliantly formulated," the Before Midnight Scholar had to acknowledge. "Unhappily, the reading matter available to me with my first wife was too shallow and silly to provide proper seasoning. Well, now I am sufficiently informed about the first two methods. But what about the last—the suggestive sounds? There's something I never heard of."

"I am referring to the passionate sounds that accompany intimate doings, not one's own but those of others. Speaking just for myself, I must own that it has always given me a fiendish pleasure, a really delightful thrill, to listen to the voluptuous sounds that lovers emit in ecstasy.

"Formerly, when my husband was still living, I used to start him up with one of the maids. Then when he was making love to her, I would remain within earshot—the sounds, his moaning, her cries of passion, would put me in a fine state of excitement. When finally the pot of my own desires was boiling and bubbling, I would clear my throat to attract his attention—that was the prearranged signal. Thereupon he would come dashing over to me and fling himself upon me like a hungry wolf. He had strict orders not to stop until I said so. Ah, what a lusty battle it was, and do you know why? Because I had arranged to get into the proper mood. When this method was observed, the battle usually ran off more smoothly than otherwise, no need for any thousand ups and downs, far from it. I was soon satisfied. All in all, this third measure is far more effective than the two others—with me at least."

"How original! How perfectly priceless! But permit me to raise one objection: you gave me to understand that your esteemed husband's performance was just about third class, that he was pretty much of a weakling. And now you tell me that he was able to take care of the two of you, first the maid and then the mistress. And to judge by your account, he must have done rather well by the maid since the sound effects put you in such fine fettle. Wasn't he exhausted by that time? How can he have joined battle with you immediately afterward, a 'lusty battle,' as you call it? That's what puzzles me."

Lady Fruit Blossom smiled knowingly.

"Why does a man have a substitute and replacement? In dealing with the maid, he sent out his substitute, and in the ensuing battle with me he let it help too—at my express demand. How else could he have managed it?"

"Aha, I see. A Little Jack Horner?"

"Right you are. I have a whole stock of the little fellows in reserve, and those of my maids who are pretty enough to be worth bothering with are similarly equipped. Today it was just a beginning between you and me; you had an easy time of it and came through on your own steam. The next time we shall ask Little Jack Horner to help us."

This was music to our scholar's ears. To whet his appetite with Lady Fruit Blossom's permission on a succulent little maid, why, that sounded like a delightful change. And yet, he felt needled in his honor. To require the services of a Little Jack Horner so soon? No, really! Did she have to say that? Was that her opinion of him? The first time, after all, he had had no need to exert himself. A bit of love play and she was done for. Did that give her a right to sit in judgment?

Suddenly he stiffened with fresh spirit of enterprise. He would show her that he was man enough to carry on a lusty tumultuous battle by his own resources. Slipping into the role of Lady Fruit Blossom's late husband when alerted by her cough, he flung himself upon her like a hungry wolf.

This time the battle was longer. He must have chalked up half a thousand ins and outs when suddenly he observed a strange change in her: starting with her hands and feet, she began to grow cold, her eyes became glassy, her mouth hung wide open, her breathing halted, all movement ceased and she lay still as a corpse.

It was the cataleptic trance of which she had spoken. It was lucky she had warned him, otherwise he would have been scared out of his wits.

The trance lasted exactly a quarter of an hour, then life, warmth, movement returned to her body. She rolled over on one side and threw her arms around him.

"You've done all right, my boy. You're terrific. You don't need any substitute to take care of me. There's nothing second class about you. You're too modest."

"Many thanks for the kind words. You will recall that I put the noble lady down on my list as extra-special-outstanding. You have been wonderfully prompt in returning the compliment."

"Ah, that list—I was just going to ask you something about that: who was it who crossed out the three names and commentaries just before where I come in? And who added that insulting quatrain?"

"I don't know," said the Before Midnight Scholar. His tact forbade him to expose Pearl as the author.

"Hm, I can imagine who it was. One of those impudent young snips. They thought they'd take a dig at me with their silly poem. They think they are too young and beautiful to be considered in the same class with me. Obviously that's the meaning of their verse. Well, granted, they are a few years younger than I; granted, they look a little fresher and snappier. But that's purely external. Yes, indeed, they are pretty to gape at when they just sit there. But when it comes to brass tacks, they can't hold a candle to me, even if—or perhaps just because—I am a little older. Not to mention what they know or don't know about the art of love. That gives me an idea: Supposing all four of us were to lie stark naked before your knowing eye. You'll be the judge. Which one's 'portal' will strike you as better built, mine or theirs?

"At the time, I saw fit to swallow their insults, to say nothing about their silly quatrain. But at the next opportunity I'm going to pay them a little visit and challenge them to a contest—four women and one man. And then we shall see who stands up better in battle, youth or mature age."

"A love contest—an excellent idea! Yes, that is something we absolutely must do. Besides, you are perfectly right, your young and inexperienced nieces shouldn't behave so impudently and disrespectfully. They should be glad to have an aunt like you for a guide and mentor. Youth requires the counsel and guidance of ripe years."

Beginning next day, Lady Fruit Blossom had recourse to her "ways and means." She had her maids fish out all sorts of vernal picture books that had lain neglected for years and all manner of gallant novels and tales, and spread them out on tables. When the time came, she and her lover studied the pictures and delved in the books for their mutual edification and the improvement of their mood.

Lady Fruit Blossom kept four lady's maids, all pretty and pert young things. Two of them, aged eighteen and seventeen, were already *p'o-kua*, "burst melons," and experienced in matters of love. The two younger, aged sixteen and fifteen, were still *ch'u-tzu*, "intact little virgins." With the consent of their mistress, the Before Midnight Scholar entrusted his servant Shu-t'ung with the rather arduous task of "opening up" the two younger maids and instructing them in the elements of love; he himself took the two older ones as succulent appetizers. And now that his honor was safe, he did not scorn to bring Little Jack Horner into the game. Thus his sojourn with Lady Fruit Blossom proved to be not only delightfully varied but instructive as well: he learned quite a good deal that was new to him about love technique.

Meanwhile the three cousins next door were getting very bored. Their horrid old aunt had already kept their darling prisoner for three days and nights. They were not even able to see him, for once the trunk was safe in her quarters, she had wisely caused the connecting door between the two properties to be locked and bolted.

All day the three grieving grass widows stood outside the bolted gate, loudly lamenting and demanding the return of the "stolen goods." But the wicked aunt let them wail and lament and hammer on the gate to their hearts' content. She remained adamant.

On the fifth day after the abduction the prisoner himself put in a plea with his stern jailer. His heart bled for the three forsaken young ladies, he was moved by their despairing cries, and besides he himself was becoming more and more eager to get back to them. They were, after all, younger.

With all the eloquence at his disposal, he tried to convince Lady Fruit Blossom that, having monopolized his person for five days, she had amply caught up with her nieces and punished them sufficiently for their cheating. He stated the case with great diplomacy and finally succeeded in softening her heart. She condescended at last to make a definite promise: when seven full days were up, she would set him free and return him to her nieces.

Her communiqué, issued through the closed gate, was received with a general sigh of relief; her nieces' anger was appeased and they desisted from their impatient pounding on the door.

The eighth day after the abduction dawned: the day of liberation!

When the gate finally opened, releasing the prisoner, it seemed to the three cousins, who had been waiting impatiently on the other side of it since early morning, as though a dense, ugly cloud that had darkened their heavens for seven days had been rent asunder and the sun which they had been deprived of for so long had burst forth in new splendor. They greeted the young man with rejoicing and besieged him with questions.

The three of them began to chirp and giggle all at once.

"How was it? Did you have a good time? What did the old bag do to you? Pretty hot and bothered, wasn't she? Did your junk manage to strike anchor in the wide Yangtze estuary? Did it find a shore to tie up at?"

The Before Midnight Scholar was cautious and tactful in his replies. He was careful not to strike up the paean of praise that he felt to be in order. It would have aroused their jealousy and put them in a bad humor; he wouldn't have wanted that. Wisely he confined his reply to a detailed report on her three recipes for mood and atmosphere, which he warmly recommended. Then he told them about their aunt's intention of challenging them to a love contest and advised them to stick together when the time came and not let their aunt get the best of them.

This announcement aroused keen excitement.

"What can she have up her sleeve? She is surely planning to put something over on us—probably she means to let us go first and keep herself for the last. Then she could warm up by watching us and be in a terrific mood for the final battle—as she herself recommends in her recipe No. 3. But we'll fool her. We shall be ever so quiet and mousy. There just won't be any sound effects. No screaming, moaning or squeaking." This was Scent Cloud's suggestion.

"In my opinion," said Pearl, "there is another way in which we can spoil her recipe without ruining our own fun. Like well-behaved nieces, we shall respectfully let her go first. Then when she is in full swing, we shall suddenly begin to shout, as though cheering her on for the final sprint. Yes, we'll give her sound effects, but not the ones she bargained for. If you ask me, that will cramp her style completely. Won't it be fun?"

"Both suggestions sound admirable," said Jade, "but I fear that our dear aunt will fool us by bringing in a proposal of her own that will prevent us from carrying them out. In my opinion the best policy would be to wait until she is here and then to act as the circumstances may dictate."

"The little one is right," the others agreed. "Let the circumstances decide for us."

Three days and nights passed, during which the three cousins sported with their lover to their hearts' content in the customary order.

On the fourth day a lady's maid appeared with a written message from Aunt Chen, announcing her visit for that very afternoon. Along with the message she had sent a money bag, including a silver piece to defray the cost of a banquet which the young ladies would be so kind as to prepare. First they would wine and dine, then there would be a love contest.

Forewarned by the Before Midnight Scholar, the nieces received the message with equanimity. The schedule, they said to themselves, called for a collective entertainment in any case; one more participant and a little more weight on the cushions would make little difference. "With due respect we accede to your exalted command"—with this brief answer they dismissed the messenger.

An hour later the visitor arrived, accompanied by four lady's maids. The Before Midnight Scholar's sharp eyes did not fail to note a slight bulge in the vicinity of her left sleeve pocket.

"What has the noble lady in her sleeve pocket? A Little Jack Horner?" he asked with a laugh.

She shook her head.

"Oh no," she replied. "Something quite different but just as nice. It is just a little game that has sometimes been very helpful at drinking bouts and bed bouts. It serves to create atmosphere. Perhaps we shall have occasion to make use of it this evening." With a sly smile she brought out a deck of drinking cards with obscene pictures on them.

"Ah, drinking cards with pictures of the different positions," cried the Before Midnight Scholar. "Usually they are just for show. But tonight our love contest will give us a chance to put them to their proper purpose. I mean . . . well, suppose each of the ladies picks a card by chance, then she tries the position indicated on the card . . . with me of course. A kind of positional lotto. It's sure to be mighty entertaining."

"That's just what I had in mind," said Aunt Chen with a nod.

"Let's have a look," Scent Cloud begged. "We ought to have some advance notice of what we are expected to do."

The Before Midnight Scholar spread the cards out on the table in front of Aunt Chen. His secret intention was that in examining the cards the young people should benefit by the guidance and learned explanations of the woman of mature years. But Aunt Chen arose from her chair and left the young folks to themselves.

"Heaven knows how many times I've looked at these cards," she remarked condescendingly. "I know all those positions by heart. When the time comes, you won't see me clinging to Buddha's feet in a fright. You look at them. I'm going to take some exercise."

The three cousins poked each other secretly with their elbows and giggled. Then they picked up one card after another and examined it. There was one card which gave them a start. The picture showed a naked girl with upraised "back yard," crouching on a rock beside a pond. A naked youth is using her in the manner of Lung Yang (favorite of one of the princes of Wei, fourth century

B.C.), as is customary among our young pansies. All three burst out laughing.

"Fooey! What kind of a position do you call that?" they cried. "Couldn't they find a more appetizing way of amusing themselves?" Attracted by their screams, Aunt Chen returned to the group.

"What is there to laugh about? Let's see." Scent Cloud handed her the objectionable card.

"Oh, the Lung Yang picture—the artist took his inspiration from literature."

"What literature?" Scent Cloud inquired.

"What? You don't know? You have never heard the old tale entitled: 'I want to get married!' That's where the artist got his idea."

"Never heard of it. What is it about? Won't you please tell us?" all three of them begged.

"Well, then. Listen. The story is about two young neighbors who loved one another. She was a beautiful, well-behaved young lady, he was a handsome, dashing young student with a rather ardent temperament. He fell in love with her, and when he could find no way of approaching her, he became so consumed with longing that he fell seriously ill.

"From his sickbed, he secretly sent her a letter, saying that if he could just once see her face to face and speak to her, he would gladly die. He assured her that she had no need to fear any improprieties on his part if she would just grant him the favor of a secret meeting.

"Touched by compassion, she granted him the meeting. She even permitted him, when they were together in a hidden garden bower, to take her on his lap, to embrace her, kiss her and caress her to his heart's content. But the fiery youth was still not satisfied and asked for more. On this point, however, she was adamant.

" 'I want to get married,' she said, 'and so I can't possibly grant what you are asking.'

"Unable to hold his passion in check, the young man

begged on his knees for mercy. But she remained steadfast in her refusal, always with the same argument: 'I want to get married.' She also pointed out that in his request for a meeting he had only expressed the desire to see her and speak to her and had promised to take no improper liberties. She had been generous enough to let him take her on his lap and kiss her and feel her all over, and it seemed to her that she had met his wishes more than halfway. But enough was enough. He just couldn't have her virginity, she wanted to keep it intact for her future marriage. What would her husband say if he found her maidenhead gone? She would be dishonored for life and rejected by society. No and again no. But the ardent youth would not desist. Again he fell at her feet and swore that he would not get up until she had heard his plea. Love, he declared, implied an intimate physical mingling. That was the law of nature. Why had nature equipped him with a certain thing three inches long? If it were not allowed to perform its natural mission, all love and tenderness, however fervent, remained incomplete and the fondest of lovers would remain mere strangers to one another.

"Thus assailed and besieged, the virgin sat and pondered. It was then that she thought up a solution compatible with the desires of both parties.

" 'I want to get married. I can't change that. And so I cannot grant you the favor you ask,' she said to the young man. 'But what if I should grant you another favor instead? What would you say to that?'

" 'I can't imagine any other favor that would fill the bill.'

" 'Ah, but I can. You don't have to do it from the front. If it must be, your certain thing three inches long can mingle with me from behind. It seems to me that that would satisfy your heartfelt wish.'

"The youth was content with the alternative solution, and so, instead of honoring her with his visit in her front yard he called on her in her back yard.

"That," Aunt Chen concluded her lecture, "is the story that inspired the artist's picture. And such an appealing story was unknown to you? I am amazed."

The three nieces did not miss the undertone of school-masterly arrogance in her final remark and it put them out of sorts. What airs she gives herself, they thought. She doesn't miss a single opportunity to show her superiority and to humiliate us. Putting down the cards, they withdrew to the next room to hold a council of war. Heaven only knew what the old battle-ax could be plotting against them. In such a situation it was imperative that they stick together and take defensive measures.

Their absence gave Lady Fruit Blossom and the Before Midnight Scholar an opportunity to fling themselves passionately into each other's arms and fondle one another. They had gone without for three days, it seemed to them like nine autumns. They would best have liked to stay by themselves and jump right into bed.

In the meanwhile dinner was announced and all five sat down to the festive board. Of course the place of honor at one end of the table was reserved for Aunt Chen; at the other end sat the "mutual friend"; the three cousins occupied the sides. Dish after dish of the choicest fare was served, accompanied by rich wines and sharp brandies. Soon the whole company was in the riotous mood which can so easily transform a merry dinner into a wild orgy.

The Before Midnight Scholar saw that a kind of chairman was needed who would take things in hand and enforce order. He suggested that they match fingers to choose a *ling-kuan*, an "order giver."

The winner, he proposed, should preside over the table and direct the subsequent entertainment. In this way confusion and quarrels would be avoided.

His suggestion was accepted unanimously—especially Aunt Chen was secretly delighted, for finger matching was her specialty. Five pairs of fists were raised at once, and each member of the company, from our scholar to Jade, the youngest of the cousins, had to show his skill at quick guessing. Quite as she had expected, Aunt Chen proved to be the quickest and shrewdest guesser. It was she who won the contest and was honored with the post of chairman, or, if you will, chairwoman. She appointed the Before Midnight Scholar *chien-ling-kuan,* her deputy. It was up to him to see that her commands were properly carried out.

From this point on all had to obey her commands. And when it came to giving orders, she was never at a loss. The first thing she did was to issue a detailed set of rules and regulations for the ensuing entertainment.

Her procedure was borrowed from the academic banquets held in the imperial Park of Rubies by candidates who have just passed the Palace examination. The *chuang-yüan,* or first victor, acts as chairman, seconded by the *pang-yen,* or second victor, and the *t'an-hua,* or third victor, who serve as his deputies.

Aunt Chen assumed the role of a *chuang-yüan.* And these were her orders: anyone whom the chairman, the *ling-kuan,* challenged to drink, must comply. Any infringement on festive discipline would be punished by punitive cups. Whenever the aunt drank or imposed a drink on one of the cousins, the Before Midnight Scholar, as a gentleman, was obliged to "keep company." Little Jade was exempted from drinking. Having come out last in the finger matching, she was treated like a candidate who had flunked his examination, exempted not only from drinking, but also from active participation in the ensuing love contest, and constrained to serve as a kind of orderly, a maid of all work, performing such menial tasks as filling the cups and standing ready with hot towels. She was expected to stay sober. This ruling was quite acceptable to our little Jade, who was decidedly weak in both subjects, drinking and bed-battling.

The regulations provided that the love contest would be organized in the form of a lotto game with cards. The deck of cards was to be placed face down. Each of the three participants—as we have seen, Jade, the youngest, was exempted—was to pick the topmost card and then proceed, with the help of the Before Midnight Scholar, to act out the position represented on the face. As to the order of sequence, the chairwoman arranged it quite arbitrarily and entirely to her own advantage. Determined to follow recipe No. 3 and improve her mood by listening to other people's sound effects, she laid down an order which was the exact opposite of what should have followed from the results of the finger matching: first Pearl, the loser, then Scent Cloud the second best, and finally the high and mighty chairwoman. Once a player had picked a card, she was forbidden to exchange it. Her regulations regarding the duration of the combat were equally autocratic. Pearl was granted one hundred ins-and-outs, and Scent Cloud two hundred, quite regardless of whether this allowance sufficed to make the cloud burst. Jade was instructed to count the ins-and-outs with the utmost precision. Any couple which exceeded or fell short of the prescribed number would be condemned to a number of punitive cups corresponding to the discrepancy. The chairwoman generously granted herself an unlimited number of ins-and-outs; the battle was to go on till the cloud burst. The participant who imitated the picture most authentically and elegantly was to be declared victor. Arbitrary deviations from the model were to be sanctioned by punitive cups and moreover entailed a reduction in the guilty party's allotted time and number.

At this point Pearl ventured a question:

"But what if the exalted *ling-kuan*, the chairman, should deviate from the model, what then?"

"Then I shall condemn myself to three punitive cups and begin again from the beginning," said Aunt Chen graciously and without much reflection. "If, in general, I should commit any breach of the regulations or injustice of any sort, you may set up a loud cry of protest. I have no wish to exert a dictatorship in the manner of the tyrant Chou-hsin of the Yin dynasty (1154–1122 B.C.)."

Here was a dangerous concession that could have grave consequences. The three cousins exchanged sly looks. Well would they mark their aunt's incautious words. But for the present they listened like obedient nieces, receiving their orders with humbly bowed heads. The Before Midnight Scholar took the liberty now and then of asking a question or raising a slight objection, and then a brief debate arose. But why were the three nieces so willing to accept regulations which obviously gave the chairman all the advantages and themselves all the drawbacks? There was a very special reason.

It was not for nothing that they had held a secret council of war. They had hatched out a plan so sly as to be positively diabolical. Just wait and see!

The rules having been established, the contest began. The chairman took a cup of wine and commanded Scent Cloud to take two; the deputy "kept company." Then Jade —this was one of her duties as an orderly—took a damp cloth and wiped the cards which had grown dusty from lying about unused for many years, shuffled them carefully in sight of all, and stacked them face down on the table.

Pearl was first to pick a card, which in accordance with the rules she showed the others. The picture represented the position designated as "dragon-fly gliding over the waves": a nude beauty lies on the bed with legs parted wide but not raised; her companion, his arms resting on the coverlet, lies over her, his torso raised a good three feet, and plays about with her in the manner of a dragon-fly which skims over the surface of the water and does not dive in.

Pearl and the Before Midnight Scholar undressed, took the position of their model, and ran through the prescribed hundred ins-and-outs. As a favor to Aunt Chen, they affected a frenzy of passion long before they had got to the point, and emitted a wide variety of rutting sounds.

Finally, Jade, who had been conscientiously counting, ordered them to stop and handed them the damp towels which she held in readiness.

Next it was Scent Cloud's turn. The card she picked and showed around represented the position known as "pushing the bark upstream." A beauty is reclining in a light armchair, the lower part of her body raised high above the edge. Her companion, standing by the edge of the chair, has lifted her legs over his shoulders. His torso bent forward, his hands propped on the back of the chair, he is pushing with all his might, at every stroke moving the chair slightly forward.

Scent Cloud and her companion took the prescribed position and set conscientiously to work. The sound effects seemed more spontaneous and genuine than those emitted in the previous performance and put Aunt Chen into so high a mood, into such a lather of excitement, that she could hardly wait for the couple to finish their stint so that she herself could go on. Since on this occasion she was able to feast her eyes as well as her ears, it seems likely that she felt even more stirred up than in times past when she had coughed to let her husband know that his preparatory efforts had put her in a state of readiness.

No sooner was the second act concluded than she sprang from her chair and proclaimed in a tone of arrogant self-importance:

"And now make way! It is my turn to perform."

Such was her haste that while one hand reached for the card, the other was already fiddling with her sash. She picked her card and looked at it. And what did she see? The hand holding it fell lifeless at her side.

"This card says . . . No, never," she cried in a raucous voice, struggling to keep her composure. "I'm going to exchange it."

Hereupon her nieces set up a loud cry of protest. They tore the card from her fingers and quickly hid the rest of the stack away. Then they put their heads together and looked at the picture on the card. Goodness, what a surprise! In one camp bitter fury, in the other malicious joy!

The picture represented the objectionable "I want to get married" position, in which the lover is forcing an entrance into his lady's upraised back yard. Was it only the malice of chance that had condemned the worthy aunt and chairwoman to perform in this position? No, it was something more.

To palm this card off on their aunt, that was the diabolical plan the cousins had hatched at their secret council of war. The execution had been entrusted to Jade, whose work it was to wipe and shuffle the cards. Once Aunt Chen had decided that the last turn would be hers, Jade had deftly smuggled the topmost card into the third position. It was the cousins' shrewd calculation that their aunt would draw this card.

However, since the card was drawn in the normal way, it seemed possible that higher powers, spirits of vengeance, had a hand in the business and had allied themselves with human wit to punish Aunt Chen for her arrogance and domineering behavior.

The nieces insisted that their aunt perform as scheduled. She put up a desperate struggle.

"Dear friends, please," she begged tearfully. "Won't you let me off? Be generous. You can't possibly expect such a thing of me."

"Let you off?" cried the nieces. "It's out of the question: Equal rights for all! What if one of us had picked this same card? Would you have let her off? I doubt it. You made up the rules. Once a card is picked, it cannot be exchanged under any circumstances. And didn't you boast that you knew all the positions by heart, that you wouldn't have to cling to Buddha's feet? Those were your very own words. If you thought that card was unsuitable, why didn't you remove it at the start? No, no. The rules are the rules. Off with your clothes. Or shall we undress you by force?"

The rebellious nieces turned to the Before Midnight

Scholar: "Hey, you. Why don't you say something? What are you deputy for? A fine deputy!"

"But my dear ladies. Far be it from me, as deputy, to take the part of our honored chairwoman—but consider, if you please, how nature has endowed me. The thing is impossible, if only on technical grounds. Let us not be too cruel. I propose that we spare our worthy chairwoman this excessive punishment and condemn her to a certain number of punitive cups instead."

But his attempted diplomacy served only to irritate rebellious youth.

"*Fang p'i!* Nonsense. If she is permitted to get away with punitive cups, why weren't we? Do you suppose we enjoyed the show we had to put on? You may be sure we would have been very glad to drain a few cups instead."

The deputy could not deny the logic of their argument. There just wasn't anything plausible he could say. He fell silent for a time and pondered. The chairwoman was also at a loss. Finally the Before Midnight Scholar found his tongue:

"I have a proposal. Perhaps your ladyships, instead of insisting that the debt be paid in full, might remit just a few farthings. Let her, if you wish, strip to the skin in plain sight of us all. Let her take the prescribed pose and forgive her the rest."

Scent Cloud and Jade raised a clamor, insisting mercilessly that the whole debt be paid. Pearl, however, declared without batting an eyelash that she accepted the proposed compromise.

"Very well, let her just undress and take the pose."

The chairwoman and her deputy heaved a sigh of relief. Though with some resistance at first, she allowed him to remove her clothing. Then, reluctantly, but spurred on by encouraging remarks from all sides, she took the position on the edge of a divan: face and belly down, rear portal upraised.

The Before Midnight Scholar sent out his ambassador

and, by way of simulating the performance demanded by the rules, let him stroll about in the valley of secret joys and sniff at the hidden rear portal, but gave him strict orders not to force the gate. Even so, the exalted chairwoman yelled bloody murder. Then assuming that enough was enough and that she had honestly fulfilled her obligations, she prepared to rise.

But the saucy young ladies wouldn't hear of it. Pearl's acceptance of the compromise solution—that she should merely undress and take the pose—had not been meant seriously. It had only been a stratagem to delude the victim and disarm her resistance. Now that she had been fooled into taking the requisite position, the show must proceed. On this the young things insisted unanimously and in no uncertain terms.

Three pairs of hands sprang into action, pushing down the victim's head, her hands and shoulders pinned fast. As though clamped in a vise, she was unable to twist or even wriggle.

There was nothing she could do. Guided by an affectionate hand, the deputy's ambassador forced his way through the narrow portal. To make matters worse, one of the three young fiends stationed herself behind the Before Midnight Scholar and pushed with all her might to increase the ambassador's impetus.

By now he was halfway in. The victim screamed and whimpered, as though under torture: "Have pity! I'm dying!" Frightened, the Before Midnight Scholar paused.

"We'd better stop. We wouldn't want to endanger her life."

"Not until the cloud bursts," cried the young fiends. "That's what it says in her own rules."

"Well, then, suppose we ask her how she's doing."

"It's burst, it's burst," moaned Aunt Chen. And then again: "It's burst, it's burst."

Finally the executioners relented and released their victim. With difficulty Aunt Chen struggled to her feet.

Speechless and broken, she staggered out, supported by her maids.

For three days she lay sick in bed, racked with fever. A painful red swelling had formed on her rear portal.

Her three days of bed rest brought repentance. She recognized the wrong she had done her nieces with her arrogance. Though still a mite resentful, she felt that her punishment had been deserved.

As soon as she was able to go out, she returned next door and celebrated a solemn reconciliation with her former enemies. From then on the five of them—four women and one man—took their pleasure in perfect harmony and friendship on the same cushions and under the same blanket.

Meanwhile more than three months had elapsed since the Before Midnight Scholar had taken his leave of Aroma and, instead of going home as he had said, moved in with the three cousins. He had promised Aroma to be back in three months. By that time her heavy hour would be over and the child would be born.

His adventure with the four beauties had detained him longer than he had expected; he had forgotten all about going back to Aroma. Then one day he remembered her and discovered to his horror that the three months had long been over.

He hurriedly sent his servant Shu-t'ung over to his house to announce his impending arrival. Shu-t'ung brought him the news that Aroma had meanwhile been happily delivered and given birth to twin girls.

Aunt Chen and the three cousins congratulated him and for three days they all celebrated the happy event. Then they took leave of him and he returned to Aroma.

When he arrived, the twins were no longer in the house. Immediately after their birth, Aroma had entrusted them to two hired nurses. She feared that the presence of two infants would hamper her personal freedom and prevent her from living her own life. She was determined to enjoy herself just as in the days preceding her pregnancy.

It was exactly a month after giving birth that Aroma's long-lost lover returned to her. She supposed that after so long an absence his host would march up with flying banners and flashing spears and challenge her to furious battle as in times gone by; she assumed that he would dutifully pay up his arrears of love.

She was in for a bitter disappointment: his armed forces, formerly so truculent, were utterly exhausted and mutinous, his treasury empty; in short, she found him flabby and listless, and all her efforts were powerless to rekindle his courage and fighting spirit. Small wonder after the four months he had spent battling with four different women. Under such circumstances the mightiest armament, be it of bronze or iron, will inevitably be blunted and the richest store of virility, be it wide as a river and deep as the sea, is bound to run dry.

From that moment on, they shunned one another. And Aroma, whose desires remained unsatisfied, began to suspect that the Before Midnight Scholar might not be the right man after all.

Whether and how she recouped her losses elsewhere you will learn in a later chapter.

CHAPTER XVII

*The daughter of an honorable family falls into the
gutter, so atoning in full measure for her husband's
guilt. Two brothers vie with one another in the enjoyment of an exclusive courtesan, thus unknowingly
repaying an old debt.*

The story of how the Before Midnight Scholar arrived, by
degrees, at the goal of all his desires has been nine tenths
told. As to the setbacks and disappointments he was to meet
with, we have thus far heard barely two tenths of the story.
Let us now stir the ink on the ink-stone, let brush dance
over paper and relate how he was to be requited in full
for the guilt he had accumulated in the course of a dissolute
life concerned solely with the pleasures of the wind-and-
moon game, how, in short, he was to reap what he had
sowed.

In Chapter XIII it has been related how Yü-hsiang,
Noble Scent, the Before Midnight Scholar's first and
legitimate wife, secretly left her home in the dead of night,
accompanied by Ju-yi, her maid, and Honest Ch'üan, her
lover.

One day in the course of their wanderings, she was
taken with labor pains. While still at home, she had tried,
by a hundred ways and means, to destroy the forbidden
fruit of her womb, but without success. Now it was her
bitter lot to be relieved of the undesired fruit on the high
road, far from home—and now, sad to say, it was too late.

If only it had happened a few days earlier while she was
still at home, all the misery and hardship of flight into the

uncertainties of the wide world would have been spared her; she would have been able to go on leading the sheltered life of an honorable daughter of an honorable family. But now a return to her father's house was unthinkable. Now it became clear that her flight had been unnecessary, that all her sufferings had been in vain. Fate had cruelly decreed that she too was to atone for the crimes of her sinful young husband.

As for Honest Ch'üan, his conduct had been inspired far less by sensual lust than by a desire for vengeance and retribution. Now that he had seduced and abducted Noble Scent, his thirst for vengeance had been stilled. He was quits with the Before Midnight Scholar, the thief of his domestic honor.

There was nothing more to attach him to Noble Scent. She had merely been the object of his vengeance, the means to an end. Now he lost all interest in her. From the very beginning of their flight he had planned to get rid of her sooner or later, by selling her into the human and social *hsia-shui*, or "quagmire."

In view of her pregnancy, however, he had decided to wait. If she should give birth to a healthy little boy or girl, he planned to marry her and stay with her. To deny his own flesh and blood, to let a child of his grow up among total strangers, no, that his sense of paternal duty and honor would not allow; that would have struck him as mean and ugly.

But now that she had brought an unripe, dead fruit into the world on the open road, he felt freed of all responsibility for her person and decided to sell her as soon as possible.

Shortly thereafter the travelers arrived in Peking, the capital, and took up quarters at an inn.

Next day Honest Ch'üan sought out a professional go-between and commissioned her to sell his "merchandise" in the "quagmire." It is customary among these traffickers in human flesh, when dealing with a well-born, unsuspecting victim, to set a trap; the poor young thing is led to believe that she will find temporary shelter at the house of a kindly "aunt," where she will be well taken care of until her husband can find suitable lodgings for both of them.

Honest Ch'üan resorted to this trick and his two companions, falling into the trap, followed the go-between to the house of the "kindly aunt."

The "good aunt" chosen by the go-between was the owner of a widely known and highly esteemed "flower garden." This "wild goose mother" was known in the world of voluptuaries by the high-sounding name of K'u-hsien niang, signifying "Mistress of the Grotto for Demigods."

After a brief introduction the wild goose mother looked Noble Scent over. Her practiced eye was quick to see that this was quality "merchandise," an unusual investment that would pay excellent interest. Without the usual bargaining, she paid the asking price for both items, Noble Scent and her maid Ju-yi. She assigned Noble Scent a spacious and pleasantly furnished boudoir and permitted her to keep Ju-yi as her lady's maid.

So far Honest Ch'üan had been possessed by an unscrupulous thirst for vengeance. Now that he had sold an innocent woman into the "quagmire" for a handsome bit of money, his conscience suddenly began to trouble him. "Have I not," he asked himself, "carried my vengeance too far?"

And his meditations continued thus: "I have heard of a saying of Buddha that is written in one of the sutras: If you wish to know of your deeds in an earlier life, consider their reward, the lot you have harvested in this life; if you wish to know of your destiny in a future life, you need only consider your deeds in this life.

"At bottom I myself was to blame for the domestic scandal I suffered: I showed criminal negligence in failing to guard my wife closely enough. And perhaps—who knows?—I was guilty of fornicating with another man's wife in a previous existence; perhaps my domestic misfortune was a punishment for that. Who knows? If I had simply accepted my punishment, my old guilt would have been expunged and I should be quits with the powers.

"What gave me the idea of taking vengeance into my own hands and of seducing this Noble Scent, another man's wife? In so doing I have burdened myself with new guilt for which I shall have to atone in a future life. And if it had to be, if my lust for vengeance was too strong for me, might I not have contented myself with a few nights of fornication? I should have been amply avenged. Why, on top of it all, did I have to drive the poor woman out of honorable society and condemn her to the 'quagmire'? Why did I have to turn a respectable woman into a public harlot? What entitles me to suppose that everyone—all her future customers—has a debt to settle with her husband? With all this I have gravely sinned and perhaps the worst offense of all was to subject a perfectly innocent little maid to the same sad fate as her mistress."

Such were Honest Ch'üan's repentant thoughts. Full of remorse, he beat his breast and stamped his feet in self-reproach and swore to devote the rest of his life to atonement. For the harm he had done was past undoing.

He took the proceeds of his sale of human flesh and gave them away to charitable institutions, hospitals, homes for the aged, and havens of refuge for the homeless. Then he had his head shorn bare, put on a shirt of coarse wool, took up a crude staff, and became a pilgrim. So he wandered from place to place, from province to province, spurred on by the pious resolve to find a holy hermit, a master of high degrees, who would be willing to take him for a disciple and show him the way to purification and perfection.

After a long wandering through the northern provinces, he reached the southern province of Chekiang. One day he came to the hut of Ku-feng, Lonely Summit, the hermit famed far and wide for his sanctity, who lived in the solitude of the *Kua-ts'ang-shan*, the "mountain swathed in azure blue." The people revered him as a Huo-Fo, a "Living Buddha," and some even regarded him as the successor of Matanga, the disciple of Buddha who, reborn after five centuries, had introduced the doctrine of Buddha into China (64 B.C.) during the reign of the Emperor Ming-ti (76–58 B.C.).

Honest Ch'üan was taken in by the holy hermit. After twenty years of the hardest asceticism, he was to achieve perfection. But that is another story. Let us get back to Noble Scent.

Before two days had passed, both she and Ju-yi had discovered what went on in the house of the supposed "good aunt"; they found out that they had been deceived and lured into a vile trap.

Escape from a flower garden with its thick walls and closely guarded gates is next to impossible even for a courageous woman with a high sense of honor. A woman like Noble Scent who had already abandoned her honor of her own free will, who had long since lost her innocence, found little difficulty in resigning herself to the inevitable and in making a virtue of necessity. She confided quite openly in the mistress of the grotto and philosophically accepted the fact that from now on she was no longer a member of respectable society but just another of the light women who live in a certain neighborhood distinguished by its shiny red, blue, and green portals.

It goes without saying that in taking up her new status, she relinquished her honorable name and took a "stage name" suitable to her new environment. The author will continue to use her old name, just as he has continued to call her seducer Honest Ch'üan, though of course this latter assumed a temple name when he entered on his life of meditation and atonement. Otherwise, the esteemed reader would doubtless be confused by so many different names and very likely see flowers dancing before his eyes.

It was shortly after her arrival at the Grotto for Demigods that the new girl was introduced for business purposes to a wealthy old gentleman. He was a regular customer, highly esteemed for the high prices he paid, and the wild goose mother was at great pains to comply with his wishes. He would usually remain at the grotto for several days and nights on end, running up quite an impressive bill. On the present occasion he stayed only one night. Early next morning he took his leave. It was in vain that the wild goose mother tried to detain him.

"Oh, no," he said. "Your *ling-ai*, 'commanding darling,' is perfectly satisfactory in point of looks and good manners. But she lacks the higher technique, she knows nothing of certain little tricks. You must absolutely teach her. For today I shall take my leave and wait until she has learned and sufficiently mastered the three artifices. Then I shall return and humbly ask for her again."

With these words the esteemed customer took his leave. You will wish to know what he meant by his remarks about "higher technique" and the three "tricks." Let me explain:

The Mistress of the Grotto for Demigods was celebrated far and wide for her mastery of three special artifices that are quite unknown to most respectable wives. She had no great outward advantages, her looks were strictly middling, and as to her cultivation, the less said the better; she had never even learned to dip a brush in an ink-pot.

And yet despite her lack of advantages, this woman had been highly esteemed by the gallant society of Peking for the last thirty years. Her admirers came, without exception, of the most distinguished circles; all were *chin-shen*, "wearers of red girdles," dignitaries in and out of office; some were dukes or even princes; commoners were not admitted to her presence. Now, at fifty, she had acquired the ownership of an exclusive flower garden; and many a gentleman of rank and wealth still found her eminently desirable and was only too glad to share her couch from time to time. How, the esteemed reader may ask, is this astonishing success to be accounted for? It was all due to her perfect mastery of the three above-mentioned artifices.

What were they? First: "Lady solicitously lowers her pleasure house toward gentleman's ambassador"; second: "Lady obligingly lifts her pleasure house to meet gentleman's ambassador"; third: "Lady sacrifices vital essence for gentleman's benefit."

Underlying principle: It is not the gentleman who should court the lady, but the reverse.

If he lies down on his back, she mounts to the saddle and guides his ambassador into the right channel. When the ambassador is flushed with enterprise, she holds him tight as a flute in a flute case. When he is listless, she rekindles the flame of his desire with deft finger play.

Other women tend to weaken in the course of a love battle; their loins are enfeebled, their limbs stiffen, and they are compelled to stop playing. With the wild goose mother it was the exact opposite. Her limbs seemed impervious to fatigue and never lost their suppleness. The wilder the fray, the more active and enterprising she became; she withstood her adversary's attacks and joyously took the counteroffensive.

She used to say: "To challenge a man to a bedtime battle is like asking a man to scratch me where I itch; but how is he going to guess where I itch? Try as he may, he is bound to miss certain spots. The best thing I can do is to help him find the spot; he will benefit and so will I. That is what is meant by the technical formula *fu yin chiu yang:* "Solicitously to lower the pleasure house toward the ambassador."

That is the first artifice. Now to the second. Ready for the fray, the lady takes her place beneath the gentleman. But she does not leave him to do all the work; full of sympathy and understanding, she assists him, taking up his movements and accompanying them. In this way she turns the game into a delightful butterfly chase, so giving herself and him twofold pleasure and at the same time making it

easier for the assailant to arrive at his main goal, the *yü-kuan*, or "jeweled enclosure."

Another of her sayings was: "True pleasure must be had in common." The two participants must meet each other halfway, then their encounter becomes a feast. If the lady does not respond to the gentleman's movements with sympathetic counter-movements, but remains passive, he might just as well resort to a wooden or cardboard woman with an artificial pleasure house. Why bother with a living woman of flesh and blood? Every first-class courtesan follows this principle, so gaining the favor of her guests and increasing her own pleasure at the same time.

This then is the second artifice. It is designated by the technical formula: "Obligingly to lift her pleasure house to meet the ambassador."

Finally we come to artifice No. 3. Here we have to do with something quite extraordinary, something bordering on magic and the black arts. When there is mutual sympathy between players and they are intimately entangled, she is animated by a desire not to waste the vital essence of her womanhood, not to secrete it for nothing, but to bestow it on her lover for his lasting pleasure. Otherwise she will regret the emission as a sheer loss, a loss of capital so to speak. And so she resolves that her secretion of essence will not be in vain but will redound to her lover's advantage. But how does she go about it?

When she feels on the verge of ecstasy, she commands her lover to bring his *kuei-t'ou*, his "tortoise head," close to her *hua-hsin*, her "flower heart," and then to cease all movement.

Clasping him in her arms and legs and pressing him close, she gives her belly a very special twist which causes her "jeweled enclosure" to open and the orifice of her "flower heart" to come to rest precisely on the orifice of his ambassador. The ambassador is thus enabled, when ecstasy sets in, to drink in her vital essence. It pours directly from her gateway into his *tan-t'ien*, his "field of cinnabar," and produces its effect.

The wonderful thing about this kind of essence is that it possesses a vitalizing power which no ginseng preparation can approach; moreover, there is nothing like it for prolonging life and rejuvenating. This then is the third and highest artifice, known by the technical formula *shu yin chu yang:* "Sacrificing vital essence for the lover's benefit."

Where, the esteemed reader will ask, did she gain her knowledge of this higher technique? I will tell you. From an itinerant juggler and magician, in whose arms she, at the age of sixteen, had met with the inevitable experience of *shu-lung*, "combing through," that is to say, loss of maidenhead. In gratitude no doubt for the favor she had shown him, a total stranger to the locality, he had given her the secret recipe, which she had studied well and conscientiously followed. However, it was not all comers but only her favorites who were privileged to nibble at her artifices.

In the course of the game, she would give her favorites various kinds of intimate advice, and those who followed it properly could be sure of obtaining pleasure such as they had never dared hope for. A man who had spent two or three nights in her arms felt as though newborn. His vital spirits were rekindled, his energies redoubled, and her powers of rejuvenation were reflected even in the freshness of his cheeks, the brightness of his eyes.

Small wonder that her fame spread far and wide and that a woman capable of bestowing such gifts came to be regarded as a higher being, a fairy who had descended for a brief time on earth. This was the reason for the flattering epithet which grateful admirers had conferred upon her: K'u-hsien niang, Mistress of the Love Grotto for Demigods.

Some of my readers may suppose that once she had practiced her higher technique with certain favorites, they were sufficiently initiated to go home and teach their wives and would have no further need of the Mistress of the Grotto. This may have been true of the first two artifices, which could be taught without great difficulty. But the third was inimitable; it remained her secret and monopoly.

And now let us get back to the wealthy customer who had been in such a hurry to leave the grotto. He had, as we may easily surmise, been attracted to the establishment by the special reputation it enjoyed. When the mistress assigned him Noble Scent, the new girl, he assumed that she must be as well versed as the mistress in the higher technique, that she would give him the utmost pleasure and enjoyment without any exertion on his part.

He was in for a disappointment. Noble Scent was totally ignorant of the higher technique and it never entered her head to try to make things easy for him. Especially as this elderly, pot-bellied gentleman was hardly the playmate she would have asked for.

And so she lay there passive and indifferent, leaving him to shift for himself. Like a great fat turtle he spread out over her jasper body. But he had scarcely got settled when he began to gasp and groan for dear life, lost his balance and slipped off. With a moan and a grunt, he rolled into a more comfortable position by her side, clutched her and pushed her up on top of him. Noble Scent was rather phlegmatic by nature; as an only child, she was more accustomed to being waited on than to wait on others. She let her companion wear himself out ministering to her in reverse position. She gave only the faintest pretense of joining in the proceedings; all she actually did was to sprinkle his wax candle a little; immediately afterward she slid off his belly and, feigning tiredness, curled up in a ball with her back to him.

He was gentleman enough to stop mauling this fragile, small-boned creature; he gave up his efforts as a bad job and left her in peace. In his disappointment, he was rather short with the wild goose mother when he took his leave of her in the morning. However, he still felt attracted by the new beauty and was determined to come back and try again. Hence his parting instructions (recorded above) to the Mistress of the Grotto.

After bowing and scraping the discontented customer to the door, she summoned the unfortunate Noble Scent.

"So that's how the land lies," she cried, "Miss Sensitive thinks she can play dead and take money for it—is that what you call service? Are you trying to scare away my best customers?" Brandishing the *chia-fa*, the "household medicine," or whip, she ordered poor Noble Scent to undress and kneel down to receive her deserved punishment.

But her anger was quick to blow over when she saw the poor sinner in all her frail beauty cowering on the floor, and heard her pleading for mercy in a voice that sounded like the sweet sobbing of a nightingale.

"Oh, all right," she said. "I'll admit you're a mere beginner. I shall be lenient just this once. Put your clothes on and listen to me attentively." And she began at once to explain the fundamentals of her method. This was Noble Scent's first lesson, but it was not to be the last. Day and night the mistress continued untiringly to instruct her pupil and initiate her in the secrets of the higher love technique. Nor did she confine herself to theory. There were also practical illustrations and exercises.

When the mistress, as sometimes happened, shared her couch with a favored customer, she sent for her pupil and bade her watch closely and observe each one of her movements. Conversely, when a customer was assigned to Noble Scent, the mistress took her place by the bed and looked on attentively to make sure that her pupil was doing things properly.

Noble Scent proved to be an eager, conscientious pupil, first for fear of provoking the severe wild goose mother's displeasure and second out of ambition, for she aspired to equal the fame of her preceptress. She made rapid progress. In less than a month she had acquired the higher technique

The wild goose mother brandished the "household medicine,"
the whip, and ordered poor Noble Scent to undress and kneel
down.

and mastered all three artifices as perfectly as the mistress herself.

Moreover, she had three advantages over her teacher: her youth, her beauty, and her cultivation. Inevitably her reputation soon outshone that of her mistress, spreading to the most fashionable circles of Peking society and even to the imperial court. Lofty mandarins and academicians, bearers of red girdles, both old and young, dukes and princes came swarming to the grotto and vied for her favor. There was no end to the stream of coaches and carriages attended by mounted retainers, that drew up before the Grotto for Demigods.

Among the distinguished visitors there were two gentlemen who willingly paid the highest prices for the honor and privilege of being received by Noble Scent. For a single night in her company they were glad to pay twenty silver pieces. Through it all Noble Scent remained cool and calculating as her father's training had made her. Cut off from her family and all good society, she was determined to provide for her future and old age. Rank and generosity —these were the considerations that guided her in distributing her favors.

Accordingly, she served the two young spendthrifts with especial zeal. And who do you suppose these two gentlemen were?

They were the young husbands of Pearl and Jade, the brothers Wo-yün sheng, "Scholar of the Resting Cloud," and Yi-yün sheng, "Scholar of the Reposing Cloud."

As related, they had recently come to Peking in the company of their indispensable tutor and drill master, the worthy Hsien-hsien-tzu, Scent Cloud's elderly husband, to attend the celebrated Kuo-tzu-chien, the "Academy for Sons of the Throne or Princes," the exclusive preparatory school for sons of distinguished families, and to prepare for the great state examination.

They too had got wind of the fame of the bewitching little nymph of the Grotto for Demigods. Once they had heard of her, there was no holding them, and secretly, each behind the other's back, first the elder, then the younger repaired to the grotto to determine, by assiduous study, whether or not the Grotto's enviable reputation was justified.

Both of them received their money's worth and each one thought the nymph was madly in love with him. It never occurred to them that she might really be interested in their pocketbooks. It must be owned that it was not exactly right of her to fornicate simultaneously with brother and brother; even in the flower garden quarter, where ethical principles were not taken too literally, such conduct was considered immoral. But in Noble Scent the spirit of business enterprise swept away all other considerations. She asked no questions about age or family relationships, and made no bones about carrying on simultaneously with son and father and grandfather; she was quite willing to sacrifice her certain little something on the ancestral altars of three generations at once.

In the end, of course, the two brothers were not able to keep their goings-on secret from each other; servants' tongues will wag, and one fine day each was apprised of the other's double dealing, which was of course his own. Far from taking the discovery to heart, they put aside all acrimony and decided with a laugh and a shrug to share their pleasure like true brothers. They even decided to give their indispensable companion and helper, their worthy tutor Hsien-hsien-tzu, a share in their delectable secondary studies.

From time to time they invited Noble Scent to their dwelling for special lessons and she instructed all three of them together in the higher love technique. The worthy Hsien-hsien-tzu discovered that she really did possess a miraculous recipe, that she really was able to refresh and revive the flagging powers of old gentlemen, and he regretted only that he had not had such a woman for his wife, for if he had, he would not be reduced to shirking his matrimonial duties toward Scent Cloud.

In the course of these hours of amorous instruction, the three gentlemen unwittingly repaid their debt to the thief of their domestic honor, the Before Midnight Scholar. And seldom has an account been settled with such accuracy, for whereas he had wronged them first seriatim then all together, now it was first seriatim, then all together that they avenged themselves.

After two semesters of study at the Princes' Academy in Peking, the two "cloud scholars" thought it might be a good idea to return home to see how their young wives were doing. Having obtained a three-month leave of absence from the rector of their institute, they set out for home in the company of their tutor.

On their return, their young wives were naturally eager to learn whether their husbands had had any exciting adventures with women while in Peking. That first night, each of the cousins plied her husband with the same questions. And each of the husbands was only too glad to relate his experience with the wonderful nymph of the Grotto for Demigods, whose amorous talents all three of them praised in the most fulsome terms.

Next morning the three young women exchanged impressions with a frankness befitting those who have sworn an oath of sisterhood. And it became apparent that the three reports were identical. The three cousins exchanged looks of consternation.

"If this is really true," said Pearl dejectedly, "if this strumpet in Peking really has such a marvelous technique, we wives might just as well pack up and leave. We are worthless."

"Come, come," Jade protested. "Those three good-for-nothings have just cooked up a story to humiliate us and spur us on to greater effort in the fulfillment of our duties. The whole thing sounds perfectly incredible."

"I have an idea," said Scent Cloud. "Suppose we ask our

young friend his opinion. He is so well informed in these matters. He is sure to know whether there is really such a sorceress of love in Peking. Let us ask him over at the first opportunity."

They did not have long to wait. It was the season of the Tsing Ming festival, "Festival of Luminous Clarity," when men celebrate the coming of spring and at the same time honor the dead. The tradition calls, at this time of the year, for long walks in the country, combined with visits to the tombs of the dear departed. Our three husbands prepared to visit the tombs of their ancestors, to sweep them clean, and perform the prescribed devotions and sacrifices. This meant that they would be absent for a whole day.

No sooner were they gone than a lady's maid was sent to the nearby dwelling of the Before Midnight Scholar, with a message requesting him to drop in for a moment. He came at once. They apprised him of their husbands' ravings about the Peking strumpet and asked him his opinion. He shrugged his shoulders and replied:

"Strange and unusual things have been known to happen beneath the heavens. Why, among the courtesans of Peking, should there not be one endowed with extraordinary gifts, a kind of sorceress if you will? I shall probably be going back to Peking one of these days. I shall seek out her grotto and spend a night with her and see for myself. And anyway what can clumsy ignoramuses like your husbands be expected to know about the art of love? I wouldn't worry too much about anything they said."

That night he gave the matter ample thought before going to sleep. All three husbands, he reflected, seemed to tell the exact same story. Didn't that suggest that there must be some truth in it? He told himself, moreover, that though he had now familiarized himself with every conceivable type of beautiful woman and every possible variant of the amorous art, this was apparently something new, a gap in his experience that he was in honor bound

The worthy Hsien-hsien-tzu discovered that she really did possess a miraculous recipe.

to fill. And furthermore, in his present state of exhaustion from having battled with five women at once for several months, it could do him no harm to let his sagging forces be revived by this unusual technique. He had been particularly impressed by what he had heard about the third artifice, the possibility of transmitting the vital essence of womanhood. His mind was soon made up: he would set out for Peking and the Grotto for Demigods.

First he would pay a duty call on his father-in-law and wife. After all, they lived in the western mountains, not far from Peking. The two projects could be conveniently combined.

How in the course of this journey undertaken out of pure frivolity a whole mountain of sorrow and shame was to descend upon him, which even the concentrated power of the western stream was powerless to wash away, you will learn in the next chapter.

CHAPTER XVIII

The measure of sins is full. With both "halls of fragrance," his first as well as his second, he experiences shame and disgrace. The wheels of repentance are set in motion. All the pleasures of the senses are exhausted and dissolve into nothingness.

Before going away, the Before Midnight Scholar took leave of his friend and adoptive brother K'un-lun's Rival.

At that time he bade him keep watch over his house in his absence and take care of his wife Aroma and the twins.

"I shall gladly keep an eye on your house, procure food and fuel, and help out with money if the treasury runs low, but I cannot undertake to guard your inner chambers, to take responsibility for your wife and children; for that I am too awkward and rough a man. That I must leave to you."

"I expected nothing of the sort. I merely thought you might help with the practical cares of the household. As far as my wife and children are concerned, I have already made my arrangements. Besides, Aroma is a woman of mature experience and exacting in her tastes; you may be sure she will not do anything foolish or immoral as an inexperienced young newlywed might. Her former husband Honest Ch'üan was a perfectly serviceable mate; in me she has a still better one. Since I have satisfied all her needs, her only desire is to belong to me forever. What better can she possibly hope for? She will be faithful. No cause for worry on that score."

"So much the better. Then everything is shipshape. And in case there is anything you would like me to do later on, you need only write me."

"Excellent."

Our young man wrote Aunt Chen and her three nieces a letter of farewell and each of his four darlings sent him a tender farewell poem in return.

He devoted the last two days to Aroma and various domestic affairs. Then he set out on his journey.

One afternoon he knocked at the door of his father-in-law's house. Nothing stirred within. He knocked again and again, with the same result. There was not a sound to be heard.

Amused and at the same time reassured, he told himself that such behavior was perfectly normal for his eccentric old father-in-law; it merely showed that nothing was changed and that there was no strange man in the house.

"Splendid," he said to himself, "it won't matter much if I stay away for another few months." And he kept on knocking undismayed, pausing now and then to rest.

Finally—meanwhile night had fallen—he heard sounds within, first the shuffling of felt slippers, then the squeaking of the rusty bolt. Finally the gate opened, but very little. Someone peered cautiously through the opening. It was Dr. Iron Door.

"Yu-chang, honored father-in-law," cried the Before Midnight Scholar, "open up. It is I, your devoted little son-in-law. I'm back from my travels." Whereupon the door opened wide and admitted him.

Silently Dr. Iron Door escorted the young man into the middle reception room. The young man performed the prescribed kowtow and squatted respectfully on a mat at his *yu-chang's* feet. He offered him first a *t'ai-an*, "sublime peace," then a *ch'ing-chi*, "pure happiness," for the absent daughter of the house, and inquired about their priceless health.

Dr. Iron Door heaved a long deep sigh.

"As for myself, old bachelor that I am, I still enjoy the same rugged health as before. But concerning my daughter I have sad news to relate. After your departure her health failed and she began to waste away. She suffered from insomnia, lost her appetite, and her mind became entangled in the thicket of melancholia. Before the year was out, she breathed away her poor three inches of life breath. So young, alas. The poor child . . ."

He could not go on, his words were stifled by sobs.

"Dead? But how is it possible?" cried the Before Midnight Scholar in consternation. Overwhelmed by grief, he could say no more. He beat his breast in despair and joined in his father-in-law's lamentations.

"Where is her coffin? Has she already been buried?" he asked after regaining his composure.

"Her coffin is still in the cold room. I didn't want to bury her until your return. Come!"

The father-in-law led him to the back of the house, to the "cold" room, situated behind the hall of ancestors. There indeed stood a coffin, flanked by incense tables with burning wax candles and smoking censers. The lid was closed and already nailed down.

The young man knelt at the head end of the coffin and for a time gave himself up to renewed lamentations.

My esteemed readers will no doubt be mystified by the presence of this coffin. Let me explain: The coffin was empty. When Dr. Iron Door discovered that his daughter and her maid had been secretly abducted by Honest Ch'üan, two considerations had guided his actions. First, he dreaded gossip, he didn't want to be talked about; second, he feared that if his son-in-law, on his return, should find his wife gone, he would stand on his rights and take the matter to the judge. That would create a public scandal. What Dr. Iron Door valued most in this world was peace and quiet. Scandal was one thing that he wished to avoid at any cost. He decided to hush the matter up.

He bought a coffin, nailed the lid down, and had it placed in the cold room. Then he spread the news that his daughter had died suddenly of an illness. In this way he succeeded in concealing the true state of affairs first from his neighbors and now from his son-in-law and in avoiding unpleasant repercussions. And he went on living as before in the undisturbed seclusion he so dearly loved.

Our young man was a simple, unsuspecting soul. It would never have occurred to him that a solemn old pedant like his father-in-law, a man who had no use for jokes and had forgotten how to laugh, could possibly be putting on an act. Besides, his account of the causes leading up to her premature death seemed perfectly plausible. When he, the Before Midnight Scholar, had left her so precipitately, she had just been awakened to feelings of love. It struck him as perfectly natural that a young woman so suddenly forsaken by a heartless husband should suffer from the fires of her just awakened senses, that her thoughts should stray into the inextricable thicket of melancholy, that she should fall a prey to mental illness and die. Assailed by feelings of guilt, he felt that he had been to blame for Noble Scent's death. In short, our young man was completely taken in by his father-in-law's playacting. He spared no expense to give the dear departed a worthy funeral; for three days and nights a group of monks intoned solemn lamentations beside the empty coffin and prayed that the deceased would soon be reborn into a happier existence where she would forget all resentment against her heartless husband.

After thus fulfilling his duties as a husband and appeasing his conscience, he took his leave of Dr. Iron Door. Once again it was his studies and the need to prepare for the great examination that provided a pretext for his hasty departure. Actually a certain grotto in Peking was the goal of his studious journey.

No sooner had he arrived in Peking and taken lodgings at an inn than he hired a coach and drove to the Grotto for Demigods. In response to his request for a certain new nymph, he was told that she was absent, that a noble lord had carried her off to his mansion a few days before. The noble lord, it appeared, was just wild about her and reluctant to let her go. But she had announced her return for the next day but one. The esteemed visitor was requested to be patient until then.

Our young man's spirits fell from dizzy heights to gloomy depths. On the next day but one he repeated his visit. The wild goose mother received him in person. Beaming, she informed him that this time he was in luck.

"My young nymph has sent another message saying that she would definitely be back this evening and expressly adding that if any estimable and attractive customer should ask for her, there was no reason not to detain him and let him wait till she returned."

Overjoyed, the Before Midnight Scholar reached into his purse and paid the wild goose mother thirty silver pieces in advance.

"Accept this fee and leave me your estimable young nymph for three nights. I also have a few personal presents for her, but those I should like to give her myself."

"Very well. But it is still early in the afternoon. Perhaps the young gentleman has an errand or two in the city; that might make the time pass more quickly . . ."

"No, no, I have come to Peking only for the sake of your commanding darling, I have no other affairs or errands —with your permission I shall wait right here."

"Just as you wish. You can wait in my little wild goose's boudoir and spend the time reading; or lie down if you prefer and take a little nap. Make yourself at home. And now if you will please excuse me, my household duties call me."

"Why, certainly. Don't let me detain you."

The wild goose mother escorted the visitor to her wild goose's boudoir and ordered a young serving maid to wait on him, to make tea, and to prepare a censer of fragrant sandalwood. Then she took her leave.

The Before Midnight Scholar preferred to lie down and take a nap. He told himself that it could do his troops no harm to gather a little strength for the impending battle. He slept for a few hours; night was falling when he awoke. Then he arose, took a sip of tea, and picked up a book. He was leafing through the first pages when a shadow at the window caused him to look up.

He saw a beautiful young woman. She stood close by the window and stared at him wide-eyed.

He approached the window to get a better look at her, but she had quickly turned away and was gone. It looked as though she wished to avoid him.

The little serving maid was just filling his teacup. "Who was it that stared at me so?" he asked her.

"Our *chieh-chieh*, the young mistress of our house, the one you are waiting for."

Could she have something against him? Why had she not come in? Was she going to refuse her services?—Tormented by impatience and uncertainty, he rushed out into the boudoir to look for her. Wherever she might be, he must get to the bottom of the matter.

Esteemed reader, let me explain. The woman who had just been staring at him and who had fled so precipitately was Noble Scent. Just returned from her sojourn of several days at the castle and informed by the wild goose mother that a new admirer had been waiting impatiently for her all afternoon in the boudoir, she resolved to give said admirer a secret looking over to see whether he was attractive enough to seem deserving of her company. To her horror she had recognized the Before Midnight Scholar, her own husband! Her bad conscience told her that he must have come to call her to account and would stir up a nasty scene. She decided to avoid him, for there was nothing she so detested as horrid scenes and domestic quarrels. That is why she had turned away from the window so quickly. She had fled to the wild goose mother, meaning to ask her advice in her distress. On the way—more horror!—she saw the visitor rushing out of her boudoir and running behind her in the same direction, toward the wild goose mother's rooms.

It was too late to ask for advice. All she could do now was to take advantage of her short headstart and hide. She was determined to avoid the unpleasant recognition scene and the scandal that was bound to ensue.

Arrived at her goal, she was breathless from running and barely able to squeeze out the words: "I cannot receive that gentleman. It's out of the question. He mustn't even see me. Not under any circumstances." Then she slipped into the wild goose mother's boudoir, bolted the door behind her and, utterly exhausted, flung herself on the bed.

At first the wild goose mother was at a loss to understand her strange behavior. The visitor, after all, was a very nice looking young man and unquestionably of noble origin. Why had she so brusquely turned her back on him? She had little time to think about it, for already the visitor came storming into her reception room, demanding his rights and his nymph in no uncertain terms. After all, he had paid in advance, quite generously it seemed to him.

The wild goose mother did not wish to offend so distinguished a customer. She attempted a diplomatic lie:

"She has just sent another message. Her noble admirer still does not wish to let her go; he insists on keeping her a few days more. I am very much embarrassed, you may be sure. I fear there is no point in your waiting any longer—I am very sorry . . . but . . ."

"Stuff and nonsense," the Before Midnight Scholar interrupted. "She has come back. I've seen her with my own eyes. She stared at me through the boudoir window. There's no use trying to pull the wool over my eyes. I presume that my price is not high enough. That's why she has chosen to run out. Very well, I can add a little more. But I ask you, is it right for her to run away like this? Is that a proper way to behave? Is she afraid I want to paint her portrait? She could greet me at least and then get rid of me, but politely at least. She might bear in mind the old rule of conduct:

If you dislike your fellow man,
Try not to let him see it.

"I saw her running in here. She is hiding somewhere in your quarters. Let me look for her. I bet you I shall find her. If I lose the bet, you can keep my thirty silver pieces and I shall ask for nothing in return."

These words made the wild goose mother's mouth water. Not a bad proposition. Thirty silver pieces for nothing. Unfortunately she could not take him up, he would be sure to find her. She tried another tack, gentle suasion:

"Very well, I won't deny it. She has indeed returned. But she is so weary and dejected from the exertions of her visit—that admirer of hers is quite a lecher, you should see how he lights into her. In short, she is in urgent need of rest. Give her two days, then she will receive you."

"Agreed. But before I go, I should at least like to see her and personally make an appointment with her for later. You must forgive me, but I want to be sure that next time I won't be dismissed with ridiculous excuses. Won't you please call her?"

"As you wish," the wild goose mother conceded, and led him from the reception room across a small inner courtyard to the nearby pavilion where her boudoir was situated. She found the door barred. There was no answer to her summons.

"Darling, the young gentleman insists on seeing you. Do be reasonable and come out, just for a moment." At first she spoke softly, then more and more insistently. But still there was no answer. . . .

Alas, it was too late for an answer. Reflecting on her predicament, Noble Scent had told herself that there was only one honorable way out: death by her own hand.

Supposing she were to appear before her husband, what could she expect? A public scandal. He would make a dreadful scene and hale her before the judge. For adultery and desertion—heaven knows how many blows she would be sentenced to. They would beat her to death. Moreover, the scandal of it would dishonor her family—was it not better to die by her own hand? Thus she would avoid the hateful scenes she so detested. By passing judgment on herself, she would expunge her guilt and no longer have to fear the reproaches of her ancestors in the Land of the Yellow Springs.

She removed the silk sash from her waist, looped it over a rafter, stood up on a stool, and hanged herself.

When shortly afterward the Before Midnight Scholar, filled with rage and impatience, kicked the door in and entered the boudoir, he found her hanging there.

He turned away in horror. He had not recognized the dead woman and had lost all desire to look at her face more closely. "Away from this abode of evil!" he said to himself. His only thought was to be gone as quickly as possible. But the wild goose mother barred the way.

"Where do you think you are going?" she cried. "You will kindly stay right where you are. How could you do such a thing to me? As far as I know, I have never injured you either in this life or in an earlier existence—how then could you hound my little girl to her death, how could you drive her to suicide? You've robbed me of my best worker, my hope, the prop of my old age. You'll have to answer to me for that." And she began to scream for help at the top of her lungs, spreading the alarm throughout the length and breadth of the flower garden.

From every side, from all the many rooms, the customers came running as though by appointment—the sons of counts and princes, all admirers of the fair nymph who had heard of her impending return and were eagerly waiting for the privilege of paying her their respects.

Their hearts bled at the sight that met their eyes; it is possible that they were even more upset than if their own legitimate spouses had passed away. Their hair stood on end with horror and rage, their caps lost their balance and began to slip or wobble.

Their unanimous rage was directed against the unknown stranger, this undesired interloper and disturber of the peace. Was it not he alone, according to the wild goose mother, who had hunted their adored nymph to her death? Could one continue to breathe the same air as such a scoundrel? No, there was no room on earth for such as he; away with him. Unanimous in this opinion, they called their servants and lackeys who were waiting outside with the horses and coaches, and incited them to make short shrift of the supposed murderer.

In vain the Before Midnight Scholar protested his innocence and tried to explain what had happened; they wouldn't even let him speak, and before he could count three he was seized by rough hands, thrown to the floor, and belabored with riding whips and broken branches.

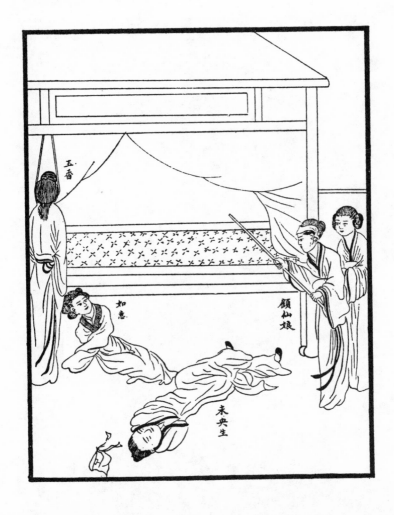

玉香

如意

顧仙娘

未央生

"Away from this abode of evil!" he said to himself. *His only thought was to be gone as quickly as possible. But the wild goose mother barred the way.*

Soon he was black and blue all over, his back and rump covered with abrasions and contusions. To make matters worse, the wild goose mother put an end to all hope of escape by fastening his ankles with foot-cuffs brought from the "cold room," the torture chamber for recalcitrant strumpets. And as though the measure of his suffering were not already full, she finally—oh cruel irony!—had him laid on a mat, side by side with the corpse which had meanwhile been cut down.

There he was to lie until the police should come for him. Left alone with the dead woman, he was seized with an irresistible desire to look at her more closely. Previously, in his desire to escape, he had not taken the time. What could she look like, this unknown enemy whose strange behavior had put him in so desperate a situation?

He turned to one side and looked at the lifeless face beside him. And suddenly he started in terror. Her features —was it possible!—were exactly those of his first wife, his Noble Scent. He looked more closely. No doubt about it, it must be she, Noble Scent. It was hardly conceivable that there could be another who resembled her to a hair—but according to her father, Dr. Iron Door, she was dead. He had shown him her coffin. Or could it be that . . .?

Under the pressure of his predicament, his mind began to work feverishly. A light dawned in his brain and from the dark chaos of doubt and error a chain of clear ideas took form: she had not died at all; she had been seduced by some wretch, abducted, and sold into the "quagmire." But in order to hush up an embarrassing family scandal and to save face, his father-in-law had staged a comedy based on an empty coffin and simulated grief. She, for her part, had spied him through the boudoir window, recognized him, run away from him in her understandable shame, and finally, driven into a corner, had taken her life. Thus everything fitted logically together in his mind, and what had been obscure and unintelligible shaped itself into a certainty. But how sad a certainty!

He had to own that speculation played a considerable part in this version. Would it convince the police? Would it convince the judge? That was the question. They would ask for proofs. How could he prove that this dead woman was Noble Scent?

Again his brain began to work intensely, and then something occurred to him: he remembered that Noble Scent had a red burn on the back of her head, where the hair had not grown back and there was still a bald spot. He turned the dead woman's head a little to one side, lifted her great knot of hair, and looked underneath. Yes, indeed, there was the bald spot, the elongated red scar he was looking for. All doubt was dispelled. Now he would be able to defend himself with a clear conscience when the police . . .

But here they were. Summoned by the wild goose mother, three members of the local police watch appeared on the scene. Two questioned him by turns, the third kept the record.

Calmly the Before Midnight Scholar made his statement, explaining in clear, logical order the events which had hitherto seemed so baffling to those present. He told them how he had come here quite unsuspectingly and only later, when lying fettered beside her on the mat, had recognized the dead woman as his legitimate wife and suddenly understood her strange behavior. It was only too understandable, he explained, that having recognized him, she had run off and finally, in despair, taken her life. Consequently, he concluded, he had no fear of the judge; on the contrary, he wished to be brought before him as quickly as possible.

The constables turned to the wild goose mother and asked her whether she could corroborate this statement. She shrugged her shoulders and said she knew nothing. The investigation proceeded:

"Who," the constables asked, "was the man who brought the girl here and sold her to you? If he was a professional procurer, he presumably did not bring you just this one, but several others at the same time. Are any of these in the house now? The dead woman, unfortunately, cannot speak, we can learn nothing from her. What we need is a living witness."

At length the wild goose mother opened her mouth.

"She had a maid with her when I bought her from a stranger. I bought the maid at the same time and let her stay with her mistress. She is still in the house. Should I call her?"

"At once. What are you waiting for?"

The wild goose mother ran out to look for little Ju-yi. She searched everywhere. After a while she came back empty-handed.

"She's not to be found."

"When and where did you see her last?"

"Just now. Scarcely half an hour ago. She returned from a journey with her mistress and followed her into my boudoir."

"Then she may still be here. Get going! Search the premises," the sergeant ordered his two men. The men searched every nook and corner of the room, looked into cupboards and clothes closets, behind screens and curtains. Finally they lay down flat on the floor and looked under the broad bed. And there she was. She had rolled up like a porcupine and made herself as small as possible. Amid raucous laughter the minions of the law tugged and pulled the trembling little girl from her hiding place and brought her to the sergeant. Even he could not repress a grin of amusement.

"Do you know this individual?" the sergeant began, pointing to the prisoner. At first she was unwilling to speak. Should she pretend not to know him? she asked herself feverishly. She was ashamed to be seen by him. But to the sergeant's practiced eye her embarrassment, the nervous way in which she kept fiddling with her mussed hair and trying to put it in order, spoke clearly enough.

"Yes or no?" he roared at her and this trusty old technique loosed her tongue.

"Yes," she said slowly and hesitantly.

"You have heard everything he said. Is it true?"

"Yes, it is true."

"Good. What more do you know of the whole affair? Go on. Talk!"

Once she had begun to speak, she shook off her timidity and told the whole truth without hesitation. Quite coherently, she related the whole course of events from beginning to end and confirmed that the dead woman, her former mistress, was the only daughter of Dr. Iron Door, who lived in the western mountains, and the legitimate wife of the accused; that a strange man, who had made himself useful as a gardener and servant and wormed his way into the household, had seduced her mistress and got her with child, that one night her mistress, for fear of discovery and of her father's anger, had taken her along and run off with the seducer, that the seducer, instead of marrying her and founding a respectable household with her as he had promised, had heartlessly dragged her off to the "quagmire" and sold her, and that today, on recognizing her own husband in the new customer, she had been driven, in her shame and despair, to take her life.

This testimony corroborated the accused's statement and sufficed, in the constables' opinion, to clear him of all suspicion.

"Clearly," said the sergeant, "what we have here is a private family tragedy. If there is guilt, it is private guilt and can be atoned for only in private. There is no ground for setting the high authorities in motion." And he added: "Remove his fetters. He is free."

Then he informed the Before Midnight Scholar that it was up to him to decide whether to leave his late wife's maid here in the house of the wild goose mother, who had purchased her in all due form, or whether he wished to take her with him, though in this case of course he must buy her free.

The Before Midnight Scholar shook his head apathetically. He was weary of everything. He felt empty and burned out. What could a woman matter to him now? Even if it had been Noble Scent herself, he would have felt no desire to take her out of the "quagmire" and try to begin a new life with her. And as for the little maid—she meant nothing to him. He was so weary and sick at heart.

"As for my former servant, my late wife's maid," he declared, "I attach no importance to her. She has had time to grow accustomed to life in a brothel, she would have difficulty in adapting herself to the ways of respectable people. Let her stay here. For the rest, I shall take no measures. I wish to let the matter drop. I might perfectly well petition the court to take action against the unknown thief of my domestic honor. But what good would it do me? Why should I stir up a public scandal and let my good name be dragged through the muck? Why should I expose myself to public ridicule?—No, I can't see the point in it."

"In that case the affair is settled," said the sergeant and retired with his men.

The wild goose mother heaved a sigh of relief. She had feared to be drawn into an unsavory trial. But now there would be no unpleasant repercussions. Of course the death of her best worker meant a considerable loss for her establishment, but it was clear, as the police hearings had shown, that she had no reason to put the blame on this strange customer. The whole incident had just been a tragic concatenation of unfortunate circumstances. Fair minded enough to recognize that she had been cruelly unjust to him in the first flush of excitement, she hastened to make amends by returning the thirty silver pieces he had paid in advance. Then she politely escorted him to the door.

Bent with pain, he hobbled with difficulty toward the coach that was waiting at the entrance. But he was not at the end of his troubles. The young noblemen who had witnessed the tragic scene were waiting for him. They still supposed that our young man was to blame that their beloved nymph had been taken from them. Lining up on either side of the roadway, they forced him to run the gantlet. One slapped him in the face, another poked him in the ribs, and all reviled him with the hallowed epithet: "*wu-kuei wang-pa*," "nasty black turtle!" In short, his departure from the Grotto for Demigods was anything but glorious.

That night there was no sleep for the Before Midnight Scholar. For one thing, his physical wounds, the abrasions and contusions on his black-and-blue back, burned fiercely and made it impossible for him to lie in any reasonable position. But there was also the torment of his conscience—the wheel of his thoughts turned and turned and would not stand still.

It was night all round him and within him as well. His heart was full to overflowing with bitter grief, burning pain, and black gloom. His mind was like an ocean lashed by a furious storm. At length, from the chaotic tumult of his thoughts groping in darkness, a logical sequence of insights struggled free and shone with a harsh redeeming clarity, like a chain of fireballs in the night sky.

"Presumptuous as I was," he said to himself, "I looked upon other men's wives as free game that I was entitled to hunt down. It never occurred to me in my blindness that my own wife might become free game for others—and so I whored and fornicated to my heart's content wherever and whenever I could—and now I have met with retribution. Never would I have dreamed that it could come so quickly and cruelly. I carried on with the wives of others, now the others have avenged themselves through my wife —and what makes the retribution all the harder to bear is that I after all carried on secretly with the wives of others, while they have fornicated openly with mine!—I, after all, took Aroma, the wife of Honest Ch'üan, for my second wife; I gave her an honorable home and a respected position in society. And what happens to me? My wife becomes a public prostitute, the property of all. Could any object lesson show more clearly that it is better not to whore with other men's wives? It is a wrong that is bitterly avenged. That is just what Lonely Summit, the holy hermit, told me three years ago! How right he was! How urgently he warned me against the dangers of carnal lust. How he pled with me to stay with him and renounce the world of red dust. And I, blind, obstinate fool that I was, I threw his well-meant advice to the winds, quarreled with him, and finally turned my back upon him in anger. Now I see that no one can evade retribution for his sins. The Prince of Heaven is just and no respecter of persons; there is no ground for supposing that he had a grudge against me in particular, that he has singled me out for punishment but closes his eyes to the activities of other sinners. And fool that I was, I made yet another mistake in my reckoning: How well I remember the argument that started up between me and Lonely Summit when he quoted the saying:

Court not your neighbor's wife
And your neighbor will not court yours.

I parried with the argument that there were innumerable women and young girls to be fornicated with, but any one man could only afford to keep a limited number of females in his household. Admitting, I said, that according to this theory of retribution a gallant were punished by the seduction of all his wives, there were far more women available with whom he could recoup his losses; despite the retribution he suffered in the person of his own wives, adultery would still be a lucrative business for him—such was my insane argument. But now I am brought face to face with the bitter truth: whereas I fornicated with a mere six women, my own wife seems to have done so with hundreds of men—with several dozen at the very least. Obviously my calculations were misleading to say the least. Indeed, I was as presumptuous in my reckoning as in my fornication. And what were Lonely Summit's last words to me as I left him? Yes, they were a prophecy, and now the prophecy has come true:

" 'My words are powerless, but experience will prove to you that my warning was justified. You will find your way to enlightenment on the Jou-p'u-t'uan, the "prayer mat of flesh." ' Now I have spent three years in abject idolatry on the 'prayer mat of flesh.' I have tasted all the sweets and all the bitterness—nothing remains untasted. What am I waiting for? The time for awakening is at hand! Did Lonely Summit not speak of the drumbeat with which Heaven wakes the sinner when his measure is full? But what have I lived through today? The public disgrace, the blows! If these were not a heavenly drumbeat, I'd like to know what is. It still resounds in my ears. Beyond a doubt that was the drumbeat with which Heaven, operating through human hands, wished to admonish and awaken me. So be it! The hour of repentance and meditation has come. What am I waiting for? The *Kua-ts'ang-shan*, the 'Mountain veiled in azure blue,' is calling. The holy man, Lonely Summit, is calling me. I hear his call, and this time it will not be in vain. I shall go to him. I will kneel down before him in repentance; a hundred times I shall beat my forehead on the ground in humility; I will confess my wrongs and beg him to receive me, to show me the ford across the furious stream of error and help me to reach the saving shore of redemption."

With these thoughts he had found his way to a decision. As soon as his wounds were healed, as soon as his health would permit, he would resume his wanderings, this time toward the southern province of Chekiang, until he should come to the cell of Lonely Summit, the holy hermit.

But first he would put his domestic affairs in order. What was to become of Aroma, his second wife, and the twins? The very next morning he dragged himself to his desk, planning to compose a letter to his friend and adoptive brother K'un-lun's Rival, giving him the necessary instructions. But alas, he had not considered the sorry state he was in. Stiff and swollen from yesterday's beating, his limbs refused to do his bidding, his bruised fingers were in no condition to hold, not to say guide, a brush. He fell back on his couch in resignation. A whole month of bed rest and medical care was needed before he was well again and his hand, otherwise so nimble at writing, was fit to use again.

Now, after a month's delay, he decided to put his plan into effect and write the letter. He had just dipped his brush in the inkpot when a messenger appeared, bearing a letter from K'un-lun's Rival. It was very brief. All it said was that domestic occurrences of the utmost importance demanded his personal presence; on receipt of this letter, he should not lose a moment but set out at once. There was no further explanation.

"Aroma must be sick," the Before Midnight Scholar reflected. "Or perhaps something has happened to the twins." These were the only ideas that came to him.

"Do you know what it's all about?" he asked the messenger.

At first the messenger was reluctant to speak. Apparently he wished to spare the Before Midnight Scholar a piece of unpleasant news. But after a little prodding, he finally disclosed the truth:

"Your second wife has run off with a strange man."

"Who is the seducer?" inquired the Before Midnight Scholar rather indifferently. The news seemed to have left him untouched. The messenger shrugged his shoulders.

"I don't know. Her maid didn't know anything either. Night after night she had been hearing suspicious sounds in her mistress's bedroom, as though she were carrying on with a man. But she saw nothing, not so much as his shadow. For some ten nights she heard the same sounds, then one morning she found the nest empty, the door to your second wife's rooms was open, she herself was gone, no one knows where; money, jewelry, clothing and linen had all been carried off in suitcases. That is why my master sent me to you. He wants you to come at once and has asked me to accompany you on the way. He himself was meanwhile going out in search of your second wife."

The news came to the Before Midnight Scholar from an utterly alien world, a world he had long left behind him. What did all that matter to him? He heaved a sigh and thought to himself:

"Another drumbeat from Heaven. And what is its lesson? Wrongs sprung from carnal lust are requited a hundred-fold. No sinner escapes retribution. If the retribution struck only me! If I were merely punished through my wives. But there are two innocent children. Perhaps the retribution will strike them too, my own flesh and blood? And will they too have to atone? Perhaps it would be better for them never to have been born. But why should I plague myself over that now? I shall seek counsel with Lonely Summit."

Once again he dipped his brush, which had meanwhile dried, in the ink and answered his friend as follows:

"A lustful second wife gets herself abducted. What is so breathtaking about that? It cannot move me:

Goods acquired unjustly and unlawfully are bound to be lost unjustly and unlawfully!

"It is a common experience. Now it is my turn to meet with it and I must resign myself. Such mishaps are just retribution for my sinful way of life. But all that is ended. My better self has awakened. The demons of temptation have departed from me. The path I mean to follow from now on leads to the shore of redemption. The one thing that still troubles me is the uncertain fate of my two help-less children. Will they too have to atone some day for the guilt of their parents? Innocent fruits of sin, they are still in need of affectionate parental care. May I ask my old friend to care for them like a father and to watch over their life breath until, grown to be a worthy successor of Buddha, I can deliver them from evil with the help of my holy blade?"

He gave the messenger the letter and sent him on his way, accompanied by his young servant Shu-t'ung. Our scholar had meant to keep Shu-t'ung with him on his journey to Chekiang, and to enter the boy in his service as a *shami*, or "spiritual servant." But then he had changed his mind, fearing that the constant company of this spry and handsome young fellow, whose nature was every bit as dissolute as his master's had been, would rekindle vain worldly thoughts in his bosom and make him backslide.

He who has once been bitten by a viper, will long fear anything that looks like a rope.

Better part with him at once and forever. Accordingly it was all alone that he set out one day on the long journey to the Mountain of azure blue. Whether Lonely Summit would have pity on the repentant sinner and receive him into his cell, you can learn in the next chapter.

[At this point there is a late gloss saying:

["With this chapter the true, profound meaning of the whole novel becomes clearly discernible. The esteemed reader need read the other chapters only once, but this chapter as well as the final chapter deserves to be read three or four times in a row."]

CHAPTER XIX

With mild indulgence Hermit Leathersack takes in
two sinners, the demon of lust and the haughty bandit.
On the wide sandalwood path to salvation two former
enemies meet without resentment.

Since the Before Midnight Scholar's abrupt departure three
years before, Lonely Summit had time and time again
reproached himself bitterly. He could not forgive himself
for his failure to win over this demon of lust, who was
outwardly so appealing and for that very reason so very
dangerous, for his failure to persuade him to stay on in his
cell. "I must still be far from perfection," the hermit told
himself. "Surely I have not developed half enough 'maternal
heart' if all my arts of persuasion have bounced so inef-
fectually off the intellectual armor of this so unusually
gifted boy. Who knows what havoc this handsome young
demon of lust will wreak in ladies' bedchambers!"

The young scapegrace, so the hermit's thoughts ran on,
was less to blame than he, Lonely Summit, who had been
incapable of curbing him and holding him fast. In need of
a whipping boy for his dissatisfaction, he lit on the leather
sack he had so carefully made himself. Had he not, while
working on it, poured into it a number of mysterious
incantations, expressing his hope that the sack might catch
some poor bewildered, but repentant soul, whose earthly
husk might become a helper to him and take his place when
he was gone?

And now that such a one had come and was within easy
reach, the magical power of the consecrated sack had

lamentably failed. "Useless thing. Out of my sight!" he cried angrily. And by way of punishment he banished it to the top of a gnarled fir tree, which stood like a solitary temple guard before the door of his cell. Let the useless thing hang up there in the wind and weather until . . .

As he climbed from branch to branch and fastened the sack to the treetop, the master had an idea. Maybe the young man would return some day repentant? Then let him see by the empty leather sack hanging up there in the branches that his place was still vacant, still waiting for him. Let him interpret the sack in the treetop as an invitation. But would he understand the symbolism of it? Eager to make the invitation perfectly plain, the master cut out a rectangular wooden slab, upon which he inscribed a few rows of fine characters; then he nailed it to the tree trunk at a height where it could plainly be seen. The inscription ran:

> *Even if the Before Midnight Scholar does not come at once,*
> *Even if the leather sack does not receive him tomorrow,*
> *The sack will not rot, the little monk's hope will not die:*
> *Let him not dwell forever on the prayer mat of flesh,*
> *Let him one day return to the leather sack.*

Strange, there seemed to be a supernatural power in this common leather sack. Since the Before Midnight Scholar's departure, three years had passed. All this time the sack had hung in the open, but wind and weather, rain and cold had not harmed it; the leather had not crumbled or become waterlogged, it had not torn to tatters as one might have expected. On the contrary it seemed to have become stronger and firmer than ever.

And then one day he had actually come! From far off he had noticed something odd in the solitary fir tree before the door of the cell, he had seen the strange bundle hanging in the treetop, swaying in the mountain breeze.

At first he had taken this something for a monk's robe,

then he had recognized it as a sack. By the tree trunk he stopped still. The wooden slab with the inscription attracted his attention. He read it and understood. The venerable master was still waiting for him.

Sobbing with emotion, the Before Midnight Scholar fell on his knees and fervently touched his forehead to the ground before the wooden slab, as though it had been a consecrated likeness of the master.

Back on his feet, he quickly climbed from branch to branch of the fir tree, untied the leather sack, and pulled it on over his head. So clad, he entered the cell's *Fo-t'ang,* "hall of Buddha."

He found Master Lonely Summit squatting on the prayer mat in pious contemplation. Again he fell down on his knees and beat his forehead audibly on the ground, not just a dozen times, no, it must have been a full hundred times. As long as the master continued to meditate, and that must have been for a good three-quarters of an hour, he did not desist from bending his neck and pounding his forehead on the hard ground.

Finally the master's meditation was over. He rose from his prayer mat, went over to the kneeling scholar, and drew him gently to his feet.

"Why this exaggerated homage? If my esteemed lay brother has found his way back to me and honors me once more with his presence, that is proof enough of his loyal affection."

"The adept's understanding was by nature clogged up and glued tight. Today he regrets with all his heart that far from heeding the master, he laughed at his well-meant advice, preferring to follow his wild ideas and lusts; he repents the unforgivable crimes which must lead him, step by step, straight to hell. He has already suffered ample earthly retribution for his sins, but retribution in the other world still awaits him. Therefore he beseeches the revered old master to have mercy on him, to receive him into the community of the holy doctrine, that he may do heartfelt penance and henceforth travel the right path to purification and redemption. Is the revered master so inclined?"

Lonely Summit replied: "Why should I, poor old monk that I am, not be willing? I see that you have taken my leather sack down from the top of the fir tree and made it yours; you have also read my inscription on the wooden slab. Since you went away I have worn out my eyes looking for you. Now that you repent and profess the holy doctrine, why should I not receive you with joy? My only fear is that your determination may not be firm enough, that you may backslide and allow yourself to be drawn back to the red dust of the world.

"Look at this leather sack; for three years I have kept it for you. All this time it hung out there in the tree, exposed to the wind and weather, the sun and the rain, yet it has suffered no harm. Will you show the same steadfastness in the face of temptation? Or will your resolution waver?"

"I have barely escaped from the jaws of hell; how, after so cruel an awakening, could I possibly waver or backslide? No, I am firmly resolved, for me there is no return to the red dust of the world! And so I beseech you once again, revered old master, take me in!"

"Very well, your wish is granted."

On a favorable day of the calendar, the Before Midnight Scholar let the master shear his head, donned a novice's robe, and took a temple name of his own choosing. Henceforth he called himself Wan-shih, "Stupid Pebble," as a reminder that he had shown no more intelligence than a hard and lifeless pebble and wasted three years before coming to his senses.

From then on he worked with the utmost zeal to cleanse and purify his self; indeed, his zeal was almost exaggerated. He systematically avoided warm clothing and insisted that the vegetable fare on which he now lived should be as tasteless and meager as possible, for fear that a copious, tasty meal might rekindle his dormant passions.

He did his best to take on the appearance of a frozen starveling to show his utter contempt for the world.

Nature, however, imposed certain limits upon his efforts to cast off the dust of this world. With all his good intentions, he was still a robust young man. Things were not so bad by day; then his thoughts were occupied by pious meditation, prayers, and the reading of the holy sutras, but at night it was very different; then his naughty, his sinful, his mutinous henchman did everything he could to attract attention. Under the coarse wool blanket, he would stretch and sprawl, rise up in defiance, or saunter haughtily about.

Good resolutions and mental commands did not suffice to put down the rebellion. What was our friend to do? He pondered. Should he help himself with his fingers? Should he resort to some cunning little novice? These are the expedients by which monks ordinarily quench the fire of their senses. But his insight forbade him to employ these methods. Self-satisfaction by means of imagination and fingerplay, sport with a member of his own sex; such *ersatz* measures boiled down to just one thing—fornication. From the imitation to the real thing it was only a short step. But the doctrine of Buddha strictly condemned all manner of fornication, all subservience to the flesh. And our Before Midnight Scholar was very serious about the restrictions and mortifications that the doctrine imposed upon Buddha's servants. And so he kept himself in check, though it was very hard for him.

One night he had an upsetting dream. He dreamt that some lady pilgrims had come to perform their devotions before the likeness of Buddha. Looking at them more closely, he recognized all six of the women with whom he had had amorous relations in the past: Aunt Hua-chen, her three nieces Scent Cloud, Pearl, and Jade, and his two faithless wives Noble Scent and Aroma. The two wives turned to run away; in a frenzy of excitement he cried out, asking Aunt Hua-chen and her three nieces to help him pursue the fugitives. But a moment later the wives had vanished and only the four others, the aunt and her nieces, remained; he escorted them to the rear of the cell to the secret little room reserved for silent meditation. There all five undressed and lay down on the prayer mats, preparing to battle and carry on as they had so many times in the past; he was already in full swing with the first of them when he was awakened by a loud barking of dogs in the nearby woods . . . Lord in Heaven, how impetuously his eternal disturber of the peace had risen up, how conspicuous his rebellious henchman was making himself! Stiff and proud, he was holding up the blanket with his head; he was peering eastward and leering westward, obviously searching desperately for one of his customary cozy hiding places.

Stupid Pebble addressed the disturber inwardly. "Infernal pest! Will you behave! You are the root of all evil, you were at the bottom of all my sinful conduct, and as though you hadn't done enough harm already, you are still at it. Quiet down there!" He tried to still his aroused senses, to distract his thoughts, by picking up a sutra scroll and reading the sacred text for a while in the flickering candlelight. When that did not help, when the evil demon continued to strut about as though he owned the place, he lost patience.

"Why should I go on dragging this accursed appendage, this mutinous henchman around with me? Especially as he is in large part of canine, bestial origin and for that alone must be highly displeasing to Buddha. How shall I attain perfection, how shall I become a worthy follower of Buddha if I go on dragging this impious, sinful appendage around with me?—Off with it! Then the source of evil will be blocked for all time." He had made his decision.

He did not wait until the following morning, no, he carried out his design that very night. Candle in hand, he crept to the kitchen, took a vegetable knife with a particularly sharp, thin blade, whetted it still more on the edge of an earthen water jug, and, scorning all fear of death, laid it on. Lo and behold, the amputation was successful. It had not even hurt very much.

With bold determination he had thus severed his last and strongest bond with the world of red dust. From then on, he was at peace, safe from nocturnal temptations. From then on there was nothing to make him deviate from the path of purification. Daily he grew in insight and illumination.

At this time Lonely Summit was much sought after as a holy man and teacher of Buddha's doctrine. Numerous young men, dedicated to the religious vocation, gathered round him and listened with pious respect to his lectures. But the most zealous and attentive of all the listeners, so much so that he revealed his interest and understanding by briskly nodding his head from time to time, was Stupid Pebble, our Before Midnight Scholar.

His first semester had been taken up chiefly with theoretical study and occasional practical exercises in meditation and other pious occupations. This was the probation period that every novice had to go through before the master found him worthy to take the ten monastic vows and to be ordained a servant of Buddha. In the course of the second semester, the master chose twenty of the most advanced among the novices who seemed to him mature enough and worthy to take their vows.

All were men of high character, unflinchingly determined to devote themselves to the service of Buddha, fully willing to submit to the ten privations, men who could be counted on to persevere in pious meditation though the earth should tremble and quake all about them.

The day came when the twenty elect, among them Stupid Pebble, gathered round the master for the ordination ceremony. They still faced one last test: the public confession of their sins. Each candidate was required to recount, one by one, every misdeed he had ever committed. Thus confessing before the assembled group, he had to kneel down before the likeness of Buddha and, pressing

With bold determination he had thus severed his last and strong-est bond with the world of red dust.

his forehead to the ground, listen in silence as the master interceded with Buddha in his behalf.

Only then was the candidate considered worthy to take the vow of the ten abstinences and to be ordained a servant of Buddha by the laying on of hands.

The confession was required to be complete; to omit a single sin was looked upon as an unpardonable attempt to deceive Heaven and lie to Buddha. Regardless how a man might labor all the rest of his life to improve himself, if he had committed this offense, he would never achieve perfection, never become a Bodhisattva.

Master Lonely Summit took his lofty seat on the pulpit and assigned the twenty candidates their places on either side, the order being determined by the date of their admission to his teaching. Accordingly Stupid Pebble took the last place, for he was last of the novices to have been received.

The master opened the ceremony with a brief address in which he once again called attention briefly but emphatically to the earnestness of the hour and to the content and significance of the vow of abstinence. Then he bade the candidates, one by one in the predetermined order, confess their sins. With lowered eyes and eagerly inclined ears, Stupid Pebble listened to what the others had to relate.

Ah, what crimes were there narrated! Murder and homicide, theft and burglary, arson and adultery. Yes, adultery, for there were several others of his ilk, who had shown a marked preference for other men's wives and whose fornications had offended against all civil law and morality.

It came the turn of the next-to-last, the candidate just ahead of him. Stupid Pebble eyed him in secret. It seemed to him that this man's features, though angular and rough-hewn, had a breath of spirituality about them.

He was a trifle over thirty years of age and the only crime he knew of was that he had seduced his master's married daughter, abducted her, and sold her into a brothel

along with her maid who was also his own wife. Fearing
that he would be punished for this sin in the other world,
he besought the master to intercede for him with Buddha.
And the master replied:

"It is a very wicked crime you have committed. From
time immemorial, forbidden lust has been regarded as the
foulest of all sins. To have been guilty of forbidden lust
and to have seduced another man's wife, that alone would
be enough to damn you. But why, in addition, did you
have to abduct the victim of your evil lust and cast her,
along with her maid, your own wife, into the gutter? Why
did you transform the honorable wife of one man into a
harlot, the venal prey of hundreds, so barring forever her
return to reputable society? I fear that I cannot intercede
with Buddha for one who has been guilty of such dis-
graceful wrongs."

"May I, with the venerable master's permission, say
something in my defense? It was not evil lust that drove
me to my sinful actions, but rather a justified desire to
avenge myself upon my victim's husband, who had previously done the same to me. He had secretly committed
adultery with my wife and then forced me to sell her to
him as a collateral wife. It was not possible for me to settle
accounts with him in an orderly, legal way. I could not
hale him before a judge, and even if I had done so, justice
would not have been done me, for my adversary had more
money and influence than I. And so I emulated the bandits
of Liang-shan Moor; I set myself up as judge and requited
like with like. Under these circumstances, in view of the
fact that I did not act out of evil lust but from affliction
and injured honor, I venture to hope that the master may
consent to intercede for me."

Stupid Pebble had listened with mounting interest. Now
he could no longer control himself; he could not restrain
the question that was burning his tongue.

"Elder brother in Buddha, what was the name of the
woman whom you seduced and carried off? Whose wife

was she? What was the name of her maid? And where are
they now, the mistress and the servant?"

"Yü-hsiang, 'Noble Scent' was her name, she was the
only daughter of a certain Dr. Iron Door in the western
mountains near Peking, the legitimate wife of a young
academician who called himself Wei-yang sheng, the 'Before Midnight Scholar.' Her maid was named Ju-yi, 'As You
Desire.' They are living in Peking, in the famous flower
garden known as the Grotto for Demigods, where they
receive gentlemen professionally. Perhaps my worthy
brother in Buddha knows them?"

"Then you must be Ch'üan, the former silk merchant,
known as Lao-shih, 'the Honest'? What brings you here?"

"May I first inquire: Are you not Wei-yang sheng, the
Before Midnight Scholar?"

"I am indeed."

Consternation was written on both men's features. In
silent awe they admired the wisdom of Buddha, which had
brought them together here on the sandalwood path to
salvation. As though in response to an inward command,
they rose from their mats, bowed politely, and solemnly
asked forgiveness for the wrong they had done one another.
Then both together they turned to Master Lonely Summit
and told him the strange story of what had passed between
them, and of the wrong they had done one another.

The master's face brightened in the course of their
narrative, until at length it became transfigured in a gentle
smile.

"I rejoice to see such high-minded adversaries, such wise
enemies. Impelled by equal remorse, both hold out their
hands in reconciliation. Praised be the day that has brought
you together here. It is only a pity that I did not foresee
this happy today, for if I had, perhaps the sorry yesterday
would never have come to pass. Praised be Buddha who in
compassion and grace has opened the broad sandalwood
path to salvation before you. If you had met on a worldly

path, your enmity would not, I believe, have turned so readily to peace and reconciliation.

"In truth the misdeeds you have both committed are unforgivable, and I should decline to intercede for you. Thank your noble wives for having already atoned for a good part of your sins, for having appreciably lightened the burden of sin that weighs on you. Otherwise, the curse of your sins would cling to you not only in this life but in the next as well—no, what am I saying?—in ten future lives of penance and atonement, and never would you escape from the inexorable wheel of retribution.

"If I now intercede with Buddha in your behalf and beseech him to treat you with compassion and indulgence, I do it chiefly for the sake of your wives. What a pity for those two noble women! What they deserve is a triumphal arch inscribed with words of praise. If they fell into sinful ways, you are to blame. The atonement they have already made for you in this world does not suffice to balance your accounts with a higher judge in the hereafter, but he will no doubt incline to mercy, considering that a part of your guilt has been expunged by your wives. But what a pity, what a pity that they should have fallen into disgrace by your fault!"

After this address, the master bade both repentant sinners kneel down before the likeness of Buddha. Then he unrolled a sutra scroll and read a certain passage. After that, he turned to the likeness of Buddha and murmured a prayer in which he begged indulgence for the two repentant evildoers. Finally he bade them take the prescribed monastic vows and stroked their heads in blessing.

In all due form they had been ordained *ho-shang*, monks and servants of Buddha.

Stupid Pebble still had something on his mind.

"Venerable *shih-fu*, may I ask one more question? Supposing the sinner for whom you intercede, whose guilt has been partly atoned for by his wife, has children, helpless little children, daughters for example, still slumbering in their nurse's bosom—will the little ones benefit by your intercession? Must they too suffer later in life for the guilt of their father? Or are they forgiven their share of future atonement?"

The master shook his head gravely.

"No, unfortunately, it is not forgiven them. The sinner's seedlings must atone for his guilt, even if they are still innocent little children. They too are lashed to the wheel of retribution."

"I can hide nothing from the revered master: the judgment you have just pronounced strikes me, your unworthy adept, and strikes me cruelly. I am the father of two seedlings, two helpless little twin girls; my second wife who ran away brought them into the world, they are living in my house, far from here, under the care of their nurses. According to your judgment, they too are condemned to suffer for my guilt in a future life—my heart bleeds at the thought. But so be it. My course is clear. I should like to take brief leave of you and return to my children. With my consecrated knife I will put an end to them, the seed of my sinful life, in order to save them from future suffering. In so doing I shall console myself with the thought that they might have drowned in the bathtub at birth and breathed out their young lives. Shall I be doing well?"

The master struck his hands together in horror.

"*A-mi-t'o-Fo!* Holy Buddha! What has got into you? Sinful words like these should not even pass your lips, let alone fall upon my ears! How can a man who has just vowed the ten *shikchapadas*, or "abstinences," who has just been ordained a monk, think of murder? And worse, the murder of his own children! Innocent babes, still in swaddling clothes! What was the first of the commandments you have vowed to obey? 'Thou shalt not kill.' What father would have it in him to commit so inhuman a deed? No, I forbid any such attempt to stop the wheel of retribution by violence."

"But what then should be done? How can the poor little

children be saved from the curse they drag about with them by my fault?"

"Just leave that to the Prince of Heaven. Pursue the path of the good and the pure. Take care not to flag in your pious zeal, to close your heart to all vain, unclean impulses. Who knows, perhaps the Prince of Heaven will feel impelled to change his mind and graciously, for your sake, release your children from their share of atonement. Who knows? No magic knife is needed for that."

Stupid Pebble nodded his head eagerly.

"I understand, the revered master is right, I incline obediently to his command."

From that moment on he banished from his mind all thoughts of home and family and the red dust of the world and devoted all his efforts to Buddha and his sacred doctrines.

Half a year went by. One day Stupid Pebble was in the meditation room, conversing on religious matters with Master Lonely Summit. Suddenly they were interrupted in their conversation by the appearance of a strange visitor.

It was a tall, powerful, imposing man who came dashing into the room unannounced and without knocking. Stupid Pebble raised his eyes and—just imagine!—it was his old friend and adoptive brother, K'un-lun's Rival. The new arrival bowed first to the likeness of Buddha and then to the master, touching his forehead to the floor in salutation and homage.

Stupid Pebble introduced him: "This is my good friend and adoptive brother Sai K'un-lun, K'un-lun's Rival, of whom I have often spoken—the most intrepid adventurer of our times and yet, with all his illegal activity, the boldest of warriors for right and justice."

"Ah, I understand, the man for whom no wall is too high to scale or too thick to bore through? The man who by his own noble decision has imposed five abstinences upon himself in his felonious enterprises. Is that the one?"

"It is he."

"In that case, I have the honor of meeting a true Bodhisattva of thieves and burglars. Would it be becoming in a poor little monk like me to accept the greeting and homage of a Bodhisattva? On the contrary, it is I who ought to bend my knee and pay him my respects."

And indeed the old man prepared to bow to the ground, but this K'un-lun's Rival would not allow. He seized him with both hands and drew him graciously to his feet.

"Oh, oh, will the venerable *shih-fu* hunt the unholy vagabond from his door? That is surely what he gives me to understand by refusing to accept my salutation and homage. But even if your devoted adept has been a robber and bandit by trade, his character is no worse, I venture to say that it might even be better, than that of certain reputable citizens who have never stolen in all their lives. If I have journeyed over hill and dale to your cell, revered *shih-fu*, I have done so for two reasons: First, I wished to see my good old friend and inquire after his health; and second, I was driven by a desire to see you, the venerable master, the Huo-Fo, the Living Buddha, face to face, and to express my sincere admiration and respect. To scorn my salutation and my homage and dismiss me from your door would be to destroy my resolve to be converted to virtue and reinforce my old inclination to evil. I cannot believe that this is what you wish to do. I should be forced to conclude that the road to salvation is closed to those who have openly committed theft and larceny, but is open to those who do the same things secretly, let us say, under the mask of respectable officialdom."

"Under these circumstances," said Lonely Summit with an encouraging smile, "the simple little monk no longer dares to decline your salutation and your homage." And he amiably invited him to be seated.

Host and guest now exchanged the usual polite formulas about the weather and each other's estimable health. K'un-lun's Rival fidgeted restlessly on his mat and replied briefly, one would have said absent-mindedly, to the old man's questions; his thoughts were obviously far away. Then he rose from his mat and by silent signs and glances gave his friend to understand that he wished to speak to him alone. But Stupid Pebble ignored his signs and remained quietly seated on his mat.

"You must know," he said to his friend, "that I have no secrets from our venerable master. I have told him all about my past life. If you have something confidential to tell me about my house and family, you can speak freely in the master's presence. In any case, a Living Buddha endowed with his supernatural vision perceives the past and foresees the future. With him no pretense or concealment is possible. You may as well speak up."

K'un-lun's Rival settled back on his mat and began to speak. First he spoke of unimportant matters. Then he paused, his face took on a look of sorrow and gloom and he continued rather hesitantly:

". . . and now I have sad news. It is all my fault that it happened, I have betrayed your trust. I had sworn to serve you as a friend and I have been remiss. When you left home, you asked me to guard your wife and to take care of your children. I promised to do so. But I failed you. Alas, alas! I betrayed your trust. I am no longer worthy to look you in the eye . . ."

"But speak, speak! Has something happened to my daughters?"

"Very well, I will tell you. I don't know how it could have happened. Both your *ling-ai,* your 'commanding darlings,' were in the best of health. They had no childhood ailment, neither measles nor chickenpox, not even the slightest cold. And yet—one night they were put to bed as healthy and chipper as ever; they went peacefully to sleep . . . and never woke up. Both their nurses told of a strange dream they had had that night—they had heard a voice crying out to the little ones: 'Your family's guilt is purged; the account is balanced. Your atonement is no longer needed. Come and follow me, I will take you home.' On

waking next morning, they had found both babies lifeless
in their little beds . . . Is it not a strange story? It sur-
passes my understanding. What do you think of it?"

Stupid Pebble had listened with profound emotion. He
made no answer, but strode with measured gait to the
likeness of Buddha, kneeling down and several times touching his forehead solemnly to the ground, he gave thanks to
the godhead. Then, returning to his mat, he turned to his
friend and explained why the news he had just heard had
been a source of consolation rather than of grief to him.
Briefly he related how dismayed he had been at the thought
that his innocent little daughters would be condemned to
atone later in life for a part of their father's guilt, how the
master had bidden him cast off all worldly and domestic
cares but turn his mind exclusively to purification and the
holy teachings of Buddha, leaving it to the Prince of Heaven
to decide whether, in recognition of his pious zeal, he might
not exchange rigor for mercy and relieve the innocent
little children of their share in their father's guilt. And he
concluded with the words:

"Now do you understand? Thanks to their early death,
my babes have been redeemed from the curse with which
they were born by my fault. There is no need to mourn.
Those are joyful tidings. Instead of offering me sympathy,
you would do better to congratulate me."

K'un-lun's Rival was a man of courage and equanimity.
But his hair stood on end in amazement at the way in which
a higher power had intervened in his friend's destiny. His
simple understanding required a good quarter of an hour
to arrange and understand what he had heard. Finally he
opened his mouth to speak:

"If that is the case, you will not be grieved at the second
piece of news I have for you. On this score, too, you surely
deserve to be congratulated. The news concerns your
second wife, Aroma.

"As my messenger has already informed you, the mon-
strous woman ran off one night with a certain individual. I

considered it my duty as a friend to track the unsavory pair
down. After a long and futile search, I discovered their
secret love-nest by pure chance. Her lover and seducer
was keeping her hidden in a cave deep in the woods."

"I beg your pardon," Lonely Summit broke in, "but how
could you find them if they were hidden in a cave?"

"It had come to my ears that an itinerant monk was
carrying on his criminal trade in those woods and making
the roads unsafe, preying on solitary travelers. He lurked
in wait for them at crossroads, fell upon them and robbed
them, as often as not taking their lives as well as their
possessions.

"It was bruited about that he had hidden a considerable
amount of stolen money in the cave. It was the money that
interested me; I was determined to take it. Meanwhile I
had located his hiding place. One night I crept into the
cave, but solely—I shouldn't want you to mistake my
motives—with a view to robbery. I found the cave well
furnished; there was even a bedroom, with a real bed, a
good wide one at that, and real bed curtains. As I was
cautiously groping about in the dark, keeping my ears open,
I noted to my surprise that there were two people in the
bed. The scoundrel had a woman with him. They were
talking. I bent an ear and listened. The woman was speaking
and I could hear her words distinctly:

" 'My former husband's name was Ch'üan, Honest
Ch'üan they called him; he wasn't much on looks, he was
stockily built with coarse, unprepossessing features, but
otherwise he did very nicely, we went very well together,
we were *yi ma yi an*, one horse, one saddle, as they say.
Best of all, he was faithful to me; I didn't have to share
his favors with anyone else. That was my former husband.
And then—never would I have expected such a thing to
happen—that fiendish K'un-lun's Rival smuggled his
friend into my bed by trickery. He became my lover. He
was a handsome young academician; Before Midnight
Scholar, he called himself. He actually managed to make

my husband give me a divorce. I became the young man's second wife—he already had a legitimate first wife, but he had deserted her soon after their marriage to go chasing around with other women. And he treated me in exactly the same way. For months he left me all alone in the empty house, while he was gadding about with other women. When he finally came home, he was all worn out, he couldn't do a thing. And then like the miserable coward he was, he skipped out again and just vanished, Lord knows where. In short, he shirked his duties disgracefully. He never troubled his head one bit about me or our children, never even bothered to find out if we were dead or alive. Wouldn't it have been just plain stupid of me to go on being faithful to that no-good lecher, that personification of infidelity . . .'

"Thus far I had ground my teeth but kept my peace while that accursed woman, your Aroma, assassinated your character. But at this point I could no longer contain myself. Righteous anger overcame me. I drew my sword, pulled aside the curtain, and killed them both, Aroma and her unsavory lover.

"Then I set fire to the bed and smoked out the cave after removing the hidden treasure. It came to some two thousand silver pieces; I have brought them with me. You can distribute them by handfuls among the poor and helpless. And now speak, venerable master, have I done right? Did this lecherous pair not deserve to die? Was I not justified in seizing the money that scoundrel had stolen?"

"They both deserved to die," the master replied, "and the stolen goods in their possession had to be taken away—but not by you, my worthy lay brother. You had no right to set yourself up as a judge! You have offended against the heavenly order and the imperial law—I fear, I fear that you will be called to account by both, by the heavenly judge and the earthly authorities as well, that you will be condemned both here and hereafter."

Grave words, but K'un-lun's Rival did not seem unduly

perturbed. "All my life I have been practicing the bandit's trade and never have I had any trouble with the authorities. The bribing of judges is one of my favorite pastimes. It hardly seems likely that I shall be caught and haled into court on account of these lousy two thousand silver pieces that were stolen to begin with."

"Don't take it so lightly, my worthy friend. The heavenly and the imperial orders both have farflung nets. Crimes do not slip so easily through their fine meshes. Offenses against the heavenly or the secular order always bring retribution, the question is only whether sooner or later. It usually turns out better when the atonement is swift rather than delayed. You had no right, regardless of the circumstances, to take up your sword in sudden anger or lay hands on other people's money. That crafty itinerant monk was guilty of many crimes: robbery, murder, adultery and abduction; that woman had committed adultery and maliciously deserted her husband, her measure of guilt was full. Do you suppose the Prince of Heaven lacks ways and means of crushing and stamping out evildoers? Do you suppose that he who governs the thunder and lightning needs your human hand as an instrument of vengeance? No, the All-Powerful requires no human aid, the fairy A-hsiang needs no assistants to help her push the chariot of the Prince of Thunder.

"Even if you should get off scot free in this life, it is sure that you will not escape judgment in the hereafter. Perhaps you will be given the benefit of extenuating circumstances because the victims of your robberies were not upright fellow citizens but scoundrels; perhaps your punishment will be reduced, who knows. But punishment there will be. So much for heavenly retribution. And now let us get back to earth. You have arrogated to yourself the right to punish your fellow men on your own, without trial or hearing. Do you call that justice?

"Furthermore, as you yourself have said, you have carried on your dubious trade for years, for heaven knows

"Righteous anger overcame me. I drew my sword, pulled aside the curtain, and killed them both, Aroma and her unsavory lover."

how long. You have made a name for yourself, you are marked down in the records of every magistrate in the country. Granted that you don't rob and steal for your own benefit but distribute your booty generously among the poor and needy. This is known to many, but there must be others who do not believe it, who are convinced that you have hidden the spoils in your house. Inevitably the constables will come one day and search the premises. If you had really hidden the booty in your house, you might at least buy yourself free, but if, as you yourself say, you distribute your wealth among the poor, how are you going to get it back again when you need it? That will be impossible. Consequently, you will not have the wherewithal to buy yourself free and save your neck from the noose. In view of all this, my worthy friend—don't be offended— I take a dark view of your future. It is not likely that you will evade earthly justice. What I particularly fear is that it will take its time and strike late, but then all the more cruelly."

K'un-lun's Rival was a man of firm character and strong will. He was no swaying reed, but a powerful, deeply rooted tree trunk, a defier of winds and tempests. He was not so easily influenced. Moreover, the esteem in which he was generally held had added considerably to his self-confidence. When well-meaning friends, as they did from time to time, tried to persuade him to give up his dubious trade and take up some reputable occupation, he had always laughed at them. And now for the first time his self-assurance was shaken.

The holy hermit's earnest, well-reasoned warning had gained admittance not only to his ear but also to his mind and heart. It had jolted and awakened his conscience. He began to understand that his mode of life had been a grievous error and that it was high time for him to repent. After an intense inner struggle he opened his mouth to speak:

"I see now that I have not conducted myself like an

honest citizen, much less a *chün-tzu* and nobleman. If there is any possible excuse for me, it is the worthy motive behind my deeds. It filled me with bitterness to observe that the wealthy do not, of their own free will, share their bounty with the poor. I thought it was up to me to provide for a more righteous distribution of the world's goods. In so doing I thought less of myself than of my fellow men who were in need of help.

"In the opinion of the venerable *shih-fu*, I have been guilty of unpardonable crimes and must look forward to retribution both on earth and in the other world. But if from now on I turn back in repentance and strive to better myself, may I not expect the master to intercede for me?"

Here was a voluntary confession and promise of repentance. No one had forced it out of him. Stupid Pebble and Lonely Summit both sighed with relief. The master pointed to Stupid Pebble and spoke:

"Take a look at this man. His burden of sins was still heavier than yours. And yet, once he had sincerely repented and turned his mind to the good, he was able to touch the heart of the Prince of Heaven; as you have heard from your friend's own mouth, the Prince of Heaven, for his sake, mercifully released his two little daughters from their share of atonement. This should make it clear to you that your fate does not depend on my intercession, but first and foremost on yourself, on your heart, your sincere striving toward the good!"

"Yes, indeed," cried Stupid Pebble with animation. "Look at me. More than three and a half years have elapsed since my first visit to the master. Then I was obstinate and refused to hear his wise counsel; I turned away from him, preferring the world of red dust, and let myself be driven headlong by my passions and lusts. And then came the day of reckoning.

"His warning was fulfilled word for word. And so once again: Look at me. Take me for a mirror."

His words of persuasion were no longer needed. His

friend had already made his decision. He threw himself at
the holy hermit's feet and swore to follow and obey him
as his superior and master. Mercifully he was received
among Lonely Summit's disciples.

In only thirty years of zealous service to Buddha he attained perfection. Then one day, while meditating on the
prayer mat, he passed gently and peacefully into Nirvana
along with his master and his friend.

Which makes it plain that every man, even the worst of
sinners, can find grace in Buddha's sight and become a
Bodhisattva.

What is it that Master Confucius says somewhere in the
Ssu-shu, the "Four Classical Books"?

Only one who has sinned can become a saint.

CHAPTER XX

*Listen and give ear. We are living in a day of un-
restrained license. It is time to call a halt. The narra-
tion of erotic episodes is not an end in itself. It serves
to gain a hearing for the voice of reason.*

This piece of ornate prose, entitled *fang-fang*, "house full
of fragrance," carries the following meaning:

Man's life, day after day and from morning to night, is
full of hardship and torment, of care and grief, which leave
little room for quiet enjoyment. Let us therefore be thank-
ful to the Creator of heaven and earth for having made two
different sexes and for providing that there should be rela-

tions between them. By so doing he has enabled men to relax from their hardship and torment, to cast off care and grief, so that we need not despair utterly of existence.

In the opinion of the orthodox adherents of the old Confucian doctrine, the entrance to woman's womb is the gateway to our life but also to our death. And according to a more modern, more progressive view, there would be reason, were it not for this same organ, to fear that we men might grow gray many years before our time and lose many years of our lives.

The adversaries of this view argue that monks of forty and fifty are far from being feeble with age and that one frequently meets with monks of seventy or eighty who are still hale and hearty and by no means decrepit.

In answer to this it may be said that most monks, although they have broken with their family ties and civil life, nevertheless pursue the same paths of sexual satisfaction as common laymen: either they fornicate secretly with women, that is the long way, or they stick to novices, that is the short way. In other words, they behave no differently from other men.

The essential is to husband the source of life, to take care of the root of vitality and keep it strong and effective. Those unable to do so are not likely to attain an advanced age.

Let us consider, if you please, an example to the contrary: the palace eunuchs in Peking. They can have dealings neither with women nor with boys, because they have been deprived of the necessary implement. According to the theory here combatted, they should live several hundred years and remain wonderfully young and vigorous. But what happens in reality? They grow gray far earlier than others, their faces become creased and wrinkled far sooner than those of normal men.

Oddly enough, the palace eunuchs are called *kung-kung*, which signifies something of the order of "man-manly." It would be more fitting to call them *p'o-p'o*, "old woman."

In the city of Peking we sometimes see memorial tablets erected in honor of citizens who have lived to be a hundred or more. We see no such tablets in honor of eunuchs.

From this it may be inferred that sexual enjoyment in itself is not harmful to man. True, it is not yet listed in our handbooks of foods and medicines, and this explains why we still have no exact scientific data on the subject and why, on the contrary, opinions are divided.

Some maintain that sexual pleasure is beneficial to man's health; others take the opposite view, that it is harmful.

Carefully weighing the pros and cons, we must decide for the former view. Sexual pleasure has something of the effect of a medicinal herb, a powerful drug; it has indeed much in common with the effect of a ginseng decoction.

Perhaps it will be worth our while to compare the two. There is one point that should be stressed above all: ginseng is a magnificent tonic and means of regeneration, but it must be taken sparingly, at reasonable intervals. It should always be regarded as a medicine and not as daily fare. Taken too abundantly or too often, it is harmful to the health.

The same is true of sexual pleasure: sparingly distributed, punctuated by sensible pauses, it has the virtue of enabling *yin* and *yang*, male and female, to give each other mutual relief and release from sultry storm pressure. Taken too frequently and immoderately, it becomes a battle to the death between the hostile elements of fire and water.

Considered as a medicine, sexual pleasure has the advantage of relaxing the middle region of the body and relieving pressure on the mind. Abused as daily fare, it causes considerable damage to the brain and heart.

Once men learn to look upon sexual pleasure as a medicine, they will not be afraid of it, but neither will they let it become a pathological drive. They will neither underestimate nor overestimate its value.

Before the act one should say to oneself: it is a medicine, not a poison, why be afraid of it? *During* the act one should always think: its purpose is healing, not greedy gluttony; why, then, let this urge destroy my will and toss me helplessly about? Where a wholesome attitude of this kind prevails, a man will not rebel against an unattractive wife, and a woman will not languish from disappointment; no longer will immoderate sexual enjoyment drive people to an early grave; there will be no neglected and embittered wives at home and the outside world will be rid of lone wolves who do nothing but prey on other people's wives. Furthermore, the population will be maintained at a suitable level—a matter of no mean importance, for according to the precepts of the wise Confucius, the political order takes precedence over the family order.

Thus far the analogy between sexual pleasure and the consumption of ginseng can be followed point for point, but in one respect there is a difference. I have in mind the source of the medicine.

A consumer of ginseng must bear one thing in mind: only the genuine ginseng root that grows wild in the Ch'ang-pai-shan, the upland forests of southern Manchuria and Korea, is sure to have the famous medicinal effect. Ginseng plants found elsewhere and those raised at home are worthless. It is quite the opposite with sexual pleasure: only the home-grown article can be counted on to give the best results. Foreign wares have proved to be worthless and, under certain circumstances, harmful.

What is meant here by "home-grown" and "foreign"?

Let us suppose that a man has his legitimate spouse at home and, if you will, a collateral wife or two; then he has no need to wander abroad, to squander his money on strange women. What he needs is right there at hand; he need only sit down to table.

Nothing in the world prevents him from lying down and taking a woman in his arms when the desire comes over him; a knock at the door need not frighten him, nothing interferes with his serene enjoyment; he can visit the tombs of his ancestors with a clear conscience and pay them his tribute of thanks. During the act he is filled with pure happiness, untempered by remorse. Is it not a fine thing? In this case may we not freely speak of a tonic, medicinal action?

And now to the contrary case. Here we have a fellow who makes unreasonable demands; she must be of a distinguished house, she must be not only beautiful but well dressed also. Chicken from his own barnyard strikes him as tasteless, his mouth waters for the gamy savor of wild duck. The charms of his aging wife are on the decline, he yearns for change, for a youthful tidbit. That is what is meant by a "foreign article."

One day he meets a "foreign article" in keeping with his ideal and it is all up with his peace of mind. By day he thinks of nothing else, by night he dreams of her, all his thoughts and actions are directed toward this one goal: he must possess her.

He begins with tender love letters; then come presents, and at length a secret rendezvous. To get there he does not hesitate to climb walls or crawl through cellars and ditches. In his desire to taste of the foreign, forbidden drug, he will perform the most daring feats, and yet he is always as frightened as a nibbling mouse. Even when no one is about, he thinks he hears footsteps, he fears to be surprised. Instead of the sweat of pleasure, it is the sweat of fear that oozes from his pores.

A wild adventure is shortlived, marriage ties are enduring; they outlast adventure. Years may pass, the evildoer may have grown a long beard, and then one day the story comes to light, the curtain is lifted from the misdeed he had thought dead and buried. Family vengeance stirs, avengers pursue him, he learns what it means to walk at the edge of the abyss. He learns what comes of tempting fate, of offending against the civil order. His conscience is burdened with secret guilt, and one day retribution overtakes him—he falls by a murderer's hand.

And what of his paramour? If she is fortunate, she may

escape with her life, but she has lost her honor, her marriage is wrecked; agitation, bitterness and grief will poison her life and send her to her grave before her time.

From this it follows that amorous adventures are not worth while. If you demand sexual pleasure, do not scorn what is close at hand; do not seek far afield and behave like the cantankerous diner who picks the lean morsel from his meat and pushes the fat aside; do not despise good everyday fare and go looking for dainty tidbits.

This brings us to the kindly, motherly intent with which our author wrote this novel: Far from wishing to encourage his fellow men to give their lusts free rein, he wishes to warn them to hold their sensual desires in check. Far from wishing to glorify the voluptary and his doings, he is determined to dispel his false and unwarranted nimbus.

It is to be hoped that the esteemed reader will not fail to understand the author's kindly, motherly intent.

Stop there!, I hear you say at this point and raise the following argument: if your intentions are so moral, my dear author, why have you not just written a treatise about moral reform? Why have you given us instead a spicy novel in which all sorts of "breezy" deviations from good conduct are described minutely?

Dear friends, let me explain: the present-day reading public has a positive horror of educational, moralistic books written in the dry, solemn style of the ancient classics and historians. They take pleasure in "wild" stories, in lively accounts of the petty human affairs which grow like weeds, as it were, between the furrows of the official history which, according to our academicians, is alone important and worth mentioning; even in a book of "wild" stories, they reject any obvious emphasis on morality and virtue as preached by Master Confucius; they are bored with sermons. What they like, on the contrary, is an imaginative and detailed account of erotic behavior which deviates— the more the better—from the strict, officially sanctioned norm. It is no exaggeration to say that certain parts of our society have today attained the peak of amorality, not to say laxity and license.

Anyone who wishes to reform his times must turn to the methods employed by the Great Yü (later Emperor Yü, 2205–2197 B.C.) in containing the "enormous flood" which menaced the country in the days of Yao (2357–2255 B.C.). How did he go about this difficult task? "... The waves seemed to rise to the high heavens. They flooded the hills and even dashed against the summits of high mountains. Yü ordered all manner of arks to be built with the help of which he was able to reach the mountains. Through forests and thickets he made his way to the summits and looked out over the countryside to find the direction in which it might be possible to guide the masses of water to the sea ..." So the ancient chronicles relate.* By adapting himself to the current, he was able, by means of canals, to guide the water into the sea and dry out the country.

One who wishes to reform his times must, like the great Yü, adapt himself to the current of the day; then his words will gain a hearing.

If nowadays a reformer were to come along with an edifying treatise, dripping morality, and expect to improve the world with it, his enterprise would be doomed in advance. Who is going to spend money on such reading matter? But even if he should imitate the pious temple patron who sends people his edifying tracts free of charge with his visiting card, what would be the good of it? The receiver would either throw his treatise unread into the waste basket, or tear it up and use the pieces to light his pipe with. The one thing that would never occur to him is to waste so much as a glance on such reading matter.

No, the direct method will not do. We must go about it very differently and try to reach the public by a detour. We must first capture the reader's attention with an enter-

---

* Cf. Kuhn, *Altchinesische Staatsweisheit*, p. 29, Verlag Die Waage, Zürich.

taining, agreeable account of erotic adventures, and so put him in a state of pleasant suspense. Once the reader's interest has been captured, once he has got into the book and can no longer tear himself away from it, he may well, in reading particularly spicy passages that are designedly scattered throughout the book, heave a sigh of unfeigned admiration and think to himself: "Ah yes, women, women! Sex! There's really something in it. That's the way to live: enjoy life, take the opportunities that offer, even far from home. Why should I not be a demon of lust, drinking my fill of the honey that pours from the calyxes of the fairest peonies? There's something worth living for. Why all this vain striving for empty fame and hollow honor?" Never mind. Let him think such thoughts. Later on, as he avidly pursues his reading, he will suddenly be pricked by the fine needles of painful but salutary acupuncture; suddenly, he will wake up in terror and say: "Gracious me! Is that how it is? Must the voluptary atone so bitterly for his brave adventures in ladies' chambers? If that's what retribution is, it's better to behave. You throw your money around for nothing and pile up debts. No, it's not worth while. Better stick to your own wife and your own collateral wives at home!"

That is what he will say to himself in the end. He will look within and admit that he was on the wrong track. He will repent and return to the path of reason; he will learn to esteem his own wife and his own collateral wives and earn their love and respect in return, and the best of order and harmony will reign once more in his soul and in his house.

That is how to fight fire with fire, to teach man by human means. This method—it is comparable to a trick of magic and might be called "conjuring up the innocent white lotus blossom from swamps and muddy pools"—is much to be recommended, and not only to the author of "wild weed stories," or novelist; even great sages of antiquity have not scorned it when they wished to carry through necessary reforms.

A classical example is provided by the famous moralist Mencius (372–289 B.C.), who used this method to convert the obstinate Prince Hsüan of Ch'i.

Mencius often carried on discussions with the young prince on the art of government and political philosophy. But the prince's interests were far removed from the affairs of government, he had five hobbies or rather foibles: he loved hunting, music, wine, rare jewels, and—women.

From time to time he applauded Master Mencius' disquisitions—but only with his lips. Inwardly he was bored; his mind was elsewhere. This Mencius noticed and called him to account with the words: "If, my Prince, you find my counsels good, why do you not follow them?" The prince replied: "Nature has given me certain faults, such as my weakness for feminine charms." With these few words, he unwittingly gave evidence of the same obstinacy and blindness as two incorrigible rulers of olden time, whose enslavement to women made tyrants of them.

These two were Chieh-kuei, the last emperor of the Hsia dynasty, who ruled from 1818 to 1766 and was overthrown by T'ang, founder of the Shang dynasty, and five hundred years later Chou-hsin, last emperor of the Shang or Yin dynasty, who reigned from 1154 to 1122 and was dethroned by Wu-wang, founder of the Chou dynasty.*

They would dismiss all the earnest admonitions and warnings of their alarmed advisors with the barren words: "It can't be done."

Now if Mencius had taken the pose of a stern educator, if, raising his voice and putting on a solemn face, he had lectured the prince as follows: "From time immemorial there have been strict laws and edicts, applicable to the ruler as well as his people, for the purpose of forestalling loose behavior with women. A common citizen found

---

* Cf. Kuhn, *op. cit.*, p. 38 ff.

guilty of such misconduct is punished by death; a dignitary loses his office; a dissolute prince of a province is deprived of his province, a dissolute Son of Heaven loses his throne and empire . . ."

If Mencius had spoken thus, the Prince might have listened in silence; out of politeness he might have kept his objections to himself. But in secret he would have exculpated himself with the thought: "Can I help it if nature made me as I am? Such are my faults and they just happen to be incurable. Why doesn't he leave me alone? His advice is useless to me." And he would have thrown all the master's warnings to the winds.

But what did Mencius do? Avoiding all pedantry, he humored the prince's weakness. In an affable, conversational tone he told him about a similar case in history, namely that of Prince Tan Fu (T'ai-wang, great-grandfather of Wu-wang), who had been afflicted with a similar attachment to women. By relating an amusing episode of gallant history and describing in detail how this Prince Tan Fu (c. 1250 B.C.) had been so dependent on female company that he could not forego it for as much as a quarter of an hour, how, even amid danger, while fleeing on horseback from an enemy, he had to have his favorite with him in the saddle, he succeeded not only in making the prince listen, but in making him listen eagerly and attentively. And then came the surprising turn. The princely listener fully expected to hear that so dissolute a prince, unable to live without women for even a quarter of an hour, who even while fleeing from an enemy had to have a woman in the saddle with him, had come to a bad end, losing his throne and with it his life. Not a bit of it; what he actually heard was that this prince, far from wishing to monopolize the pleasures of the bed, helped his people to share in these very same pleasures. He did everything in his power to encourage marriages throughout the land and see to it that there should be no grieving, neglected spinster daughters in the homes, nor out in the world any young bachelors of a marriageable age. When he celebrated a festive occasion with his wives at court, he wanted the people as well to celebrate, to share in his enjoyment of life, and with this in mind he organized popular festivals. So he became for his people a veritable "springtime on feet," a bringer of joy and life, practicing a principle of age-old statecraft that was put into writing by the philosopher Kuan-tzu (seventh century B.C.): "Heaven is just and selfless and impartial. It shelters all men, whether beautiful or ugly. The earth too is just and selfless and impartial. It supports the little as well as the great."*

In order that streams of fruitful blessing should lave all men alike, the ruler takes third place after heaven and earth. The ruler is like heaven which selflessly shelters all men. He is like the earth who selflessly bears all. Self-seeking government leads to anarchy.

Who among the people would not have offered up thanks and praise to such a prince? Who would have dared to find fault with him for his weakness and accuse him of injustice? So spake Mencius.

Prince Hsüan of Ch'i listened with pleasure. He took the words to heart and followed them. From then on he governed wisely. And thereafter when Mencius came to him with well-meant advice, he did not reply with evasions or offer his "weakness" and his "natural faults" as excuses.

The author has tried his best to follow the classical example of Mencius and to make the innocent white lotus blossom grow from swamp and morass. May his esteemed readers judge his novel in this light; may they appreciate it not for the swamp and morass, that is to say, its lurid, realistic picture of manners, but for the pure lotus blossom, that is to say, its good and wise teachings, its earnest summons to repentance and reflection.

If the author incidentally gives crass descriptions of intimate "bed curtain" scenes and sometimes, admittedly, comes

---

* Cf. Kuhn, *op. cit.*, p. 34.

very close to pornography, let it be said in justification that he wished, by such tasty trimmings, to hold the reader's attention until curtain fall. Only in this way could he bring his readers to take in the serious idea of retribution which is expressed quite emphatically toward the end of the novel, and to think it over. Without the trimmings in question, the book would leave the bitter, acrid, unpleasant aftertaste of the olive in the reader's mouth. By describing the intimate details of "bedcraft," the author wished, as it were, to offer the reader the bitter taste of the olive embedded in the sweet flesh of the date, and so prevent his novel from incurring unfavorable criticism and from being rejected as "dismal, tedious slop."